The Family
He Didn't Expect

Shirley Jump

P9-CSB-583

H HARLEQUIN SPECIAL EDITION

Recycling programs
for this product may
not exist in your area.

ISBN-13: 978-1-335-57396-4

The Family He Didn't Expect

Printed in U.S.A.   www.Harlequin.com

New York Times and *USA TODAY* bestselling author **Shirley Jump** spends her days writing romance so she can avoid the towering stack of dirty dishes, eat copious amounts of chocolate and reward herself with trips to the mall. Visit her website at shirleyjump.com for author news and a book list, and follow her at Facebook.com/shirleyjump.author for giveaways and deep discussions about important things like chocolate and shoes.

Books by Shirley Jump

Harlequin Special Edition

The Barlow Brothers

The Homecoming Queen Gets Her Man
The Instant Family Man
The Tycoon's Proposal
The Firefighter's Family Secret
Winning the Nanny's Heart

Harlequin Romance

If the Red Slipper Fits...
Midnight Kiss, New Year Wish
How to Lasso a Cowboy
The Princess Test
Family Christmas in Riverbend
One Day to Find a Husband
How the Playboy Got Serious
Return of the Last McKenna
Mistletoe Kisses with the Billionaire
The Matchmaker's Happy Ending
The Christmas Baby Surprise

Visit the Author Profile page
at Harlequin.com for more titles.

To Barb and Donna, two of the smartest and best friends I could ever ask for. Here's to more laughs and a lifetime of cocktail Fridays.

Chapter One

Dylan Millwright sat in his Jeep, parked on a slight hill. Stone Gap, North Carolina, lay before him, lazy, content and still in the late October sunshine. When he was eight, he'd climbed the side of this hill with his older brother and felt like he'd conquered Mt. Everest. When he was sixteen, he'd brought Mary Alice Hathaway to this very hill and mistaken lust for love. At seventeen, he'd quit high school and crested the hill once again, but this time vowing to leave the small town where he'd grown up in his rearview mirror forever.

Forever had lasted a little over ten years. Then Uncle Ty had called, said *I need you, kid*, and Dylan had dropped everything. There were very few people in the world that Dylan would do that for. Uncle Ty was at the top of the list. Dylan had no idea how long he was going to be here, or what Uncle Ty needed, but that was okay. Dylan was used to living by the seat of his pants, with no more formal commitment than a handshake.

He looked out over the town one last time, then drew in a deep breath. Then he climbed back into his Jeep and headed down the hill and into downtown Stone Gap. Not much had changed, as if the whole town was caught in a time warp. Sadie's Clip 'n' Curl still marked the beginning of Main Street, followed by the ice cream parlor, a couple diners, Gator's Garage, Betty's Bakery, Joe's Barbershop...

Small-town America, on a first-name basis with everyone.

Hopefully he wouldn't be caught in this Norman Rockwell painting for very long. Dylan paused at the intersection with Juniper Street, took a left, then pulled into the parking lot of a long, low-slung building. The white paint was fading, peeling, and the roof had a few broken shingles. The morning rain had left the grass richly green and knocked a few light branches to the ground. The sign out front looked brighter than Dylan remembered, but still said the same thing, like a promise he could depend upon:

Millwright Family Children's Community Center

Uncle Ty and Aunt Virginia, who'd never had children of their own, had opened the center two decades ago. Kids from all over came here, filling the game rooms and the basketball courts out back, mostly after school and always on Saturdays. Dylan himself had spent many an afternoon here, often after a fight with his parents or yet another grounding for breaking a rule (or ten). Uncle Ty and Aunt Virginia had always welcomed him with open arms, providing a refuge for kids who really needed one.

A month ago, Aunt Virginia had died. Dylan had been hiking in Colorado and didn't get the message until after the funeral. Then Uncle Ty had called, his voice breaking with grief, and asked Dylan to come help.

He headed inside, his eyes adjusting to the dim interior, and his ears to the din. A couple of teenage boys were playing ping-pong at the scarred table with the Swiss cheese net in the rec room. Two others were immersed in an older generation PlayStation or Xbox. Another few were sprawled across the battered leather sofas, watching a football game. The teenagers, a motley, kind of scruffy crew, barely noticed him enter. At a set of small chrome and laminate tables on the left, a quartet of little kids were making some kind of craft with Mavis Beacham that involved a whole lot of glue and a tub of colorful beads.

As soon as she saw Dylan, Mavis got to her feet and opened her arms. "Dylan Millwright, as I live and breathe! What are you doing here?"

Before he could answer, she was drawing him into a tight hug. Mavis was an ample woman, the kind that embodied welcome. She'd been his neighbor when he was growing up, and had always made time for both the Millwright boys, keeping a jar of their favorite peppermints by her door for whenever they passed by.

"Tell me you're staying at the inn while you're here,"

Mavis said. "Della Barlow and I turned Gareth Richardson's house into something amazing. You'll love it there."

Leave it to Mavis to not even ask Dylan about staying with his brother. She knew him well, and had seen the squabbles between the boys. He smiled at her. "I wouldn't dream of staying anywhere else, Mavis."

She cupped his face between both her palms. "I'm glad you're home, Dylan. Real glad. Your uncle needs you."

"I'm glad I'm here, too, Mavis," Dylan said. He didn't correct her on calling Stone Gap home. She loved this town far more than he ever had, so he let that go and instead gave her a quick kiss on the cheek.

Uncle Ty was sitting in his office, behind a wide plate-glass window. He looked up, saw Dylan and started waving as he got out of his seat and came around the door. "Dylan! You made it!"

Dylan crossed the room and gave Uncle Ty a big hug. His uncle was five foot nine, a few inches shorter than Dylan, and used to be nearly as wide as he was tall. But since the last time Dylan had seen him, his uncle had lost at least twenty pounds. He had a friendly, open face, and though his graying hair was thinning a little and receding a lot, he still looked younger than his sixty years. As long as Dylan had known him, Uncle Ty had been a kid at heart. "Good to see you, Uncle Ty."

"You too, son. You too." He patted Dylan's back. "I've missed you."

"I've missed you too." Dylan drew back. "I'm really sorry about Aunt Virginia."

Ty's eyes filled. "She was one of a kind. Lord, I loved that woman."

"Everyone who met her did, too," Dylan said. Aunt Virginia had had one of those larger-than-life personalities. The kind of woman who welcomed perfect strangers into her home and fed them pork and beans on a Saturday night. The kind of woman who knitted blankets for the homeless and baked pies for the poor. She'd been the lifeblood of the community center. Even though the rooms were still teeming with activity, it felt as if some of the air had gone out of the space, but Dylan didn't want to say that. "Looks like the place is as busy as ever. And exactly the same as when I was here."

Uncle Ty chuckled. "You know me. Change is a four-letter word. I don't like to mess with a winning formula." Then his uncle sobered and draped an arm over Dylan's shoulder, lowering his voice as the two of them walked toward the office. "Thank God you came when I called. I can't manage this place on my own. You know Virginia—she was my right *and* my left hand here. I'm just…lost without her."

Dylan could see that in his uncle's eyes, hear it in his voice. He'd never known anyone who loved another person as much as Virginia and Ty had loved each other. They'd had movie love, the kind you only saw in some Nicholas Sparks flick. And now, Virginia was gone, and Uncle Ty looked like he was marooned on a deserted island.

"Whatever you need," Dylan said. "I've got a couple weeks where I don't have to be anywhere. I can start on some of the maintenance or—"

Ty drew in a deep breath. "Actually, I want you to

work with the kids. At least for today. I'm just having a…well, a rough afternoon and I can't do it."

The statement hung in the stale air of Ty's office. For a second, Dylan thought he hadn't heard his uncle right. "Work…with the kids? Me?"

Uncle Ty ran a hand through his thinning hair. His face was lined, his eyes tired. His usual smile had disappeared, as if he'd lost it and couldn't remember where it was. "I just can't. It's not that I don't still love all these kids and love my job, but it's too much right now. How am I supposed to tell these kids how to get their lives on track when mine is so far off the rails? I'm doing all I can to manage the books and clean the bathrooms once in a while."

"Uncle Ty, I don't have a degree in child psychology like Aunt Virginia, or a background in social work like you do."

"No, but you have life experience. And sometimes, that's what gets through to the tough cases better than any therapy you throw at them."

Yeah, he had life experience, but it wasn't the kind he figured these kids should have. Like running away from home at seventeen. Hitchhiking from here to California, funding his way with odd jobs. He'd been picked up by the cops a few times—mainly for loitering and underage drinking—and wound his way around the country ever since, never staying in any one place long. He'd worked fishing charters in Florida, potato farms in Idaho, building projects in Minnesota. He'd feel like a hypocrite if he told the kids that settling down and working hard would make them happy in the end. What did he know about settling down—or finding happiness? "I don't think I can do this, Uncle Ty. I'm not cut out for it at all."

"I know you think that," Ty said, "but you're more suited than anyone I know. You grew up here—"

"And didn't exactly turn out to be a Nobel Prize winner."

"No, but you did turn into a hell of a good man."

Dylan shook that off. If there was one adjective he'd use for himself, it sure wasn't *good*. "Can't you hire someone? Someone with a degree or something?"

"You know this place has always operated on a shoe-string budget, Dylan. Anyone I hired would have to be working for almost nothing." Ty put a hand on his nephew's shoulder. "Just give it a try for a little while. For me, please?"

Dylan took another look at his uncle. Ty's shoulders sagged low, and there was a blankness in his features that Dylan had never seen before, as if Uncle Ty was a fading photo. He'd lost the love of his life, and it had drained every bit of the color out of his world.

"All right. You can count on me, but only for a temporary gig, okay?" Dylan said, with a lot more conviction than he felt. Dylan never had been the kind of guy anyone—especially anyone in this town—had counted on for anything more than a ride to the liquor store on Friday night.

Relief flooded Ty's face. "Thank you, Dylan. It's just for a few days. I need to…find myself again, you know? Without Virginia, I'm…half of who I used to be."

Ty and Virginia had loved each other in that way most people aspired to and never found. Dylan had no such aspirations. He didn't want to be tied down, to any one place or any one person. He was here now, but he wasn't planning on staying one second longer than necessary.

Dylan slung his backpack into the corner beside a teetering stack of boxes and the world's largest supply of colored construction paper. He still wasn't sure he was cut out for this, but maybe if he gave Ty a day or two off, things would get back to normal. "Just tell me what to do."

"The little kids are doing okay. Mavis has them making some kind of rainbow thing with beads." Ty gestured toward the round table, headed by the generously sized, warm and affectionate African American woman. The kids gravitated to her like ants to honey, and from the smile on her face, Mavis loved every minute with them.

"She was awesome when I was a kid," Dylan said. "I'm glad she's still volunteering here."

"Me, too. Though she has fewer hours to spare, since she's running the inn with Della Barlow." Ty nodded, then he waved toward the sofas. "Take the teen circle, will you? The rest of them will be here any minute. All you have to do is prompt them to talk, and believe me, they'll talk your ear off. Remind them to keep it positive."

"Uncle Ty—"

Ty put a hand on Dylan's arm, cutting off his protest. "You've walked the walk and talked the talk and broken the same rules these kids have. But then you turned yourself around, got a great job with that company up in Maine… I can't think of a better person than you to connect with them."

His uncle had a point. If there was one thing Dylan had succeeded at in life, it was being a rebellious teenager. He'd broken pretty much every rule his parents had set forth, and quite a few put in place by the state of North Carolina. If there was a way to get away with doing the wrong thing, Dylan knew it. These kids, sprawled across the sofas like human afghans, weren't going to be able to get anything past him. And whether they knew it or not, they shared some common ground with him.

The door to the center opened and a leggy brunette woman carrying a briefcase strode in, followed by a singing four-year-old and a sullen teenage boy who looked like he'd rather disappear inside his gray hoodie than be here. The smaller kid peeled off and beelined for Mavis's table, while the teenager propped himself against the wall closest to the door. But Dylan's gaze remained on the brunette.

Stunning. That was the only word that came to mind.

She had long brown hair that tumbled around her shoulders. Her eyes were masked by sunglasses, but they couldn't hide a face that had that kind of delicate bone structure that made him think of Aunt Virginia's porcelain teacups. The woman was wearing a dark navy skirt, a white button-down blouse with the cuffs turned back and a bright red beaded necklace swinging down to her waist. Then there were the heels—tall, spiky, dark blue shoes that offset incredible legs and made something deep inside Dylan go hot.

"Ty, sorry I'm late." She strode forward, passing

Dylan as if he didn't even exist. "I got out of work late and then had to track down Cody, who, as usual, wasn't where he was supposed to be." She blew a lock of hair off her face. "I swear, that kid is going to be the death of me."

Uncle Ty put a hand on her shoulder. "It's fine, Abby, really. Cody will settle in soon and Jacob is already up to his elbows in glue."

She glanced over at the table, where Jacob—the youngest one, Dylan assumed—had already taken a seat and was sprinkling beads across bright blue construction paper. Mavis sent up a little wave, signaling *I've got this, honey.*

"Okay." Abby let out a long sigh. "If you don't mind, I have a proposal I need to work on. Can I…" She waved toward the office and gave Ty a smile.

For some weird reason, that smile—directed toward his uncle—sent a little flicker of jealousy through Dylan.

"Of course. Use my office. But first, I want you to meet my nephew, Dylan." Ty turned to Dylan and gestured between the two of them. "Dylan Millwright, meet Abigail Cooper, but everyone calls her Abby. Abby, my nephew. He's going to be helping out with the teen program."

For the first time in his life, Dylan wished he was the kind of guy who wore a suit and tie. His battered jeans, faded concert T-shirt and black leather boots didn't exactly match the polished, pressed woman beside him. "Nice to meet you," he said, extending his hand.

She gave him a surprisingly firm handshake, considering how delicate she seemed at first blush. She was all business, not a spark of interest in her eyes. "You, too."

He was about to say something witty back, but before he could come up with a handful of words more charming than *uh, you're beautiful*, she was picking up the briefcase and heading for Ty's office. A second later, the glass door closed and Abby settled herself behind Ty's desk. She pulled a laptop out of her bag, set it up and started typing.

"I can see you watching her," Uncle Ty said, putting a hand on Dylan's shoulder. "And I can read interest in your eyes. I'm tellin' you right now, Abby isn't…"

"Isn't the kind of woman who would date a guy like me?"

Ty turned to his nephew and the lines around his eyes softened. "I wasn't going to say that. You're a good man, Dylan—"

Dylan scoffed.

"*A good man*," Ty repeated with emphasis, "or I wouldn't have you here. As for Abby, she's…complicated. One of those women juggling a whole lot of balls and not interested in having a man help catch a single one of them. Her ex was a real jerk, who let her and her boys down in a big way."

"I'm not here to date anyone," Dylan said and turned away from the office to prove his point. "Don't you worry about that."

But as he walked away and crossed toward the teenagers waiting on the sofas, Dylan wondered if he'd still be singing that tune if Abby Cooper had looked at him with even an ounce of interest. Either way, the last thing he needed was a small-town single mom with workaholic tendencies. If anything screamed *complete opposite from you*, that fit the bill.

He dropped into the lone armchair sitting in front of the sofas and propped his elbows on his knees. "Hey, guys, I'm Dylan. How about we talk about breaking the rules?"

Abby stared at the report in front of her. She'd spent the better part of the day putting it together, but it still didn't feel right. Had she missed some data points? Forgotten to add the case study? She scrolled through the document, checked it against her list, then read the pages over again.

Ever since she'd taken the promotion to director of brand development at Davis Marketing, she'd worried that she'd bitten off more than she could chew. Worried that they were going to see her as a fraud, as a woman who was only pretending to be up to the job.

Because she was.

Hell, her whole life seemed to be about pretending she could handle everything, whether she actually could or not. Get up in the morning, drag Cody out of bed, feed Jake, shoo Cody out the door and pray he made it to high school this time instead of heading for the park or the mall or somewhere with his friends. Then drop Jake off at preschool, making sure he'd taken his snack and a change of clothes for just in case at daycare later and that he didn't have anything after school that she was supposed to go to. After all that, finally head off to work. Eight or more hours later, head home and repeat the process in reverse. Sometime in that window, she was supposed to cook healthy dinners, make the house spotless, draw baths and read bedtime stories. Oh and have "me" time, with rose-petal filled bubble baths and meaty novels.

Because that was what the magazines said "women who had it all" managed to do. She'd yet to find a way to even come close to that, but it didn't stop her from trying.

Tears sprang to her eyes and a burst of panic made her heart race. Abby drew in a deep breath, counted to ten, then whisked the tears away. There was no time to get distracted or lose her focus.

She read the pages once again, hit Send on the report, then closed the laptop. There was more on her To Do list, but it could wait until after Jake went to bed. That would mean another late night again, but her Mommy Guilt was kicking into overdrive, especially after Jake had asked in the car if she was going to work "again," with that pouty sound in his voice and disappointment swimming in his big brown eyes.

She emerged from Ty's office and crossed to the little kids' table. Two more kids had arrived and now seven of them sat in pint-size chairs on either side of Mavis. She loved those kids and welcomed them like they were all her own little ducklings.

"How are you, Mavis?" Abby said. She placed a hand on the older woman's shoulder. Mavis covered it with her own and gave Abby's hand a friendly pat.

"Just fine, just fine." She turned to the kids and grinned at them. "I have the best table of kittens—"

"We're not kittens, Miss Mavis," Jake said with a

laugh in his voice. He was the happy one of her two boys, always ready with a smile or a laugh. Abby loved that about him and reached over to ruffle his hair.

"Well, I don't know about that, Jakester," Abby teased. "You drink milk, right?"

"Uh-huh."

"And you like to sleep a lot."

Jacob laughed and cocked his head to the side, causing one lock of hair to do a little flip-flop. "That's cuz I'm tired."

"And you have a big old mop of fur—" She nuzzled his dark hair.

"Mommy, that's hair! I'm a boy!"

She leaned back and pretended to study him, tapping a finger against her lip. "Well, now, I think you might be right about that. Now that I look a little closer, I see you are indeed a boy. A cute one at that." She gave Mavis a smile, then placed a kiss on her son's forehead. "Keep on working on your picture, Jake. I'll be back in a minute."

She crossed the room, pausing by the watercooler, filling a paper cup and pretending to get a drink, but really trying to see how Cody was doing. Of the two boys, Cody had taken their father's sudden departure the hardest. It had been easier when Keith had left the first time, because Cody was only two, but ten years later, when Keith had returned to try again, Cody had started to put trust in his father. The problem was Keith had never fully committed to his family and had never really intended to stay forever.

The second time, Cody had turned twelve the day

before and gone to sleep believing the world was perfect because he had a new bike and another game for his Xbox. When he got up the next morning, there'd been an empty spot at the kitchen table and a dark oil stain on the driveway where Keith's Malibu used to be.

Keith had walked out the door, leaving her with a newborn baby, forty dollars in the bank, a sheaf of bills as high as her elbow and the Herculean task of explaining why to two boys who didn't understand.

There were days when she wanted to throttle her ex-husband for what he had done to their family, for how he had hurt his children. She had known he'd wanted out for a long time, but had never thought he'd up and move, to live with the twenty-year-old college student who was the "love of his life."

Keith Cooper had been irresponsible and selfish, two traits that Abby had been blind to for far too long. She'd kept thinking he would change, that he would settle down, find a career, not just a job, and become the family man she'd foolishly hoped he'd be.

She'd been wrong.

Abby leaned against the wall beside the watercooler, a paper cone of cool water in her hand, and watched Cody. He was hunched into the corner of one of the sofas, looking angry and sullen. Par for the course with a sixteen-year-old who thought his life sucked.

To his left sat Dylan Millwright, Ty's nephew. He was a good-looking guy—tall and lean, with dark hair and green-brown eyes. She hadn't really noticed him before, but she did now.

He had a roguish look to him, with the scuffed black

boots, the battered jeans, the faded T-shirt. Like one of those guys in a modern-day fairy tale who roared up on a motorcycle and whisked the bored debutante away for a life of adventure.

Except Abby knew full well those kinds of guys didn't make good boyfriend or husband material. They were as temporal as spring weather, gone with the next gust of wind.

"Hey, Cody, want to join us?" Dylan asked.

Cody shrugged and hunkered down more, as if his hoodie could hide him from the world.

"We're just talking," Dylan said.

One of the other kids, a fair-haired tattooed kid wearing a T-shirt with Kurt Cobain's picture, leaned forward. "Yeah, like about girls and crap."

Another boy, with long dark hair and a dirty white T-shirt, leaned back against the couch. "My girl's all mad at me today. I spent the day in solitary and she's acting like I did it on purpose."

In solitary was slang for in-school suspension, something Abby knew all too well from Cody's frequent trips down that hall. She leaned back against the wall, waiting to see where the conversation would lead.

"Well, did you?" Dylan said.

Long Dark Hair snorted. "No. Who gets suspended on purpose?"

Dylan chuckled. "Some of us have done that. So I can sympathize."

"What do you know about our lives, man?" Cobain Fan scoffed. "What'd you do, skip a class? Blow off an essay?"

"I was a lot like you guys. One of those angry kids who thought he knew better than any adult. Now I—"

"Let me guess," Cody said. He had pushed the hoodie off his head. He had the same mop of dark brown hair as his little brother and his father, except he wore his long on the top and shaved on the sides. "You grew up, got a good job, bought a sweet house in the suburbs where you mow the lawn on Saturdays and crap like that. Matt's right. You don't know anything about how tough our lives are."

"I'm not claiming to be an expert, even if you all think I'm too old to understand," Dylan said. "Just someone who has made my fair share of mistakes."

"Doesn't mean you know anything about us," Matt—previously known as Cobain Fan—said.

"True. But it doesn't hurt to talk about your lives, does it? Maybe I can learn a thing or two from you guys, too." Dylan shrugged. "So let's talk."

Cody cursed. "Talking doesn't change jack. Waste of time."

"Hey, I get it that you all don't really want to sit here and go on and on about your lives. I'm not exactly Mr. Conversation myself. But I don't think sitting around here—" Dylan waved at the motley set of battered sofas "—pissed at the world is going to change anything. And I'm betting every one of you has something he wants to change about his life. So let's talk."

Abby couldn't have been more surprised if Dylan had stood up and started singing "The Star-Spangled Banner." She never would have imagined—given his appearance—that he would be so smart and intuitive with how he handled these kids. There was color in Cody's cheeks, interest in his eyes—

Two things Abby hadn't seen in a long, long time. Abby clutched the paper cup so hard it crumpled, praying her son would open up, stop shutting himself off from the world.

"Whatever, dude," Cody said finally, then got to his feet, flipping the hoodie back over his head as he rose. "I'm not here to have a Dr. Phil moment with some guy I don't even know. I'm just trying to survive."

Then he headed out the door, snagging a basketball from the bin as he went. The door shut behind him with a solid *thunk*.

Abby looked at Dylan. She could see the same disappointment in his face that she felt herself. For one brief second, Abby had felt like she had an ally.

And that was a dangerous thing to depend on, Abby reminded herself. She knew full well how a man could let her—and more, her sons—down. So she went back into the office and went back to work, doing the only thing she knew how to do, to—

Survive.

Chapter Two

Dylan straightened the sofas, replaced the cushions and pillows and picked up the empty soda cans from the scarred coffee table. The rest of the teenagers had headed outside after Cody, a sort of group mutiny. Dylan could hear the ping-ping of a basketball hitting the pavement.

Well, that hadn't gone too well. He'd hoped maybe he could connect with the teenagers, have an open discussion, maybe warn them off from making the same mistakes as he had. But so far, his batting average at being a teen group leader was pretty close to zero. For the hundredth time, he wondered why Uncle Ty had thought he could be good at this.

The little kids had finished their craft project, and were sitting in a circle on the carpet while Mavis read them a story about a lost kangaroo. Maybe that was the age when Dylan should be telling them to stay in school. When they still thought books and stories held magic, and when they weren't scarred by the world.

Uncle Ty came over and picked up a cushion that had fallen on the floor. "That went pretty well. I liked how you handled them."

Dylan turned to his uncle. "Really? They all walked out on me."

Ty waved that off. "It happens. The last thing teenagers want you to know is that they're listening to you and agreeing with you. The first time I led a teen group, it lasted maybe ten minutes before the whole lot of them walked out the door. I didn't have the basketball court or the game stations then, so they all went home. Your group lasted a lot longer than that."

"Maybe. But they still left." Dylan sighed.

"No, they're still here." Ty pointed to the boys outside the window, shooting layups and teasing each other between shots. "Getting teenagers to listen is like turning a cruise ship. You don't yank the wheel hard to the right. You nudge it, a little at a time, so the passengers don't even feel the turn."

Dylan chuckled. "Covert counseling?"

"Exactly."

"I'll keep that in mind." Talking to the teenagers had been like talking to his former self, if he could have done that fifteen or sixteen years ago and with better results. Of course, Dylan hadn't listened to anyone back then, not even his uncle. Dylan had been so angry at the world, so ready to leave Stone Gap. Maybe if he'd listened years ago, his path wouldn't have been so rocky, and he wouldn't be thirty-two and still trying to figure out what he wanted to be when he grew up.

"Don't worry so much. You're doing great." Ty looked around the room and let out a long breath. "There's so much to do here. I put everything on hold when Virginia got sick because I kept thinking she'd get better and I'd have time, but…" Ty shook his head. "I need to repaint. Replace that carpet. Repair a few of the chairs and sofas, fix the kitchen cabinets, replace a chunk of countertop that rotted when we had a water pipe burst. One of the toilets is leaking and there's a hole in the roof, two broken windows, a big hole in the hallway wall and another over there. That's just the big stuff, not to mention all the little things that need to be done around this place. I don't even know where to start."

He could hear the stress in Ty's voice. The center was, indeed, in need of a major overhaul. Major overhauls—of buildings at least—were something Dylan could do. He draped an arm over his uncle's shoulders. "It's like steering a cruise ship, Uncle Ty. One thing at a time. Show me where the tools are and I'll start on the repairs today."

Gratitude eased the worry in Ty's face. His uncle looked tired, worn down by the last few weeks. "I'll get my toolbox. I have a list as long as my arm of things I need to buy at the hardware store—"

"Give it to me. Go home tonight, let me lock up. The center's only open for another hour, and I'm sure I can handle things for that long. I'll run over to Ernie's hardware store in the morning and start the repair work tomorrow." It was the least he could do for his uncle during his time here. And, it would keep Dylan busy, which would also keep him from running into his brother. Or think about what he was going to do next, after he was done in Stone Gap. He had a job offer from his boss to manage a construction project in Maine. It was a multi-year commitment starting in the spring, for a slew of new housing. His boss had taken Dylan under his wing a couple years ago, even paid for Dylan to take the contractor's exam, to make him official. Jay was a good man, who had a similar history to Dylan's, and they'd hit it off from the start. It was the longest Dylan had ever stayed with one job, and most of that was due to Jay's support.

Dylan had put off the decision, telling Jay he needed to go to Stone Gap first. Be there for Uncle Ty and then…

Dylan would see. Taking the job from Jay would mean staying in one place, something Dylan wasn't so sure he wanted.

"Thank you, Dylan." Ty's eyes watered. "If Virginia and I had ever had a son…"

The emotion chafed at Dylan. He never knew quite what to do with emotions, his own or other people's. "Don't go getting all sentimental on me, Uncle Ty. Or I'll be the one heading out to the basketball court."

"Point taken." Ty chuckled. He dropped his keys into Dylan's palm. "Thank you. I'll see you in the morning."

Dylan squeezed his uncle's shoulder. "Don't worry. I've got it all under control. See you tomorrow."

As his uncle walked out of the building, the brunette—Cody's mother, Abby—emerged from Ty's office for the second time. Dylan had noticed her standing by the watercooler earlier. He didn't know how much, if any, she'd overheard of the conversation between him and the teenagers, or if she'd just been standing there to get a drink of water.

Abby and Mavis talked for a moment. Then Abby gave Mavis a nod and headed over to Dylan, with her little boy in tow. He was a younger version of Cody, but with a bright, inquisitive face and a ready smile.

"Mavis asked me to set up the snack for everyone because she has to leave early today. And she suggested I get some help, because there are a whole lot of hungry kids here."

He grinned. "So you're asking me to be crowd control?"

"Pretty much, yes. But if you're busy…"

"No, not at all." He could have been in the middle of building the Taj Mahal, and he would have told her he had plenty of time. Something about her blue-green eyes drew him in, made him want to know more about her. They were…

Intoxicating.

A tug on the hem of Dylan's T-shirt drew his attention. He glanced down and saw Abby's youngest son peering up at him, with eyes a deeper green than his mother's. He was a cute kid, only three feet tall, wearing a Transformers T-shirt, jeans and sneakers that blinked red lights when he walked. "I wanna snack. Miss Mavis said you're gonna make me one."

Abby put a hand on her son's shoulder. "Jake, that

isn't what Miss Mavis said. Mommy's gonna make the snack."

Jacob gave his mother a doubtful look. "But you don't cook very good, Mommy."

Abby's cheeks flushed. Dylan liked that. The blush made her seem open, vulnerable. "I'm going to head into the kitchen now before my son spills any more family secrets."

Dylan chuckled. "That's okay. I used to do that to my older brother all the time when we were kids. Especially if he had a girlfriend over. I once told Wendy Simmons about the time Sam got a hornet stuck in his shorts. I thought Sam was going to kill me."

That made Abby smile. She had a nice smile. Warm, friendly. "Sam… Sam Millwright? He's your brother? I've met him a couple times. He sold my boss the property that houses our offices."

"Yup. Sam's my brother." Dylan fell into step beside her as they walked toward the small kitchen at the back of the community center. "Almost five years older, but he thinks he's twenty years older. Like he's my father and needs to remind me how to be responsible."

Okay, so maybe a little more resentment leaked into his voice than he would have liked. No need to spill his own family secrets to a person who was, essentially, a stranger.

"I have a younger sister like that. She's the one who did it all right. Married the perfect man, works the perfect job at a magazine, lives in the perfect house in Connecticut." Abby sighed. "According to her, I'm…a mess." Then she blushed again, as if she wanted to suck the words back inside.

It was another moment of vulnerability, a chink in her armor. He suspected she rarely let anyone see her with her guard down.

"For what it's worth, I don't think you are a mess at all. When you walked in, it made me wish I was wearing something a little less…rock-concert-leftover, just so I could impress you. Like a suit or something." Damn, where had that come from? When was the last time he'd confessed anything like that? Maybe it was because she'd given him a peek inside. Or maybe it was the way Abby carried herself, all poised and confident, that had him feeling like she was, well…a little out of his league. Okay, a *lot*.

She arched a brow. "A suit?"

"I do own one, contrary to what my current attire suggests. Last time I wore it was at my grandfather's funeral and I think my mother still has it in a box somewhere. But I was ten, so I'm not so sure it would still fit me."

She laughed, then pushed on the swinging door. As soon as the three of them entered the kitchen, Jacob scrambled onto one of the stainless steel stools and sat at the counter. He set the picture he'd been working on aside, propped his elbows on the counter and sat up tall. "I'm ready to help, Mommy."

"That's great, Jakester. We're making peanut butter and jelly sandwiches." She tossed Dylan a look. The laughter had disappeared from her voice, and she was all business again. "Despite my son's one-star rating, I can handle those. Really. I'm sure you have other things to do and I hate to put you out. I'll be fine on my own. Really."

The teenagers had finished their basketball game and began to file into the building in a hum of conversation and heavy footsteps. As they headed for the couches, they glanced over at the kitchen. "Yo, man, where's the food?" Matt called out.

"Coming soon," Dylan said. He turned back to Abby. He got the distinct feeling she was giving him the brush-off. She had, after all, asked for his help, then promptly changed her mind. "I don't mind helping at all. And, I have the skills. I have, after all, been making my own sandwiches for almost twenty years now. In fact, I even have Expert Sandwich Maker on my résumé."

"And did you actually get hired somewhere because of that?"

"I think it was my Great Ninja Skills section that impressed the bosses." He winked at Jacob. "I bet you're a great ninja, Jake."

"I am. I scare Mommy all the time cuz I go like this." He hopped down off the stool, then tiptoed forward, with his hands bent like T. rex arms. "I'm super quiet."

Abby ruffled his hair. "You're four, Jake. I don't think *quiet* is an adjective for you yet."

Jake squirmed in his seat, as if proving the point that he was neither stealthy nor quiet. "Did you see my picture I made?"

Abby glanced at the paper. "Very good, Jake. I like your doggy."

From where Dylan stood, he wasn't sure how Abby

discerned the brown blob on the paper was a dog, but then again, Dylan wasn't exactly an art critic. Nor could he draw worth a damn. The pot couldn't exactly pass judgment on the kettle here.

"You know why I drew it?" Jake bounced up and down on his knees. "Cuz I love dogs."

Abby smiled. "I know. If there's one thing you talk about more than dinosaurs, my little non-ninja, it's dogs."

Jake studied his drawing, his lips thinned in concentration. "Can we get a puppy, Mommy? Mrs. Reynolds next door said her dog had puppies and I can has one if I want."

"It's *have*, and no, we're not getting a puppy right now. I have my hands full with you guys." She waved toward the sink. "Go wash your hands, buddy, then sit down again and you can lay out the bread. I'll put on the peanut butter and jelly."

"Or, I can do the peanut butter and you can do the jelly," Dylan said. Somehow, they had ended up inches apart. He could catch the floral notes of her perfume, see the lower lashes that dusted under her eyes. "Assembly-line style."

Why was he trying so hard? Even though Mavis had the little ones under control, Dylan did need to check on the older kids in the center and keep working on that list of repairs, and making sandwiches wasn't a job she couldn't handle.

"I've got it." She handed Jake the loaf of bread, then retrieved the peanut butter from the shelf. "Thanks."

The *thanks* was a clear dismissal. She had obviously

changed her mind about his help. She was also intelligent and beautiful and light-years out of his league. He should take the hint and leave her be.

Instead, he reached into the fridge for the jelly before she could grab it. "An extra set of hands makes the job go faster," Dylan said. "I have no doubt you are fully capable of making a couple dozen sandwiches all by yourself. But there are hungry kids out there who don't care who's slapping on the peanut butter, just as long as it's ready yesterday."

She glanced at the teenagers, who were watching the whole conversation from where they sat. At the same time, Mavis finished the book she was reading, and the little kids scrambled to their feet and dashed to sit at the tables. Mavis waved toward the door, a question in her face, and Abby nodded. "Okay. But only because the kids shouldn't have to wait."

It wasn't exactly her saying she'd been so charmed by his smile that she couldn't say no, but he'd take it.

Dylan slipped in beside her. Jake handed his mother a piece of bread, Abby slathered peanut butter on it, then Dylan spread jelly across the surface and topped it with a second slice of bread. "Are you always this difficult to help?" he asked.

"I'm not difficult. It's just…" She handed him the next piece of peanut-buttered bread. "In my experience, it's better to do things on my own than to count on someone else to help."

Someone had let this woman down. More than once. Dylan wouldn't consider himself Mr. Dependable, but he was the kind of guy who kept his word. He made three more sandwiches before he spoke again. "Well, maybe you've been counting on the wrong people."

She sent him a sideways glance. "Or maybe it's just better to count on myself. No surprises that way."

"Maybe. Or maybe not." He slapped the last piece of bread onto the final sandwich, then pulled a knife out of the drawer and cut the stacks in half.

"Diagonal," Abby said softly. "That's how my mom did it."

"Mine, too."

They shared a glance for a heartbeat, heat filling the space between them, then she spun toward the fridge and filled a tote with juice boxes. A second later, they'd put the snacks onto the sill between the kitchen and the main room. The kids descended like locusts, and before Dylan could blink, every last crumb was gone. Jacob wolfed down half a sandwich, then dashed off with the others to play with a bucket of Legos. That left Dylan and Abby alone in the kitchen.

"Well, I'd say you got a five-star rating on your peanut butter and jelly sandwiches." Dylan retrieved the empty tray and put it in the sink.

A grin flickered across her face. "Maybe I should add that to my résumé."

"Seems to me like you're the kind of girl who already has one hell of a résumé."

Interest sparked in her eyes. "And what makes you say that?"

"Because you are smart and talented. Not to mention beautiful, which isn't a résumé thing, I know, but—" He stopped before his mouth ran away from him.

Her gaze narrowed. "Are you making a pass at me?"

"I'm…" Was he? He wasn't sure. He wasn't in town long, and even if he was staying, he wasn't a guy who did long-term. Abby was completely out of his league and definitely had *long-term* written all over her. That reality reined him back in. "Just making an observation."

"Oh. Well, uh, thank you. That's…that's very nice of you to say." She spun away from the sink and started loading the leftover juice boxes back into the refrigerator.

Dylan knew a brush-off when he saw one, and Abby had just flicked him off like a cobweb on her shoulder. Dylan gave Abby one more look, then headed back out to the main room.

Abby washed the platter and knives, then dried them and stored them on the shelves of the kitchen. She glanced around the room and noticed the peeling paint, the nearly bare shelves, the broken cabinets, the missing chunk of countertop. She'd been bringing her kids here for a year and had never seen it this…lonely. When Virginia had been alive, the kitchen had been full and sparklingly clean. Now it just seemed tired.

Dylan stuck his head in the door. "Hey, we're closing soon. Do you need anything?"

"No. But I think this place does." She let out a sigh. "Things started falling apart when Virginia got sick, but since she died…it just hasn't been the same around here."

Dylan came inside and let the door swing shut behind him. "My aunt Virginia was one of a kind."

"I didn't know her long, but I'd agree with you. She was like a second mother to the kids." Abby folded the dish towel in thirds and laid it on the counter. Maybe it was his help with the sandwiches, maybe it was seeing him try so hard to talk to Cody, but Abby found herself opening up ever so slightly. "When I first started coming here with the boys, Virginia was the one who connected with Cody. Jacob, he's the kind of kid who connects with anyone, but Cody…he hasn't been the same since his father left."

Dylan leaned against the counter and crossed his arms over his chest. He looked so solid there, like the kind of guy she could lean against. "My aunt was like that with me, too. I didn't get along with my dad, and Uncle Ty and Aunt Virginia became more like my parents." Dylan shifted his weight. "How long has it been since Cody's dad left? Sorry. Ty told me a little about your situation."

She should have been angry. Abby tended to keep her personal life to herself. But she saw something in Dylan, something that reminded her of her boys. He had, after all, gotten Ty's stamp of approval which wasn't given to just anyone. Maybe this guy knew something about how hard it was for her to be mom, dad and breadwinner all at the same time. Or maybe she'd just liked the way he smiled at her earlier. In a day filled with stress, that had made her feel good for a second.

"You want to hear about the first or the second time?" She shook her head. "I was stupid enough to take him back and try again. He was gone again the day I found out I was pregnant with Jacob. Despite all the promises he made, when it came down to it, my ex wasn't exactly interested in being a father." She shrugged, like it was no big deal. She'd gotten over the hurt long ago, but there were days when she wanted to throttle the boys' father for the looks of disappointment in their eyes. He'd barely done more than send a birthday card while Cody was growing up, but she'd thought Keith had changed during those few months when he came back. Believed him when he said he wanted a second chance. She'd foolishly thought maybe having Jacob would change things. It hadn't.

"Well, at least the boys got a great mother," Dylan said.

She didn't feel that great on the days when she got truancy notices about Cody and difficult questions from a curious Jake who was beginning to notice he didn't have a father. "And how do you know I'm a great mother?"

"I don't. But your kids seem to be good kids, and that doesn't happen by accident." He pushed off from the counter and crossed to her. "I've never had kids, but I know how important it is to have a good influence in your life."

This was not a topic Abby wanted to discuss. All it did was remind her of how she had picked the wrong man—twice. She averted her gaze and concentrated on wiping up some crumbs. "It's great that you're helping Ty."

"Yeah, well, I'm not really doing much."

He seemed embarrassed by the praise. She wanted to know why, if he was just a naturally humble guy or if he didn't think he deserved it. But she didn't ask, because she had enough on her plate and caring about one more person would tip her over the edge.

Cody was a minute away from being kicked out of school. Jake was doing okay, but he was having trouble paying attention in preschool, and she was worried that he was going to end up following his older brother down a difficult path.

At least they have a great mother—she wasn't so sure about that. She glanced through the half window at Jake, sitting in a chair by the window, no longer interacting with the other kids, while Cody was draped across an armchair, lost in his phone, sullen and angry again. Whatever momentary good mood he'd experienced earlier was gone now.

She sighed. This was why she couldn't get involved with anyone. Couldn't even think about a personal life, no matter how nice Dylan's smile was or how kind his eyes seemed. Because she was barely holding her own life together.

Chapter Three

The Stone Gap Inn looked like the kind of home Dylan had seen on the cover of *Southern Living* magazine. A wide, welcoming front porch with twin rockers, a gorgeous oak door with a brass knocker, opening into a picturesque foyer with a curved staircase.

Mavis grabbed Dylan as soon as he walked in the door that night and gathered him into another big hug. "Oh, it was so good to see you this afternoon," she said. "Your uncle was sure glad you came back to town."

"I'm glad to be here." He pressed a kiss to Mavis's cheek, then drew back. "Tell me you're still making your rhubarb pie."

"You know I am." She grinned. "And I have a piece waiting for you."

"I've been looking forward to it all day." He followed

Mavis down the hall into a sunny yellow kitchen. "You guys have done amazing work with this place."

Mavis beamed, clearly proud of the B&B. "That was all the doing of Della's boys and her new daughter-in-law. They put in a whole lot of blood, sweat and tears to take this place from decrepit to delightful."

Dylan had grown up with the Barlow brothers. He wasn't surprised they'd all pitched in together to help Della rebuild this place. He'd always thought he and Sam would be close like that, but…

Ancient history. There was no sense wishing for things that weren't going to change. "How's business been?" Dylan asked.

"Getting better every day, as word spreads and people hear about my rhubarb pie." She winked as she laid a hearty slice before him.

"I take it the pie is in the Yelp reviews?"

"Of course." Mavis settled into the chair opposite him. "So, I bet you being back in town has the ladies down at Sadie's Clip 'n' Curl buzzing."

Dylan shook his head and chuckled. "Stone Gap hasn't changed a bit."

Mavis's hand covered his. "That's what makes it so great."

He scoffed. "For you, maybe. I'm only in town to help Uncle Ty and then—"

"Back to running away."

"I'm not running away, Mavis. I'm too old to do that."

She peered at him over her reading glasses "You most certainly are. So maybe this time you could consider staying. You've got family here, Dylan, and that's not something you can find growing like blueberries in Maine. Your uncle told me you were thinking about taking a permanent job up there. It's no Stone Gap, you know. Now, enjoy your pie. I already made up your room, second one on the left at the top of the stairs. You're staying in the Asheville. Oh, and don't forget, there'll be waffles in the morning."

She left Dylan to finish his pie. He washed his plate and fork, loaded them into the drying rack, then went to bed. Mavis was wrong about him, but he knew her well and knew trying to change her mind was like trying to shift the direction of the Mississippi River.

The next morning, Dylan headed into the community center shortly after eight, his belly full of homemade waffles and rich maple syrup. He'd planned to arrive earlier, but he'd had to wait for Ernie's hardware store to open up so he could buy the list of supplies Uncle Ty had given him. His uncle had kept the list at a bare minimum, so Dylan added a few things—okay, a lot of things—to the cart before he checked out. Dylan had enough savings to cover the costs, because he suspected Uncle Ty didn't have any kind of budget. Some of the bigger items would have to be ordered from a big-box store, but Ernie carried enough to get Dylan started.

Uncle Ty wasn't in, so Dylan used the key from yesterday to let himself into the building. He flicked on the lights, pausing a moment in the doorway to notice the quiet. He'd never been in the community center when it was empty. The place seemed sad, as if all the life left it when the kids went home.

He decided to start with the projects that were safety issues. The list of things to do was long, but if he worked his way backward from the areas where the kids congregated first, he could minimize the risk of anyone getting hurt. First, he tackled a broken electrical outlet, then moved on to repair a wonky light switch. The community center didn't officially open until two, when the older kids got out of school, so that gave Dylan a few hours to work.

Dylan was getting ready to patch a hole in the wall when the front door opened. He pivoted, expecting Uncle Ty. "Cody. What are you doing here?"

The teenager shrugged. He slid his backpack off one shoulder and dropped it in the corner. "Just needed a break."

Dylan glanced at his watch. "It's only ten in the morning. Aren't you supposed to be in school?"

Cody shrugged again. He dropped onto a love seat and propped his boots on the opposite end. He draped an arm over his eyes and leaned his head back.

Dylan watched him for a minute. He recognized that don't-care attitude, the slouched shoulders, the ripped jeans and faded concert T. "Yo, this isn't a motel."

Cody didn't respond.

Undoubtedly, the kid was skipping school. Dylan debated whether he should call Abby and realized he didn't have her number. And Cody probably wouldn't give it up.

"Listen, let me take you back to school. Finish up the day, then come back here."

Cody shook his head. "No. No way."

"You can't skip school, Cody," Dylan said.

"Why not? I'm practically failing anyway. What's the point?"

"Getting a diploma so you won't be stuck serving fries to ten-year-olds when you're fifty?"

"I don't care about that. All I care about is being left alone." Cody jerked up his backpack and turned to go. "I don't need a lecture from you, too."

Dylan sighed. He could see what was going to happen as soon as the boy walked out the door. It was pretty much Dylan's history repeating itself. Dylan knew that look and knew it well—

Cody would leave here and get into trouble faster than the wind could shift on a fall afternoon.

He thought of the stress on Abby's face the day before. How overwhelmed she seemed, being both father and mother. The last thing he wanted to do was add to her troubles. Cody was safe here—albeit skipping school—and if Dylan kept him occupied, at least there'd be something good to come out of the whole thing.

"Before you go, Cody…" Dylan unloaded his supplies and set them beside his toolbox. A square of Sheetrock, a small handsaw, some plaster and a putty knife. He looked at the hole in the wall—a deep circular indent that was probably from some angry teen's fist—and then back at Cody. "I could use a hand, if you have a minute."

Cody didn't move. "Where's Ty?"

"Not here." Dylan wasn't about to explain to a sixteen-year-old how his uncle was mourning the loss of the love of his life, and doing what he had done ever since Virginia died—sitting in his house, trying to get the motivation to go to the center she had loved so much and that echoed without her presence. Dylan had stopped by last night for a little bit, and seen the loss of the love of his life hanging over Ty like a cloud. At Cody's age, relationships started in homeroom and ended by sixth period. "Come on, dude, help me out."

Cody stood there a moment longer, then let out a long sigh, then dropped his backpack into the corner again. He glanced over at the wall. "That wasn't my fault, you know."

"Whose fault was it?"

"Leon. That dude's got an anger management issue. Meaning, he doesn't manage it at all." Cody traced the outline of the hole. "He got pissed because somebody changed the channel without asking him first, like he's the warden around here."

Dylan tried to think back to the names of the kids who'd been in the circle last afternoon. "Was he here yesterday?"

"Nah, Ty kicked him out and told him not to come back. He does that with any of us who break the rules."

Dylan chuckled. "Some things never change." Uncle Ty had been a little more lenient with Dylan, but there'd been times he'd skated on the edge of banishment.

Cody gestured toward the wall. "So, uh, what do you have to do here?"

"The hole is too big for an ordinary patch," Dylan said. "I'm going to trim the Sheetrock to fill in the space, then attach it to the stud behind the hole. We'll put a patch over that, and in a few hours, it'll dry and be good as new."

"Sounds pretty simple."

"It is. Here, hold this." Dylan handed him the Sheet-rock without asking if he wanted to help. Keeping the kid busy was a good policy regardless, Dylan figured.

Cody held the square of Sheetrock, bracing it against the floor, while Dylan sawed off a piece big enough to fill the hole. A couple times, he glanced back over his shoulder to assess the right shape, then perfect the cutout.

"How do you know all this stuff?" Cody asked. "Did your dad teach you?"

His dad. Jonathon Millwright had favored Sam, the eldest. Sam was the one who could do no wrong, who got good grades, who married his high school sweet-heart, had a career and a couple of kids. Dylan spent his entire childhood being compared to his brother—and always came up lacking. No one had been on his side. Their mother had supported her critical, control-ling husband, no matter what.

"My dad and I didn't exactly get along. He was never real hands-on, especially with me." Dylan shrugged. Better to keep the story short and simple than to explain decades of troubled history. "Uncle Ty taught me some stuff, and I learned the rest along the way."

Cody slipped the piece into the space in the wall, then held it while Dylan screwed it into place. "What do you mean, along the way?"

Should he tell Cody the truth? Would the kid see it as a journey to be emulated or an example of what not to do? "I dropped out when I was your age. Hitched a ride out of here and took whatever jobs I could so I could afford a place to stay warm and something to eat."

"Sounds awesome."

"It was the exact opposite of awesome." Dylan lowered the screw gun. "Some nights I slept on the ground or in a doorway. Many days I didn't have anything to eat because I couldn't catch a ride or find a job. It sucked, a lot."

"Yeah, but it worked out okay for you. Didn't it?"

"I took the long road to get here. If I had been smart and listened to the advice I was given, I might have taken a few less detours." Dylan peeled the lid off the plaster and held out the putty knife to Cody. "Here, you do this."

"I don't know how." Cody scuffed at the floor. The hood of his sweatshirt obscured his face. "My dad didn't show me anything, either. He's never been anything more than a sperm donor."

Dylan could hear the hurt in the kid's voice. Dylan might have had a strained relationship with his father, but at least he'd had one, and he'd had Uncle Ty to pick up the slack. Cody looked like he could use an Uncle Ty of his own, or at least a reasonable facsimile.

Dylan, however, was the only one here. He didn't even begin to think he was role model material, but maybe he could at least teach Cody a couple things and steer him away from the bad decisions Dylan had made at his age.

That was a lot to ask from a piece of Sheetrock and some plaster, but he was going to try.

"Here," Dylan said, placing the putty knife in Cody's palm. "I'll show you."

Cody brushed the hood back, then glanced over at Dylan. "For real?"

"Yeah." Dylan grinned at Cody. "I might not know everything, but I do know how to fix a hole in a wall."

Not a hole in a kid's life. That was a task way out-side of Dylan's skill set.

Abby rushed into the community center, breathless and angry. She'd gotten the call from the high school truant officer a little after eleven and spent the better part of her lunch hour trying to find Cody. He wasn't at home, he wasn't at the park. Finally, she thought of the community center. Ty was known to let the kids hang out during the day if they wanted a place to chill, usu-ally calling their parents so they wouldn't worry. She hadn't gotten a call, so she'd worked on the assumption Cody was spending his hooky time elsewhere. But she'd run out of other places to look.

There was a car in front of the building, not Ty's green pickup but a battered red Jeep. She remembered seeing the same car yesterday and realized it must be Dylan's. She parked and hurried into the building.

Then stuttered to a stop.

Dylan and Cody were working together, repairing a broken window screen. Dylan was holding the frame while Cody rolled some tool along the edge, that rein-serted the plastic line that held it in place. Dylan was explaining how the tool worked while Cody listened, his eyes bright, his face attentive. They were so engrossed in the task, they didn't hear her enter.

"So, what did you mean earlier about taking the long road?" Cody asked.

Abby started to open her mouth to yell at Cody for

skipping school when she heard Dylan start to speak. She hung by the door, watching and listening.

"I was young and stupid. I thought it didn't matter if I graduated high school or went to college," Dylan said. "You start ditching class when you're young, and it gets easier to ditch the other important things in life. Like a job. Like an interview. Like a date. I became someone who quit. A lot."

Cody snorted. "Is this going to be one of those *kid, you should stay in school* speeches? Because I get enough of that already."

"Nope. I'm not telling you what to do. You probably wouldn't listen any better than I did." Dylan sighed. "I will tell you, though, that I learned my lesson when I was washing dishes until my hands bled from the hot water—or when they were frozen stiff from hauling hundred-pound bags of potatoes off of trucks for hours in the cold. That's when I wished I had stayed in school."

She wouldn't have thought Dylan had a past like that. He was a little rough around the edges, but he seemed responsible, smart, strong. Or maybe it was just his smile that blinded her to everything else.

"I hate school," Cody said. "I just wanna blow that place so bad."

Dylan turned to Cody. "Stick it out. I know it's hard, dude. At the time, it's going to seem like the hardest thing you've ever done. But if you stay with school and graduate, that's success."

"Success? What, graduating at the bottom of the class?" Cody snorted and shook his head. And this was where Abby usually lost the argument. Because his grades were so bad, Cody saw graduating as a lost cause. Instead of trying hard to change that, he gave up.

"You gotta learn to finish what you start." Dylan shifted the screen and stretched the material over the frame. "Dropping out puts you behind the curve before you even get out of the gate. It's a hell of a lot harder to get where you're going if you start five steps behind than if you start in the middle."

Cody didn't say anything, but Abby could see that he was mulling over Dylan's words. They were the same ones Abby had said, over and over again, but this time, Cody actually seemed to be taking them in. Maybe it was because it was advice from a stranger, given in a rougher language than she would have used. Maybe because Dylan had been down Cody's path already and spoke from experience.

Dylan stepped back and assessed their work on the screen. "Looks good. We'll just trim the extra bit of screen along the edge, and it'll be good as new," Dylan held out the tool to Cody. "Here, you want to try? Be careful. The blade is sharp."

Cody took the retractable knife from Dylan, then slid it along the edge of the new rubber spline, trimming the extra sliver of mesh. "Hey, that was pretty easy." Cody leaned back, and looked the window over. "It looks like it was never torn."

"The magic of a good repair job. Let's hang this—" Dylan cut off the sentence when he turned and noticed Abby standing there. "Oh, hey, Abby."

Cody let out a low curse, then turned toward his mother. "Mom, I can explain—"

"And you'd better. You know what the principal said about you skipping." She crossed to her son, taking a moment to be glad he was okay and not drinking or doing drugs or getting into some other kind of trouble. The last couple years with Cody had been rocky at best, which was why she had started bringing him to the community center. She'd hoped he'd find a good outlet for all the angst and anger that came with being sixteen and essentially abandoned by his father. Up until now, Cody hadn't done much more than make a token effort at being involved here. Seeing him working with Dylan had been a revelation…but it didn't stop her frustration.

"Don't you understand that you are one bad move away from being expelled? You only have one job, Cody. Go to school."

The light in Cody's eyes dimmed. "I know. I just got all stressed because Mrs. Deets was on my back again, so I ditched and came here."

"We talked about how you can't just do this, Cody." She ran a hand through her hair and let out a gust. "I'm worried about your future."

Cody cursed under his breath. "I heard the lecture already, Mom. I don't need another one."

She spun toward Dylan. "And why didn't you bring him back?"

"Because I figured he'd be gone again five minutes later. So I thought I'd give him something constructive to do. I let him stay, but he had to promise me he'd go to school every day next week. He's been helping me with the repairs around here. We fixed the small hole in that wall, tightened a leaky faucet in the kitchen, and now we're working on the window screens. He did a great job."

The praise lifted Cody's head. He shot Dylan a look that was a mixture of surprise and joy. Cody had had very few male role models in his life, and none that he had warmed to as quickly as he had warmed to Dylan.

"I even learned how to patch a hole, Mom," Cody said. He gestured toward the wall. "You wouldn't even know Leon put his fist through there."

She could see pride in her son's face. Interest. It was more than she'd seen in months, and the moment caused a little catch in her throat. Her anger evaporated. "That's great, Code. Really great."

"I know you're probably going to drag me back to school," Cody said, his voice low, his gaze on the floor. "But Dylan really needed some help with the windows today. One of them is broken, and Dylan's worried somebody might try to break in."

She opened her mouth to protest and to tell Cody she had, indeed, been here to bring him back to school. But she took one look at his face, at the enthusiasm written all over him and decided one more missed day wasn't going to hurt anything. Maybe a little bit of success would help Cody find his footing again. It was, after all, only one day. "Sure. That sounds like a good thing to do. Why don't I run out and get you guys some lunch? I bet you're starving."

"You mean I can stay?" Surprise lit Cody's voice. He almost sounded like he was Jake's age again, shocked she had let him stay at the playground for an extra half hour. There was no argument in him, none of the sullenness that was usually part of his daily wardrobe. For a split second, he was Cody again, the son she had been missing for a long, long time.

And that was worth one missed day of school.

"Yeah, you can stay." She glanced at Dylan. "As long as that's okay with you."

Dylan nodded and turned to her son. "Totally cool with me. As long as you go to school next week, like we agreed. No skipping."

"Deal," Cody said.

"Great. I'll be back with some subs." She turned away, before Cody saw the tears that were threatening at the back of her eyes. She pushed on the door and stepped out into the North Carolina sunshine.

"Hey, thanks for letting Cody stay."

She spun at the sound of Dylan's voice behind her. She tried to work a smile onto her face, but it wobbled. Her composure was on the brink of disappearing. She fumbled for her sunglasses in her purse and slipped them on. "Thank you for letting him help. He's never really gotten to do any of that stuff before, and he looks like he's enjoying the work."

"He's a good kid." Dylan eased the door shut and stepped out onto the porch with Abby. "I know you've had some problems with him lately, with cutting class and getting in trouble."

"He told you that?"

"Not in so many words. I…" Dylan looked back over his shoulder at the door. "I see a lot of myself in him. I was like that at his age. Mad at the world, ready to run at the slightest hint of a problem."

In a few words, Dylan had summarized all the fears and worries that Abby had been keeping to herself. She shook her head, and the tears she'd been trying to hold back began to spill onto her lashes.

Abby worked so hard to be strong, to handle everything herself. But right now, the stress, the worry, seemed too heavy, too much. Jake wanting a puppy, something normal kids all over the world asked for, had been something she couldn't even entertain. She was barely holding herself together, never mind her kids and her life. When the school had called, it had crushed the very fragile hold on her stress. And now, the relief that Cody was okay, that he was actually doing something constructive—that had her teetering on the edge of a sob. "It's been hard, you know? Being mom and dad at the same time. My friends don't understand, because they've all got partners or grandparents around to pick up the slack, but it's just me, and Cody is at that age where he needs a man who can be a good influence. Ty was a good role model to him, but then Virginia died—Ty started withdrawing and Cody went off the rails again and…"

Dylan took her hand, and her babbling brook of words ceased. His touch was warm and strong, comforting. He gave her a little squeeze. "Hey, it's going to be okay. He's a good kid."

Abby raised her gaze to Dylan's. For just a moment, she needed that reassurance. In a second, she told herself, she'd go back to being strong and independent. "You really think so? I mean, that he'll be okay?"

What was she doing? Asking a perfect stranger to predict her kid's future? Maybe she was hormonal. Or maybe it was simply that Abby was exhausted, drained by the simple task of raising two boys on her own while trying to build a career at the marketing agency and keep everyone fed and clothed—and feeling like she wasn't doing any of the above well.

"I don't have a crystal ball, but I do think he's ready to find a better way to do things," Dylan said. "Maybe spending some time helping out around here will give him a sense of accomplishment. I know I found my way by going into renovation and new construction work. There's just something about seeing a room or a house or even a table take shape under your own two hands that makes you feel like you have control over your world."

She liked how Dylan described his work. And for Cody, she got a sense that that feeling of control and accomplishment was important. Her oldest had struggled so much with having a father who barely cared. The therapist she'd taken him to a few times had said that Cody really needed to find an outlet for his emotions, a way to express himself. Jake did that through his art, but Cody tended to bottle up his feelings. Both times he had been with Dylan, she had seen Cody come out of his shell and quite literally come out from under the security of his hoodie. A wave of reassurance swept over her, because for a moment, she wasn't alone. "Cody needs that. He needs it a lot."

"Then let him hang here with me. Tomorrow's Saturday, and if he wants to come over here bright and early, he can help me fix the broken cabinet in the kitchen and some busted tiles. Ty's got a long list of needs for this place, and I want to do as much as I can to help him while I'm here."

"I noticed that things had gotten out of hand when I was looking around the kitchen. I was thinking maybe I could go to the store and get some supplies for the center this weekend. It seems like Ty is out of everything."

"Virginia did all the ordering for him. He's kinda lost without her. I think everyone is." Dylan released her hand, as if he'd just realized he'd been holding it.

A little flutter of disappointment went through her, but she was determined not to show it. She knew better than to depend on anyone other than herself. Already she was starting to like this guy, to crave more time with him. She could see why Cody liked him so much. Dylan was confident and quiet, yet patient and warm. Not to mention, he cared—about Cody, about his aunt and uncle. That caring nature was something she could get used to—and even considering getting used to counting on someone meant she was treading on dangerous ground. "Uh...what kind of sub do you want?"

"I'm not picky." He grinned. "Surprise me."

"I'd hate to disappoint you."

"You won't, Abby. Believe me." He started into the building, then turned back and put a hand on her arm.

This time, his touch sent a flutter through her veins. She lifted her gaze, surprised at the electricity, the intensity that a simple touch could bring. She had the strangest urge to press her lips to the slight dusting of stubble on his chin, to inhale his cologne.

"I have an idea," Dylan said.

"Oh, yeah?" Her voice shook a little, damn it.

"Why don't I pick you and both the boys up tomorrow morning? That way, I can help you get the supplies for the kitchen, and you all can go with me to the home improvement store. I need to order some things that Ernie doesn't carry, and I'm sure both boys will love being around power tools and forklifts."

For a second there, she'd thought Dylan was going to ask her out on a date. It took a moment for her brain to process what he was saying. That it wasn't a date at all. Disappointment sank in her gut, which was completely insane. She didn't have time or room in her life for another person with testosterone. "Sure. If you don't mind. The boys would love that."

"Great." He grinned. "Then it's a date?"

No, it's not. She worked a smile onto her face. "Of course."

But as Abby climbed into her car and headed away from the community center, she did her best to ignore her disappointment. She ignored it. The last thing she wanted to do was fall for another man with a charming smile and all the right words. Because in the end, the words were empty and the ones who got hurt were the boys she was trying so hard to protect.

She flicked a gaze at the rearview mirror and saw Dylan, talking to Cody by their newly repaired window. Her heart cracked a little, and she whispered a silent prayer that this time she was wrong about that man and his smile.

Chapter Four

Dylan borrowed Ty's extended cab pickup truck early the next morning. The Ford rattled and shook its way down the road, yet another thing on its last legs. Dylan made a mental note to take a look under the hood later this afternoon. He was no mechanic, but he knew his way around basic engine maintenance.

He pulled into Abby's driveway. She lived in a small bungalow on Peach Street, a cul-de-sac filled with kids' bicycles, swing sets and a basketball hoop at the end of the curve. Her house was older, maybe built in the fifties, but it was neat and tidy, with a row of red geraniums along the front. A wooden swing hung from eyehooks on the porch and swung gently in the breeze.

He half expected a white picket fence and a golden retriever to come running out the door. Abby lived in the kind of house he'd expect to see in some sitcom. The kind of home he'd avoided all his life. It smacked of commitment, domesticity and—

Shackles. Expectations.

Jake poked his head up from the porch. He had a gold-colored dog in his arms, as if providing the final key to Dylan's view of the perfect family life. He waved like crazy at Dylan, keeping the puppy balanced in one hand. Abby came out onto the porch, bent down and scolded her youngest son, who trudged next door, dropped the puppy into an outdoor playpen, then headed back, his eyes downcast and his face full of pout.

The front door opened again, and Cody emerged, looking half asleep and angry to be woken up so early on a weekend. At the door, Abby touched Jake's shoulder, and the little boy turned around. Abby bent down and zipped the front of Jake's spring jacket. She placed a hand on her son's chest and gave him a smile. He smiled back, then leaned forward on his toes and wrapped his arms around his mother.

Something in Dylan's heart squeezed. The whole scene—Abby and her sons in the shade of the front porch, a dark-haired trio framed by the pale yellow house—smacked of domesticity. Dylan should have felt more cynical. Jaded.

Instead he felt...

Envy.

Crazy thoughts. He lived his life like a tumbleweed. He wasn't the kind to get wrapped up in geraniums and porch swings. Dylan jerked his attention back to the present, rolled down the passenger-side window and leaned across the cab. "Good morning, everyone. You all set?"

"Yup." Jake beamed, his frown gone. "Mommy says we're gonna see a fork truck."

Dylan chuckled. "A forklift, and yes, we'll see at least one of those today."

Abby gave Jake a nudge. "Boys, why don't you get in the truck so we don't keep Dylan waiting?"

At his mother's reminder, Cody opened the back door for his little brother, installed a booster seat, and then the boys climbed in back. "Hi, Dylan," Jake said, leaning over the seat and halfway into the front. "I can't wait to build stuff today. Can we build a doghouse someday? In case I get a puppy?"

Abby shot him a glance and shook her head.

"Uh, maybe," he said, then directed his attention to the teenager. "Hey, Cody."

Cody gave Dylan a half nod. "Hey."

Well, at least he hadn't turned into a zombie. For a second there, Dylan wasn't sure. And he might not be peppy, but Cody's usual attitude seemed to be at a minimum. All good signs for the day ahead.

Abby climbed into the passenger's seat. She'd dressed in jeans, a worn gray T-shirt and a blue hooded sweatshirt that was unzipped. Her hair was in a ponytail that swung along her neck and her makeup was light. She looked beautiful. Sweet.

Damn. He was turning into a walking poem. Had to be the early morning and lack of caffeine. He'd been running late and he'd headed out of the B&B without his usual cup of joe. Yeah, that was it.

"Good morning," Abby said.

"Good morning." He shot her a grin. "I see you're ready to work."

"I have almost no handyman skills, but I do have a good attitude."

"That's half the battle. The rest can be taught." He glanced in the rearview mirror at Cody. The teenager was sitting with his arms crossed over his chest, a scowl on his face. Apparently the good attitude hadn't taken root in all members of the Cooper family.

"Hey, Jake, Cody, buckle up. Okay?"

Cody rolled his eyes but did as he was told. Jake sat back in the seat, dragged his seatbelt across his lap, clicked it into place, then crossed his arms in his lap, his face eager.

A big-box grocery store and a home improvement store were located just outside of Stone Gap, about twenty minutes away. Jake started chattering before the truck even left the driveway. "What are we gonna build, Dylan? Do I get to use a hammer?"

He chuckled. "Maybe. First we have to pick up the supplies. Then we'll decide what we want to fix first."

"I don't know how to hammer stuff," Jake said.

"That's okay. I'll teach you." Dylan glanced over at Abby. She had a slight smile on her face, and when she caught him looking, she averted her gaze. "I can teach your mom, too."

She laughed. "I might be a hopeless case. Give me a marketing presentation to write, and I'm in my element. But fixing a leaky toilet or hanging a picture…

Let's just say I've used a lot of superglue and duct tape to repair stuff in my house."

"Hey, those are valid home-repair tools." He shot her a grin. "Seriously, though, if you need help with something at your house, I'd be glad to step in. Fixing houses is pretty much how I make a living."

"I'll keep that in mind."

He wondered if she was being polite or if she really meant that. And why he cared when he wasn't planning on staying in Stone Gap. He reminded himself that Abby was one of those women who settled down, planted geraniums. And he was the kind of guy who moved on before the geraniums bloomed.

Jake kept up his chatter, asking about hammers and nails and doors and pretty much anything he could think to ask about. The conversation went in loopy circles, detouring from hammers to dogs then back again to nails. Dylan glanced at Abby, who clearly was used to Jake's roundabout style.

"Is this pretty much how it always is with a kid?" he asked her, keeping his voice low.

She chuckled. "Yup. Jake's mind moves a million miles a minute, and he's one of the most creative kids I've ever met. You'll get used to it."

Dylan wanted to contradict her, but figured if he announced he wasn't staying long, he'd spoil the light mood in the truck and also indicate that he cared more than he did. Abby was a friend, and her kids were just... help for the day. Albeit, chatty, inexperienced help.

Once they parked at the home improvement store, Jake and Cody got out of the truck and followed along behind Dylan and Abby. Dylan grabbed a bright orange cart, then headed down the aisles. Jake kept on talking as Dylan shopped, picking up Sheetrock, some plywood, a box of replacement tiles for the bathrooms and a stack of other supplies. "Well, I think we've about emptied the store," Dylan said. "Let me just drop off this order for the countertop at the front desk and we can check out."

Cody hadn't said two words the entire time. He'd barely shown any interest in anything Dylan bought, eyes glued to his phone. Abby tried to engage her teenage son several times but didn't receive much more than grunts in return.

"Cody, why don't you help me load the truck while your mom and Jake grab us some hot dogs?" Dylan turned to Abby and handed her some money. "If you don't mind. There's a vendor right outside the store."

"Not at all." She took Jake's hand. "Come on, Jakester, let's get some hot dogs."

"I love hot dogs!" Jake looked up at his older brother. "Do you love them, Cody?"

Cody shrugged. "They're okay."

"I'll get you one. Okay?" Jake gave his brother a wide grin, which Cody half returned, then Jake headed outside with his mother.

Dylan placed his order, paid for his purchase and walked to the truck with Cody. "I know you probably don't want to be here—"

"Are you really going to do it?" Cody spun toward him.

"Do what?"

"Teach Jake how to fix stuff? You're not going to just ditch him at home or something, are you?"

"No, of course not. Why would I…?" Dylan's voice trailed off as he put the pieces together. The absentee father, the boys who had been raised by a single mom. The stoic, seemingly emotionless teenage boy, making sure his little brother wasn't disappointed again. Dylan saw so much of Sam and himself in these two boys—or at least him and his brother when they were younger and got along. He could see the flicker of hope in Cody's face, gone almost as fast as it appeared.

"I meant what I said, Cody." He met the teenager's gaze and held it. "I'm going to teach both of you how to fix things. And your mom, if she wants to learn, too."

Cody considered that, then slid the plywood into the bed of the truck. "Okay. Good."

They put the rest of the supplies in the truck, finishing up just as Jake and Abby returned with the hot dogs. She glanced at her oldest son, then at Dylan. Cody hadn't said much, but his mood had considerably brightened and Dylan could see the relief in Abby's face.

"Hey, thanks for grabbing lunch," Dylan said.

"You're welcome. Though your arteries might argue with the menu choice." She handed him one of the hot dogs. "Isn't stopping me from having one, though. I swear, it's been years since I ate a hot dog. I'm not big on junk food, as my boys will attest."

He shifted closer to her. "Life is short, Abby. You should have some really good junk food once in a while. It makes you appreciate the healthy stuff later."

She laughed. "I don't know if I agree with that logic. But I'll give it a try."

Cody took his lunch and climbed into the truck cab. Jake clambered up beside his big brother and started talking a mile a minute about the hot dog vendor, the bird he saw in the parking lot, the dollop of mustard on his shirt.

Abby watched her sons with a bittersweet look in her eyes. "Those two boys are like night and day. I swear, Jake was born happy and talkative. Cody was always my quiet one. The good kid when he was a baby—a good sleeper, good eater. Jake had enough energy for ten kids—always squirming, never wanted to sleep. Now Cody's become…" She sighed. "Maybe it's just teenage stuff."

Dylan gave the cart a shove and sent it sailing into the corral. It nestled with the others with a soft clank. "They're both good kids, Abby."

"Thanks." A shy smile filled her face, and he could tell, this was the place where she was most easily touched. When it came to her kids, Abby allowed that wall to wobble ever so slightly. He liked that.

He wasn't going to slip into their lives and become Ward Cleaver, but he could enjoy a Saturday morning in her company and make it fun for her kids. Dylan took her trash and tossed it in a nearby can. "Let's get back to the center. I can drop you off at home on the way, if you want, then bring the boys home when we're done working. You don't have to help."

"I want to. The center is important to me, too." Abby climbed into her side of the truck and waited while

Dylan got in the driver's seat. "I've been trying to get Ty a grant so he can do some big improvements, maybe even expand. But grant writing isn't my specialty, so I haven't been successful yet."

He glanced over at her. Abby was the first person outside his aunt and uncle who seemed to care as deeply about the center as he did. It was an encouraging sign. A team effort, after all, worked far better than a solitary one. For the first time since he arrived, Dylan had a flicker of hope that maybe the center could be saved after all. "That's great. I didn't even know there was such a thing."

Abby shrugged. "It's only great if it works out."

Dylan pulled into the parking lot of the grocery store. Abby was an efficient shopper and they were in and out of the first stop in less than thirty minutes. The boys helped load everything, then hopped back in for the short ride to the center. In the back seat, Cody had his head back, asleep, while Jake was working a handheld game. Quiet, for now. "I'm sure you'll get that grant," Dylan said. "Either way, everything you're doing today is going to be appreciated. Ty can use all the help he can get, especially when it comes to getting that place back in shape."

"Even if it's from people who can barely hold a hammer?"

He shot her a grin. "By the end of the day, you'll be an expert and the boys will be ready to open their own renovation business."

"I'm counting on that, Dylan." She turned her attention to the window, her gaze on the passing houses.

She didn't share any of the troubles on her mind, not that he expected her to. Abby was clearly a woman used to shouldering her burdens alone, and given what little he'd heard about the boys' father, Dylan suspected she'd been doing so for a long time.

Abby glanced over at her sons from time to time, as if making sure they were still there. She checked her phone but otherwise kept to herself. A few minutes later, they pulled into the parking lot for the center.

On Saturdays, the center didn't open until three, a big departure from the early morning opening time that Dylan remembered. The hand-lettered sign announcing the new weekend times was undoubtedly put there by Ty, to minimize his hours at the center. In the old days, Ty and Virginia had planned game days and movie nights for Saturdays, but the schedule on the door was blank. Dylan wondered how long it had been since the center had been running at full speed. That river of guilt flowed over him again. If he had been here…

But he hadn't been, and there was nothing he could do to change that fact. Nothing except make the present better.

When Dylan parked, Cody jerked awake. "We're here, guys. Let's get the truck unloaded and get to work. We only have a few hours before the kids arrive."

Cody slipped out of the truck without a word, and stood by the tailgate, perfecting his teenage attitude. Jake bounced up and down beside Dylan. "What are we gonna work on first? Are we gonna build something? Should I wear a tool belt? I don't have one, but I can make one." He tugged on the belt loops of his jeans.

Dylan chuckled. "You're good, Jake. And the first thing we're going to work on is repairing the broken cabinets in the kitchen so that we can load in all the food and stuff we bought this morning."

"Cool!" Jake grabbed a bag of supplies and hurried over to the shelter door. He kept on bouncing, impatient for Dylan to grab a load and unlock the door. As soon as the door was open, Jake beelined for the kitchen.

"I wish everyone who worked with me was that eager," Dylan said to Abby.

"Heck, I wish he was that eager about cleaning his room." She shed her jacket once inside the building, then motioned to Cody. "Come on, Code. Let's get started."

Cody muttered under his breath about it being too early, but came inside and dropped his coat on one of the sofas. He followed Dylan into the kitchen, where Abby was already waiting with Jake.

Dylan laughed. "Okay, it's only one cabinet, so I don't need that much help. So why don't I get you and Cody working on removing the broken tiles in the bathroom? It's pretty easy and foolproof because the tiles are already broken and the grout is old and dried out."

"A job I can't screw up?" Abby grinned. "Put me to work, sir."

The *sir* had his mind derailing down a whole other path. Dylan yanked himself back to the present, and to the toolbox. He found a couple hammers, chisels and a putty knife and handed them to Abby and Cody. "Jake, can you find me four of these screws—" he held up a wood screw, then handed Jake a small plastic tub "—while I show your mom and Cody what to do?"

"Sure!" Jake scrambled onto one of the stools and started sorting through the container.

Dylan, Abby and Cody headed for the single restroom. Down the road, Dylan would love to add another bathroom, just to help handle the amount of traffic. When Ty and Virginia opened this place, they converted an old house, which meant it also had old plumbing, old wiring and an old layout.

Then he remembered that down the road, he'd be moving on. Which meant someone else would worry about the additional bathroom, the major changes the center would still need, even after he repaired and updated what he could in the space of a couple of weeks.

"Okay, how do we do this?"

He glanced at Abby and Cody, the two of them waiting in the small room for him to get his act together. He took a set of tools from her and knelt on the floor. "We only want to remove the broken tiles. First, you have to scrape out the grout." He showed them how to do that with the edge of the chisel. "Be careful not to chip the nearby tiles. Then, use the hammer and chisel to break it up and remove it."

"Looks easy enough." Abby put her hands out for the tools.

"Not yet. You both need these." He reached into his pocket and took out two pairs of safety glasses.

"No way, man," Cody said, warding them off. "I'm not wearing those dork goggles."

"You will if you don't want tile chips in your eyes. Trust me, that's no fun." Dylan handed Abby a pair. She slipped them on, and he thought no one in the world had ever looked as cute with safety glasses on as she did. For a second, he imagined being alone in the close quarters of the bathroom with her. Then he glanced at her and remembered that Abby came with an entire package that he had no business being around.

"Well, uh, you guys let me know if you run into any problems. I'll be in the kitchen."

Then he headed back to the cabinets before he lingered too long with a woman who made him think about everything but the reason he was really here.

Abby knelt beside Cody and started working on the first tile while her son worked on one a few feet away. "I think we can handle this. What do you think, Cody?"

Cody grunted.

Abby sighed and sat back on her heels. "Cody, will you talk to me?"

"I am."

"A grunt and two words is not talking to me. How's school, how are your friends, how's—"

"School sucks. My friends are cool and I don't want to talk about anything else." He bent down and started chiseling away at the grout.

"Be careful, remember what Dylan said—"

"I'm not a baby, Mom. Quit telling me what to do."

Abby sighed again. When had everything shifted between her and Cody? When had the boy who had rushed into her arms at the end of the school day turned into this distant almost-man?

A part of her was envious that Dylan had gotten through to her eldest. What secret was she missing?

They worked together for the next half hour. Abby tried, over and over, to get Cody to talk, but he'd gone back to grunts and single-word answers. The chisels made more noise in the bathroom than her son did.

"I've finished my section." Abby got to her feet and wiped the dust off her jeans. "I'm just going to check on your brother. Or do you want me to help…?"

"I've got it, Mom." Cody kept his back to her and went on working.

Abby headed toward the kitchen, her mind still heavy with worry about her eldest son. Every day, he seemed to grow more and more detached. Did he blame her for his father's absence? For the long hours she worked to make ends meet? Or was it all normal teenage attitude?

As she neared the kitchen, she could hear Jake talking to Dylan. Her youngest was, as always, excited and chipper, going a mile a minute, telling him all about the puppies next door and how he'd named them and thought the littlest one was the cutest and the loneliest. Dylan was indulgent and patient with Jake, which made Abby like him even more. He had a way of relating to her kids that was nice. Reassuring.

Easy to get attached to.

That sent the red warning flag up in her head. Something she had better pay attention to, regardless of how a few conversations went.

"Can we fix more stuff, Dylan?" Jake was saying. "Can we fix my window? Cuz Mommy says it's broken and when it's hot, I wanna open my window. And if I get a puppy, he'll get hot, too."

Dylan chuckled. "I can fix that later. But right now,

let's fix the stuff we have here. Now, do you want to help me replace the wall outside the office?"

"A whole wall? Sure!"

Dylan emerged from the kitchen and drew up short when he saw Abby. "Hey."

"Hey." She stood there like an idiot for a long second, then remembered why she had sought him out. "We finished taking out the broken tiles."

"Great. I'll lay the new ones when the center closes for the night. They need time to set before people start walking on them."

"Did you finish the cabinet repair?"

"Yup. Me and my trusty helper. Then we put the groceries away. They might not be exactly where Ty expects them to be but—"

"I'm sure it's all fine. Thank you, Dylan. It was really sweet." She shifted closer to him, intrigued, attracted, despite her common sense. This man, who connected with her kids, did thoughtful things to help her out… Every time she saw him, all she did was crave more of all that.

He shrugged, but his gaze locked on hers, held. A heartbeat filled the space between them. Another. "No problem."

Jake sauntered out of the kitchen then, a kid-size hammer tucked in his jeans pocket. "I was a big help, Mommy. Dylan said so."

"That's right. And now he's going to help me fix a wall." Dylan looked at Abby. "You want in on that fun, too?"

"Sure." She flexed a biceps. "I'll add it to my list of skills."

"Stick with me and you'll have a killer handywoman résumé in no time." Dylan grinned, then headed out to the truck.

Stick with me. Why did those words impact her? Why did her gaze linger on him, and more, her thoughts? She'd found herself smiling a hundred times more today than she had in weeks. She told herself it was because she was spending time with her boys. Nothing more.

When Dylan returned with two panels of Sheetrock, with a thrilled Jake rushing to hold the door and start up his endless stream of questions again, Abby found that smile returning. Even though she had a stack of work waiting for her at home, she felt light, happy. Unstressed.

Dylan laid the Sheetrock against the wall, then popped his head in the bathroom. "Cody, wanna help do some demo work?"

"Does that mean I get to destroy something?" Cody said.

"Yup. Bring your hammer."

"Cool." Cody ambled into the room, his hammer tucked in his pocket, just like Jake. His little brother ran up beside him, mimicking Cody's stance. Cody leaned over and ruffled Jake's hair.

Well, heck, if that's what it took to get her teenager to come out from under that perpetual dark storm cloud, maybe she should have Dylan come over and figure out something they could demo in her house. Of course, that would probably mean Dylan would get sweaty and have to take off his shirt—

Not productive. Not one bit.

Dylan positioned the three of them along the long wall in the hallway. Water damage from a leak in the roof last spring had crumbled part of the wall, left the rest a rusty tan color. "All right, Cody, you start here. Jake, you start over here, and Abby, you start here."

"Wait, me?" she said when she realized Dylan had moved her to a place at the end.

Dylan shifted closer to her. His smile drew her in, like the proverbial moth to the flame. He had an easy smile that fit him well, like a comfortable pair of jeans. "You have a little stress you want to work off?"

"Uh…yeah." Except it wasn't stress burning in her right now. It was the curiosity about kissing him. Wondering what it would be like to be in his arms.

This man was all wrong for her—a charmer, a wanderer. A man who didn't seem to want or need any ties.

Yet that didn't stop her from wanting more. From fantasizing about him. From wanting him. And from "accidentally" bumping into him a couple times today. All of which left her discombobulated and flustered.

"Yeah, uh, I have some stress," she said. "Where do I hit?"

Dylan pulled a marker out of his back pocket and drew three X's on the wall. "Right there. After you punch a hole in the wall, start tearing out the old Sheetrock. Trust me, this is going to be better than therapy."

"What about the electricity?" She pointed at the wall

socket. "The mom in me doesn't want to make any emergency room trips today."

"I turned off the power already, and I'm handling the section with the wiring, as a double precaution. You guys should be just fine." He waved toward the wall. "So…have at it."

Jake hit the wall first, making a hammer-size dent. Cody followed, sending his hammer through with a crash. A chunk of wall tumbled onto the floor. Dylan and Cody turned to look at her.

"Have at it, Abby," Dylan said. "Let her rip."

Abby gripped her hammer with two hands, took a deep breath, then swung it at the X. She hit a little wide of the target, but hard enough to punch a hole in the wall. Sheetrock cracked, then dropped to her feet. "Wow. I did it."

"You did." Dylan's eyes held a measure of pride and wonder. "Now let's rip the rest of the wall down."

They went at the damaged Sheetrock like a pack of wolves, hitting, tearing and yanking, then tossing the debris on the floor. Most of it yielded easily, softened by the water leak. Abby latched on to an edge, pulled, then leaned back and pulled some more. The wall tore in one giant, satisfying piece.

A few minutes later, the four of them stepped back and assessed their work. All that remained was a few wires from the electrical outlet and the studs.

Abby had had no idea how awesome it would feel to tear something apart. The whole experience was… liberating. Powerful. Unleashed. Wild. All the things she had avoided in her life for so long.

"Well, that was great," Abby said. "More therapeutic than I expected."

"Can I say I told you so?" Dylan said.

She laughed. "I think I deserve that. Okay, what do we get to demo next?"

"Hold on there, Bob Vila. Let's clean this up, hang the new wall, then move on to another project."

"That was so cool, Dylan!" Jake said. "I hit it with my hammer. Lots of times!"

"You did great, Jake," Dylan said, then turned to her oldest. "You, too, Cody. You're a natural at this."

"Thanks." Cody toed at the floor. "Can I, uh, help you hang up the new wall?"

Abby glanced at Dylan. Cody had been an unwilling participant today until just now. She half expected Dylan to do what her ex always did, tell the kids no, and do the job himself. Her ex-husband had been around so little that the boys were perpetually hopeful whenever he was home that he'd let them spend time with him—help out while he did stuff around the house. He'd always said it was easier, faster to do the work himself. And the boys would be left watching from the outside while their dad hung a picture or changed the brake pads in his car.

"Sure, Cody. Let's just get the old stuff cleaned up and then I'll show both you and your brother how to hang the new wall." Dylan swung a trash can into place. "The least fun part of demo—cleaning up."

Cody nodded, then grabbed a big dustpan and scooped up the chunks, dumping them into the trash without complaint. Jake did his best, but his littler hands didn't do the job of his older brother. When they were done, Cody took the initiative to grab the first piece of Sheetrock.

Dylan nodded toward the wall. "Go ahead, put it up. Then the three of us will nail it into place." He dropped some nails into Abby's palm.

They worked together as a team. Cody held the wall while Abby hammered on one end and Dylan and Jake did the other end. Dylan would drive a couple nails, then hold one for Jake and let him take a swing at it. Even when Jake hit Dylan's thumb a few times, Dylan went on letting Jake try. It was sweet, and for a moment, Abby found herself wondering what their childhoods would have been like if Dylan had been around the boys in those days without a father.

Then she drew herself up and faced reality—she already knew what happened with men like him. Men who had no real ties or commitments. They might be good for a while, but eventually, they left. And they let her down. More than that, they let her sons down.

And that was the one price Abby wasn't willing to pay, no matter how much she liked Dylan's smile.

With his motley crew, Dylan managed to make his way through a lot of the repairs before three. For sure, the wall demo had been the most popular activity of the day. The boys had been cooperative—Jake clearly eager to learn; Cody unable to pretend he didn't care. Even Abby had been enthusiastic and, in the process, picked up a few skills.

Abby.

Every time he'd looked at her, he lost his concentration. She had this way of knitting her brows when she was struggling to understand something. He thought it was…

Cute.

Okay, so he really was becoming a softie. It had to be being back in this town. Being around all these kids. Even now, several hours after he'd brought Abby and her boys back home, and he'd returned to run the center for the rest of the day, he found his mind straying to her. Wondering what she was doing.

At six, he said goodbye to the last of the teens as they left, shut the doors and turned off most of the lights. He spent an hour laying the new tile in the bathroom, then picked up his phone. No texts from Abby. No contact at all.

He didn't know why he was disappointed. After all, they weren't dating, weren't even really friends. She was a woman he'd met a couple days ago who'd helped him tear down a wall. Nothing more. And either way, he wasn't the kind of man who settled down with a dog—as soon as Jake wore Abby down—and kids. He wasn't even remotely cut out for that. He needed to remind himself of that.

He locked the building and headed out to the parking lot. And saw his older brother, Sam, waiting for him.

Sam hadn't aged much in the years they'd been apart. His hair was a little shorter, his frame a little heavier, and the scowl Dylan had come to know well still sat on Sam's face.

"When were you going to tell me you were in town?" Sam asked.

Dylan rolled his eyes. Why was he surprised Sam had started with criticism? "Hello to you, too."

"I would have said hello if I didn't have to find out from Sadie at the grocery store, who found out from Mavis Beacham, that my long-lost brother has returned to Stone Gap. And is staying at the Stone Gap Inn, but apparently forgot to call and let his older brother know."

As usual, Sam had attacked first, assuming the worst. When had their relationship turned into this adversarial clash of swords? It seemed like one day they'd been normal brothers, the next, antagonists from different planets.

"I didn't call you because I'm pretty sure the last words you said to me were *don't bother calling me, I won't pick up.* Forgive me if I didn't want to rush into a confrontation with you." Dylan shook his head. Every time he and Sam got together, it was an argument.

Sam let out a gust. "It's the same old thing with you, isn't it? Blame everyone but yourself."

Dylan threw up his hands. "I don't have time for this conversation."

Sam looked away. He stood there for a long moment, as if mulling his next words. His gaze swung back to Dylan. "What are you doing here anyway?"

Dylan debated not answering. He thought about just getting in his Jeep and leaving. His relationship with Sam had been rocky for years, and that wasn't going to change anytime soon. Sam still saw him as the family screwup, while Sam was the one who did it all right. Settled down, got married, had kids. Even after his wife died, Sam had stayed here, juggling kids and work and now, a new fiancée. The storybook life—the same one Dylan had stayed away from. Because he'd learned years ago that family could let you down. Family could hurt you. And family could turn away when you needed them most.

His older brother was the one who was supposed to support and protect him. Be there, no matter what. But Sam's love had limits, it turned out. The last time Dylan had gotten in trouble and Sam had gone to the Stone Gap Police Department to pick him up, Sam had been by his brother's side. But when it was all over, Sam stood in the driveway and shook his head in disgust. "I give up. Nothing gets through to you," Sam had said. The words had hurt then, and still did.

Yet, there was a part of Dylan that remembered the older brother who had given his little brother a hoisting hand up into their tree house. The older brother who had skipped math to sneak out to the playground and confront a bully preying on Dylan at recess. The same older brother shielded him from their father's anger, who had tucked Dylan in on the nights when the house reverberated with shouting and anger. Was any of that still there, in Sam? Or was it a lost cause? Was Dylan an idiot for hoping again?

"I'm working at the center," Dylan said. Maybe if he told Sam about that, his brother would offer to pitch in. The two of them, working together, like when they were young. "Helping Uncle Ty out. He's not up to running it since he lost Aunt Virginia."

Sam arched a brow. "Ty put *you* in charge?"

"Yeah." Dylan bristled. "Why wouldn't he?"

"Because you're not going to be here in five minutes, Dylan. I know you, and I know you have all the sticking power of wet tape."

Dylan let out a gust. Why had he let himself get sentimental? "Same old Sam. Telling me all the ways I screw up my life. Thanks for the reminder, big brother, that I'm not as perfect as you."

"I'm not saying that." Sam took a step closer. "I just don't want to see Uncle Ty left in a bind when you leave."

The implication was clear—that Dylan would let the family down again. He'd had a long day and didn't need to deal with this. Not now, not ever. Sam had been here to deliver a lecture, not a reunion.

Dylan thumbed the remote for his Jeep and unlocked the doors. "Thanks for the vote of confidence. See you around, Sam."

Then he climbed in the truck and left, before he said something he'd regret. In the rearview mirror, he saw Sam, still standing in the parking lot and watching him leave. For a second, Dylan debated turning around. Then he caught a green light and the urge disappeared.

Chapter Five

Dusk had fallen over Stone Gap, broken by porch lights flicking on and streetlights that dropped yellow pools on the road. Dylan stopped at the intersection in the center of downtown. Left took him back to the Stone Gap Inn. Right took him to Abby's house. After the conversation with Sam, a part of Dylan just wanted to go to a bar and forget it all with a few beers. But all that would give him was a headache and a few more regrets. He hesitated and then turned right.

He made one stop before he got there and pulled into Abby's driveway a little before eight. The lights were still on, and he could hear the sound of a radio. He climbed the porch steps and through the large front windows, he saw Abby.

Dancing. With Jake.

She swung back and forth, laughing, while Jake kept time with his mother, the two of them holding hands and stepping together. The radio was playing an old seventies song, one of those catchy one-hit wonders that struck a familiar chord.

What hit him hardest, though, was how…homey the whole scene was. How warm. Just a mom and her son, dancing in the living room on a Saturday night. It was a world so foreign to him, something he didn't think really existed. If he'd been a different man, maybe he would have dreamed of such a scene. But he wasn't, and he shouldn't.

He almost hated to ring the doorbell. Came close to turning around and leaving, because he didn't want to intrude on Abby and her sons. Then he remembered the stop he'd made and figured he had a good enough reason for being here.

Dylan pressed the doorbell. Abby flicked off the music and peeked through the window, her face narrow with suspicion. By the time she opened the door to him, the suspicion had been replaced by a smile. "Dylan. What are you doing here?"

It was the second time he'd been asked that question in the space of twenty minutes. But coming from Abby, the words sounded sweet, genuine. "I, uh, wanted to thank you guys for your hard work today. So I brought ice cream." He held up the bag in his hand.

"Ice cream!" Jake raced to the door and poked his head outside. "What kind? I love ice cream! I love chocolate the best. Or maybe cookie dough. I love that one, too."

Abby blushed and put a calming hand on Jake's shoulder. "Sorry. You just happen to have brought over Jake's favorite dessert."

Was it also her favorite dessert? He wanted to ask but figured that would show interest, and Dylan wasn't interested in Abby.

Uh-huh. That's why he was on her doorstep with three melting quarts of ice cream instead of back at the bed-and-breakfast, getting a good night's sleep after a very long day.

"I did get cookie dough, Jake," Dylan said. "And chocolate. And vanilla. Just in case."

Abby smiled. "Something to make everyone happy."

"As long as I grabbed your favorite, that is." Then he caught himself and added, "and, uh, Cody's."

"Cody is out with his friends. And I'm a chocolate kind of girl." She hesitated a second, then opened the door wider. "Come on in, Dylan."

Abby's house was just as welcoming as he'd expected it to be. Wide wood floors, pale cream walls, and a dark brown leather couch that looked as soft as a marshmallow. Framed photos of her boys filled the walls of the hallway, and dominated the fireplace mantel. A pile of clean, folded shirts sat on the second step, with a basket of toys on the first. The house was organized but comfortable.

He felt both at home and out of place, following her down the hall to the sunny yellow kitchen with a bright spray of flowers in the center of the round maple table. Before they reached the kitchen, Abby's doorbell rang again. Jake spun on his heel and barreled for the door.

"I get the door, Jake, not you." Abby put a hand on his shoulder, then opened the door. "Besides, buddy, it's past your bedtime."

An elderly woman stood on the other side, holding the same puppy Dylan had seen before. "I thought I'd bring this little guy by for Jake to play with."

"Mrs. Reynolds, it's late and Jake has to get to bed. Besides, we can't get a dog. I work so many hours—"

"I know, dear." The older woman had a kind face behind cat's-eye glasses. She put a hand on Abby's and gave her a soft smile. "But Jake loves these dogs so much, and if he can play with them a little, it wears the little guys out and gives Jake his puppy fix."

"Can I, Mommy? Can I? Please?" Jake bounced up and down, all but lunging for the dog.

"Okay, but only for a few minutes. Bedtime, remember?" Jake leaned forward, took the dog from Mrs. Reynolds, then spun around. "And keep him in the kitchen. I don't want any accidents on the carpet."

"I'll be back in a little bit," Mrs. Reynolds said.

"Thanks." Abby shut the door, then let out a long sigh. "How can I keep telling him no? He's going to get attached."

"That might not be such a bad thing," Dylan said. "Dogs teach kids responsibility."

"He's four years old, so let's not pretend most of the responsibility would fall on him. I have my hands full, Mr. Single and Unattached to So Much as a Potted Plant. The last thing I need is another mouth to feed and clean up after." Abby shook her head. "You wouldn't understand."

She was right about him. He had no attachments. But as he watched Jake love on that puppy with tight hugs and hundreds of kisses, he wondered if that was such a good thing. Jake talked to the dog nonstop for a solid five minutes, clearly attached despite Abby's wishes, before Abby said it was time to bring Dudley—the dog's name, according to Jake—home. "He needs to go to bed early," Abby said. "And then you can come back and have ice cream."

"Okay." Jake frowned. He plodded behind his mother, and the two of them returned the dog while Dylan waited in the kitchen. By the time they returned, Abby must have said something because Jake was back to his usual bouncy self. He spied the tubs of ice cream melting on the counter and reached for one of the containers. "I want a lot of ice cream," Jake said. "Please, Mommy?"

She grabbed three bowls out of the cabinet and set them on the counter. "First, wash your hands."

Jake rose on his tiptoes and rubbed his hands under the water from the kitchen faucet. Abby dished up the ice cream, chocolate in one bowl, cookie dough in another. She hesitated over the third bowl. "Which is your favorite, Dylan?"

"Oh, I..." He looked at the sunflower-printed dish towel hanging off the stove. The refrigerator peppered with Jake's drawings and candid photos of the boys. The carved wooden sign above the window that read simply Family. "I wasn't planning on staying. I just wanted to drop that off as a thank-you."

"You're not staying?" Jake pouted. "But I wanted to show you my dinosaurs."

Dylan arched a brow. "Dinosaurs?"

"Jake's favorite thing in the whole world, besides a P-U-P-P-Y, is dinosaurs." Abby ignored his answer about not staying and put a bowl of half chocolate and half vanilla in front of him. "I'll warn you, though, once you get him started talking about them, it's hard to get him to stop."

Dinosaurs.

Dylan saw another kitchen in his mind, heard another boy's voice. The memory slid through him, crystal clear and just as biting all these years later. His father, coming home after a long day at the office. He could still see Dad setting his briefcase in its customary place by the front door with one hand while he loosened his tie with the other. Dylan had been four or five, still caught in that world where he believed his father would one day just come home and be a dad like the ones on TV. With piggyback rides and baseball lessons and campfire stories. *Dad, look at my dinosaur! Mom bought it for me today. Because I was good in the store. It's a T. rex and he's mean! Rrrr!*

His dad had given the toy a half a glance, then told Dylan to go outside to play. *I need a moment to breathe when I get home, not a kid and a bunch of toys all over me. Where's Sam? I want to see his book report.*

Maybe that was when Dylan had started to pull away. When he'd stopped believing in happy homes and loving parents. When he'd realized that, beside his brother, there wasn't going to be a male role model there to make a big deal about his new dinosaur or teach him how to pop a fly ball or tell him a ghost story on a camping trip.

As Dylan ate his ice cream, he looked over at Jake, who was sitting at the bar, a ring of ice cream around his mouth, his eyes wide and waiting. And hopeful.

How could Dylan let him down? The kid had just had to give back a puppy, for Pete's sake. Dylan couldn't say no to this request. Even if Dylan was far from father material, he could at least do this.

"Sure, I'd love to see your dinosaurs. They're my favorite, too," Dylan said. "I used to have some when I was your age."

Jake's eyes widened. "You did? Did you have a bron-o-saurus?"

"I did. My favorite was Tyrannosaurus rex. Do you have one of those?"

"I do! Lemme go get him!" Jake scrambled off the chair, the last of his ice cream forgotten. He barreled out of the room, then ran back in five seconds later, his arms stuffed with plastic dinosaurs of all shapes, sizes and colors. He stopped in the center of the kitchen and let the pile tumble to the floor. "Look at all my dinosaurs, Dylan."

Dylan gave Abby a grin. "You weren't kidding about the collection."

"Makes birthday gifts pretty easy." She nodded toward her son. "Jake, why don't you show Dylan your triceratops?"

Jake dug through the pile of plastic toys until he found the three-horned dinosaur. "I named him Joe."

Dylan chuckled. "Joe's a great name."

"And this one is Mack and this one is…" Jake went through every single dinosaur—maybe three dozen in all—and told Dylan their names and explained what he knew about what they ate. Kid clearly knew his dinosaurs. Maybe better than Dylan had at that age. Jake then started going on about movies with dinosaurs— apparently there was one with many sequels—and scientists who studied dinosaurs, and books that had dinosaurs in them, until his mother put a hand on his shoulder.

"Jakester, why don't you take the dinosaurs back up to your room and get ready for bed? I'm going to talk to Dylan for a minute, then I'll come tuck you in."

Jake pouted, but did as he was told and gathered up his toys. "Do I have to brush my teeth?"

Abby smiled. "Always."

Jake trudged out of the room and up the stairs. A second later, they heard the clatter of the dinosaurs hitting the floor, followed by the sound of running water.

"Thank you for indulging him." Abby said. "I'm sorry he ran on so much."

Dylan waved that off. "I was just like him when I was young. My dad didn't really care all that much, and I always wanted him to. Uncle Ty was the one who would listen to my stories about dinosaurs or ask me to draw a picture and hang it in his office."

"Your uncle is such a great guy. Everyone needs an Uncle Ty."

He nodded. "They do indeed." As far as he could tell, Abby's boys didn't have a close male relative. And given how depressed Ty had been lately, he probably wasn't being much of a surrogate relative to Abby's kids, either. If listening to Jake talk about dinosaurs for a little while could help with that, Dylan would do it.

"Also, thank you for the ice cream," Abby said. She was leaning against the counter, her empty bowl beside her hand. "It was a nice thing to do."

He shrugged. "It was no big deal. I wanted to thank you all for helping me so much." And have a chance to see her again, though he didn't say that out loud. Because that would mean admitting he was interested in her, that he was thinking about her—and wishing he wasn't leaving at the end of his two weeks.

Abby had changed into a fresh pair of jeans and a soft coral sweater with an enticing V-neck. Her feet were bare, bright red toenails a contrast to the light tile.

There was something both innocent and sexy about her standing there barefooted. That drew him to her, like a chain coiling into a winch. He got to his feet, grabbed his empty bowl, then closed the distance between them. Abby raised her gaze to Dylan's, her eyes wide. Her lips parted and her cheeks flushed, but she didn't move.

The heat from her body merged with his. Her perfume floated in the space between them, something darkly floral. It enticed him, drew him even closer. He leaned over her shoulder and reached behind her to ostensibly put down the bowl. "I should put this in the sink."

She stayed where she was, her chest rising and falling with each breath. "Thanks." The word escaped in a whisper.

As he drew back, Dylan paused and pressed a kiss to the valley of her neck. Damn, she tasted good. Better than the ice cream. Better, in fact, than anything he could remember tasting in a long, long time. He kissed farther up her neck, her skin soft and sweet and warm. Another kiss, a fourth, inching his way along that delicate curve, then the underside of her jaw.

Abby let out a little mew, then drew in a sharp breath and leaned toward him. Dylan planted his hands on either side of her, then kissed her jaw, the soft fullness of her cheek, then drifted closer to her mouth. Her breathing hastened but she stood stock-still, waiting, anticipating.

When his lips finally met hers, Abby opened to him. Her arms slid around and up his back. Dylan planted his legs on either side of her, and she shifted into that space. Desire surged inside him, overriding common sense, the dozens of reasons he had for not getting involved. All he knew right now was Abby. All he wanted was Abby. Their kiss deepened, becoming hotter, faster, hands sliding along backs and waists and—

"Mommy? You coming to tuck me in?" Jake's voice, echoing in the staircase.

Abby jerked back and put her hands on Dylan's chest. "Uh, yeah, Jake." She turned back to Dylan. Even though her cheeks were flushed and she was still breathing hard, cool distance had replaced the warmth in her. "You should go. I have… I have…"

"People to tuck in," he finished for her.

"Yes." She stepped to the side and smoothed her

hair. She cleared her throat. "Uh, thank you for the ice cream. It was a nice thing to do."

"You said that already." Dylan grinned. Was it possible that the strong and confident Abby was just as flustered as he was by that kiss? A little part of him hoped so.

"Oh, well, yes, uh, I forgot." She started walking out of the kitchen, with Dylan following behind. She opened the front door, the message clear—*leave now, we're not returning to that kiss*. "Thank you again."

"Anytime." The word was one of those throwaway ones, the kind people said without really thinking about it. But when Dylan thought of stopping by Abby's *anytime*, a little rush ran through him.

Insane. She represented home and hearth and kids— and he was unattached, unburdened, unhomey. Just because he enjoyed a dish of ice cream in her kitchen or got a little sentimental when he watched her dance with her son didn't mean he walked in the same world she did. Or even should.

"See you at the center." Dylan reached for the door handle.

"Mommy, can Dylan read me my story tonight? Please?"

Dylan turned and saw Jake, wearing dinosaur pajamas, the buttons a little askew, and holding a hardcover book. Dylan could see himself in those pajamas, with that book, waiting for a dad who was never going to get involved, never going to take the time to read a story. His mom had done the work of two parents, always excusing her husband from his parental duties with excuses about stress or exhaustion. *Dad's tired tonight.* Or *Dad had a hard day at work.* Or *Dad's grumpy because he's stressed about work.*

Sam had read Dylan stories at night—the two of them propped up against Dylan's headboard in the room that they shared. Sam had read about pirates and lost treasures, adventurous dogs and amateur detective twins. Then Sam had gotten older, found girls and basketball and moved into his own room that had been cobbled together from an unused corner of the basement. By then Dylan could read on his own, of course, but he remembered being hurt and wondering why his brother no longer hung out with him in the evenings.

Can Dylan read me my story tonight? Please? He could see the hope in Jake's face, the need in his voice.

"Jake, Dylan's going home," Abby said. "He—"

"Would love to read a story," Dylan said.

She turned toward him. "Really, you don't have to. I mean, it's a lot for Jake to ask."

"I don't mind, Abby. I remember being that age and wanting the same thing." Besides, how hard could it be? Dylan could read—way better than when he was a kid, after all—and Jake was just a little boy. It would take five, ten minutes, tops.

Besides, Jake was kind of growing on Dylan. He was a cute kid, who was curious and bright and funny. And reading to Jake might make Dylan a little more comfortable relating to the kids at the community center.

Yeah, that's why he was doing it. To relate better. Not because he could hear the echoes of his own childhood in Jake's voice.

"Okay," Abby said to Jake. "But just one story."

"Aw, Mom…"

"One." She and Dylan made their way up the stairs to the first room on the right. It was a small bedroom, with a twin bed in the shape of a red race car, a set of bookshelves filled with toys and books, and two toy chests overrun with stuffed animals and cars and robots. Jake's dinosaurs were in a pile at the foot of his bed, with Joe the triceratops on Jake's nightstand, basking under the light of a dinosaur-themed lamp.

Jake scooted over on his bed. "Dylan, you can sit here. I mades room."

"Uh, okay." Dylan lowered himself onto Jake's bed and sat back against the headboard. He settled in, while Abby went back downstairs to load the dishwasher.

"Here. I wanna read this book." Jake gave him a hardcover copy of a book about a lonely dinosaur who goes on a cross-country adventure.

Dylan opened the book and started to read. At first, the words were as stiff as Dylan's posture, but as he read, he settled into both. Jake shifted, then snuggled up against Dylan, his little head resting on Dylan's left arm. Dylan hesitated for a moment, caught in the middle of a sentence.

"Uh, and then the dinosaur said…" Dylan looked at the page, then over at Jake's head, nestled into the soft cotton of Dylan's T-shirt. It could have been him and Sam, years ago. And something in Dylan's heart melted.

"He said he wanted a friend," Jake said. "And then he meets a friend. And then he's happy. And then they go on adventures. I love this story. Mommy reads it a lot."

Which made Dylan wonder anew why Jake wanted him to read the book. Had Jake tired of his mother's reading? Or was there something more here, something that Dylan didn't want to see?

That maybe Jake had already latched on to Dylan and begun to see him as a pseudo-father figure? If so, that was far from the role Dylan, of all people, should be playing. Sam was the one with kids, the one who had settled down, made a life in this town. Dylan was only here for a short time, and then he'd be gone. And with his past, he wasn't cut out to be anyone's father, substitute or otherwise.

But was it worse to let Jake down tonight or to give him this time to be happy and then let him down weeks from now? Either choice would leave this little boy with heartbreak. The last thing Dylan wanted to see on any child's face.

Or on the face of that child's mother.

Abby paused outside Jake's bedroom door. Her breath caught in her throat, lodging with a thick lump. Jake sitting there, curled up against Dylan, a smile on his face, while Dylan read about the lonely dinosaur traveling the world to find a friend. The book was a favorite of Jake's, one she herself had read to him, oh, two hundred times.

The scene before her was one she had prayed for a thousand times when she'd been married to Keith. She'd always thought, given the chance, that he would step up and be a good dad. Take Jake on piggyback rides and shoot hoops with Cody. But in the end, Keith had checked out, spending more of his time away from home than with his family.

But this was just a scene, a blip in time, and she knew better than to put her stock in a man who was only going to let her down. And worse, let her sons down. They had had enough of that for one lifetime. Even today, seeing Jake's face when they brought back the dog, she'd wanted to cry. She felt like a terrible mother, saying no when she really wanted to say yes. Her baby had had to give up so much already—she hated the thought of him losing even more.

Her tender feelings were about more than that, she knew. She was starting to care about Dylan. Enjoying spending time with him, seeing the way he smiled at her, the way he patiently taught her how to work on the floors and the walls, and the way being around him made her heart race like it hadn't in a long, long time.

Dylan finished the book and closed the cover. Jake had nodded off, so Dylan slid out from under him and pulled the covers up to Jake's shoulders. He turned, then noticed Abby. "Oh, hey. Didn't see you there."

"I was only here for a second." Long enough to see the look of adoration and hope on Jake's face, the little smile that lingered after he fell asleep. Long enough to know that men like Dylan didn't hang around and that she was going to be the one left to pick up the pieces in his wake, for her kids and herself. Better to remember that than to let a smile and a racing pulse affect her decisions.

Dylan stepped into the hall, leaving Jake's door ajar. "He's a busy kid, but fun and smart."

"He is." Abby smiled. "I got lucky. A lot of women say their second child is more difficult but Jake has been sweet from the day he was born."

"I think a lot of that is due to you. You're so great with him, with both boys."

Here, in the dim hall, Abby was a hundred times more aware of Dylan. Their kiss still simmered on her lips, and the desire still rumbled in her veins. A part of her wanted to take his hand and bring him down the hall to her bedroom and finish what they had started.

The insane part, clearly. Her son was starting to lean on and believe in a man who wasn't going to stay—but he still believed in Santa Claus and the tooth fairy, too. It was crazy of her to do the same thing.

"Well, thanks again," she said. "I'll show you out."

"No problem." He followed her down the stairs and back to the front door. At the last second, he pivoted back to face her. "Tomorrow, the center is closed, so I have a rare day off. I was going to do some reno work in the morning, but what do you think about going fishing later in the morning? Uncle Ty has a pontoon boat he keeps down at Stone Gap Lake, and he said I'm welcome to use it. I'm hoping I can get him out, too, to get some sun and maybe catch a few bass."

"Fishing?"

"It'll be fun. I'll even bait your hook for you."

She put a fist on her hip. "Do you think I look so girly I can't do that?"

"Well, no, but you know, most women I've known don't like to handle worms and stuff like that."

She gave him a sassy look. "I'll have you know I've

been fishing since I was five years old. In fact, I bet I'll be the first one to catch a fish."

He grinned. "Are you challenging me? Because I've been fishing all my life, too. And Uncle Ty has won a few titles, in the years he isn't beaten by Ernie Morris."

This was where she was comfortable, with teasing and jokes and activities. Not with those quiet moments in her kitchen when she imagined things that were never going to come true. When she started to fall for a man who wasn't going to be here down the road. So she'd fish with him and leave it at that.

She put out her hand. "Want to put a wager on it?"

"Okay." He thought a second. "Ten bucks says I catch a fish faster than you do."

"Make it twenty and I'm in." They shook and she laughed. As she watched him leave, she realized she was feeling light, happy and, most of all, anticipating spending another day with Dylan.

Damn it. Just when she had convinced herself to let him leave and not see him again, Dylan had come up with an idea she couldn't resist. She didn't want to like this guy—

But she did.

And the worst part? Her sons liked him, too.

Chapter Six

Uncle Ty put his feet up and shook his head. "You kids go without me. I've got a football game to watch later."

Dylan looked around at Ty's ranch-style house. He and Aunt Virginia had lived here for their entire marriage. When Aunt Virginia had been alive, the house had been bright, merry. But now, it seemed as if the light had gone out of the space. The curtains hung despondent and limp and the air held a musty, sad scent. "I need you on my team, Uncle Ty. I made a bet with Abby that I could catch the first fish."

Uncle Ty scoffed. "Dylan, you know I love you like a son, but your fishing skills suck."

"Exactly why I need you along." And one of the things Dylan didn't want to admit to Abby. Call it manly pride, but he didn't want her to think he was bad at anything. "Your superior fishing ability should balance out my inability to hook anything."

Ty sat back in his recliner and fiddled with the remote. He'd muted the TV when Dylan came in. The images of Bruce Willis and Sylvester Stallone filled the screen in one of those guy movies with a lot of guns and not a lot of plot. "I wouldn't be good company," Uncle Ty said finally.

"And sitting here all day is better?" Dylan sighed. "Aunt Virginia would be mad as hell at you for doing that. She'd want you to get out of the house and go fishing with Abby and her boys. Not to mention your favorite nephew."

Ty let out a short laugh and shook his head. "You're a pain in the butt, you know that?"

"Yup. I do indeed." Dylan held out the canvas hat he had grabbed from the hook by the door earlier. His uncle didn't take it. "Here's your lucky fishing cap. All it needs is you to be wearing it."

Ty didn't say anything for so long, Dylan was sure he wasn't going to go. Then Ty flicked off the TV, popped the footrest back into his recliner and got to his feet. He reached for the cap and plopped it on his head. "How much money do we have riding on this bet?"

Dylan chuckled. "With you on my side, not nearly enough."

There was a small shift in Uncle Ty's mood as he headed out of the house. His steps hesitated when he approached the truck, but he got in and made small talk while Dylan drove.

On the way over to the lake, Dylan stopped at the

community center to show Uncle Ty the renovations he'd done so far, hoping maybe that would bring his uncle out of his funk. Ty made all the appropriate sounds and words, but his enthusiasm for the center was still low. *Give it time*, Dylan told himself. Soon enough, Ty would be back at work, and that meant Dylan could get back up to Maine and to the job waiting for him there.

All of this—the ice cream, the fishing, the work at the center—was temporary. His real life was far from Stone Gap, far from women like Abby Cooper. Yet he forgot all of that the second he saw her and started thinking about the kind of life he was far from equipped to have.

They pulled up to the dock and got out of the Jeep. Abby and her sons were already waiting there, Cody leaning against Abby's car and texting on his phone, Jake holding his mother's hand and dancing from foot to foot. "Dylan! We're goin' fishin'!"

Dylan chuckled. "Yup, we are. But first, you're gonna need this." He reached over and into the pontoon and pulled out a life jacket.

Jake pouted and argued, but in the end, Abby told him he had to wear the life jacket or forget fishing. Abby bent down and fitted the life jacket around a wriggling, impatient Jake. When she was done, Jake looked down at the thick orange vest with a pout. "But Cody isn't wearing one."

"Cody, you know how to swim?" Dylan said.

Cody shrugged. "Sorta."

Dylan grabbed a second life jacket and tossed it at Cody. The teenager caught it with one hand. "Then you get to wear one, too."

"Yay! Me and Cody are the same now!" Jake ran over to his brother. "Mine has a whistle on it. Does yours have a whistle? Can we blow the whistle?"

"That's just for emergencies, Jake," Dylan said. "Like if you fall in and you need us to come get you."

Jake's eyes widened. His gaze darted from Dylan to Abby, to the water and back again. "Am I gonna fall in?"

"No, sweetie, you won't fall in." Abby put a hand on her son's shoulder and knelt down to his level. She checked the belt on the life jacket and tightened it a bit. "Just be sure to listen to Dylan and Ty, okay? They're the bosses today."

Dylan had to laugh at the idea of being the boss of anyone. Sure, he'd run construction crews before, but that was different than commanding a family of three on a fishing trip. Uncle Ty was the one used to being in charge, but as he glanced at his uncle, he saw that Ty still wore a look of disengagement. Somehow, Dylan had to get his uncle to plug in today. Maybe then the cloud over Ty would begin to lighten.

Dylan glanced at the group, all of them waiting on him to do or say something. "Well, it looks like everyone's all set. How about we get on that boat and catch us some dinner?"

"Wait. I brought a cooler," Abby said. She reached into her back seat and pulled out a small dark blue container. "Snacks and some water bottles, in case we're out here a long time."

A smile flickered on Ty's face. "And that, nephew, is why you always invite a woman on a fishing trip. They think of the important things like food and drinks.

Your Aunt Virginia always made me two ham-and-cheese sandwiches and tucked my favorite soda into the cooler." His eyes misted and he shook his head. When he spoke again, his voice was thick, and his hands trembled. "I sure miss those sandwiches."

Abby put a hand on Ty's shoulder, kindness and understanding filling her features. "I thought you might be feeling that way, Ty, so I made you two ham-and-cheese sandwiches and packed a Dr. Pepper."

Ty's eyes widened. "How did you know?"

Dylan wondered the same thing. It was such a sweet gesture from Abby, and one that left Dylan feeling a weird bit of envy. He'd never dated a woman who paid attention like that, who did thoughtful things for him, with no expectations in return.

"You're not the only one who talked about your spouse with a whole lot of love." Abby's smile was tender, soft. "Virginia used to tell me how much she loved taking care of you."

"And she did a wonderful job of it." Ty cleared his throat, then resettled his fishing cap on his head. "The fish are biting, so we better get a move on while they're still hungry."

The shift in his uncle was nearly imperceptible, but it was there, and it gave Dylan hope that maybe things were starting to turn around. And maybe this outing was going to go better than he expected.

Uncle Ty boarded first, then put out a hand to help Jake and Cody up the gangplank and onto the pontoon boat. Dylan reached for Abby's hand as she stepped onto the wobbly crossing. She glanced at him but didn't take his hand. "Thanks. I've got it."

Of course, she was a grown woman, not a kid like Jake. And from what she'd said the previous night, he knew she had been on a boat before and knew how to steady herself. Even knowing all that, a little shiver of disappointment went through Dylan. He shook it off and climbed onto the boat, unlatched the gangplank and released the ropes holding the boat to the dock.

Uncle Ty hadn't stepped up to start the engine or steer the pontoon out into the water. He dropped the keys into Dylan's palm, then took a seat on one of the cushioned benches at the front of the boat. Jake clambered up beside him, kneeling on the seat to look over the bow. Abby sat down beside her son and put a cautionary hand on his back. Cody joined them, still immersed in his phone.

Dylan started the boat and began to back away from the dock, then pivoted the pontoon toward the open water of the lake. It was a sunny day, and the deep blue lake sparkled with gold. A few boats dotted the expanse of Stone Gap Lake, most of them fishermen out for an afternoon of fun and maybe a good catch.

"Uncle Ty, where's that great fishing place you always go to?" Dylan knew the answer but figured asking might engage Ty a little more. The melancholy mood was washing over Ty in waves. For a second, the waters would be calm, then his grief and depression would roll in again and the light in his eyes would dim.

His uncle sat there, staring out at the lake, sadness heavy on his shoulders. "Wherever you think, Dylan."

"I remember this spot over by a little grove of trees

that we used to go to a lot. Sort of tucked away? Which direction is that?"

Ty waved vaguely toward the east side of the lake, and Dylan turned. The old pontoon boat—not made for speed—putt-putted across the lake, its cranky engine clearly in need of a tune-up. Item number 753 on the things Dylan needed to do for his uncle before going back to Maine.

Abby came up beside him. The breeze made her hair dance around her shoulders, and the slight chill in the air added a little color to her cheeks. She was wearing jeans and a thick sweatshirt. The outfit made her look casual, comfortable, like the kind of woman a man could come home to at the end of the day and share a pizza with.

Where the hell had that thought come from? It was the ham sandwiches, Dylan told himself. One touching moment, and he got all hearth-and-home.

"In case I forget to say it, thank you for today," she said.

He shot her a grin. "We haven't even started fishing yet."

"I know. But Jake is already having the time of his life. Even Cody is starting to loosen up a little."

At the front of the boat, Cody had moved next to his little brother. The two of them were talking, with Ty throwing in a word or two, about the water, what kind of fish they would catch, how fast the boat was moving. Jake did most of the talking, of course. Still, Dylan could see the engagement in Cody's face, the relaxed posture. And the phone that was now tucked in his back pocket.

Abby sighed and leaned against the railing beside Dylan. "It's been hard, being both mom and dad. And working full-time." Then she shook her head. "Sorry. I don't usually complain about my life."

"Or rely on anyone else?"

She let out a short laugh. "You noticed that?"

"I do believe you gave me a good lecture about that when we were making PB&Js." He didn't add that it had intrigued him, the way she had been both stubborn and confident. He'd met very few women who challenged him like Abby did. He liked that. A lot. Maybe too much.

"I'm sorry. I've just been let down so many times…" She shrugged. "It's just easier to have no expectations. I grew up relying on myself and I guess it was easier just to keep on doing that."

Dylan wanted to shake some sense into the man who had left Abby to raise her sons alone. Even though he wasn't a father, if he'd had children of his own, he never would have done that. Kids required parents who were there, parents who supported instead of criticized. Abby was like that, and Dylan had no doubt her sons were lucky to have a mother like her.

He thought about what she'd said, growing up and relying on herself, and realized he had more in common with her than he'd thought. "Where were your parents when you were a kid?"

"In a bar or on the road." Abby shrugged, like it was no big deal, but he could see the lingering pain in her eyes. "My mom was busy with her things and my dad traveled for work. Most of the time, it was just me and my sister, home alone. I learned how to make my own breakfast at five, and by the time I was ten, I was getting myself ready and out the door for school every day."

"That had to be tough." It was a life he understood, a childhood that seemed deflated, empty of the essentials other kids had. "You turned out pretty well, though, considering."

She shrugged again. "I grew up, I became a different mom. It all worked out."

"My parents weren't too plugged in, either. I had an older brother, as you know, but once he got to high school... I was kind of left behind, being a not-so-cool middle schooler still. When I was seventeen, I went out on my own and pretty much never looked back." His gaze scanned the water's edge. Stone Gap lay just beyond the trees, a small town so many people loved—so many people other than him. "I've lived everywhere but here."

"Why not here?"

"I'm not much for small-town life." The expectations that came with that. The disappointments. Far better to keep his roots loose and movable.

"So neither one of us relies on other people." She gave him a half smile, her eyes unreadable behind dark sunglasses. "I wouldn't have thought we had that in common."

He wouldn't have, either. From the minute he met Abby, he saw her as the two-point-five kids, white-picket fence, house and husband type, the kind who built connections and relationships with everyone around her. But she was far more complex than that, and ten times more independent. Every layer of her that he uncovered made him like and admire her more. She'd done things he couldn't imagine doing—like raising two kids alone.

"For the most part, I'm the kind who doesn't rely on others, but I have found that sometimes people surprise you." Dylan turned a little more north, aiming for the outcropping of trees that marked the edge of Uncle Ty's fishing spot. "First time I ever ran a construction crew, I had a hard time letting go, letting the guys do their thing. I only trusted myself, you know? I had this one kid who worked for me. He was maybe nineteen or twenty and a real go-getter. Always trying to go above and beyond, prove himself to the guys who had a few years on him. He'd ask me, over and over, for more responsibility."

"Did you give it to him?"

He chuckled. "Eventually, he wore me down. So I put him in charge of a tile job that had to be done over the weekend. Figured he could handle it—he'd laid tile with me dozens of times and this job was fairly small. I took the day off, thinking I'd come back and check on his progress that afternoon." Dylan slowed the boat as they neared the trees. A few more minutes, and they'd drop anchor.

"What happened?"

"When I got there in the afternoon, the kid was gone. The guys said he was there for an hour that morning, then said he was going to grab coffee and never came back. I was really ticked off. I finished up the job with the other guys, then went to his house. He wasn't there. His mom said he hadn't come home." Dylan turned a little left, to avoid the stump he knew lurked underneath the lake's tranquil waters. Uncle Ty had hit it more than once. Dinged up the boat one time badly enough that they'd had to do an emergency repair before heading for home. "I decided I wasn't going to trust anyone again. Do it all myself, you know, and not let anyone let me down again. A month later, who comes back to work, but the kid."

"Really?"

"Yup. A part of me was mad as hell at him, but another part was glad to see him. Because you know what?" Dylan stopped the boat and shut off the motor. At the bow, Uncle Ty was showing Jake the best place to cast his line. Dylan paused a moment, watching a stick float by them. "I saw myself in that kid. I used to be the person no one could depend on. The one who would take off at the slightest issue. He got scared that day, he said, worried that he would screw up and ruin the job, so he left. I did that once, too, when I was around his age. Responsibility mixed with someone whose age still ends in *teen* doesn't always work. Eventually, I grew up. Realized that wasn't the way to live my life. Though some would say I'm still as undependable as I was when I was a teenager."

Some people like Sam. His parents. Dylan's family had never seen him as anything other than an irresponsible, fickle kid. Yeah, maybe he'd switched from job to job more than the average person, and maybe he did move often, but once he'd grown up and got a clue, he'd never walked out on a job, never let a boss down. Never walked away from someone who needed him.

"Did you hire the kid back?"

"Yup." Dylan tossed the anchor over, then leaned

back against the console. "Turned out to be one of the smartest things I ever did. I gave him a second chance and a big lecture, and he turned out to be one of the best workers I've ever had."

"That gives me hope," Abby said quietly. Her gaze was on the water, far from him.

"Hope for what?" Dylan asked.

But she didn't answer. Instead Abby pushed off from the railing and crossed to her boys. "Who's ready for Mom to teach them some killer fishing skills?"

Abby concentrated on fishing and not on Dylan. Or at least, she tried to. The five of them were at the bow of the boat, a wide and generous space because the steering wheel was close to the rear. Ty, Dylan and Cody were fishing on one side of the boat while Abby and Jake fished from the other side.

Jake was eager to learn but impatient with the fish. Every ten seconds he thought he had a nibble and yanked his pole up. "Mommy, when am I going to catch a fish?"

"When you sit down and wait a bit," Abby said. "You have to be patient."

Jake sighed and plopped onto the seat. "Okay."

Abby glanced over at Dylan. He'd surprised her, with the story about the kid who worked for him. Based on how he was with the teens at the center and with Cody, she could see him doing exactly that with one of his workers—but she understood how he had seen himself in that kid, too. He seemed to be a good guy, but there was a lot of wanderlust in him. Ty had mentioned once that his nephew Dylan had worked all over the country, the kind of guy who got tired of the day-to-day grind and would constantly set off on another adventure.

Exactly the kind of man she didn't need in her life. Nor did she need her boys relying on someone like that. At the same time, she couldn't deny the connection the boys had with Dylan. The way they talked to him, asked him for advice, and interacted with him. Cody was engaging with them, and Jake was slowing down, paying attention, learning whatever Dylan had to share. For the first time in a long time, she was seeing a change in her sons, and she wasn't ready to walk away from that yet.

Not to mention the attraction she felt for him. He was sweet and tender, and a hundred times she caught him watching her. She found herself glancing at him just as often, wondering if he was thinking of her as much as she was thinking of him.

Across from them, Cody let out a whoop. "Hey! I got one."

"Great job, Code," Dylan said, clapping him on the back. "You beat your mom, too."

"Let me see!" Jake ran across the bow just as Abby grabbed his pole and saved it from landing in the water. "Wow! It's a big fishy!"

"Awesome, Cody," Abby said. "You might beat us all."

"There's a competition?" Cody asked.

Dylan grinned at Abby, and she smiled back. "Well, it was a bet between Abby and me, but I think we should include everyone. Whoever catches the most fish…" His voice trailed off, leaving her to fill in the blanks.

"Gets to decide where we go for dinner," Abby said.

Cody perked up at that. "Even if it's fast food?"

The forbidden food that Abby only allowed her boys to eat once in a while. Most nights, she had something healthy that she made in the slow cooker, which constantly earned complaints from Cody, who would live on a diet of cheeseburgers and pizza if she let him.

Fast food or not, this was one of the few times she'd seen her son interested and she wasn't about to let that go over some fries.

"Even if it's fast food," Abby said. She cast her line into the water. "But if I win, we're going to that vegetarian place on Fourth Street."

Cody groaned. "God, Mom, I hate that place."

"Then you better get fishing." She grinned at her son, and for just a second, he smiled back. It was a start. A really nice start.

Dylan's gaze connected with hers. For a second, she thought how nice this was, a family moment, with her boys laughing and having fun. But it was, she reminded herself, just a moment. Dylan wasn't her husband or even her boyfriend. He was just a guy, a guy who would one day be far away and not here to depend upon.

When they pulled back up to the dock, Dylan would leave and she would go back to being a single mom. Far better to focus on that than imagine a future that was never going to happen.

Chapter Seven

Dylan stowed the fishing poles in the storage bins on the pontoon boat, then grabbed Abby's cooler and joined everyone on the dock. Uncle Ty looked tired, which surprised Dylan, who remembered a constantly moving, optimistic uncle with more energy than a roomful of preschoolers. Ty said a quick goodbye to Abby and her boys, then headed off to Dylan's truck, climbed inside and laid his head against the headrest.

Dylan sighed. The day had been a moderate success. Uncle Ty hadn't been his usual jovial self, but he had helped Jake fish and taught Cody a few things about giving the line well-timed tugs to entice the fish closer. After Cody noticed the lures attached to Ty's lucky cap, they had a long talk about the benefits of spinnerbaits over crankbaits.

But it was Abby whom Dylan noticed the most. She hadn't been kidding—she was a great fisherman. For the first time since he'd met her, he saw her truly relax, her mood light, her smile wide, as she hooked one fish after another. Cody had the lead until the very end, when his mother nabbed two fish back-to-back. They threw all their catches back into the lake, mostly because Jake worried that the fish were going to miss their families. It was kinda cute and something Dylan remembered saying when he was Jake's age.

He was stacking the life jackets in the bin at the front of the boat when Cody came up beside him. "Hey, Cody."

"Thanks for the fishing," Cody said. "I had a good time. I've never gone, and it just seemed so…peaceful." The teenager shook his head. "That sounds all weird and nerdy."

"Nah, it doesn't," Dylan said. "When the water is as smooth as glass and the sun is warm on your back, it feels like the world has stopped for a second. Now *I* sound weird and nerdy and like some Walt Whitman poem."

Cody laughed. "Yeah, I get that. Makes me forget about homework and grades and stuff like that."

Dylan arched a brow. "Are you saying homework is usually the first thing on your mind?"

Cody scoffed. "Yeah, I guess not. But I was thinking about it a lot and I kinda want to change that. I guess I need school to have a job doing stuff like building houses or something."

The thought that Cody might follow in Dylan's career footsteps warmed him. He wondered if that was what it was like to be a parent, to see your child admire and emulate you. Then a part of him remembered he was no role model for a troubled kid. Dylan may have gotten his life back on track but not without a lot of effort and missteps.

"Building houses is all about figuring out angles and reading blueprints and negotiating contracts. If you want to get a contractor's license, you have to take a test. So yeah, you kinda need to pay attention in school."

Cody toed at the deck, his face shadowed by the hood of his sweatshirt. "Can I ask you something?"

"Sure." Dylan straightened and leaned against the railing.

"You said you and your dad didn't get along and, like, he wasn't there much."

"Yeah. I mean, he lived with us, but he worked a lot. And when he was home, he was closer to my older brother and I was the one who always seemed to be in trouble. But I had my Uncle Ty to take me fishing and teach me how to fix stuff."

"So, like, did you ever—" Cody let out a breath "—did you ever tell your dad that bothered you?"

"Yeah." It had been more than a decade, but Dylan could still hear the words ringing in his head, words he had flung at his father before Dylan packed his bags and hit the road. *I was never anything but a disappointment to you.*

His father had stood there, silent. Even after the door shut and Dylan climbed in his car, Jonathon had stayed inside, stubborn to the very end. In the years since, there'd only been a handful of stilted phone calls on holidays and birthdays. In every one of them, his father had talked about how good Sam had turned out, with the implication that Dylan was still nothing but a disappointment.

"I was hoping he'd change," Dylan said, "but some people never do. The only way you find out if they're gonna change, though, is to give them the opportunity." He thought of the kid he had hired, the kid who had screwed up but come back twice as good after Dylan gave him a second chance.

"I don't think my dad's gonna change," Cody said. He shrugged, as if it didn't matter, but clearly it did. "Thanks for the fishing."

"Anytime, Cody." The teenager ambled off. Dylan waited a few minutes, busying himself with tidying up the pontoon boat, before following.

Dylan stowed the coolers in the back of Abby's car, then turned and noticed her holding a sleeping Jake in her arms and struggling under the weight of the four-year-old. Cody was already sitting in his mother's car, ready to leave. The hoodie was over his face, and he was glued to his phone.

"Here, let me take Jake," Dylan said to Abby, reaching for her son.

"You don't have to—"

"I know I don't." He put his arms out. Abby relented and transferred her son, who barely stirred.

Jake's weight settled over Dylan like a thick, heavy blanket. Dylan had never held a kid like this before. He'd had friends who had babies and kids, of course, but he'd never held any of them. There was something warm and nice about the way Jake nestled into Dylan's shoulder, his arms going tight around Dylan's back. He smelled of Johnson's Baby Shampoo, which rocketed Dylan back to after-dinner baths and water fights with his brother.

He followed Abby to her car and waited while she unlocked the doors. As he moved to lower Jake into his booster seat, the boy stirred. "T'ank you for fishing," he said. "I had fun, Uncle Dylan."

Uncle Dylan?

"Glad you had fun, Jake," Dylan said, because he didn't know what to say to the uncle thing, so instead he latched Jake's seat belt.

"Can we go again? Soon?" Jake asked. Beside his brother, Cody watched for Dylan's answer, feigning teenage indifference.

"Uh, sure." But as Dylan made the promise, he realized he couldn't necessarily keep it. Another week, and he was due to be in Maine. The projects at the center would be done by then, and hopefully Ty would be back at work, which would let Dylan hit the road. Leave Stone Gap.

Leave Jake and Cody. And Abby.

It would be best for all of them, he told himself. Before they all got too attached. Like Jake with the puppy. Except…the little boy had become attached to that dog within seconds.

Abby stowed her purse in the car, then slipped into the driver's seat. "Thank you, Dylan. I agree with Jake. It was a great day."

"You're welcome. Glad you all had fun. And congrats on winning the fishing contest." He gave her a grin. "I might have exaggerated my fishing skills."

She laughed. "You caught one. That's better than none. And you still get to partake in the winner's prize, if you want to come to dinner with us."

"Do we really have to go to that vegetarian place?" Cody leaned over the seat. "I hate that food, Mom. It makes me want to barf."

Abby chuckled, her mood still light and fun. Dylan liked her like this, unfettered, unstressed. "How about a compromise," she said to her eldest son, "since you were one heck of a fisherman yourself today. Burgers on the grill?"

Cody brightened, then he dimmed the emotion as if he was afraid to be caught looking happy. "Sure, that would be okay, I guess."

"Dylan, are you comin' to our bar-b-cue?" Jake asked.

Dylan hesitated. Abby had invited him to the restaurant a second ago, but he wasn't sure if it was a real invitation or one of those people threw out to be polite. He should probably get some more work done anyway. The clock to his departure was ticktocking away. And the more he tied himself up with this family—this woman—the harder it would be to leave.

"Jake, I'm sure Dylan has other things to do tonight," Abby said. "We've already taken so much of his time."

"But I want him to come, Mom. He's my friend."

The word hit Dylan smack in the chest. *Friend. Uncle Dylan.* In just a few short days, Jake had bonded with Dylan.

The little boy didn't see Dylan's past or Dylan's shortcomings. He took him at face value and saw him as a buddy. Someone with a shared affinity for dinosaurs and burgers.

Which Dylan realized wasn't such a bad feeling. He glanced over at Cody and saw the older boy was also waiting for Dylan's answer. The two of them, depending on him. He wasn't the kind of guy they could depend on, but he didn't say that. There was something… magical in the air right now, that floated in the happy mood between the Cooper family and himself. Dylan didn't want to be the one who brought that back to earth.

Besides, it was just a barbecue, he told himself. Not a lifetime commitment.

"How about I bring some potato salad?" he said.

A smile curved across Abby's face. "Sure. That would be nice. Come by after five."

"Great. See you then." He waved to the boys, then shut Abby's car door and headed back to his truck, his steps lighter. A barbecue. It didn't get more American, apple-pie than that. Dylan climbed inside his Jeep and started the engine.

"She's a keeper," Uncle Ty said.

"Who?"

His uncle gave him an unamused look. "Just because I'm old and a little slow doesn't mean I'm dim-witted, too. Abby is who. She's the kind of woman a smart man keeps for a lifetime."

Dylan put up his hands. "Whoa, whoa. I'm just going to a barbecue, Uncle Ty. Not a wedding."

"Then be careful. I saw how those boys look at you. They already see you as part of the family. And Abby…"

"Abby what?" Dylan prompted. He was curious and also didn't want to know at the same time. Because he already knew how Jake felt—*Uncle Dylan*—and if Abby was starting to depend on him, think about a future…

Ty didn't say anything for a moment. Dylan turned out of the parking lot, heading in the opposite direction of Abby. A moment later, her car disappeared from his rearview.

"Just don't break her heart," his uncle said finally. "She's a good woman, and like I told you, she's been through a lot."

Dylan let out a gust. "Why does everyone expect the worst of me?"

Ty shifted in his seat and gave his nephew a hard look. "I never said you were no good for her. I just said be careful and don't hurt her. I know you're not planning on staying around, and Abby is the staying-around kind."

"I know that already." It was the exact war he'd been having in his own head.

"I see how you look at her. It's the same way I looked at Virginia when I first met her."

Dylan took a right, then a left, winding his way through Stone Gap and back to Uncle Ty's house, a few blocks away from the center. When the weather was good, Ty and Virginia would walk to and from the center, hand in hand, talking the whole way, their laughter so frequent, it seemed to bubble between them with each step. Dylan had always thought his aunt and uncle had it right and perfect, one of those rare relationships where the two made for perfect complements.

"Well, what you and Aunt Virginia had is about as common as a two-headed penny."

"That doesn't mean it can't happen to you, if you ever decide to stay in one place longer than five minutes and hitch your star to one woman."

Dylan scowled. "How did a simple fishing trip turn into a lecture about me settling down and getting married?"

Ty grinned, the first smile Dylan had seen in hours on his uncle's face. "Don't you know, Dylan? Sometimes when you go fishing, you catch something completely unexpected. A real prize."

Abby took a long hot shower after she got home from fishing. She shaved her legs, curled her hair, spritzed on a little perfume and redid her makeup.

For a barbecue.

She changed her outfit twice, finally settling on a pair of skinny jeans and a navy blue loose flowy blouse. She straightened a house that didn't need straightening, rummaged through her pantry for a boxed dessert that she could whip up, then made the hamburger patties.

When her phone rang at four thirty, Abby steeled herself, sure it was Dylan calling to cancel. Telling herself that would be best, because she was already starting to fall for him.

Instead of Dylan, her sister Melanie's name lit up

the phone. "Hey, Mel," Abby said when she answered. "How are you?"

"Driving home from work in rush-hour traffic from hell. I thought leaving a little early would help me miss it, but no." Melanie sighed. "I've got to go to a big meeting with an advertiser tonight. You know, fancy restaurant, the whole schmoozing thing."

"I can't remember the last time I was in a fancy restaurant," Abby said. "So how's Adam?"

A hesitation on Melanie's end. "Everyone's great. Just great. You know, the usual, working a lot, spending a lot, sleeping too little. I think we might take our winter vacation in Europe this year."

"Europe, huh?" Abby had to admit she felt a pang of envy. That was the kind of vacation she'd never be able to afford for her kids. Melanie was free and loose, without kids to tie her down. "Glad everything is going well. You sound great."

"Yeah, yeah. I am."

There was something off in Melanie's voice, though, something that nagged at Abby. Maybe her sister wasn't as happy as she made herself out to be. Or maybe the traffic just had her off center. "You doing okay?" Abby asked. "I mean, you don't call me that often and—"

"I'm just catching up, Abs." Melanie let out an irritated sigh. "Why are you giving me the third degree?"

"Sorry." Abby switched topics, and forced a brightness into her tone. "Your birthday is coming up. Why don't I buy you a plane ticket, and you can come down here and visit me? I know the kids would love to see you. Oh, and do you remember Harris McCarthy from high school? He's been back in town recently. He's a builder or something and was working on a project nearby for some retired baseball player. I saw it in the paper the other day. Small world, isn't it?"

Her sister seemed to hesitate. "Harris McCarthy? From high school? I... I hardly remember him."

Abby laughed. "Right. You were head over heels for him in high school. I always thought you two would end up together. Guess you hit the jackpot elsewhere, though."

"Yeah, well, happy endings don't always come true." Melanie let out a breath, then her voice brightened. "Anyway, I should go. I've got...traffic. Meeting. All that stuff. Bye, Ab!"

Her sister was gone. Abby worried about Melanie's out-of-the-blue call for a second, then brushed it off. Melanie had that jet-set life, was editor of a major magazine, married to a man who used to be a model. So what if she rarely called? Maybe reaching out signaled a change in their relationship. Besides, if there was one thing Melanie didn't need, it was someone worrying.

A little before five, her doorbell rang. Abby checked her hair and makeup in the hall mirror, then cursed herself for worrying what she looked like. This wasn't a date, it was a cookout—a cookout her son had invited Dylan to attend. But when she pulled her door open and saw Dylan, it was a little hard to remember that.

Dylan had showered and changed, too, and she could smell the soapy freshness of his skin. His hair was still damp, the longish dark brown locks curling at his neck and by his ears. He had on jeans and a dark green T-shirt that hugged his chest, rolling and dipping over muscles that seemed to beg her to touch. Abby had to remind herself to breathe.

"Potato salad," Dylan said, handing her a ceramic bowl topped with plastic wrap.

She arched a brow. "Did you make this yourself?"

"Nope." He chuckled. "I have no cooking ability, remember? I asked Della where to find the best potato salad in Stone Gap, and she said, 'right here in my own kitchen.' Then she made up a batch and told me to make sure Jake and Cody got these for later, and for just them, not us grownups." Dylan handed her a plastic sandwich bag stuffed with chocolate chip cookies.

"Good thing I made brownies too, so I get my chocolate fix. Della is awesome. She spoils my boys rotten. I swear, she's like everyone's grandma." Abby opened the door wider and waved Dylan in and then started talking a mile a minute to cover for her nerves. "For a while, she was babysitting your brother's two kids. Jake and Henry got along really well. In fact, Henry and Libby are at the center at least once a week. You'll probably see them soon. You should see how big Henry's gotten. He talks as much as Jake, and when they're together at preschool, they go on and on more than a Congressional debate. It's nice to see how Sam's kids have blossomed since Katie came into their lives."

"I've, ah, never met Libby or Henry." Dylan grabbed the tray of hamburger patties and followed Abby into the backyard. "And who's Katie?"

He didn't know about his brother's fiancée? That seemed strange. Then she remembered he had said he didn't get along that well with his brother anymore. She wondered what had driven them apart. She'd met Sam briefly—she knew his kids and fiancée much better—and found him to be a nice guy, sort of an older version of Dylan.

"Katie is a sister to one of the Barlows and moved here a little while ago." Abby pressed the button to light the grill. Flames whooshed under the steel grate. "Sam hired her to be his nanny, and five minutes later, he fell in love. You should see him. Sam goes around town, grinning like a total fool. They're getting married at the end of the month."

"Guess I have been gone a long time." A mix of emotions ran across Dylan's features. She could see he was hurt that his brother had left him out of the loop about his life. Maybe, given enough time in Stone Gap, Dylan and Sam could mend their broken fences.

Jake came barreling across the yard and plowed straight into Dylan's legs. "You came to our party!"

Abby laughed. "Jake, one guest doesn't make a party."

Dylan bent down to her son's level. "Thank you for inviting me, Jake," he said. "And I think it's a party if you have balloons."

Jake pouted. "I don't have any balloons. Cuz it's not my birthday."

Dylan fished in his pocket and pulled out a handful of brightly colored uninflated balloons. "If you help me blow these up, then we'll have balloons. Even if it's not anybody's birthday."

Abby tended the burgers while Dylan and Jake competed to blow up balloons the fastest. In minutes, they had a dozen filled, and Jake took off, playing kickball with one of them and laughing when it floated away from his foot. Cody helped, too, tying the balloons for Jake and inflating a few of his own. Mrs. Reynolds came over and brought the puppies, who tumbled over their big feet, running after Jake and the balloons. Jake's smile was as wide and bright as the North Carolina sky. Dylan dropped to the ground, while the puppies and Jake climbed all over him.

She watched them and had the same feeling she'd had out on the lake. That this was what a family with two parents—two involved, caring parents—could look like. It was a dangerous thought, a very dangerous thought. She knew better than to dream of an impossible future.

She'd always thought of herself as pragmatic, sensible. But when it came to her boys and the family she dreamed of having, the hopeless romantic kept trying to make her believe in some white picket fantasy. This was just a barbecue, just a handful of balloons. Not a life.

And this man, no matter how much she was attracted to him or how much she craved his touch, wasn't interested in anything permanent.

"That was thoughtful of you to bring those. The kids are really having fun," Abby said to Dylan. Such a simple thing, a handful of balloons, but the joy on Jake's face caused a lump in Abby's throat.

How she didn't want to like this guy, or rely on him, or bring him any further into their lives. Every time she thought she had resolve, he did something sweet, and all her resistance melted.

Dylan shrugged. "I used to be a kid once. I saw these at the center when I stopped by there this morning with my uncle and thought Jake might like them. They're not puppies, but they're still fun."

Damn him for being so considerate. She turned away and concentrated on the burgers. Because that was easier than dealing with the conflicting emotions running through her.

Dylan moved into the space beside her. The heat from his body mingled with the heat from the grill. She wanted to reach out and touch him, feel the muscles underneath his shirt. Lean into him for another of those amazing kisses.

"Hey, you had a hard day," Dylan said. "Hell, a hard week, between working, helping at the center, and taking care of the boys. Why don't you let me grill?"

"I thought you couldn't cook."

"I can't. But when it comes to tending something on a fire, I'm your man." He flexed a biceps and gave her a grin.

I'm your man.

The words hit her hard and carved a chink in that wall Abby had kept around her heart for years. How she wanted to believe those words, even if he was saying them as a joke. How she wanted to trust that he was the kind of man who would stay around, who would be a role model for her boys, who would share the workload that weighed heavy on her shoulders, who would treat her with kindness and love.

But she knew better. Dylan himself had told her he

wasn't hanging around. That he wasn't the kind of guy to put down roots.

"Thanks for the offer, but I'm okay on my own," Abby said and pivoted away before Dylan could see the truth in her eyes.

Something had shifted in Abby after Dylan had given Jake the balloons. For a second, he'd seen her open up, warming to him, then that wall went up again and she was cool and distant.

Maybe she'd read the change in Dylan after hearing about Sam's fiancée. It had taken him a moment to absorb the news about the upcoming wedding—to which he hadn't been invited—and to push his disappointment to the side. A part of Dylan was hurt that this information hadn't come from Sam, but he knew that was par for the course. They rarely talked, and their last few exchanges had been terse.

He was happy Sam had found love again. He and his older brother might not get along, but Dylan still wanted to see Sam and his kids happy and content. If Dylan hung around town long enough, maybe he could at least meet this fiancée, even if he wasn't invited to the wedding.

Wait. Hung around town long enough? He only had a week left before he had to drive to Maine. After these next few days, Dylan would be hundreds of miles away from Sam. From Jake and Cody. From Uncle Ty.

From Abby.

And that fact, Dylan was pretty damned sure, was the reason why Abby kept putting distance between them. He had made her no promises, nothing beyond his short stay here. But as he watched her, helping Jake dish some potato salad onto his plate, he caught her glancing at him, and something in his chest leaped.

Cody left a minute later, as soon as his plate was clean, saying he was going to hang out with a friend. With dinner over, the still tired Jake went inside, sat down to watch TV and promptly fell asleep on the sofa, a plastic dinosaur clutched in his hand. Dylan helped Abby carry the dishes into the house, then started the water to wash them before she could.

"You don't have to do that," she said.

"I know." He nodded toward the dish towel. "You want to dry?"

He half expected her to make up another excuse to be away from him like she had earlier. When they'd all sat down to eat, Cody and Jake had sat together on one side of the picnic table, leaving Abby and Dylan on the other. But instead of sitting beside him, Abby had gotten up to shut off the grill, then bring everyone refills of their drinks, then extra napkins they didn't need.

He wondered if she'd done that because she wasn't interested in him or because she *was* interested and was afraid to take it any further. He knew he hadn't imagined the undercurrent between them, her responses to his kisses, his touch. He didn't want the day to end, and if doing the dishes, heck, cleaning her whole house, kept him here a little longer, he was game. Even if he knew he was only prolonging a connection he couldn't keep.

Abby hesitated a second, then grabbed the towel and slipped into place beside him. He caught the dark floral notes of her perfume, a compliment to the sweet scent of the dish soap. Earlier, when the evening had been hotter, Abby had put her hair up into a clip, and he'd had the strongest urge to kiss the valley of her neck, then peel back the edge of her shirt and kiss the divot beside her shoulder—

He turned, halfway through washing a plate. "Go out with me."

"Outside? We brought everything in already."

"I meant on a date." The words had been spontaneous, but the sentiment had been there since the day he'd met her. Abby intrigued him, with the way she was both strong and fragile at the same time. The side of her that danced with her four-year-old son to oldies was such a beautiful contrast to the resilient, confident woman who baited her own hooks.

He knew he was asking a lot. Knew he was leaving town soon, and there was no way this relationship could progress, and that a man like him shouldn't be in a relationship, especially not one that was a package deal. But he also didn't want to head to Maine without spending at least one night alone with Abby. Hearing her laugh. Seeing her smile. Holding her in his arms.

Abby took the plate he'd washed and dried it. "I don't know, Dylan. I mean, I suppose Cody could watch Jake, but he's not always the most reliable teenager…"

"Della could watch Jake. She told me herself she loves that kid. Or my uncle Ty. He's great with kids, and having Jake around might bring him out of his grief for a little while." He rinsed another plate and handed it to her. "When was the last time you went on a date?"

She scoffed. "I can't remember. How sad is that?"

Pretty damned sad if you asked him. Abby was a smart, beautiful woman. Any man with half a brain cell in his head would ask her out. For the hundredth time, Dylan wondered what had made her ex-husband so blind to how amazing she was.

"That's all the more reason why we should go out." He handed her another plate. She dried it in slow, concentric circles, turned to put it away and paused.

"Why?" she asked. "Why go out on a date when you told me yourself you're not staying in town? That this is a temporary stop for you?"

She'd nailed the truth about him in a few words. The thought of leaving caused an ache in his chest, but Dylan told himself that feeling would ease. For right here, right now, he wanted to get to know Abby more. Find out what made her laugh. What she felt like beneath him. He wanted more—even though he knew she was right and he had no business asking her for anything.

"Does everything in your life have to be permanent, Abby? We can go out, have fun and leave it at that." One night. That would be enough. Wouldn't it? He turned off the water, let it drain and put his back to the sink. "Loosen the reins a bit, Abby."

She shook her head. "I don't do that, Dylan. I don't change my schedule, I don't take impromptu trips. This whole thing here—" she waved to indicate the house, her kids "—is like a well-oiled machine. Take one cog out and it falls apart."

"You spent a Saturday tearing down a wall, took

an impromptu fishing trip, had a last-minute barbecue. Nothing fell apart." He leaned closer to her, caught those blue-green eyes with his own. "I think you're just scared."

She raised her chin. "I'm not scared to go out on a date."

"Then prove it. The center closes at six, so I'll pick you up at six thirty tomorrow night. Wear something comfortable."

"I have a presentation to work on—"

He leaned toward her, kissed that valley of her neck, then her lips. The protest died in her throat.

She let out a soft sound as his lips continued their path along her neckline. That simple sound almost undid him. Her hands went to his waist, and her body swayed into his. Everything in him wanted to sweep her into his arms and carry her into her bedroom and take his sweet time exploring the lines of her curves. Instead, he pulled back, aware that a sleeping Jake was only a room away. Later, he told himself, later they could see where this led. "I'll see you tomorrow night, Abby."

A smile curved across her face. "You're stubborn, you know that?"

"That's what my mother tells me." He almost hated to go but knew there was work to be done at the center yet tonight, so it could be ready for the kids tomorrow. And maybe getting out of this house, with all the toys and bedroom stories and warmth, would keep him from dreaming of things he couldn't have. "Thanks for dinner."

"You did the cooking. And brought the side dish. All I did was provide a picnic table."

"And brownies. Don't forget the brownies. It's always nice to end with something sweet." He grinned, then took Della's clean dish and headed toward the door with Abby walking beside him. Jake was still sleeping on the couch as they walked by, so Dylan leaned over and gave Abby a quick kiss goodbye. "See you tomorrow."

"See you tomorrow, Dylan." She said his name with a soft lilt in the middle. A lilt that almost had him staying.

He left Abby's house, his chest filled with anticipation. She lingered in his mind as he went to work at the center, repairing loose floorboards, grouting the new tiles and painting the wall the four of them had put up two days ago.

He headed back to the inn a few hours later, his muscles tired, but his brain still running a mile a minute. That alone was a sign he was in too deep with Abby. He couldn't remember the last time a woman had occupied his every waking thought. Hell, she'd been in his dreams, too. If he was honest with himself, he thought about her pretty much all the time.

When he walked into the bed-and-breakfast, he saw the kitchen light burning. He headed down the hall and found Della Barlow sitting at the table, a pile of recipe books and a notepad beside her.

"Oh, hi, Dylan. I'm just working on the menu for next week. We've got a few more visitors coming in on Friday."

Dylan put the clean dish away, then sank into the opposite chair. "That's great. Business is doing well?"

"Better than expected." She pushed a covered plate toward him. "More of those chocolate chip cookies I made for the boys."

"Thank God." He grabbed two and took a bite out of one. "I have to admit, I was a little jealous watching Jake eat them. Your cooking is the best, Della. The potato salad was a huge hit, too." He was sure he'd gained at least five pounds in the time he'd been here, eating Della's cooking. Not to mention the little treats Mavis often brought into the center.

"You're welcome." She set her pen down and crossed her hands over the notepad. Her reading glasses slipped down on her nose, and she took them off. "How was the barbecue? How's Abby?"

"It was great. And Abby is…" He shrugged, as if he was blasé about the whole subject, but then a smile winged its way across his face. Hell, he could feel that smile all the way to his toes.

"Something special, isn't she?" Della gave him a knowing glance. "She's only lived in Stone Gap for a few years, but she's really been a great addition to town. She worked with Mavis and me on some marketing materials for the inn when we first opened. Wouldn't take a dime for her time, either."

That sounded like the woman he knew. Stubborn yet generous with her time and talents. Like the way she helped at the center, kept applying for those grants, despite a demanding job and life as a single mom. "Well, whatever she did, it seems to be working if you're booking up that fast."

"So," Della said, fiddling with the pen. "Are you

thinking about extending your stay here? There's always plenty of renovation work in this area, especially being so close to the city. I know you're only booked through the end of next week, but it seems you've fit back into Stone Gap like a missing puzzle piece."

"I never fit this puzzle, Della," Dylan said. "I'm not a small town kind of guy."

"And what's so bad about small towns?"

"They close in on you. I like space, room to move and breathe." He thought of all the judgment and expectations that came with this place.

"And you can't find that here?"

"There's not much for me here, Della. That's why I left a long time ago." There was his uncle, of course, and now Abby, but all of that came with the one thing he didn't do—settling down. Staying put.

Della covered Dylan's hand with her own. He often wondered what it would have been like to grow up as a Barlow instead of a Millwright. "There's a lot more than you think. Your uncle, the community center, your brother—"

Dylan scoffed. "We don't exactly get along. Uncle Ty will eventually get back to running the center alone and I'll…"

"Move on, leave." Her kind eyes met his. As long as he'd known Della, she'd been a surrogate mom to everyone she met. Wise, kind and giving. "Or is it more running away again?"

And right on the money. He kept telling himself this wasn't running away…

Except wasn't that exactly what he was doing? Running before he got too close? Running before he found himself stuck here? Running...because it was easier than facing all the things he'd left in the first place? All those fears meeting Abby had awakened in him?

"I'm too old to run away," he said, though he wasn't sure if he was telling Della or himself.

Della nodded and got to her feet. "Good. I'm glad we agree on that. So, put you down for another week? Until you find a place of your own?"

Dylan put up his hands. "Whoa, whoa. I'm not moving back to Stone Gap. I have a job waiting for me in Maine—"

"And a family needing you here." Della stacked up her recipe books and stowed them on a shelf. "If there's one thing I've learned in my life after raising three boys and welcoming a stepson and a whole bunch of daughters-in-law into the family, it's that family is the most important thing in your life. You can find a new job. You can find a new house. But finding a new family... That's not something you can just pluck out of the classified ads."

"I have commitments in Maine, Della. I can't just break them."

"Okay. Can't blame me for trying to keep you around, and don't think this means I won't mention it again sometime. You've always been like an extra son to me." Della put a hand on his shoulder. "Good night, Dylan. Mavis is making waffles for tomorrow morning's breakfast. She knows you like them." Della went home to her husband Bobby every night while single Mavis lived at the inn. They took turns doing the cooking and cleaning, with Mavis mainly handling the morning routines and Della taking over at night.

"Thanks, Della." He waited until he heard her leave. Then he snagged another cookie and headed up to his room. But the last chocolate chip cookie didn't taste as sweet. And sleep took a long time to come.

Chapter Eight

Abby spent her workday distracted. Twice, she'd been caught daydreaming in a client meeting. Her mind kept drifting to the date she had tonight. With Dylan. A man who was all wrong for her, but she couldn't seem to remember that whenever he was nearby.

She left work a few minutes early, then headed to the community center to pick up the boys. When she walked in, Jake scrambled to his feet, leaving his craft project on the table. He plowed into her legs and gave her a tight hug. She hoisted Jake onto her hip—he was almost too heavy for her to keep doing this—then asked him about his day.

Cody was sitting on the sofas with the other boys, in a repeat of the other day. Dylan sat in the armchair at the center of the group, talking with the teenagers about the latest *Star Wars* movie. He looked up, saw her and gave her a quick, private smile. A little thrill ran through Abby and she felt her face heat.

Dylan excused himself from the teen circle and crossed to her. "Hey. You're here early."

"I wanted to get the boys over to Ty's house so I'd have time to change out of my work clothes." Just the thought of changing clothes had her mind derailing to thoughts of being in a bedroom with Dylan, taking off her shirt—

She cleared her throat. "Are you sure Ty is okay with watching them?"

Dylan nodded. "I talked to him earlier today. I think the fishing trip really helped bring him out of his dark mood. The boys are good for him."

"Good." She shifted Jake's weight, aware her youngest son was paying attention to every word of the adult conversation. "Well… I…uh, should get going. See you at six thirty?"

"You can count on it." He smiled at her, and heat rushed through every inch of Abby.

Oh, this was bad. Very bad.

But that didn't stop her from humming under her breath as she gathered her sons and headed out of the community center. She drove over to Ty's house with the boys, her mind on Dylan instead of on the continual stream of chatter from Jake, who interjected *can we get a puppy* in between every sentence.

Ty came out onto the porch when she pulled in. He still looked too thin and too pale, but there was a little more spring in his step. "How you doing, Abby?"

"Great. Brought you a couple of troublemakers to keep you company."

Jake looked up at his mother. "I'm not a troublemaker."

Abby laughed. "I know, Jakester. I was just joking."

Ty chuckled. "Well, they're my favorite troublemakers in this whole town. Boys, I rented a movie and ordered a pizza. Sound good to you?"

Cody nodded. "Yeah, sure."

She'd expected Cody to complain and ask to go to a friend's house. But he seemed okay staying here with his brother, so she didn't question it. "You guys all set? I have to run home and change before I go out tonight."

Jake nodded, then bounced up and down when he noticed the video in Ty's hands. "I'm gonna help Ty put the movie on! It's about dinosaurs!"

"Somebody told me they're your favorite thing," Ty said. He glanced at Abby. "My nephew apparently was very impressed with Jake's knowledge of T. rexes."

Dylan had remembered and thought to tell Ty, so Jake would have a good time. Every time she thought she had this guy figured out, he did something that surprised her, like kissing her in her kitchen and leaving her breathless and thinking of him long into the night.

Abby gave Jake a kiss and a hug, then Ty and Jake headed down the hall. Abby turned to go.

"Wait, Mom." Cody reached in his backpack. "Can you, uh, sign my progress report?"

By the end of the last school year, Cody had been on the edge of failing. After multiple meetings with his teachers, they'd finally settled on a weekly progress report that Abby had to sign, so everyone could keep an eye on his grades. She'd asked the teachers for his junior year to keep the practice in place, so she wouldn't be caught off guard and end up having to send Cody to summer school again.

She took the paper from him, expecting the same report as always. Lots of Ds and Fs, and a whole lot of *needs to participate more*, *missing assignments*, *negative attitude* in the comments column. She hadn't seen a grade with any of the first three letters of the alphabet in at least a year.

She scanned the pink sheet, then read it again. Four Ds, no Fs, and one C in math. *Attitude improved. Did all homework this week.* Abby raised her gaze to her son. "You brought up your math grade?"

Cody shrugged. "Dylan helped me with my homework. I finally get the Pythagorean theorem. It's not really that hard. He just told me to think about it like building a house."

Abby stared at Cody. Was this the same son she'd been nagging a week ago to bring a book home once in a while? The same son who had told her he wanted to drop out? The same son who said math was pointless? "That's…that's great, Cody. Way to go. I'm really proud of you."

Cody toed at the floor. "Yeah, like I said, it was no big deal."

Before her son could escape, she drew him into a tight hug. Cody stood there, stiff, for a moment, then eased into his mother's embrace. "Well, it's a big deal to me, Cody. And I'm really, really proud."

Cody untangled himself and stepped back. "Yeah, well, I'm gonna go see what Ty has to eat." Cody ambled off, and Abby had to choke back some tears when she got back in her car.

Dylan was changing her son's life. Redirecting her lost teenager. Bringing light into her world.

And making it extremely hard for Abby to remember why she shouldn't get involved with him.

Dylan had never been a man who was known for romantic gestures. That kind of thing had always befuddled him, and he'd usually opted for the easy way out, with a fast casual dinner in some chain restaurant. But tonight, with Abby, he wanted to make it special. To make *her* feel special.

He'd debated all afternoon between some big grand gesture, a few smaller ones, or just eschewing the romantic part all together. But then he'd think of Abby and how hard she worked to raise her sons, to do her job and to help other people, and decided she deserved far more than a half-hearted effort on his part. Not to mention a part of him wanted to impress her, to see her smile light her eyes.

At 6:29, he was standing on her doorstep, a thin bead of sweat on his forehead and a too-tight collar on his neck. He'd run around like a crazy man after he left the center and barely made it to her house in time. There was no music coming from inside, no dancing this afternoon. The boys, Dylan knew, were already at his uncle's house. He'd stopped by there first, to make sure Ty had it under control, and was surprised to see his uncle sitting at the coffee table, playing Monopoly with Cody while Jake watched a cartoon movie about dinosaurs.

Abby opened the door, and Dylan had to remind himself to breathe. She looked stunning, in hip-hugging dark jeans, a blue patterned V-neck shirt and a soft cream cardigan. Her hair was down, curling loosely around her shoulders, and she was wearing a soft red lipstick that begged him to kiss her.

"Hi," she said, her voice quiet and shy.

"Hi." It was like they hardly knew each other. He blamed it on the collared shirt, so foreign to Dylan that it might as well have been a straitjacket.

"Nice shirt." Abby smirked.

"Figured I'd try to impress you." He held out his hands. "Did it work?"

"Well, to be honest, even though you look handsome—"

He heard the *handsome* and figured that was worth this strangulation collar.

"—what someone wears doesn't impress me." Abby grabbed her purse and pulled the door shut behind her. "Actions do."

It was a good policy. Dylan had always hired workers based on the way they handled the job, not on what color their hair was, how many piercings they had, or whether they had a sleeve of tattoos. But her words had him wondering if his actions had been the impressive type, because he was really starting to fall for this woman. "So how am I doing in the actions department?"

The shy smile filled her face again. "Not bad, Dylan. Not bad at all."

Damn. When she looked at him like that, it took all he had not to run up the stairs with her and make love to her. He cleared his throat. "Are you ready to go?"

She locked the door and pivoted toward him, nearly colliding. She caught her breath, her eyes wide and luminous in the dim light from the porch. "Am I, uh, dressed okay? You said to wear something comfortable."

"You're perfect, Abby. Absolutely perfect." The words hung in the tense, heavy air between them. He wanted to say more but was afraid the words would trip in his throat, make promises he couldn't keep.

A blush filled her cheeks. She held his gaze for a moment, then looked away. "We should probably get going. I don't want to leave the boys at Ty's too late."

He led her down to his Jeep, opening the door for her before coming around to the driver's side. He'd taken it to the car wash early this morning, scrubbing down almost every surface inside and out until the leather and glass resembled its much-former new self. As he drove, they exchanged small talk about the center, the nice weather Stone Gap had been enjoying all week, Jake's newest toy dinosaur.

"So, you grew up here?" Abby asked.

"Yup. Born and raised."

"Did you like Stone Gap when you were a kid?"

Dylan thought about that for a moment. "I guess I did when I was little. The town, anyway. My school. My friends. My brother. It wasn't until I got older, high school age, that my mind changed."

She shifted in the seat to face him. "So what happened? I'm not trying to pry, I'm just…trying to understand my own son."

"Because you see a lot of Cody in me?"

"In who you used to be," she said.

Who he used to be. Had he really changed all that much? He thought of what Della had said, about how he was only running away again. Was he really? Or was he just moving on to the next opportunity?

He liked to think he had grown up, changed, evolved. But he was in his thirties and had yet to put down roots or even have a relationship that lasted longer than a few months. He'd never really fallen in love, never really connected with anyone too much. His entire life, it seemed, was transitory. For years, he'd liked that, but now, admitting it out loud made it all sound…sad.

"It was gradual," Dylan said. "I was always close to Sam, and he made life here good. We'd go fishing, build forts in the woods, stay up too late watching movies and eating junk food. Then my brother grew up, got a car and his own life. My dad was never much of a father, especially to me. I think he resented having a second child because it meant he had to work more, you know? Sam was always the one who could do no wrong, and when Sam was gone, my father laid into me twice as hard. So instead of trying harder, I rebelled. Flunking out of school, committed a string of petty crimes, that kind of thing."

"A rebel without a cause?"

He chuckled. "Yeah, I guess that's how you could describe it. But really, I spent more time with the truant officer and talking to the Stone Gap cops than anyone should. I guess I just felt like Stone Gap had all these rules and restrictions, and I just wanted to escape them."

"Like you wanted to with your father," Abby said softly.

He'd never thought of it that way. When he'd run away, he'd told everyone it was because he was sick of being held down, of being told what to do, of being in trouble. He'd thought he was escaping the town that seemed to judge his every move, the neighbors who shied away because they thought he was trouble. The brother who had rejected him.

He'd never seen it as an escape from his father.

"I understand that," Abby said. "I was so anxious to get out on my own and get away from my parents that I married the first guy who asked. I'd say it was the biggest mistake of my life, but I was blessed with two sons from that relationship so... I guess it had its pluses."

"Everything in life has an up and a down side." Dylan shook his head. "Now I sound like some fortune cookie philosopher."

It was being around Abby and her boys that had him thinking like that. Had him questioning his choices, decisions. Made him wonder how his life would have been different if he had followed the same route as Sam. Would he be married to a woman like Abby? Raising a couple of boys? Maybe a little girl?

Speculation, that's all that was. His life was what it was, and he liked it. He wasn't lacking for anything. And he certainly wasn't cut from the same cloth as Sam, who seemed made for the role of family man.

But as he glanced at the beautiful woman beside him, he had to wonder if he was fooling himself.

They wound their way through the town and at last Dylan turned onto a dirt road that led to the edge of Stone Gap Lake, away from the few private homes on the lake and the dock where Ty's pontoon was parked, and down to the western side of the lake. The Jeep bounced a little on the rough surface, sending Abby's arm crashing into his. He didn't complain.

A quartet of small cabins sat on either side of the road's end. To the right, stacked logs formed a circle around a stone firepit. The rest of the buildings had fallen into disrepair, but these four still stood strong. Maybe they'd been built later or with better materials. Whatever the reason, he was glad they were still here. There were some things in Stone Gap that he liked to be able to count on. This place was one of them.

"Where are we?" Abby asked.

"It used to be a campground. I went here in the summers with my uncle, my brother and some of my friends. It was a group outing that Ty organized every year. The campground shut down about ten years ago when the owner died."

He had hundreds of happy memories from those years. When he and Sam had first started going to the Little Otter Summer Camp, Dylan had been only five, his brother almost ten. He and Sam had roomed together, staying up late long into the night talking or playing card games. Those were the years filled with swimming and boating and fishing and bonds Dylan was sure would never break.

But just like the campground had fallen apart, so, too, had his relationship with Sam. *I give up on you*, Sam had said as the police left after Sam had gotten Dylan out of yet another scrape. *You're just going to let everyone down again.*

Dylan wasn't that kid anymore. He'd cleaned up his act, stopped doing stupid things like knocking over mailboxes or spray-painting the sides of buildings. That night in the police station had been the wake-up call he'd needed. The problem? Sam didn't see any of those changes in Dylan and probably never would. And until Sam stopped seeing him as the family screwup, their relationship was destined to be a failure.

"This must have been a great place to camp," Abby said. "What a view."

"It was. It's one of my favorite places in Stone Gap." He parked, shut off the car.

The lake spread before them, blue and deep. The sun was setting, and the lake began to tint with purples and pinks. They got out of the car and Dylan came around to the passenger's side. He took Abby's hand and led her down the trail to the water's edge and to the little tableau he'd set up earlier.

He'd borrowed a thick blanket from Della and spread it on the grass. He'd set a cooler on one corner, then laid two wineglasses and a chilling bottle of white wine in the center, flanked by a spray of wildflowers. It was simple and rustic and he prayed she liked it.

"Wow. This is really nice, Dylan." Abby gave him a smile. "I love it."

The praise warmed him. He hadn't realized until then

that he'd been holding his breath, waiting for her reaction. All that told him that he was in too deep, but right now, in this place, with this woman, the first woman he'd ever taken here, Dylan didn't care.

"Thanks. I… I didn't know what you liked so I got a few different things to eat." He knelt on the blanket, pulled a book of matches out of his pocket and lit two candles sitting in mason jars. The gold light flickered over the blue patterned quilt. "There. Ambiance."

"Perfect." Abby lowered herself into a sitting position on the blanket, then leaned back on her hands. "The lake is so quiet and still."

Dylan sat beside her. "This used to be my favorite time of day when I camped here in the summers. I'd sneak out after dinner started and sit here to eat. Most of the fishermen were gone, and the swimmers were out of the water, so it was just me, a few loons and the occasional fish jumping. I liked the quiet. I still do."

"Do you find a lot of that where you live?"

"Yeah. When I'm not working, I'm doing the same thing. Either camping in the woods or fishing in a lake. I've always loved being outdoors."

"Me, too. Though I spend far too much time indoors. When I was a little girl, my grandpa would take me fishing. My dad was never much for that kind of thing, nor was my sister, so it was just me and my grandpa." Abby smiled. "Whenever I visited him in Connecticut, I made sure to get at least one afternoon out on the water with him. He died five years ago, and I haven't been fishing since you took us out on the water. I was so glad to share that with my boys, especially Jake, who has never gotten to do those things."

"Is that where you grew up? Connecticut?" He couldn't imagine her in a place like Connecticut, which had always seemed so upper crust to him. Abby was more like…

Well, more like Stone Gap. At least the good parts of it. The parts he used to love.

He'd never met a woman like her. He'd dated all kinds of women, but none had that calm centeredness mixed with sweet temptation that Abby had. It was a contradiction that intrigued him and attracted him in ways he'd never felt before.

"I grew up in a little town much like this one," Abby said. "I moved down here after I got divorced. I really wanted a small town for my kids to grow up in, and when I got the job offer at the marketing agency a couple towns over, I looked at a house here in Stone Gap and fell in love with the area. I've been here ever since."

He scoffed. He didn't get people who said they fell in love with this sleepy North Carolina town. "All I wanted to do when I got older was leave this place. I can't understand anyone who wants to stay."

"But why? Stone Gap is a great place. You have a job that can go anywhere. And you have family here—"

"I'm only close to my uncle. My parents moved to Arizona a few years back and I rarely see them. That leaves just my brother, Sam, and my niece and nephew."

"Why not try to make amends with Sam?" Abby said. "I've met him, and he seems like a really nice guy."

You're just going to let everyone down again.

"My brother still sees me as the same headstrong foolish seventeen-year-old who dropped out of school and took off on his own." The teenager who hit the road and never looked back. The adult who hadn't been there when Sam's wife died, or when Aunt Virginia died. The man who had let his family down too many times to count. If he could go back and make amends for all that, Dylan would. But life just didn't work that way.

"That's…sad," Abby said. "I don't get along really well with my sister, but I am glad she's part of my life. We talk a couple times a month. We can trade stories about my mom's apple pie or what our uncle Sal is up to now. There's no one else you can do that with but family."

Dylan turned and reached in the cooler. The topic of his family was a sore one for him, the kind that made him question all his life choices. Maybe if things had been different… But they hadn't been, so dwelling on that didn't do anyone any good.

"So, I brought some roast chicken, a salad and this pasta thing that looked good at the market."

Abby laughed. "Change of subject?"

"Yup." He held up the container of chicken. "Do you want some?"

"Let's start with the wine and watch the sun set."

"Sounds like a plan." Dylan pushed Play on his phone, sending a soft undertone of Sinatra into the air while he poured two glasses of wine. The music calmed the tension in his chest, recentered him to the quiet of the setting, the beauty of the woman beside him. "To unforgettable evenings," he said and clinked his glass against hers.

"Sinatra? Wine? A sweet toast? You surprise me, Dylan Millwright."

"Good. That was my plan." He was sure there were other men who could do something far more romantic and memorable, but when Abby settled against his shoulder, he figured he'd added just the right amount of romance. They sipped their wine and watched the world ease into dark while Frank Sinatra crooned in the background.

Being with Abby was so enjoyable, unpressured, unhurried. He liked being around her, having her close. She was the kind of woman he didn't feel he had to force conversation with. The silence between them felt...relaxed. A first for him on a date. At the same time, every inch of him was acutely aware of her, of the scent of her perfume, of how close she sat, close enough to be warmed by the heat from her body.

"This is nice," Abby said with a long, happy sigh. "Really nice. I can't remember the last time I just...sat and enjoyed an evening."

"Me, either. Most days I'm too exhausted to do much more than eat and go to bed. The projects I get hired to work on are usually so time-consuming, I haven't had too many weekends off." He also hadn't had the desire to have time off. Work kept him from thinking, kept him from dwelling on his choices, his life. Nor had he had a woman he wanted to spend time with as much as he wanted to be with Abby. He'd seen her every day since he arrived in Stone Gap, and still it didn't feel like enough.

She turned to him, her eyes bright in the moonlight. "You're a good man, you know that?"

The words took him by surprise, especially since Uncle Ty had said them just a few days ago. The praise didn't feel as if it fit him, like an oversize suit. "What makes you say that?"

"The way you pitched in with your uncle, how you led the teen group. And how you're changing my boys' lives."

He shook his head. She had him all wrong. "I'm not doing anything really."

"You're doing more than you know. Cody's math grade went up." Abby clasped Dylan's hand and met his gaze. "I haven't seen that boy get anything higher than a D in a *year*. This week, he has a C in math. He did all his homework for the week and he said he finally understands the Pythagorean theorem, and all because of you."

Dylan hadn't been sure that Cody was listening when they'd talked. The conversation about solving triangle problems came up when they'd been working together on the repairs for the center. "I didn't do much. Just put it into terms he understood. He really likes working with his hands and doing construction work, so when I rephrased the word problems into that kind of thing, he understood it."

"It's more than that, though, Dylan. My boys have been...lost for a while. I really do the best I can, but I'm a mom, not a dad. And I think it's important for them to have a strong male role model. It's why I started bringing them to the community center. By then Ty pretty much checked out, and it wasn't until they met you that I saw real changes, especially in Cody." Her eyes welled. "I thought I'd lost him. And now... I think he's coming around."

Dylan wanted to tell her she was putting her faith in the wrong man, that he wasn't this picture-perfect man she painted him out to be. And strong male role model? He was the last man on earth anyone should hold up like that. "I told you, you're a great mom. That's important, more important than a fishing trip or a few minutes repairing a wall and talking about math problems."

She shifted to sit up and lean over him. "You made a difference, and I can't begin to tell you how much I appreciate that."

"You're...welcome." The words didn't feel right, because he didn't feel like he'd earned them. And yet, he wasn't going to argue any further with her because he had to admit he really liked seeing the gratitude in Abby's face, seeing her so happy. And all because he'd helped Cody solve for C in a triangle. "I just... I really like you, Abby, and hanging out with your kids seemed natural."

"You really like me?"

He grinned. That was a lot easier to say than *you're on my mind all the time and I'm not sure what to do about that.* "You think I break out the Sinatra for every girl I meet?"

"Well, I don't know. Do you? For all I know, the Little Otter Summer Camp could be your secret love nest." Her smile was edged with something devilish. Something he liked very much.

He cupped her jaw and ran his thumb along the edge of her lips. "It's most definitely not. It is my favorite place in this town, but I've never taken anyone I dated here before."

"Why me?"

"Because I wanted to give you something…special. Because… I'm falling for you, Abby Cooper."

Damn. He'd said that out loud. The words hung in the air. He shouldn't have said them, shouldn't have taken this any further, knowing he was leaving in a week. But every time he looked in her eyes or felt her touch, all rational thought fled.

"I'm falling for you, too, Dylan," she whispered.

His heart soared and he didn't give a damn about timelines or expectations or anything other than being with Abby. He'd worry about tomorrow in the morning.

He pulled her down to him, until she was on his chest, and her mouth was inches from his. "This could get dangerous."

"I'm kinda hoping it does." Then she smiled again, and that was all the answer Dylan needed.

He kissed Abby, not a soft, easy kiss like before, but hard, hot, fast. The desire he'd tamped down from the minute he met her surged to the surface. She met his fire with equal passion, running her hands down his shirt, over the buttons, then as his kiss deepened and the desire became a full-on inferno, she fumbled with the buttons, undoing them one at a time.

Dylan was tempted to rip the shirt off, but there was

something sexy and sweet about her unbuttoning his shirt. He vowed to wear this kind of shirt around her often. A lot more often.

She parted the panels of his shirt, then slid a hand along his chest. "God, your chest is…amazing," she said. "So sexy."

"Hang enough Sheetrock and you can have these muscles, too."

"No thank you, sir. I'll stick to my computer and my weak biceps." She straddled him. "And running my fingers over your chest instead." She did just that and he groaned. Her hands were smooth and soft, her touch igniting every nerve she brushed against.

"I think we should be equal in that regard." He slipped off her sweater, then slid his palms under her shirt and lifted it over her head. She wore a lacy pink bra underneath, and he wondered if she had done that on purpose, for him. He sure hoped so.

His fingers danced above the lacy edge, and her nipples hardened against his palms. Damn. "You are beautiful."

She blushed, and for some reason, that made him fall for her even more. Abby had no idea how mesmerizing she was, how amazing, and he liked that little bit of vulnerability. It was damned sexy.

Dylan rose into a sitting position, with Abby settling in his lap. He kissed her again, his hands tangling in her long, dark hair, then slid his palms down her back, to the tiny clasp at the back of the bra. Abby gasped when the lace cups fell forward, exposing her skin to the cool night air.

He was hard beneath her, his body urging him to hurry up, to quench the need burning inside him, but he didn't want to rush this. He wanted to savor her, to savor this moment, the beauty of her in the moonlight. He bent his head, kissing a trail from her shoulders to the top of her breasts. When he brushed against her nipple, Abby arched against him.

He took her nipple in his mouth, tasting it delicately at first, then harder, teasing the bud until she was gasping and writhing against him. "Good Lord, Dylan," she said. "Just that…and oh…oh my. Yes, that."

She ran her fingers through his hair, urging his mouth closer. He switched to the other side, and in an instant, she was moaning again. He lifted his head, cupping her jaw with his hands, and kissed her, deep, slow, easy. Then he pulled back and shifted to the side, laying her down on the blanket.

The moonlight danced on her bare skin, and he took a moment just to drink in that image. Then she smiled that sexy, devilish smile again, and he forgot all about moonlight and savoring. He undid the clasp on her jeans, slid them over her hips and tossed them to the side, then did the same with his own jeans.

"Are we really doing this?" Abby asked.

"Do you want to?"

She nodded. "But…it's been a long time for me, and… I may be out of practice."

"Then I say we practice." He ran a finger under the edge of her pink lace panties. "A lot."

"That sounds like an incredibly good idea, Mr. Millwright." Her laughter was throaty, sexy, and when she surged into his arms, he lost all rational thought. A second later, they were both naked under the moonlight, the food and wine forgotten, and he was fumbling for the condom in his wallet.

When he entered her, she arched and gasped, digging her fingers into his back. Being inside Abby felt like coming home, warm, sweet, delicious and perfect. She matched him, stroke for stroke, their lovemaking hard and furious and hungry. She cried out, her voice lost among the trees and the night birds.

He increased his pace and she gasped his name in his ear, over and over again, until her orgasm crested and she let out a long, happy sigh. He came a minute later, holding tight to her long after they were finished. For those endless sweet minutes, the world was perfect, and there was nothing in his mind, in his heart, except for Abby Cooper.

He rolled to the side, curling her against his chest, and realized one thing. Dylan had fallen hard for Abby Cooper—

And leaving Stone Gap was not going to be as easy as he'd thought.

Chapter Nine

Abby woke up the next morning, long before the alarm rang. Her day stretched before her, filled with To Do lists and lunches to make and kids to worry about, but her mind lingered on the night before. On the picnic with Dylan. The lovemaking that had left her more satisfied than she could ever remember—twice.

He had been a considerate and tender lover, especially the second time. In those moments under the moon, she had felt special and treasured and—

Hooked.

As much as she hadn't wanted to, Abby had fallen in love with sweet and considerate Dylan Millwright. The man who was all wrong for her, and was undoubtedly going to leave her brokenhearted. Except there was the tiny part of her that saw the way he connected with this town, with his uncle, with the center and with her and her boys, and began to hope that maybe he was going to stay.

She got up, pulled on a robe and went out to the kitchen. The coffeepot, set on a timer the night before, already had fresh hot brew waiting for her. She poured a cup, powered up her laptop and got to work, first checking on the status of a grant she'd applied for a month ago for the center, then on a client presentation she needed to make on Friday. She had about an hour before the boys had to get up for school, and instead of trying to chase elusive sleep, she'd be smart to work.

Because when it came down to it, focusing on a man wasn't going to pay her bills or feed her children. The only one she could rely on to do that was herself.

Uh-huh. Then why did her thoughts keep roaming to last night? To being touched by him, kissed by him, and wanting so much more in that private little grove by the campground. Abby shook her head and refocused on work. On being practical.

She answered what felt like a thousand emails in between typing up presentation notes and creating a few more PowerPoint slides. Three cups of coffee later, Jake came bounding into the kitchen. "Morning, Mommy!"

"Morning, Jakester." Abby refilled her coffee again, then set a cereal bowl on the kitchen table. "You're up bright and early and all by yourself. Good job, buddy."

He'd even dressed himself, in a striped T-shirt and a worn pair of jeans. His socks didn't match, but she let that go. Just the fact that Jake had taken the initiative to get ready on his own told her that her littlest son was growing up. As proud as she was, a tiny part of her was sad.

Jake climbed into the chair and waited for his mother to pour him some cereal. "I wanna go help Dylan build more things today!"

"You can't sweetie. It's a school day. You and Cody have to get ready." She grabbed the milk and added some to Jake's bowl, then got him a spoon. "After school, you can go to the center. Mavis will be there, so you can make a new craft."

"I wanna build things. Like a house. For my dinosaurs!" Jake dug into his cereal, hurrying through his breakfast. "Can I do that? I don't wanna do a craft."

Abby chuckled. "Well, let me talk to Dylan later and see if he needs your help. Right now, I need you and your brother to get ready for school." She dropped her attention back to the presentation. Just one more slide—

"Cody's not goin'," Jake said between spoonfuls. "He came in my room and told me. He said he had to go somewhere else."

The hairs on the back of Abby's neck rose. She froze. "Somewhere else?"

Jake nodded. "Can I watch SpongeBob?"

Abby flicked on the TV, breaking her no-television-during-meals rule, just to keep Jake distracted for a minute. There was no way Cody was going to skip school again. He'd promised her, promised Dylan. His grades were improving; he'd be crazy to start skipping again. Maybe Jake had misunderstood.

She headed down the hall toward Cody's room. The door was closed, as usual, with its bright red Keep Out sign tacked outside. Abby knocked twice. "Cody? Time to get up for school."

No reply.

She knocked again, harder. "Cody? Come on, wake up. I'll make you some eggs if you want. Or one of those burritos you can eat in the car. Let's go, I don't want to be late for work."

No response. Par for the course with a teenager who slept like the dead and hated waking up before seven. Abby turned the handle, opened the door and poked her head inside. Cody's room was dark, save for the soft blue glow coming from his computer's power supply. She took a few steps into the room. "Cody? Hey, sleeping in is—"

The bed was empty. The covers shoved aside, the pillow on the floor.

And the bedroom window open. A chilly breeze floated the dark blue curtains in, out, in, out. She crossed to the window and saw nothing outside except for the deep impression of two footprints in the dewy grass, then a trail leading around to the side of the house.

That couldn't be from Cody. He had to be here somewhere. He'd never run away before. And things were going so well—why would he do that now?

Abby spun on her heel and darted into the bathroom the boys shared. Empty. She checked Jake's room, her bathroom and bedroom, the living room. No Cody. She paused on the stairs, looked out into the yard and noticed Cody's bike wasn't in its customary spot propped against the side of the shed.

Abby ran into the kitchen, her heart in her throat, panic rising in her chest. Jake was still at the table, eating while SpongeBob prattled on about Krabby Patties. "Jake? What did Cody say to you this morning? *Exactly.*"

Jake shrugged, his gaze on SpongeBob's debate with Mr. Krabs. "I dunno. He said goodbye."

Goodbye didn't mean anything. Cody could have gone to school early or to a friend's house—

But there was no text on her phone, no note on the table. Not that Cody told her when he was going to skip school. Something about this departure, though, felt different, wrong, and Abby's Mom SpideySense was tingling.

"Did he say where he was going?" Every word got shriller, worry hitting her in a wave. Cody skipped school, broke curfew and snuck out at night when he was grounded, but never had he left early in the morning, without a word.

Jake turned and looked at his mother. "Mommy, what's wrong?"

"Cody's not in his room," Abby said, and saying it made it real, and the feeling of wrongness multiplied. *Calm down*, she told herself, *don't get Jake all worked up. It's probably nothing.* "He's not in trouble, but I do need to know where he told you he was going, because moms should always know where their kids are, right? So, Jake, can you think really hard and tell me everything he said to you?"

Jake thought a minute. "He said, 'Bye-bye, Jakester.

I gotta go. I'm gonna go see Dad.' He said Dylan said he should."

Keith lived two states away, in Georgia. She wasn't even sure Cody had his father's address, since it had been at least a year since the boys had received so much as a Christmas card. Cody had no money, no means of transportation beside his bike. How on earth was he going to get there?

"Come on, Jake, we have to go now." She picked up the half-empty bowl and put it in the sink. "Go get your shoes on as fast as you can. We're not going to school today."

"Yay! Are we gonna go see Dylan?"

"Yes," Abby said, the word ground out between her teeth. "We are definitely starting with Dylan."

Dylan had arrived at the community center shortly after six in the morning, his To Do list long and full, the pressure to finish doubled after a late-night phone call from his boss in Maine. The job's timeline had been moved up, and Jay wanted him back as soon as possible—and if Dylan wasn't able to return to take on the role, he'd need to immediately hire someone else. Which meant instead of a week before he had to hit the road, Dylan had two days.

Today was Tuesday. He needed to drive back to Maine on Thursday, meet with his boss as soon as he got back and be ready to break ground on the first house in the development on Monday.

But after last night with Abby, Dylan's desire to leave quickly had been cut in half. He wanted the full week, wanted every minute he could have with her. He knew it was impossible to make this new relationship last once he returned to Maine, but—

He still wanted to see if there was a way. Abby was strong and confident and beautiful and unlike any woman he had ever met. She lingered in his mind, hung on the fringes of every thought, every breath.

So he got to work, because that was the only thing that kept him from running back over to Abby's house, just to see her smile, or even better, kiss her, touch her again. Given how often that urge hit him, he was going to end up renovating the entire building in a single day.

The door to the center opened, and even though Dylan knew it was too early and that she was undoubtedly either dropping kids at school or heading to work, his heart hoped to see Abby walking in. Instead, Uncle Ty headed inside and Dylan had to pretend he wasn't disappointed.

"Hey, Uncle Ty." He put down his paintbrush, crossed the room and gave his uncle a quick hug. "What are you doing here so early?"

Ty rocked back on his heels, paused a minute before he spoke. "Here to help, if you want a hand."

Dylan swallowed his surprise. "That would be great."

"Sorry it took me so long to get back on track." His uncle drew in a deep breath. "I always believed life was a journey on a winding road, you know? You hit a bump, you get up and keep going. Until I hit a detour and lost my Virginia and I came to a dead stop." His eyes watered. "But I gotta keep moving, even if it's harder than hell. Like you said, Virginia wouldn't want me sitting around, living in shadows the rest of my life. She'd want me to…"

"Move forward." Instead of staying in one place. That had always been Dylan's reasoning for moving from place to place, job to job. He'd told himself he was moving forward. But for some reason lately, it felt an awful lot like staying in the same place.

His uncle glanced around the center, at the newly repaired walls, the fixed window, the broken door that had been rehung. "You've done a great job here, Dylan, in a really short amount of time."

Uncle Ty had always been more of a father to Dylan than his own father, and his uncle's praise warmed him. "Thanks."

Ty brushed his hands together. "All right. Enough of that emotional crap. Where do we start?"

"Actually, I have to run over to the home improvement store and pick up the replacement piece of countertop I ordered." Dylan thumbed toward the paint and brush he had left in the corner. "If you want to finish painting that game cabinet while I'm gone, that would be great."

"Sure. Sounds good."

"When I get back, I have a few things to finish up here, then I thought I'd check out your truck this afternoon. Sounds like you need a tune-up. And then…" Dylan took in a deep breath. Better to say it sooner than later, even if the anticipation he'd felt earlier when he'd talked to Jay had begun to wither. "I've got to go back to Maine a little sooner than I expected. The timeline for the new build got moved up. My boss wants to put me in charge of the entire project, but only if I can get there in the next few days."

"That's great," Ty said, beaming at his nephew. "I always knew you'd be a success."

Dylan scoffed. Success? He wasn't sure he even thought of himself that way. Sure, he'd gotten his GED, advanced in the construction world until he became a general contractor, but it wasn't like he'd cured cancer or anything. "*Nobody* thought I'd be a success."

Ty put a hand on his nephew's heart. "Doesn't matter what anyone else thinks. If you're a success in here, then you are. As long as you're proud of yourself, that's all that matters."

Dylan had never thought about that before. Was he proud of who he was? What he had become in those years since he'd left this town? The man he'd been for the last couple weeks?

The same man who was leaving all this in his rearview mirror soon?

Instead of answering those questions, he nodded toward the door. "I should get the countertop."

Uncle Ty reached in his back pocket and tugged out his wallet. "Let me pay you for—"

"You don't owe me anything, Uncle Ty. Not a single dime." Dylan pushed the wallet away. "You changed my life when I was younger, and that's payment enough."

"Success, right there." Ty gave his nephew a wide smile. "That's what makes me proud of myself, Dylan. It's not the money I've made or the house I've bought. It's opening this place and changing a life, one person at a time. It's why Virginia and I put so many years into this place and why I'm back again. You change one kid's life, and I'll tell you, it's the best feeling in the world. It's the kind of feeling that makes you want to stay around and keep on doing that."

Dylan grinned. "Is that a hint?"

"Well, I'm not getting any younger, and this center's going to need someone to keep it going. Someone young and enthusiastic." Ty arched a brow. "Hint, hint."

Him? Run the center? Dylan had enjoyed his time here, no doubt about that, but he didn't see himself as the kind of person who should be influencing kids. He didn't have the steady way that Ty had or Aunt Virginia's experience. "Nobody could replace you, Uncle Ty."

"No, there's one somebody who could." Ty gave him another smile, then gestured toward the door. "Go ahead, go get the countertop. I'll hold down the fort here. But think about what I said, okay?"

"Yeah." Dylan walked out of the center and climbed in his Jeep. Uncle Ty was crazy if he thought Dylan should be the one to take over the center. Dylan certainly hadn't done much to change anyone's life here in the past week or so—one changed grade for Cody didn't equal a life-changing moment—and he doubted he'd ever be the kind of role model Ty had been to him.

No, it was best if he got on the road and got back to Maine. Before he got any more wrapped up in a fantasy life he wasn't made for having.

Abby tried Dylan's phone but there was no answer. She tried calling Cody, leaving several messages, but he didn't answer, either. She drove through town toward the community center, frantic, looking for her son and his bike.

Nothing. She told herself Cody couldn't have gone that far. It had only been, what, at most an hour since he left? She didn't know for sure, and that was what scared her most. Cody could be anywhere by now.

Maybe he was just blowing off some steam. But no matter how many times she checked her phone, she didn't see a message from Dylan or Cody.

"Mommy, where are we going?"

Jake had sat in the back seat, playing with one of his dinosaurs, unaware of the rising worry in Abby's mind. "I was thinking we'd stop by and see Dylan, then maybe you can play at Ty's house today." She tried to keep her voice light, happy, in the this-is-an-adventure tone. She glanced at Jake in the rearview mirror. "Does that sound good?"

"Yup. I like Ty. He's really nice and he made me popcorn. And he likes dinosaurs, too."

"That's great," Abby said, barely hearing as Jake went on about Ty's favorite prehistoric creatures. Her mind raced while her gaze darted from one side to the other, peering down every street she passed. No sign of her son, of his bike.

A little after seven, Abby pulled up to the community center. Dylan's car wasn't in the lot, but Ty's was. She parked, not bothering to stay within the lines, then unbuckled Jake and dashed inside. She slowed her steps when she got inside, said a quick hello to Dylan's uncle, then plopped Jake in front of the TV. "Why don't you watch a cartoon while I talk to Ty?"

"SpongeBob?"

"Sure, sure." She handed Jake the remote, then crossed the room to Ty. "Has Cody been here?"

Ty paused in touching up the paint job on a cabinet that usually held games and books. "No, I haven't. Isn't he supposed to be in school?"

Abby lowered her voice and tried to curb her growing worry and impatience. "He told Jake he was leaving to go see his father. He said that Dylan told him to do it."

"Dylan?" Ty's brows creased. "He wouldn't tell Cody to run away."

But hadn't Dylan been a runaway himself? Had he told Cody about his life and Cody had taken that as a sign he should do the same? Didn't it stand to reason that if Dylan could persuade Cody to do his math homework, he could also influence him in running away? Or was she just being overly suspicious because she was worried and scared?

"Maybe he didn't. But maybe he just made his choices sound glamorous to a teenager who didn't need a negative influence." She let out a gusty sigh. She should have known better than to trust a man who had wanderlust in his blood. "I never should have fallen for him."

"Whoa, whoa. Don't blame this all on Dylan. Let's talk to Cody first—"

Abby threw up her hands. "I don't know where he is. He's on his bike and he doesn't have any money, and I don't know what to do." Tears burned the backs of her eyes, but she willed them away. She had to hold it together, had to think. "I tried calling Dylan, but he didn't answer."

Ty nodded toward the table. "Left his cell here when he ran over to the home improvement store. He should be back in about a half hour."

"I don't have that kind of time, Ty. I need to find Cody before he does something stupid." She glanced around the center again, as if she could find her eldest son asleep on a sofa, unnoticed by everyone. All she saw was Jake, thankfully engrossed in the cartoon and unaware of her worry. "Can you stay here, watch Jake and call me if Cody shows up?"

"Of course. And when Dylan gets back—"

Dylan. The mistake she'd made. He had gotten close to her and her boys and just when she'd let down her defenses, he'd gone and told Cody something stupid. Or if he hadn't said the words, he'd at the very least set the example.

"He's made things bad enough. I don't need his help." Then she turned and headed out of the building.

Doing exactly what she should have done all along— relying on herself and no one else.

Chapter Ten

They were a family.

Dylan sat at the stop sign in downtown Stone Gap and watched his brother with his fiancée and his kids in the park. Laughing, smiling. Having fun.

The kids, both brown-haired like Dylan and Sam had been as kids, were dressed in jackets, with book bags and lunchboxes set on the bench. Probably making a quick stop at the park before school. It seemed like something Sam would do. Sam always had been the nurturing kind. Dylan had no doubt he was an excellent dad.

Dylan sat at the stop sign, his Jeep idling, for a long time, debating. Then someone pulled up behind him and beeped, forcing him into a decision. Dylan went through the intersection, pulled into a space on the right, then jogged across the street.

He didn't know what made him enter the park. Something deep inside him urged him closer to his brother, to that picture-perfect family on the swing set. Maybe it was the sense of things unfinished or the urge to set things right before he left again. Or maybe it was seeing Sam's kids, laughing and playing together, that reminded him of days like that decades ago.

When Dylan neared, Sam stopped pushing the swing his daughter was on and raised a brow in surprise. "Dylan. What are you doing here?"

The distrust in Sam's voice almost made Dylan turn around. But then he looked at the two kids, a girl about eight and a little boy the same age as Jake, and he saw himself and Sam in their curious faces. Dylan thought of Jake and Cody and how awful it would be if the two of them grew up and stopped talking to each other. Jake clearly idolized Cody, and Cody had a way of being protective and tender with his little brother, much like Sam had always been with Dylan. Before Dylan took several wrong turns and their relationship went south.

Why had he gone so many years without talking to Sam? Did it really matter what they had said to each other when they were both still young and hot-headed? Dylan's heart ached for the connection he'd once had with Sam. The memories he'd missed out on, the conversations they hadn't had.

More than a decade had passed. Wasn't it time to let go and move on?

Dylan took two steps forward. "Meeting my brother's family, if that's okay. Sorry it took me so long to get here."

Sam glanced at the brunette woman beside him—Katie was her name, Dylan remembered. She gave Sam a slight nod and a tender smile. Sam stepped away from the swing, and Katie slipped into his place and started pushing Libby first, then Henry, alternating between the kids.

Dylan held his breath. Sam stood there another minute, assessing Dylan. Finally, the steel in Sam's face eased. The two of them, so alike, so close. Dylan could almost feel the years of animosity rolling back.

"Better late than never," Sam said. He reached forward, and drew Dylan into a hug. Dylan held stone still for a second, surprised, then as Sam kept on hugging him, he was five again, scared of the sounds of yet another argument floating up the staircase. Sam telling him it was all going to be all right. Making up a story about a pirate and a hidden treasure, until Sam's voice drowned out the anger on the floor below them.

His older brother. Not just a sibling but a friend. A friend he had missed more than he realized.

"Damn, I'm sorry, Sam, for everything," Dylan said, drawing back. All the words that Dylan hadn't spoken, words that had lain in wait for the moment when he was ready to face his past, repair his mistakes. "I didn't mean to drag you into my trouble all those years ago. I should have called Dad the night I was arrested instead of you but you were...you were my best friend."

Sam had been the only one Dylan trusted. The only one he'd ever felt was on his side.

"Don't apologize. I'm glad you called me," Sam said. "Dad would have just yelled at you and probably left you in that police station overnight. I never understood why he had such a beef with you."

Dylan had done a lot of thinking about that very fact ever since he'd left home. It had taken years for him to see his father clearly, to understand the anger and criticism. Now he was older, presumably wiser, he could see his father's viewpoint. Didn't mean he agreed with it, but it brought some peace to Dylan to know it wasn't really personal. "I heard him and Mom arguing one time and he said he would have left her a long time ago, except she got pregnant again. I think he just always saw me as the reason he had to work so many hours and not get whatever life he wanted."

Sam shook his head in disgust. "That's just wrong. I'd never think that about one of my kids."

"That's why you're the kind of dad everyone wishes they had." Dylan glanced at Henry and Libby, who were clearly happy and content. How would Dylan's life had been different—or for that matter, Jake and Cody's lives—with two loving, supportive parents? "That's why I called you that night. I knew you'd take care of me."

And Sam had. After he'd bailed Dylan out, he'd talked to the police and the shop owner, getting them to drop all charges so that Dylan could go free. Then Sam had come home and started lecturing Dylan, not out of some need to emulate their father, Dylan realized now, but out of fear that his little brother was going to end up in jail or worse. Dylan had been too angry in those years to see what his brother had done for him. Too immature to realize that leaving town wasn't the answer to his problems. Facing them and tackling them was.

Sam smiled. "You think I'm a good dad?"

"You know I do. But if you ask me in public, I'll deny everything."

The brothers laughed, then Dylan sighed and faced all the things that he had avoided for so long, all the mistakes he had made. Sam hadn't let Dylan down— he'd been trying to protect him. Whereas Dylan, caught in misguided resentment, had left Sam alone when he needed support the most. "I'm sorry I missed out on getting to know Libby and Henry earlier. Or not being here after your wife died. I was too caught up in my own crap to be good brother. I'm so, so sorry."

"I don't blame you. Hell, I wouldn't have talked to me, either." Sam shook his head. "I said a lot of things to you that night that I never should have. I was young and I was just…"

"Just what?" Dylan prompted when Sam stopped talking.

His brother watched his kids swinging for a while. "I was mad. You were leaving, Dylan. Leaving me, leaving me with them. And I was mad that you were getting out of here and I was…staying behind."

Dylan had never looked at it that way. For so many years, his own hurt feelings had gotten in the way of him seeing things from Sam's point of view. When Dylan was away, Sam had handled their parents, dealt with them almost daily. Helped them move to their retirement home in Arizona. "I had no idea. I didn't leave town because I was mad at you. I left because I didn't see another way out."

Sam considered those words, then waved a hand in dismissal. There was the Sam that Dylan had known as a kid, quick to forgive and forget. "It's been more than ten years. I think that's long enough, don't you?"

"Yeah," Dylan said. "More than long enough."

Sam's face broke into a wide grin. He clapped Dylan on the shoulder, then drew him into another hug. And just like that, the brothers erased years of distance. The renewed connection to Sam settled over Dylan like a warm summer day. It was nice. Really nice.

"Come on, Dylan." Sam thumbed toward the swing set. "I'd like to introduce you to my family."

As they crossed to the playground, Dylan saw Katie's face light up. She smiled at Sam first, one of those private smiles of someone in love. His brother had the same goofy grin on his face. A little surge of envy ran through Dylan. What would it be like to come home to a woman who smiled at him like that every day? Who made his world light up?

Like Abby had, in the few days they'd been together. He pushed that thought away, to deal with when he wasn't feeling all dorky and sentimental.

"Dylan, this is my fiancée, Katie," Sam said. "She's related to the Barlows, but it's a long story. I'll tell you sometime over a beer." Sam said that as if Dylan was putting down roots. Planning on being here for the next family barbecue or birthday party. The Barlows had— well, every one of them had settled into town. They'd been here for generations, the kind of people who put down roots. Like Sam had.

Dylan had no doubt that he could return to Stone Gap in ten years and still find the Barlows here, and see Sam and Katie, happier than ever. And where would Dylan be?

He had no idea. He could be in Maine, he could be in Florida, he could be in Timbuktu. For the first time that he could remember, that thought didn't fill him with anticipation.

"Nice to meet you, Katie," Dylan said. "You must be a patient woman to put up with my brother."

Katie smiled up at Sam. "Oh, he's not so bad."

"Yeah, he's not," Dylan said. "I'm happy for you both."

Sam called over his kids and introduced them. Libby and Henry were both cute, amiable kids. "You guys must know Jake Cooper," Dylan said. "His mom said you two come to the community center sometimes."

Libby nodded. "We go on Tuesdays, when Mom Katie works late. She helps my daddy with his company."

Sam chuckled. "I don't think being a corporate Realtor means I have a company of my own, but yeah, Katie helps me with the accounting." He wrapped an arm around his soon-to-be-wife. She beamed up at him and put a hand on his chest. "She's brilliant with numbers."

For a second, Dylan wanted to tell Sam about Abby, to add that his girlfriend was brilliant at marketing, that she had helped put the Stone Gap Inn on the map. But calling her his girlfriend implied something more permanent. Something that meant staying in town.

As he said goodbye to his brother's family, promising to stop by for dinner the next night, he had to wonder if maybe taking the road out of town had taken him in the wrong direction. Away from the very thing that Sam had and Dylan hadn't thought he wanted until he saw how precious it was.

Abby spent another hour scouring Stone Gap and calling Cody's cell phone. No response and no sign of her son. She called his school, texted his friends, but no one had seen or heard from him. She swung back by the community center, relieved to see Dylan's car back in the parking lot. Finally.

He was just getting out of his truck as she pulled in. He gave her a wave, then opened the back of his Jeep to pull out the section of countertop he'd ordered a few days ago. "Hey, Abby."

"Don't you 'hey' me," she said. Her temper was full-on now, powered by an almost frantic worry about where Cody could be. "What did you say to my son?"

Dylan gave her a confused look. "Say to your son? Which one? Jake? Cody?"

"Cody. He ran away and told Jake it was because of what *you* said." She came closer, pointing at his chest. "What did you say to him? Did you tell him how great it was to run away? How it would be some kind of cool adventure or something?"

Dylan shook his head. "I never told him to run away, Abby. That's the last thing I'd say to any kid."

She let out a gust. "Did you tell him to go look for his father?"

"No. We never really talked about his father." Dylan thought a minute. "Wait, yeah, we did one time, but only briefly."

"And what *exactly* did you say to him?"

"He asked me if I'd ever confronted my dad about how he treated me when I was a kid. I told him that I had and that it hadn't gone well. Cody asked if there was hope for his dad, and I said he wouldn't know until he asked him. I'm sorry, Abby. I never thought he'd take off and go do that."

Cody, still aching for the father he'd never really had. The man who had provided him with DNA and not much else. Her heart broke for her son, who was looking for answers he might never get. "So you told him to go see his father and confront him?"

"No. I didn't. And Cody didn't mention that he wanted to." Dylan put the countertop down, then took Abby's hands in his. "You have to believe me, Abby. I would never tell him to leave."

She wanted to lean into his touch, into the comfort of someone who knew Cody, someone who wanted to support her, but Dylan was the whole reason she was here. Maybe his intentions had been good, but the results were disastrous. She pulled her hands out of his. "Whatever you said, it made my son sneak out of the house before I woke up and get on his bike. His father lives in *Georgia*, Dylan. Is he planning on riding all the way there? Or God forbid, hitchhike? He has maybe ten bucks to his name. What do you think is going to happen to him out there?" Her voice had risen into that shrill panic again. Her heart thudded in her chest, the worry quadrupling as she realized how much she'd counted on Dylan having the answers she needed.

Another dead end. Her son was out there, some-where, and she couldn't find him. Oh, God.

She had already called the police, but they were non-chalant about a sixteen-year-old who had a history of not showing up at school. She was going to call again, and maybe they'd take her seriously this time.

"Calm down, Abby. I'm sure if we think about it to-gether, we can figure out where he is or what route he might have taken."

Calm down? Didn't he realize what she was going through? The catastrophe his "words of advice" had cre-ated in her life? If something happened to Cody while he was out on the road…

"I'm not doing anything together with you, Dylan. All you did is show up in this town, screw up my life and now you're going to leave again, like a storm that blew through. Do me a favor and stay away from me and my boys." She got back in her car and left the park-ing lot, then headed for the streets again.

Alone. Because that was the best choice for her, all around.

Dylan watched Abby go, and for the second time in his life, felt like he had failed at everything. Had an in-nocuous conversation really driven Cody to try to make his way to Georgia? On a ten-speed and with ten bucks?

He replayed the words he'd exchanged with Cody in

his head again and again. There'd been nothing in their few words at the end of the fishing trip that said, *run away and settle this*, Dylan was sure of it.

Cody was a smart kid. He would know he couldn't travel through two states on a bike. And even if he was trying, chances were good he was still close by. But where?

And if Abby hadn't been able to find him, what made Dylan think he'd have better luck?

He grabbed the countertop and headed into the center. Jake was sitting at a table, working on some kind of craft with glue and construction paper while Uncle Ty was fixing a loose door handle. When he saw Dylan, Ty stopped what he was doing and gestured toward the kitchen.

Dylan laid the replacement countertop into the open slot, then turned to face his uncle. He kept his voice low, aware Jake was just a room away. "What happened? I just saw Abby in the parking lot and she said Cody ran away?"

"I don't know much more than you." Worry etched the lines in Ty's face. The kids at the center were Ty's family, and whenever one of them got in trouble, got sick or hurt, it hit his uncle as hard as it did the parents. "She came here about an hour ago, looking for you. You'd forgotten your cell—"

Dylan patted his pocket and cursed. Of all times to not have his phone on him.

"So she left Jake here and went out searching." Ty shook his head. "I told her you'd never say anything like that to Cody."

"And I didn't. Not exactly." Dylan recounted what he had told Abby in the parking lot. "I didn't mean anything other than calling his dad up and having a conversation, if he thought it would help. Not take off and go there on his own. Even if he tried that, I don't think Cody could have gotten very far."

"Unless he ditched the bike and started hitchhiking. Like you did."

The thought made Dylan shiver. Would Cody do that? Would he, like Dylan once had, think that thumbing his way from here to Georgia was a cool idea?

Two years before Dylan left Stone Gap for good, he'd had a blowout fight with his father over his grades and lack of ambition and whatever else his father was mad at him for that day. Dylan had taken off on his bike, riding hard until the sun went down and the road ahead seemed endless. He'd hit a rock, blown a tire and been forced to leave the bike on the side of the road, then stick out a thumb.

In the movies, hitchhiking always looked so cool. Some guy with an interesting story to tell picked up the lonely wanderer and they embarked on an adventure, building a lifelong friendship as the miles passed. But the first car that stopped was driven by a man who gave Dylan a long look that made his hair stand on end. He'd refused the ride and walked away, feeling the dark crowding in on him.

A second set of headlights came up behind him a few seconds later and Dylan had started to break into a run, sure the creepy guy was coming to get him. Grab him and drag him away, in one of those hitchhiker scenarios that didn't end with a fun adventure.

But when he'd turned, he'd seen the headlights of a pickup truck, not a sedan. And behind the wheel, a much welcome and familiar face.

"You brought me home that night," Dylan said to his uncle. The gratitude he'd felt on that stretch of road still rung in his heart. "Somehow you found me, and you picked me up."

Before anything bad happened. The words were unspoken but had always hovered in the air. It was one of hundreds of tiny moments that had tied Dylan's loyalty to his uncle. Ty was a good man, a good role model and one of the best things in Stone Gap. When Dylan had left town, he'd missed his uncle every single day.

"It was easy to find you, Dylan. I knew you and figured you'd head for that campground on Stone Gap Lake. We did that group camping trip there every summer. You always loved that campground and said it was your favorite place in the world." Ty shrugged, like it was no big deal, but for Dylan, who had grown up with a father who'd never understood him, Ty's perceptiveness mattered. A lot.

"I'm glad you remembered that, Uncle Ty. I don't know what I would have done if you hadn't come along."

"Well, I'm glad I did. Though I'm not so sure you liked the lecture I gave you on the way home about making smart choices. About staying around instead of running from your problems."

"I guess I didn't really listen, since I was on the road again two years later." He had hurt his uncle, hurt his brother, and now, he realized also hurt himself by severing these relationships that meant so much to him.

Ty smiled. "You always were a stubborn learner, Dylan, but you came around. And hopefully you've stopped running."

Dylan didn't know how to answer that. Was going back to his job in Maine running away? Or was it just doing the sensible thing? "I honestly don't know, Uncle Ty."

"Did I ever tell you how I ran away from home when I was about that age?" When Dylan shook his head, Ty continued, "Probably because I didn't want you to think it was a cool idea. But I'd had a fight with my parents, probably over the same things kids fight with their parents about now, and I decided I was better off on my own. I made it two miles out of town and spent the night camping in the woods. By the time I got back home, my mother was a mess and my father was talking to the police in the driveway. I've always regretted hurting them like that. When I saw the worry on their faces, I knew running away was the wrong choice. So when you did the same thing, I found you by thinking like I had when I ran away. That's how you can help Abby find Cody. Which direction do you think he would go? And where do you think he would stop when it got scary and lonely?"

Dylan didn't know Cody that well. He'd only met the kid a little over a week ago. But from the start, he'd felt like they were kindred spirits. Loners with troubled relationships with their fathers.

It wasn't much to go on. But it was a start.

Chapter Eleven

Abby sat in her house and cried. She'd been all over Stone Gap, up and down every single street, then driving the outskirts, even hitting the highway for several miles in each direction, trying to find any sign of her son. She'd called all his friends, then the friends' mothers, searched the penny candy store and the arcade and the bowling alley—

No Cody.

She picked up her phone and made the last call she wanted to make. When her ex-husband picked up, Abby braced herself. "Keith, I just wanted to let you know Cody might be on his way up to see you."

He sighed. "Did you kick him out or something?"

The implication that it was her fault. "No. He's just upset with you and I think he wants to talk to you in person. He didn't think it through and just took off on his bike."

He cursed. "Can't you keep an eye on those kids? I don't have time to deal with this."

"Those kids are your *sons*, Keith." How many times had she said those words and it hadn't changed anything?

When they first met, she'd been fresh out of high school and seen city-born and much older Keith as charming, exciting. A man who traveled the world, lived for experiences and spontaneity. It wasn't until she was married and pregnant that she'd realized all of those things rotated around the very small axis of Keith. When he'd come back into her life, begging for a second chance, she'd convinced herself that he had changed, that the fairy tale she had dreamed of was finally coming to life. In the end, Keith had gone right back to focusing on the only thing that mattered—himself.

"I'm the one who is here with them full-time, feeding them, raising them, so yes, I do keep an eye on them."

"Here we go again." He sighed. "The bad-dad lecture."

"I don't have to give you a lecture. You *know* you're a terrible father. You haven't been there for either one of them for longer than five minutes." Keith had had brief moments of clarity when he'd come back into her life, vowing to be different, to try again to create a family with her. To stop wasting money on gambling and alcohol and idiocy. She'd thought the change was real, something to depend upon. But in the end, he'd gone right back to his old behavior, leaving her with two kids and a nearly empty bank account.

"I have to work, Abby. It's not like I just sit around all day. I'm busy."

"Too busy for your children?" She drew in a breath and bit her tongue before she said anything more and re-tread an argument she'd had five thousand times. None of that brought her son home. "Will you please just let me know if you hear from or see Cody?"

"I don't think I'll see him. I've got meetings and sales calls and—"

"Just text me or call me. Please." She hung up, even more frustrated than she'd been before she had dialed. Keith was never going to step into fatherhood and be a good role model. The kind who read bedtime stories and took his sons fishing and showed them how to fix whatever was broken.

Only one man had done that. Dylan.

But he'd also given her son advice that had put her sixteen-year-old out on the road alone. Cody had been gone for five hours now, and she was no closer to finding him than she had been this morning.

Abby sank into a chair and started to sob again. She'd failed as a parent. Failed to keep her child safe. Failed to be there when he needed her. And now, she may have lost Cody altogether.

When Dylan left Uncle Ty at the shelter with Jake, the two of them were working together to install the new countertop. The activity kept Jake distracted, kept him from asking every few minutes where his mother was and when his brother was coming back. On the other hand, the little boy peppered Uncle Ty with so many questions about the installation process—and everything else under the sun, including Ty's favorite kind of dinosaur and whether he thought Jake should have a puppy—that the older man had no time to dwell on his grief. Dylan could see Ty's enthusiasm for working with kids returning the more he interacted with Jake.

Which meant Ty no longer really needed Dylan. He'd finished all the repairs on the center except for the roof and an engine tune-up for Ty's aged pickup. If he had enough time before he left, he wanted to give the pontoon boat a spruce-up. And there was also the broken window at Abby's—

If he wanted to, Dylan could easily find enough things to keep him busy in Stone Gap for a month. The problem—he didn't have a month. He had two days. And right now, the entire To Do list was on hold until he found Cody.

He thought of what Uncle Ty had said, about trying to see Cody's perspective and using that to figure out where he might have gone. For a while, Dylan drove aimlessly, while his mind turned over every conversation he'd had with the boy.

Then, as he made his second loop of Stone Gap, his mind latched on to an idea. It was a long shot, but maybe...

Dylan turned right, and as the Jeep left the main areas of Stone Gap, he began to accelerate. The long shot became more of a possibility the farther he drove. He turned off the main road, down a path he had taken just a couple days ago. His battered Jeep bumped and lurched over the dirt road, squeaky axles protesting the rough treatment.

There was a flash of silver ahead of him. The frame of a bike, left in the grass of a ditch. Dylan's chest squeezed. For a second, that was his bike and he was back on the road and trying to get away from the scary man in the sedan.

What if the same thing had happened to Cody? What if Dylan was too late?

The pocked road forced him to slow the Jeep. It had rained the night before, and the path that had been smooth just twenty-four hours earlier was now filled with muddy divots that were hardening in the North Carolina sun. He braced himself on the roof while he urged the Jeep farther down the path.

Finally, Dylan rounded a corner and stopped. Stone Gap Lake lay before him, blue and sparkling and inviting. On any other day, the sight would have made Dylan feel peaceful.

But when he noticed the empty dock, the space where Uncle Ty's pontoon boat usually sat, any sense of peace evaporated. Undoubtedly the key tucked in the box under the steering wheel was used to start it, by a kid who had paid attention on a fishing trip.

Dylan debated calling Abby. But he wasn't sure that was Cody's bike, and the pontoon could have been borrowed by one of Ty's friends. Still, Dylan's instincts told him otherwise. He'd check it out, then call her if he found something.

Better to be sure than disappoint her again. He'd seen

the look in her eyes, the hurt, the betrayal. Why did it seem that no matter how hard he tried, he still ended up hurting the people he cared about?

Dylan jogged down the shore, until he reached the spit of land that held Ray Prescott's cabin. At the top of the hill, he saw Jack Barlow, installing a new back deck on Ray's house. His old friend from high school still had the haircut and lean body of his military days. "Hey, Jack!"

The youngest Barlow son turned and gave Dylan a wave. Jack put down his hammer and the board in his hands, then ambled down the embankment. "Dylan! Nice to see you. My mom told me you were back in town."

He wasn't surprised Della had mentioned his return to her sons, probably thinking they would all get together. Now was not the time to catch up, though. "Yeah, I've been here for almost two weeks. Listen, can I borrow Ray's boat?"

Jack shrugged. "Sure. I don't think he'd mind. Is Ty's broken down?"

"No." Dylan sighed. "I think Abby Cooper's son Cody is out on the water in it. Abby's been looking all over for him, and she's frantic."

"Come to think of it, I did hear a boat go by maybe a couple hours ago. I was busy and didn't look to see whose boat it was. But it went to the eastern side of the lake."

"Thanks, Jack." Dylan turned to go back down the hill. Eastern side? Maybe Cody had taken the boat out fishing. Or maybe it wasn't Cody at all and Dylan was chasing his own tail.

"Hey, Dylan?"

He turned back. "Yeah?"

"It's good to have you back in town. Maybe after you get this Cody thing straightened out, you could come to dinner at my house. Meri would love to see you, too."

Meri, clearly now Jack's wife, given the gold ring on Jack's left hand. "Sure. That'd be great." He didn't want to tell Jack that his time in Stone Gap was limited and the chances of dinner with them were slim. He thanked him again, then jogged down to the pier and untied Ray's flat-bottom fishing boat from the cleats.

There was water in the boat, from the rainstorm. Dylan scooped it out with furious moves, then turned to start the motor. The engine took a couple good pulls before it finally roared to life.

Dylan steered the boat through the lake, scanning the wide expanse of water. He headed east, passing Uncle Ty's favorite fishing spot on the way. No pontoon. No Cody.

Dylan pushed the little outboard to go faster. He skirted the outside of the lake, then slowed to skim past the thick pocket of lilies that carpeted the water between the tiny island in the center of Stone Gap Lake and the water's edge. Just as he rounded the island, he saw the pontoon.

And Cody, sitting on the seats at the bow, his head on his knees. Relief flooded Dylan. He took out his cell phone to call Abby, but out here on the lake, he didn't have a signal.

Dylan pulled up alongside the pontoon, tied the fishing boat to the railing, then climbed aboard. "Cody! Hey, dude, we've been looking all over for you."

The teenager scowled. "I didn't want to be found. I wanted to get out of here for a while."

He could have been parroting back Dylan's exact words when he was that age. He could see the anger and distance in the set of Cody's jaw, the hardness of his shoulders.

Was anything Dylan could say going to make it better? Or would he only send Cody in the wrong direction again?

He thought of that long drive home with Uncle Ty all those years ago, the words his uncle had said. Words Dylan hadn't been ready to hear then, but maybe Cody would respond differently.

Dylan lowered himself to the bench seat beside Cody. "Your mom said you were thinking of going to your dad's house in Georgia."

"Yeah, well, he doesn't want to see me. I called him and he said he was busy and maybe he could get me a plane ticket sometime instead." Cody cursed. "I should have known he wasn't going to change."

Dylan's heart broke for Cody. He knew that disappointment. He wished he could wave a magic wand and make everything better, but life wasn't a movie that ended with happy tears and rolling credits.

"Some people never change," Dylan said. "But if you ask me, your dad is the one losing out, not you. You're a great kid, Cody. You're smart and strong and so good to Jake." Much like Sam had been with Dylan.

Cody lifted his head. "You think I'm a great kid?"

"Yeah, I do. I've really enjoyed getting to know you and spending time with you while I've been here."

Cody picked at the railing, his gaze averted. "My mom says you're leaving."

"I have a job in Maine. So yes, I am leaving." But the thought made Dylan's chest ache. He looked out over the glass-smooth water, sparkling in the bright sun. It was a perfect day to be out here, absorbing some peace and quiet. He was going to miss this lake. Miss—

This kid. His brother. And most of all, their mom.

"So you're gonna be just like my dad and bail." Cody cursed and got to his feet. "Why don't you just leave already? We don't need you."

The sharp words slivered through Dylan. He could see the wall going up in Cody again, the boy adding the bricks as fast as he could, to head off another hurt. "I'm not bailing, Cody. I have a job and—"

"There are jobs here, fixing up houses and running the center and things like that. You told me so yourself. That if I graduated and learned more of this stuff, I could work with a construction crew like you do."

"Yes, I could work here. But…" Dylan searched for an explanation, one that Cody would understand. And came up empty. "Maine is where my job is. I'm sorry."

"Just go, Dylan." Cody's face darkened and he waved Dylan off. "You don't have to stay here and babysit me. I'm fine."

"Then why were you sitting on the bow? Not fishing or moving?"

"Engine died." He shrugged. "But I'll just wait a

bit and start it again. I mean, I don't know much about engines, but I figured maybe it was just overheated or something."

There was no way Dylan was going to leave this kid on the water in a boat that wasn't working. Though honestly, he wasn't about to leave him until he was safe and back home with his mother.

"Let me look at the motor." Dylan waved to Cody. "Come on, you can help me."

They went to the back of the boat. Dylan tried starting the outboard himself, but it wouldn't catch, so he tipped it forward and removed the cover. "We can check the spark plug and the fuel lines. See if the plug is bad or if one of the fuel lines is leaking." He pointed out the parts to Cody as he went through the engine. "All of this seems to be okay."

"Then are we stuck out here?"

"Nope. Couple more things we can check." Dylan lowered the engine back into place, then pointed at a hatch. "Open that up and we'll check the fuel vent."

Cody lifted the hatch, looked at the tank below him, then up at Dylan with confusion. "Uh, where's the fuel vent?"

"See that circular thing right there, attached to the fuel line? When that gets blocked, the engine can't draw any fuel and it won't start."

Cody looked inside, peered at the vent. "It looks like there's some mud in there."

"Mud daubers—they're kind of like wasps—like to build nests in there." Dylan took out his penknife and handed it to Cody. "Be careful, but go ahead and clean that out."

"Me?"

"You can do it, Code." Dylan sat back and watched while the teenager cleaned the vent, then closed the hatch. "Okay, try to start it."

Cody turned the key. The outboard sputtered for a minute, then roared to life. Pride lit Cody's face. "I did it."

"Yup." Another victory in the life of a kid who'd had way too much disappointment, especially today. Dylan couldn't repair all that, but he could fix this moment. "Now, let's head for home."

Cody shook his head. "I can't do that. My mom's gonna kill me."

"She'll be mad, yes. But she'll also be so glad to see you that she's probably going to hug you for a year." Now whether Abby would forgive Dylan that quickly was a whole other story. He wasn't going to put a wager on that, not after their argument this morning.

Cody fiddled with the steering wheel. "She's not such a bad mom, is she?"

"She's one of the best." The kind of mom every kid deserved to have. A woman unlike any other that Dylan had ever met.

Cody let out a long breath. "Is my dad ever going to change?"

The question hung in the warm October air, heavy and thick. Dylan heard his own voice in Cody's and would have done anything in that moment to fix everything for the boy. "I don't know the answer to that,

Cody. My dad is still the same as he was when I was a kid. I don't know if people really change all that much."

"But you did, didn't you? My friend Matt said his mom used to know you. She said you, like, dropped out and stuff, and people thought you were going to end up in jail, cuz you got arrested a lot when you were a kid."

Yeah, that was his reputation. People didn't forget in this town, and he might as well have tattooed the information on his forehead.

Except there were some people—Sam, Abby, her sons, Uncle Ty—who didn't see Dylan's past when they looked at him. They just saw him, as he was. *You're a good man*, Abby had said.

Words that Dylan still wasn't sure he believed. He wondered if Abby still believed them, or if he'd let her down too much, too.

"Once. I got arrested once," Dylan said to Cody. "I was young and stupid and didn't listen to anyone. My brother bailed me out and the charges were dropped, but it could have ended much, much worse, Cody. And yes, I did drop out, and floated around for years before I finally figured out what I wanted. If I could go back and do it all over again, I'd do a lot of things differently."

Cody waved that off. "All adults say that."

"Because it's true." Dylan glanced out over the water. "You know, you've got a great mom, a great life here. And a great future, if you just accept it instead of running from it. I ran from my life for too long, and I don't want to do that anymore. There's something nice about knowing where you're going to be tomorrow and the day after that."

Cody thought about that for a second. "And where are you going to be, Dylan?"

Dylan didn't answer. He just took the wheel and steered the pontoon boat back to the dock.

Abby grabbed her car keys and headed out the door. She needed to make another sweep of Stone Gap, and if she still didn't find Cody, she was going to call the police. Keith had texted to say he heard from Cody and told him not to come to Georgia. That they'd see each other another time.

At least that took a two-state hitchhiking journey off the table. But it didn't tell her where her son was.

She pulled out her phone to call Ty and ask him to keep Jake a little longer when a Jeep pulled in her driveway. Dylan's car. With Cody in the passenger seat. Thank God.

Abby barreled down the stairs and flung open the car door. All the worry and anger disappeared the second she saw her son's face.

"Mom, I'm sorry—"

"Thank God you're okay." She grabbed Cody in a bear hug, the tightest hug she'd given him since the day he was six and fell off the monkey bars and banged his head on the ground. She'd picked her son up that day and held him tight and long, thinking she would have died if she'd lost him. And now, ten years later, she felt exactly the same way. "I love you, Cody. I'm so glad you're home."

Cody hugged his mother, just as he had when he was six. For the first time in a long time, Abby felt like she had her son truly and totally back. Gratitude overflowed in her heart and spilled out in her tears.

"Don't you ever do that again, Cody. You worried me so much." Her words were muffled by his shoulder.

"I won't, Mom. I'm sorry. I wasn't thinking."

"You're home now. That's all that matters." She hugged him tighter still. Over Cody's head, she saw Dylan. She mouthed *thank you*. Dylan nodded in return, his face unreadable.

After a while, Cody drew back. "Hey, where's Jake?"

"Over at the community center with Ty." Abby brushed Cody's hair off his forehead. He looked embarrassed but didn't stop her. "We can go over there. I know he'll be glad to see you."

"Why don't we all go over there?" Dylan said. "Hop in, Abby. I'll give you a ride."

She climbed in the back of the Jeep and the three of them made the short drive to the community center.

Abby could hardly take her eyes off her son. He'd only been gone a few hours, but it had felt like a lifetime. Later, they would talk, maybe one of those late-night conversations she used to have with Cody before Keith left and Jake came along. She'd make him some hot cocoa and they'd sit at the kitchen table and get back to where they used to be before the schedules and the organization and the turmoil over grades and curfews.

If there was one thing she'd learned in the last couple of weeks, it was that ditching the schedule sometimes didn't necessarily result in catastrophe. It was in those moments when she'd had unscripted fun with her boys—fishing, barbecuing, tearing down a wall—when she had seen the connection knit more tightly between the three of them. In the future, she vowed, there'd be far more of that and far less of the rigid lines that had filled her life before.

As soon as Dylan parked, Cody hopped out and headed inside. Abby lingered by the car. She'd loosened up with her kids in the last few weeks, and it had changed things in good ways, overall. Maybe it was time she loosened the cage she kept around her heart, too, and let someone in again. "Dylan, wait. I wanted to talk to you."

He turned back. "Sure."

"Thank you so much for finding Cody." Abby could tell Dylan thank-you a thousand times and it still wouldn't be enough to express the depths of her gratitude. He didn't have to help her, didn't have to come back here, knowing how she blamed him. But he had, and that meant a lot. "How did you do it? I looked everywhere, called all his friends."

"I was like him one time, and my uncle found me by thinking about where I would go. So I did the same with him. He said something to me on the fishing boat about how when he was out on the water, nothing bugged him. I thought he might have borrowed Ty's boat."

The fishing trip. Of course. Cody had been open and relaxed that day, back to the son she remembered before his father had left for the second time. "Thank God you did. I was about to call the police and demand they put out a missing person report." She shook her head, and now that the elation had passed, regret filled all the spaces inside her. "I feel like such a bad mom. How could I not see that he was hurting so badly?"

Dylan put a hand on her shoulder and met her gaze. "At that age, they're pretty good at keeping their feelings to themselves. Don't beat yourself up."

She leaned into his touch, into the confidence he had in her. For so long, Abby had felt alone, struggling to balance a thousand things at once. But this man understood her, understood what she was going through. "It's hard not to. When you're the mom, you feel responsible for everything."

"Cody thinks you're a great mom, Abby. Actually, he said, 'she's not a bad mom.'"

She laughed. "Well, there's a rousing endorsement, but I'll take it." Coming from a sixteen-year-old, that was the equivalent of a gold medal, Abby figured.

Dylan stepped forward and tucked an errant lock of her hair behind her ear. She wanted to hold on to that moment, but his hand was already gone. "I think you're not a bad woman myself."

"You're a good man, Dylan. You really are." She held his gaze and felt her body warm, responding to him as easily as a flower opening to the midday sun. She liked this man, liked him a lot.

No, not just liked. *Loved.*

She had fallen in love with Dylan Millwright somewhere between tearing down the wall and casting the first fishing line. He was considerate and tender and, most of all, welcomed the package deal that was Abby and her boys. She loved his smile, loved the way he touched her and the way he looked at her. Like maybe…

he loved her, too. But instead of asking about that, she slipped into the easier space of a joke. "Not a bad woman, huh? I'll take that as a compliment, too."

"Actually, you're pretty incredible, Abby." He cupped her jaw, and his thumb traced over her lips. She wanted him to kiss her. Wanted him to hold her. Wanted him to hold on and never let go. "I'm gonna miss you when I leave."

It took a moment. Then the reality of those words hit her, hard and cold. He was leaving. It wasn't like she hadn't known this all along, but some silly part of her had hoped he would fall in love with Stone Gap—fall in love with her—and stay. "So you really are going to Maine?"

He gave her a sad nod. "The job's starting earlier than I expected so I'm leaving Thursday afternoon."

Less than forty-eight hours. She'd thought he would be here at least until the end of the weekend. But he hadn't made her any promises, hadn't made any plans for the future. She should have known better than to fall in love with a man who had no intentions of staying put.

"That's what you do, isn't it? You leave?" She shook her head and willed the tears threatening her eyes to stay back. "Why did I think there was a chance you'd change your mind?"

"I never promised you anything, Abby. You knew all along that I had to go back to my job."

"No, you didn't promise me. But I thought—" She shook her head, cursed, then drew in a breath. "I thought you had found something here that you couldn't find in Maine or Virginia or Iowa."

Something like me. And my boys.

Dylan started to protest, but she cut him off. "I've got to get inside. My boys and I need to go home. We'll get a ride from Ty. We've had a long day, and I think we just need to order some Chinese food and chill tonight and go back to being a family of three."

She didn't invite him over. Didn't ask him to join them. They were back to being just three, and Abby told herself that was fine. She was fine. Or...

She *would* be fine. Once she forgot about Dylan.

Just when she'd started to fall for him. To see him as the kind of man she'd always wanted. Before Dylan could stop her, or twist her heart into another knot, Abby turned on her heel and went inside the center. It wasn't until the door shut behind her that she allowed her tears to fall.

Chapter Twelve

Dylan sat in his Jeep on the hill overlooking Stone Gap on Thursday afternoon. The town lay before him, sleepy and still in the warm sunshine. It was the third time he'd sat here and looked at this town. Once to say goodbye, once to say hello. And now—

The Jeep idled while Dylan debated. If he said goodbye, it would probably be for a long time. The project in Maine was two years' worth of work, and the scale of the project meant it was something that would undoubtedly eat up all his free time.

That's what you do, isn't it? You leave?

Abby's words had haunted his thoughts ever since Tuesday night. When she'd confronted him, a part of Dylan had wanted to leave right then and there, get back on the road, where no one expected anything of him—

And where he wouldn't let anybody down.

That was the crux of it, wasn't it? That he didn't want to disappoint anyone again. But who had he really disappointed?

Not Uncle Ty, who had said to him this morning that Dylan had brought him back from the edge of his despair. Ty had given him a long hug and thanked his nephew over and over again for all he had done. There'd been tears in Ty's eyes and genuine love in his voice.

Not Cody, who had come up to Dylan at the center today to show him his math test, with a very proud B in red at the top. Cody thanked Dylan for making the equations understandable. *And for turning me around when I got lost*, the teenager had added.

Then there had been Jake, who had run into the center this afternoon, calling out *Uncle Dylan* with such joy in his voice that it nearly made Dylan choke up.

And Abby—

Dylan couldn't even think about her without his chest tightening. She was the one person he had let down, and hurt. He could still see the tears in her eyes, hear the catch in her words. Damn. He sat in the Jeep for a long, long time, watching Stone Gap wind down for the day, families going home to each other, sitting down at the dinner table, passing rolls and jokes.

Then he put the Jeep in gear and started to drive.

As soon as Abby pulled into the driveway on Thursday night, the boys were out of the car, dashing inside with the pizza she had picked up on the way home and the latest superhero movie she had rented. For all her talk about wanting to enjoy more spontaneity with her boys, though, all Abby wanted to do right now was crawl into bed and cry.

Dylan had stopped in at the center this afternoon, said goodbye to both her sons and Ty, then stopped to say goodbye to her. His words were short, to the point. Nothing flowery, nothing romantic. He could have been saying goodbye to his dentist for all the emotion in his sentences.

Her heart ached, her eyes burned, but she kept putting one foot in front of the other. Kept being the responsible one, the one who stayed and built roots.

After she set the boys up with the movie, she poured a rare midweek glass of wine and went out to sit in the rocker on her front porch. How long had it been since she'd sat here and enjoyed watching Stone Gap ease into night? She used to love seeing the streetlights wink on, the parents coming home at the end of the day, the families getting in one last game of catch before bedtime.

But tonight, all that made her incredibly sad. She sipped her wine and wondered if it was worse to try to go back inside and pretend she actually cared if a group of superheroes saved the world.

Her phone rang, and her sister's name lit up the screen. Two calls in the space of a week? Melanie must be either bored or homesick. "Hey, Mel."

"What's up? You don't sound like yourself."

"Just…" What was she supposed to say? *I was let down by another charmer? I fell for Mr. Wrong again?* "Drinking some wine and trying to forget a guy."

"It's always about a guy, isn't it?" Melanie sighed. "Was he nice?"

"Yeah. And smart and good with the boys and... gone."

"Gone for good or just for now?"

"I don't know." She didn't quite want to accept yet that Dylan might never return to Stone Gap. A stubborn part of her clung to hope. Stubborn and stupid. She'd learned this lesson once before. She needed to let go of the fantasy of Dylan and accept the reality.

"If you find a guy who's smart and good with the boys and treats you well, hold on tight," Melanie said. "Trust me, those men don't come along every day."

"Good advice," Abby said. But the words stung her throat. The man had come along and left again. There was no way to hold on to him—because he didn't want to stay.

"Listen, I think I will come down and visit you. Let me take a look at my schedule and see when I can fit in a visit, okay? I really need..." Melanie paused "...some sister time."

Abby thought of yesterday, of how overjoyed Jake had been to see his brother home again. She prayed her sons never lost that connection and stayed close long after they were adults. "I do, too, Mel. I really do."

They chatted a little while longer, while Abby went down to the box, retrieved the mail, then returned to her seat. After she hung up with her sister, Abby went through the envelopes—a thick stack because she'd forgotten all about getting the mail in yesterday's madness.

Bills, flyers, catalogs, an ad for a spa opening in a

nearby town, then a letter. She opened the envelope and scanned the contents. She had to read it twice before she believed the words before her.

She got up, opened the front door to go inside and make a call when a pair of headlights swung into her driveway. She blocked her eyes from the sudden glare, then blinked. She knew those headlights. Knew that vehicle.

Knew that man.

The engine cut off, the headlights blinked into darkness. The Jeep's door opened and Dylan stepped out. He hesitated a second, reaching into the truck for something. Abby's heart leaped, but she cautioned herself not to get too excited. He could be here because he forgot something or wanted to say goodbye to the boys again. She put down her wineglass and got to her feet.

"So," Dylan said as he approached, his voice still making her heart flip, "turns out I had a little trouble leaving town."

"Car trouble?"

"Nope." Then he came into the light and she saw what he had in his hands. One of the puppies from next door. Not just any puppy, but the puppy that Jake had named Dudley. The dog had fallen asleep but stirred when Abby approached. "I sat on the hill outside of town for a good hour, trying to find the motivation to get on the road and head to Maine. But as I looked down into Stone Gap, I realized everything I ever wanted was at the bottom of that hill, not a thousand miles away from here."

"Everything you ever wanted? As in a dog?" She

didn't dare let the hope come to life again. Almost didn't dare to meet his gaze. She wanted to tell him about the letter she had received—the grant that had come through for the community center—but if he wasn't staying, it wouldn't matter to him.

"I've been an idiot, Abby," Dylan said. He put the dog on the chair on the porch, then took her hands in his and held tight. "I've spent my whole life running from this town because I thought I hated it. What I really hated was the person I used to be when I lived here. I was running away from him. From the mistakes I made, the reputation I had. But I couldn't put enough miles in between all that. Not until I came back here and faced my past. And met you and your boys."

She held her breath, not sure where the conversation was going to go next. Only knowing she wanted him to keep talking. Even the yellow Lab was watching, tail beating a soft tune against the cushions. The hope in her chest began to bloom again.

"You changed my life, Abby. From the minute we met, you looked at me and you saw just me. And you made me crave the very things I never thought I wanted. A family. A dog. And most of all, a woman who looks at me the way you look at me."

Her breath caught in her throat. "And how do I look at you?"

"Like you love me."

She dipped her gaze. What if he didn't love her in return? What if she was still being the foolish one? Because she did love him and couldn't bear it if he didn't feel the same.

The puppy scrambled down from the chair and pawed at Dylan's leg. He picked the dog up with one arm, then turned back to Abby. Dylan tipped her chin until she was looking at him. "And I look back at you like I love you, too."

"You do?"

He smiled. "I do. I love the way you laugh and the way you smile. I love how you love your sons. I love how good you are at fishing and how easy you are to please, and most of all, I love how I feel when I'm with you."

"And how is that?"

"Like I've come home, Abby. For the first time in my life." He brushed away a tendril of her hair, and had such tenderness in his eyes, she nearly cried. "So I decided it's about time I put down some roots and stayed here in Stone Gap. With you. And Dudley, if you'll have us."

She wrapped her arms around him and the puppy, and laid her head on his shoulder. Everything she had dreamed of was all coming together in this one instant. She thought of her sister's words, about finding a good man and holding on tight. She intended to do that, starting right now.

"A PUPPY!!" Jake came barreling down the hallway, slamming into Abby's legs. "I knew it!"

Or maybe she'd do that in a minute, when they were alone again.

Dylan bent down and handed the little dog over to Jake, making sure he had a solid grip on the squirming bundle of fur. "Dudley needs a home," he said. "Think you can give him a good one?"

Jake nodded. And nodded again. And nodded until Abby thought her son's head might bounce off. "I can. I promise."

"You know, Jake… I think you're going to need some help with this puppy," Dylan added. "Walking him, training him. I should tell you, I am a pretty good puppy trainer."

"You are?" Jake's eyes widened. "Can you help me?"

"I'm planning on it, kid." Dylan ruffled Jake's hair.

Cody stood in the hallway, watching it all, his face hopeful and scared and vulnerable. His chin jutted up and he eyed Dylan with a flicker of mistrust. "You mean it?"

Dylan rose. He took Abby's hand and drew her to his side. "I do."

Cody studied him for a long time, then gave Dylan a nod and a flash of a smile. An understanding passed between them, and the guardedness that Cody wore like an extra shirt began to melt. Cody put a hand on Jake's shoulder. "Hey, squirt, what's this mutt's name again?"

"Dudley. And he's not a mutt."

Cody laughed. "I know. Come on. Let's take him outside and let Mom talk to Dylan."

The boys headed outside, a burst of conversation flowing between them about the dog and a dog house and who was going to walk him first. When the back door opened, a breeze whispered through the house. Abby could swear it carried the scent of happiness.

"Now where were we?" Abby asked.

"I was right..." He pulled her against his chest. "Here. Exactly where I should be." He kissed her then, long and slow and sweet, while the night birds began their evening calls and the families around them wound down for the day. Her grandfather used to call it the magic hour, and as Abby curved against Dylan, she thought that was a perfect description. An absolutely perfect description.

Epilogue

The grant for the community center had given them enough money to expand, adding a game room, a second bathroom and a bank of computers for the kids to use for homework. The center buzzed with life every day, just as it should. Ty was a new man, dividing his time between working there and working on his fishing skills.

Dylan stood in the middle of the center and saw happy, busy kids. He'd started his construction business last month and already had contracts to build two new houses in nearby towns. He worked part-time at the center with his uncle, keeping his hours on the construction sites flexible enough to be here most afternoons.

"Hey, Dylan, I had an idea."

Dylan turned to Cody. The kid had filled out in the last couple months. His grades were up, his eyes brighter, his face happier. He worked with Dylan on the weekends and really seemed to have a knack for building. "Sure. What is it?"

"How about I lead the teen group today? I was thinking, you know, the whole peer-to-peer thing might work well."

Dylan nodded. "I think that's a great idea. Go right ahead."

Cody grinned, then headed over to the center of the sofas. He got the attention of the other teenagers and exchanged a little small talk before turning the conversation to school and grades. "You know, I hate to say it, and probably wouldn't in front of my mom, but doing homework actually does make the rest of it easier. I'm even thinking about going to college."

The other kids scoffed. "Why go to more school?" Matt asked.

"Because it opens up doors," Cody said. "Opportunities. Choices. And I like the idea of more choices. I like having more options?"

The others nodded agreement, and the conversation shifted to jobs, then colleges. There were still several naysayers in the group, but Dylan heard many of the boys chiming in, supporting Cody.

"He's becoming quite the leader," Uncle Ty said.

"Yep. I'm proud of him." And he was. It was weird, because Dylan wasn't really Cody's dad, but every day he spent with the two boys, he fell into that role more and more. There'd been more fishing trips, a couple overnight trips to the old campground, and a trip to a dinosaur museum with Jake. Every time he saw them, the bond between them grew until it felt like Cody and Jake had always been part of his life.

"He reminds me of someone else I knew at that age." Ty clapped Dylan on the back. "Good job, Dylan. You've really turned this place around."

"I'd say that was a team effort."

Ty smiled. "We do have one heck of a great team here, don't we?"

Dylan grinned. "We do indeed." Between the boys, himself, Ty and Abby, the center had become a new place, even better than before. Aunt Virginia's picture hung on the wall, her smile seeming to say she was well pleased with how her legacy was continuing.

The door to the center opened, and Abby hurried in, with Jake by her side. Dudley brought up the rear, still all gangly puppy legs and too-big paws, but perfectly content to trot along beside Jake, who spoiled the dog rotten. Truth be told, Abby and Dylan did, too, and Cody had sneaked him bites at dinner more than once. The Lab had made a perfect addition to their family, and although Dylan came by every day to let the dog out and walk him, it wasn't the same as actually going to sleep in the same house with Abby, Jake, Cody and Dudley.

Abby stopped when she saw Dylan and smiled that smile he loved. Dylan patted his pocket and worked a smile to his own face, then strode forward to greet her. "Glad you're here."

"Sorry I'm late. That presentation ran over, but it worked out well anyway. The agency landed the contract and put me in charge of the new account." Abby beamed.

"That's great, Abby. I'm thrilled for you." He ruffled Jake's hair. "And how was school today?"

"We talked about dinosaurs! Did you know a person who studies dinosaurs is called a pale-o-tologist?" Jake said. "That's what I want to be when I grow up. Or maybe a vet...vetra-narian. Cuz I love dogs."

"Or maybe both, Jake." Dylan pointed to the craft table. "Hey, I think Mavis is waiting for you."

"Great! Thanks!" Jake bounded off. His dog bounded after him, then settled at his feet under the table.

Dylan grabbed Abby's hand before she could head into the office to do any last-minute work. "Hold on a second. I want to show you something."

She gave him a curious glance. "Okay."

He led her through the center and into the hall where the four of them had installed a new wall just a few short months ago. His heart pounded in his throat, but the rest of him felt sure and confident. In fact, he'd never been surer about anything in his life.

"There's a problem with the wall we put in," he said. "I don't know if it's going to last. It might need a stronger foundation. Why don't you take a look at it and tell me what you think?"

Abby stood back and assessed the wall. "I don't see anything wrong, Dylan." She paused, looked closer. The confusion on her face yielded to something tentative, cautious. "Wait. Did you write something on here?"

By the time Abby read the words he'd scrawled on the unpainted wall earlier today, Dylan was already on one knee, the velvet ring box propped open. She turned to him and stared, mouth agape. "Dylan…what…what are you doing?"

"The second smart thing I've done in a long time. The first was not going to Maine." He leaned toward her. "Will you marry me, Abby?"

Her smile bloomed into the biggest one he'd ever seen. She barely hesitated before the joy lit her eyes. "Yes, Dylan, yes! Of course I'll marry you."

He let out a whoop, then rose and slid the ring onto her finger. He leaned around the corner and called out to his sons. He'd sat both of them down yesterday and asked them for permission to marry their mom. If the boys hadn't been on board, Dylan would have waited. But both kids had been as overjoyed as Abby. And when Jake asked if he could call Dylan Dad, he almost broke down and cried. They were his sons, now and forever, and this was his family. Dylan was a bit overjoyed himself. "Cody, Jake, she said yes!"

The boys rushed in and gathered Abby and Dylan in a celebratory hug. The four of them stood in the hall where they'd once rebuilt something that had been torn down, and now began to build a new family together. The family Dylan had always wanted, and the home he'd searched the world for and only found when he came back to the very place he left.

* * * * *

Look for Melanie Cooper's story,
Their Last Second Chance,
the next book in New York Times
bestselling author Shirley Jump's miniseries,
The Stone Gap Inn.

Available August 2019,
wherever Harlequin books and
ebooks are sold.

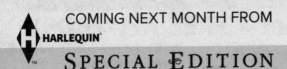

COMING NEXT MONTH FROM

HARLEQUIN®

SPECIAL EDITION

Available July 16, 2019

#2707 RUST CREEK FALLS CINDERELLA
Montana Mavericks: Six Brides for Six Brothers
by Melissa Senate
When Lily Hunt, a plain-Jane Cinderella chef, gives herself a makeover to spice up her flirtation with a sexy cowboy, she finds herself contending with his past heartbreak and his father's matchmaking scheme!

#2708 ONE NIGHT WITH THE COWBOY
Match Made in Haven • by Brenda Harlen
Soon-to-be-exes Brielle Channing and Caleb Gilmore said goodbye after a night of passion—until a surprise pregnancy changed all their plans. Could their baby be their second chance for happily-ever-after, or will their feuding families once again come between them?

#2709 THEIR INHERITED TRIPLETS
Texas Legends: The McCabes • by Cathy Gillen Thacker
To give the orphaned triplets the stability they need, guardians Lulu McCabe and Sam Kirkland decide to jointly adopt them. But when it's discovered their marriage wasn't actually annulled, they have to prove to the courts they're responsible—by renewing their vows!

#2710 HIS UNEXPECTED TWINS
Small-Town Sweethearts • by Carrie Nichols
It was supposed to be a summer romance between friends, but a surprise pregnancy forces Liam McBride and Ellie Harding to confront their feelings for each other—and their fears of the future.

#2711 THEIR LAST SECOND CHANCE
The Stone Gap Inn • by Shirley Jump
When Melanie Cooper runs into her first love, her picture-perfect life is unraveling—unbeknownst to her family. Harris McCarthy is hiding a few secrets of his own, but exposing them could save Melanie's career and torpedo their last second chance at love.

#2712 A BABY BETWEEN FRIENDS
Sweet Briar Sweethearts • by Kathy Douglass
After their friendship is ruined by a night of passion, Joni Danielson and Lex Devlin have to find a way back to being friends. Will her unexpected pregnancy lead them to love?

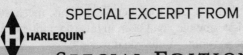
"The two of you are still married," Liz said.

"Still?" Lulu croaked.

Sam asked, "What are you talking about?"

"More to the point, how do you know this?" Lulu
demanded, the news continuing to hit her like a gut punch.

Travis looked down at the papers in front of him.
"Official state records show you eloped in the Double
Knot Wedding Chapel in Memphis, Tennessee, on
Monday, March 14, nearly ten years ago. Alongside
another couple, Peter and Theresa Thompson, in a double
wedding ceremony."

Lulu gulped. "But our union was never legal," she
pointed out, trying to stay calm, while Sam sat beside her
in stoic silence.

Liz countered, "Ah, actually, it is legal. In fact, it's still
valid to this day."

Sam reached over and took her hand in his, much as he had the first time they had been in this room together.

"How is that possible?" Lulu asked weakly.

"We never mailed in the certificate of marriage, along with the license, to the state of Tennessee," Sam said.

"And for our union to be recorded and therefore legal, we had to have done that," Lulu reiterated.

"Well, apparently, the owners of the Double Knot Wedding Chapel did, and your marriage was recorded. And is still valid to this day, near as we can tell. Unless you two got a divorce or an annulment somewhere else? Say another country?" Travis prodded.

"Why would we do that? We didn't know we were married," Sam returned.

Don't miss
Their Inherited Triplets *by Cathy Gillen Thacker,*
available August 2019 wherever
Harlequin® Special Edition books and ebooks are sold.

www.Harlequin.com

SPECIAL EXCERPT FROM

*Read on for a sneak peek at
the first funny and heart-tugging book in Jo McNally's
Rendezvous Falls series,* Slow Dancing at Sunrise!

"I'd have thought the idea of me getting caught in a rainstorm would make your day."

He gave her a quick glance. Just because she was off-limits didn't mean he was blind.

"Trust me, it did." Luke slowed the truck and reached behind the seat to grab his zippered hoodie hanging there. Whitney looked down and her cheeks flamed when she realized how her clothes were clinging to her. She snatched the hoodie from his hand before he could give it to her, and thrust her arms into it without offering any thanks. Even the zipper sounded pissed off when she yanked it closed.

"Perfect. Another guy with more testosterone than manners. Nice to know it's not just a Chicago thing. Jackasses are everywhere."

Luke frowned. He'd been having fun at her expense, figuring she'd give it right back to him as she had before. But her words hinted at a story that didn't reflect well on men in general. She'd been hurt. He shouldn't care. But that quick dimming of the fight in her eyes made him feel ashamed. *That* was a new experience.

A flash of lightning made her flinch. But the thunder didn't follow as quickly as the last time. The storm was moving off. He drove from the vineyard into the parking lot and over to the main house. The sound of the rain on the roof was less angry. But Whitney wasn't. She was clutching his sweatshirt around herself, her knuckles white. From anger? Embarrassment? Both? Luke shook his head.

"Look, I thought I was doing the right thing, driving up there." He rubbed the back of his neck and grimaced, remembering how sweaty and filthy he still was. "It's not my fault you walked out of the woods soaking wet. I mean, I try not to be a jackass, but I'm still a man. And I *did* offer my hoodie."

Whitney's chin pointed up toward the second floor of the main house. Her neck was long and graceful. There was a vein pulsing at the base of it. She blinked a few times, and for a horrifying moment, he thought there might be tears shimmering there in her eyes. *Damn it.* The last thing he needed was to have Helen's niece *crying* in his truck. He opened his mouth to say something—anything—but she beat him to it.

"I'll concede I wasn't prepared for rain." Her mouth barely moved, her words forced through clenched teeth. "But a gentleman would have looked away or…something."

His low laughter was enough to crack that brittle shell of hers. She turned to face him, eyes wide.

"See, Whitney, that's where you made your biggest mistake." He shrugged. "It wasn't going out for a day hike with a storm coming." He talked over her attempted objection. "Your *biggest* mistake was thinking I'm any kind of gentleman."

The corner of her mouth tipped up into an almost smile. "But you said you weren't a jackass."

"There's a hell of a lot of real estate between jackass and gentleman, babe."

Her half smile faltered, then returned. That familiar spark appeared in her eyes. The crack in her veneer had been repaired, and the sharp edge returned to her voice. Any other guy might have been annoyed, but Luke was oddly relieved to see Whitney back in fighting form.

"The fact that you just referred to me as 'babe' tells me you're a lot closer to jackass than you think."

He lifted his shoulder. "I never told you which end of the spectrum I fell on."

The rain had slowed to a steady drizzle. She reached for the door handle, looking over her shoulder with a smirk.

"Actually, I'm pretty sure you just did."

She hurried up the steps to the covered porch. He waited, but she didn't look back before going into the house. Her energy still filled the cab of the truck, and so did her scent. Spicy, woodsy, rain soaked. Finally coming to his senses, he threw the truck into Reverse and headed back toward the carriage house. He needed a long shower. A long *cold* one.

Don't miss
Jo McNally's Slow Dancing at Sunrise,
available July 2019 from HQN Books!

www.Harlequin.com

PHJMEXP0719

The Shadow Queen

"A strong romantic fantasy."　　　　　　　　—Alternative Worlds

"Anne Bishop does not disappoint. I have not read a book of hers that did not immediately captivate me and draw me immediately back into her world. . . . [She] weaves her spell so well. . . . Her characters seem so real and engaging."　　　　　　　　—SFRevu

"*Black Jewels* fans won't want to miss this installment, which offers a different look on the realms of the Blood."　　　—Dear Author . . .

"If you are a fan of high fantasy with some romance and a limited amount of spell casting, Bishop is a good choice for you."
　　　　　　　　　　　　　　　　　　　　　—BookSpot Central

"*The Shadow Queen* is in many respects the best book set in the world of the *Black Jewels* since the original series. . . . If you're a fan of the series, you will very likely enjoy this trip back into Bishop's world."　　　　　　—Fantasy & Sci-Fi Lovin' Book Reviews

"In this stand-alone novel set in the evocative *Black Jewels* world, Bishop tackles surviving various horrors head-on. . . . It's a difficult subject, but one that Bishop writes about sensitively, with compassion and without blinking or pulling punches." —*Romantic Times*

Tangled Webs

"Bewitching. . . . With feverish pacing and terrifying twists, Bishop's surefire spell craft will leave readers' hearts pounding."
　　　　　　　　　　　　　　—*Publishers Weekly* (starred review)

"[Has] enough plot to interest series fans and newbies alike."
　　　　　　　　　　　　　　　　　　　　　　　—*Booklist*

"An excellent action-packed tale that grips readers . . . and never slows down. . . . The story line is fast-paced and the cast seems real."　　　　　　　　　　　　　　—*Midwest Book Review*

"Bishop is one of those wonderful writers who get steadily better as they grow more experienced, and I have no problem saying this is the most enjoyable of her books to date, but I doubt it will stay that way for long."　　　　　　　　　　　—Critical Mass

continued . . .

"Fans of Bishop's *Black Jewels* series will delight in this stand-alone foray into the world of the Blood with the SaDiablo family. . . . There's plenty of sly humor and action to keep the reader well entertained."   —*Romantic Times*

"Reading *Tangled Webs* was like meeting up with an old friend. . . . The humor brought a smile to my face . . . and I will always appreciate how Bishop can make even the most superpowered characters seem like those eccentric neighbors next door."
—Dear Author . . .

"A nice visit back into the world of Blood."
—Monsters and Critics

Queen of the Darkness

"As engaging, as strongly characterized, and as fully conceived as its predecessors . . . a perfect—and very moving—conclusion."
—SF Site

"A storyteller of stunning intensity, Ms. Bishop has a knack for appealing but complex characterization realized in a richly drawn, imaginative ambience."   —*Romantic Times*

"A powerful finale for this fascinating, uniquely dark trilogy."
—*Locus*

Heir to the Shadows

"Daemon, Lucivar, and Saetan ooze more sex appeal than any three fictional characters created in a very long time."
—*The Romance Reader*

"*Heir to the Shadows* isn't as dark as its predecessor. . . . All the other elements that made the first book such a gripping read are present: vivid and sympathetic characters, a fascinating and fully realized magical system . . . lavish and sensuous descriptions, and interesting world building that turns traditional gender roles and concepts of dominance and submission on their heads. . . . It's a terrific read, and I highly recommend both it and *Daughter of the Blood*."   —SF Site

"Bishop seems to delight in turning fantasy conventions on their heads. . . . still darkly opulent, often exotic."   —*Locus*

"The fabulous talent of Anne Bishop is showcased in *Heir to the Shadows*. . . . Ms. Bishop's striking magical concepts and powerful images are wonderfully leavened with unexpected dash and humor, creating an irresistible treat for fantasy fans."

—*Romantic Times*

Daughter of the Blood

"A terrific writer. . . . The more I read, the more excited I became because of the freshness of [her] take on the usual high-fantasy setting, the assurance of [her] language, all the lovely touches of characterization that [she slips] in so effortlessly."

—Charles de Lint

"Darkly mesmerizing . . . [a] fascinating, dark world."   —*Locus*

"Vividly painted . . . dramatic, erotic, hope-filled."

—Lynn Flewelling

"Lavishly sensual . . . a richly detailed world based on a reversal of standard genre clichés."   —*Library Journal*

"Intense . . . erotic, violent, and imaginative. This one is white-hot."   —Nancy Kress

"A fabulous new talent . . . a uniquely realized fantasy filled with vibrant colors and rich textures. A wonderful new voice, Ms. Bishop holds us spellbound from the very first page."

—*Romantic Times* (4½ stars)

"Dark, intricate, and disturbing."

—Josepha Sherman, author of *Forging the Runes*

"Has immense appeal for fans of dark fantasy or horror. Most highly recommended."   —Hypatia's Hoard

"A high-voltage ride through a new realm. Bishop draws her characters with acute emotion [and] leaves the reader lusting for her next novel."   —Lois H. Gresh, coauthor of *The Termination Node*

"Dark, morbid, sinister, and yet it holds you completely fascinated and spellbound by its beauty. Once I'd begun reading . . . I couldn't bring myself to put down the book and leave the world that Anne Bishop had magically spun around me . . . rich in both positive and negative emotions and intense in its portrayal of human behavior and human desires . . . one of the most original and readable books in the fantasy genre."   —The 11th Hour

ANNE BISHOP

THE SHADOW QUEEN

*A **Black Jewels** Novel*

ROC

A ROC BOOK

ROC
Published by New American Library, a division of
Penguin Group (USA) Inc., 375 Hudson Street,
New York, New York 10014, USA
Penguin Group (Canada), 90 Eglinton Avenue East, Suite 700, Toronto,
Ontario M4P 2Y3, Canada (a division of Pearson Penguin Canada Inc.)
Penguin Books Ltd., 80 Strand, London WC2R 0RL, England
Penguin Ireland, 25 St. Stephen's Green, Dublin 2,
Ireland (a division of Penguin Books Ltd.)
Penguin Group (Australia), 250 Camberwell Road, Camberwell, Victoria 3124,
Australia (a division of Pearson Australia Group Pty. Ltd.)
Penguin Books India Pvt. Ltd., 11 Community Centre, Panchsheel Park,
New Delhi – 110 017, India
Penguin Group (NZ), 67 Apollo Drive, Rosedale, North Shore 0632,
New Zealand (a division of Pearson New Zealand Ltd.)
Penguin Books (South Africa) (Pty.) Ltd., 24 Sturdee Avenue,
Rosebank, Johannesburg 2196, South Africa

Penguin Books Ltd., Registered Offices:
80 Strand, London WC2R 0RL, England

Published by Roc, an imprint of New American Library, a division of Penguin
Group (USA) Inc. Previously published in a Roc hardcover edition.

First Roc Mass Market Printing, March 2010
10 9 8 7 6 5 4 3 2 1

PUBLISHER'S NOTE
This is a work of fiction. Names, characters, places, and incidents either are the
product of the author's imagination or are used fictitiously, and any resemblance
to actual persons, living or dead, business establishments, events, or locales is
entirely coincidental.

The publisher does not have any control over and does not assume any responsibility for author or third-party Web sites or their content.

FOR

CASS, MAGGIE, CHERYL,

AND

DEE

ACKNOWLEDGMENTS

My thanks to Blair Boone for continuing to be my first reader, to Debra Dixon for being second reader, to Doranna Durgin for maintaining the Web site, to Anne Sowards and Jennifer Jackson for being enthusiastic about this story, to Pat Feidner just because, and to all the friends and readers who make this journey with me.

JEWELS

WHITE
YELLOW
TIGER EYE
ROSE
SUMMER-SKY
PURPLE DUSK
OPAL*
GREEN
SAPPHIRE
RED
GRAY
EBON-GRAY
BLACK

*Opal is the dividing line between lighter and darker Jewels because it can be either.

When making the Offering to the Darkness, a person can descend a maximum of three ranks from his/her Birthright Jewel.

Example: Birthright White could descend to Rose.

BLOOD HIERARCHY/CASTES

MALES

landen—non-Blood of any race

Blood male—a general term for all males of the Blood; also refers to any Blood male who doesn't wear Jewels

Warlord—a Jeweled male equal in status to a witch

Prince—a Jeweled male equal in status to a Priestess or a Healer

Warlord Prince—a dangerous, extremely aggressive Jeweled male; in status, slightly lower than a Queen

FEMALES

landen—non-Blood of any race

Blood female—a general term for all females of the Blood; mostly refers to any Blood female who doesn't wear Jewels

witch—a Blood female who wears Jewels but isn't one of the other hierarchical levels; also refers to any Jeweled female

Healer—a witch who heals physical wounds and illnesses; equal in status to a Priestess and a Prince

Priestess—a witch who cares for altars, sanctuaries, and Dark Altars; witnesses handfasts and marriages; performs offerings; equal in status to a Healer and a Prince

Black Widow—a witch who heals the mind; weaves the tangled webs of dreams and visions; is trained in illusions and poisons

Queen—a witch who rules the Blood; is considered to be the land's heart and the Blood's moral center; as such, she is the focal point of their society

PLACES IN THE REALMS

Terreille

Dena Nehele
TAMANARA MOUNTAINS
GRAYHAVEN — BOTH A FAMILY ESTATE AND A TOWN

Ebon Askavi (aka the Black Mountain, the Keep)

Hayll

Zuulaman

Kaeleer (The Shadow Realm)

Askavi
EBON ASKAVI (AKA THE BLACK MOUNTAIN, THE KEEP)
EBON RIH — VALLEY THAT IS THE KEEP'S TERRITORY
RIADA — BLOOD VILLAGE IN EBON RIH

Dea al Mon

Dharo
WEAVERS FIELD — BLOOD VILLAGE
BHAK — BLOOD VILLAGE
WOOLSKIN — LANDEN VILLAGE

Dhemlan
AMDARH—CAPITAL CITY
HALAWAY—VILLAGE NEAR SADIABLO HALL
SADIABLO HALL (THE HALL)

Nharkhava
TAJRANA—CAPITAL CITY

Scelt (*shelt*)
MAGHRE (MA-GRA)—VILLAGE

Hell (The Dark Realm, The Realm of the Dead)
EBON ASKAVI (AKA THE BLACK MOUNTAIN, THE KEEP)
SADIABLO HALL

PROLOGUE

Terreille
Two years ago

Still shaken by the storm of power that had destroyed half the Blood in Dena Nehele only a few days before, the rogues came down from their camps in the Tamanara Mountains to face an unexpected enemy.

The landens, who had been brutalized for generations by the "caretakers of the Realms," hadn't wasted time. When they realized the surviving Blood were stunned by the violent loss of Queens and courts, they rebelled—and decided that dying by the thousands was an acceptable price to pay in order to wipe out the Blood in Dena Nehele.

So the landens died during those first days of the uprising. Oh, how they died.

But so did the Blood.

The males in the Blood's towns and villages died as they exhausted the power that made the Blood who and what they were, until even the ones who wore Jewels and had a reservoir of power had used up everything they had in the effort to defend the women and children who didn't have the strength or skill to defend themselves.

When that power that lived within them was gone, they fought with weapons like any other man. But the landens kept coming, kept fighting—and the Blood, outnumbered, had no chance of surviving.

Women and children died, along with the men. The landens, steeped in their hatred for the Blood, set fire to the buildings, turning entire villages into funeral pyres.

Then the rogues, trained warriors who had refused to

serve any Queen, came down from the mountains—and
the battle for Dena Nehele really began.

He rode with one pack of rogues, a leader committed
to slaughter in order to defend what was left of his people.
But as they reached a walled estate on their way to the
town that served as Dena Nehele's capital, he pulled his
horse aside and stared through the iron bars of a double
gate at the big stone mansion.

Grayhaven.

It was his family name. This was his family's home.

He had never lived in that mansion because the Queens
who had controlled Dena Nehele had claimed it for their
own residence, their own seat of power. And like the rest
of the Territory, the house and the land had declined under
the rule of bitches who had stood in the shadow of Dorothea SaDiablo, the High Priestess of Hayll.

He had grown up in the mountain camps ruled by the
rogues because he was the last of his line, the last direct
descendant of Lord Jared and Lady Lia, the Queen who,
like her grandmother before her, had been called "the
Gray Lady." And if there was any truth to the family stories, he was the last person capable of finding the key that
would reveal a treasure great enough to restore Dena
Nehele.

Lord Jared had told his grandsons about the treasure
the Gray Lady and Thera, a powerful Black Widow, had
hidden somewhere around Grayhaven. While the family
still lived in the house, every male had searched for it, and
the story had spread to trusted advisers who shouldn't have
been trusted. When the family line failed to produce even
a minor Queen, Dorothea's pet Queens had descended on
Dena Nehele like scavengers fighting over a fresh carcass.
What was left of his family abandoned Grayhaven and
spoke the family name only in secret.

Generations had tried to hold on to something that was
Dena Nehele, that was the Blood as they had been when
the Gray Lady had ruled. Generations of the Grayhaven
line had been "broken into service" as a way of keeping the
people yoked to the rule of unworthy Queens.

Generations of suffering—until that witch storm swept
through Terreille. A fast, violent storm, terrible in its cleansing, it had swept away Dorothea SaDiablo and everyone

who had been tainted by her, but it had left the surviving Blood prey to the landens' hatred.

"Theran!" one of the Warlords shouted. "The bastards have set fire to the south end of the town!"

He wanted to ride through those gates, wanted to protect the only thing left of his own heritage. But he had been trained to fight, had been born to stand on a killing field. So he turned away from the house and land he wanted to reclaim.

But as he rode away, he promised himself that when the fires of rebellion were finally smothered, he would come back to his family's home.

If there was anything left.

ONE

Reaching the broken-down stone wall and the double gate that was half-torn from its hinges, Theran Gray-haven planted his feet in the exact spot where he'd stood two years before. Now, finally, the landen uprising had been completely smothered, and the Blood—those who were left—could set about the business of trying to restore their land and their people.

If there was any way of restoring their people.

"Since you invited them here, you're going to feel like a fool if you're still standing at the gate when the other War-lord Princes arrive."

Theran looked over his shoulder. He hadn't heard the other man approach, hadn't felt a warning presence. Even a month ago, being that careless would have gotten him killed.

"You shouldn't be up before sunset," Theran said. "It drains you too much."

The old man scowled at the wall and the gate—and all the other signs of neglect. "I'll manage."

"You'll need blood tonight."

The scowl deepened. "I'll manage."

"Talon . . ."

"Don't be using that voice on me, boy. I can still whack some sense into that stubborn head of yours."

Talon was a grizzled warrior who was missing two fin-gers on his left hand and half his right foot—evidence of the price paid for the battles won. He was also a Sapphire-

Jeweled Warlord Prince. Since Theran was a Warlord Prince who wore Green Jewels, Talon was the only man in Dena Nehele who was strong enough to "whack some sense" into him.

But only after the sun set.

Talon was demon-dead. If he was forced to act during daylight hours, his strength drained at a terrifying speed.

"Did you ever wonder if it was worth it?" Theran asked, looking away from the man who had raised him.

He had never known his father. The man had mated to continue the Grayhaven bloodline and had been caught, broken, and completely destroyed before Theran had been born.

When he was seven, his mother had brought him to the mountain camps to keep the Grayhaven line safe from Dorothea's pet Queens.

He never saw her again.

Talon looked at the mansion and shook his head. "I was in this fight for three hundred years, give or take a few. I knew Lia, and I knew Grizelle before her. I stood with Jared and Blaed when we were all among the living—and I stood with others when I became demon-dead. So I never wondered if bringing Dena Nehele back to the way it was when the Gray Ladies ruled was worth the blood and pain and lives that were lost. I *knew* getting that back was worth the price."

"We didn't win, Talon," Theran said softly. "Someone else eliminated the enemy, but we still didn't win."

"A Grayhaven is standing once more on the family land. That's a start. And there is a marker on the table."

A marker Talon hadn't told him about until a few days ago. "A dangerous one, assuming the man who owes us a favor is still alive."

"There's no way to win unless we gamble," Talon said. "Come on. We'll bring the Coach onto the grounds and camp out here tonight. Tomorrow you can go through the house and see what needs to be done."

"We'll be lucky if we find anything intact," Theran said bitterly. "I can't imagine the bitches who ruled from here *not* trying to find the treasure."

"But the key wasn't in the house," Talon said. "That's part of the legend. And without the key that begins unlocking the spells, they could have ripped up every floorboard and knocked down every brick in every fireplace, and they still wouldn't have found the treasure even if they were looking right at it."

"Doesn't mean we're going to find a safe floor or a working fireplace," Theran grumbled.

"Do your pissing and moaning later," Talon said. "We've got company. I'll fetch the Coach. You give yourself a kick in the ass and get up to the house."

"Yes, sir."

Surrogate father and protector of the Grayhaven line, Talon had held him when he'd cried and hadn't hesitated to give him a smack when it was deserved—at least, deserved according to Talon. Everything good that he knew about the Blood, about honor and Protocol and what a Warlord Prince should be, he had learned from a man who remembered Dena Nehele as it had been. Who remembered what it meant to have honor. To wear, as Talon put it, the Invisible Ring.

Bracing himself for the discussion ahead, Theran strode toward the mansion.

Was the honey pear tree still in the back gardens somewhere? Could the tree have survived that many centuries? There had been a few honey pear trees growing in one of the rogue camps low in the mountains, and there was a grove of them—or so he'd heard—tucked away in the southern part of Dena Nehele, in one of the Shalador reserves. Having heard stories about Jared's mother growing the honey pear trees for her sons and how Jared had gifted Lia with his tree and given another to Thera and Blaed, he'd been disappointed when he'd finally gotten to taste one of the hard little fruits. But Talon said the trees didn't grow well in the mountains, that something they needed was lacking, and that was the reason the fruit didn't taste right.

Well, the trees weren't the only things that had felt a need that had gone unanswered.

Talon set the Coach down on the scrubby front lawn, while Theran watched the Warlord Princes appear near the gate as they dropped from the Winds, those webs of psychic roadways that allowed the Blood to travel through the Darkness.

It wasn't until Talon limped over to join him that the first Warlord Princes came through the gate, walking up the weedy drive in pairs, the lightest-Jeweled males coming first.

★I count about a hundred,★ Talon said on a psychic thread.

★That's probably every Warlord Prince left in Dena Nehele,★ Theran replied.

★Probably. And a better response than I'd hoped for.★

What wasn't said was that only a handful of those men wore an Opal that was considered a dark Jewel. He and Talon, wearing Green and Sapphire, were the strongest males in the Territory. Everyone else wore lighter Jewels.

They formed a semicircle around him and Talon, the lighter Jewels leaving spaces so the darker-Jeweled males could stand in the front.

Except for one Opal-Jeweled Warlord Prince who stood apart from the others—a Prince whose golden brown skin marked him as having a Shalador bloodline. Maybe even being pure Shalador.

Lord Jared's coloring. Lord Jared's race.

Theran resisted the urge to look at his own hand and see the similarities.

"Would you care to join us, Prince Ranon?" Talon said.

"I can hear from where I'm standing," was the chilly reply.

Talon nodded as if the less-than-courteous response made no difference.

Prince Archerr, another who wore Opal Jewels, stepped forward. "You called us here, and we answered. But none of us can afford to be gone long. The landens have to be held on a tight leash, and some of us are the only trained warrior left in our piece of Dena Nehele."

Theran nodded. "Then I'll come to the point. We need a Queen."

A moment of disbelieving silence before several men made derisive sounds.

"Tell us something we don't know," Spere said.

"We've got Queens, more or less," Archerr said.

"Would you serve any of them?" Theran asked.

"When the sun shines in Hell."

Mutters with an undercurrent of anger.

"We have Queens," Theran said. "Women who, even in their prime, weren't considered strong enough to be a concern to the Queens who whored for Dorothea SaDiablo. And we have Queens who are still little girls, barely old enough to begin training in basic Craft. And we have a handful who are adolescents."

"One being a fifteen-year-old who's turning into such a ripe bitch she may not live long enough to be sixteen," Archerr said bitterly.

"We need a Queen who knows how to be a Queen," Theran said. "We need a Queen who could rule Dena Nehele in the same tradition as the Gray Lady."

"You won't find one of those within our own borders," Spere said. "Don't you think we've all been looking? And if you look beyond our borders to find a Queen mature enough to rule, the males in that Territory aren't going to give up anyone *good*. And since I live in a village along the western border, I can tell you the Territories west of us aren't doing any better."

"I know," Theran replied.

"Then where are we supposed to find a Queen?" Archerr asked.

"In Kaeleer."

Silence. Not even embarrassed coughs or shuffling feet.

"There's no way into Kaeleer except through the service fairs," Shaddo said. "At least, no other way to get into the Shadow Realm and stay alive long enough to state your business."

"Yes, there is," Theran said, grateful that he and Talon had considered this possibility. "Someone goes to the Black Mountain."

Ninety-eight men stared at him.

"And does what?" Archerr asked quietly.

Theran glanced at Talon, who nodded. "There's a Warlord Prince who owes my family a favor." That wasn't exactly the way Talon had phrased it. More like, *For Jared's sake and memory, he might be willing to do the family a favor.* "If I can find him . . ."

"You think this Prince can get us a Queen *from Kaeleer*?" Shaddo asked. "Who has that kind of influence and power?"

Theran took a deep breath. "Daemon Sadi."

Ninety-eight Warlord Princes shivered.

"The *Sadist* owes your family a favor?" Archerr asked. Theran nodded.

A dozen voices muttered, "Hell's fire, Mother Night, and may the Darkness be merciful."

"Talon and I talked it over and figured asking at the Keep is the simplest way of finding out if anyone knows where Sadi is."

"He could be dead," Spere said, sounding a little hopeful. "His brother disappeared years ago, didn't he? Maybe Sadi got caught in that storm like the rest of the Blood."

"Maybe," Talon said. "And maybe he's no longer among the living. But even if he's demon-dead, he still might be able to help. And if he's among the demon-dead who went to the Dark Realm, going to the Keep is still our best chance of finding him."

"What happens if we do get a Queen from Kaeleer?" Shaddo asked.

"Then at least twelve males have to be willing to serve her and form her First Circle," Theran said. "We'll have to form a court. Some of us will have to serve." The next words stuck in his throat, but on this too, he and Talon had agreed. "And Grayhaven will be offered as her place of residence."

"You say we'll have to form a court," Ranon said, still sounding cold. "Will Shalador be asked to serve? Will Shalador be allowed to serve? Or will the blood that also flows through *your* veins, Prince Theran, be held to the reserves, ignored unless we're needed for fodder?"

Before anyone could draw a line and start a fight that would end with someone dying, Talon raised his hand, commanding their attention.

"That will be up to the Queen, Ranon," he said quietly. "We're all going to hone the blade and offer her our throats."

"Hoping we won't end up with someone who will crush what is left of us?" Ranon asked.

"Hoping exactly that," Talon replied.

A long silence. Ranon took a step back, then hesitated. "If a Kaeleer Queen comes to Dena Nehele, some of the Shalador people will offer themselves for her pleasure."

Talon looked thoughtful as they all watched Ranon

walk back to the gate. Nothing was said until the Shalador Warlord Prince caught one of the Winds and vanished.

"If you can get a Queen from Kaeleer..." Archerr didn't finish the sentence.

"I'll send a message," Theran said.

The Warlord Princes retreated to the gate. No breaking into groups, no talking among themselves. Some looked back at him and Talon.

"Looks like you're going to the Keep," Talon said.

Theran nodded as he watched the last man vanish. "Which do you think worries them more? That I won't be able to find Sadi—or that I will?"

TWO

Kaeleer

Cassidy sat back on her heels and brushed her chin with the tail of her long red braid.

"So," she said as she considered the ground in front of her. "Does the rock stay or does the rock go?"

Since the question had been offered to the air and the patch of garden in front of her, she didn't expect an answer. Besides, it wasn't really her decision. She'd volunteered to clear the weeds out of this bed as a way to have something to do—and a way to work with a little piece of land. But this was her mother's garden, and whether the rock was an unwanted obstacle or a desired, important part of the whole depended on how one looked at it.

Which was true of so many things.

"It's done and can't be undone," she muttered. "So enjoy your visit here, do what you can, and let the rest go."

Let the rest go. How long would it take before her heart let go of the humiliation?

"Well, at least I found out *before* I put in all the spring work on *those* g-gardens." Her voice wobbled and tears blurred her vision.

Swallowing the hurt that wanted to spill out every moment she didn't keep her feelings chained, she reviewed the containers of seeds she had collected last year from the Queen's garden in Bhak. *That* garden wasn't hers anymore, so her mother would benefit by having a few new plants this year.

"Your mother said I'd find you here."

The voice, always rough because the vocal cords had

been damaged in a boyhood accident, made her smile as she looked over her shoulder at the burly man walking toward her.

Burly in body, Burle by name. A simple man. A handyman. Twice each month he would stay at a landen village for three days and take jobs to fix whatever needed fixing. Most Blood thought it was beneath a Warlord's dignity to work for landens—even if the Warlord wore a Jewel as light as Tiger Eye. He'd always said, "Work is work, and the marks they pay me with are as good as any that come from some snot-nosed aristo family."

That attitude didn't get him work in houses owned by Blood aristos here in Weavers Field, their home village, or in other nearby Blood villages, but the rest of the Blood didn't care what Burle said about aristos, and the landens liked having that little bit extra that came from a man who could use some Craft along with a hammer and didn't talk down to them. The fact that Lord Burle always gave them that little bit extra—and more—meant he had as much work as he wanted.

Her heart warmed to see him—and a moment later began hammering with alarm. "Why are you home? Is something wrong?"

Burle made a show of looking at the sky before focusing on his daughter. "Well, Kitten, it's midday. Food's on the table. You're still out here. Your mother has that look. You know that look?"

Oh, yes. She knew that look.

"So," Burle continued, "I was sent out to fetch you."

Not likely. Sent out, maybe. But not to fetch her. She loved her mother, Devra, but there were some things she could say only to her father. She just wasn't ready to say them.

"All right, Father. What are you up to?" She put enough emphasis on the word "Father" to tell him she *knew* he was up to something. When the only response she got was his frowning at her under those bushy eyebrows her mother subtly kept subdued with grooming Craft, she tried not to sigh as she said, "Poppi."

He nodded, satisfied that he'd made his point. "Your mother said you came out here right after breakfast. Seemed like a long time to be digging up weeds, so I thought I'd give you a hand. But it looks like you've got that bed in good order." He frowned at the gloves lying on the ground beside her.

Cassidy held up her hands. "I wore the heavy gloves. I used a tight shield to protect the palms. And I used a little Craft to turn over the bits of the garden that were obstinate." And if it really was midday, she'd spent far more time staring at nothing and trying not to think than she'd spent on actual labor.

Burle crouched beside her, took her hands in his, and studied her palms. "Nothing wrong with a few calluses, but a hand that's torn up can't serve." He gave her hands a gentle squeeze and let go. "Still, you didn't need to do all of this yourself."

"My father taught me that there was nothing wrong with hard work or sweat."

Laughing, he stood up, bringing her with him. "I used to wonder if your brother, Clayton, heard half of what I said. And I used to worry that you heard too much." He rested a hand on her shoulder. "You're a good woman, Kitten. And you're a good Queen."

"Good Queen?" Control broke, and the pain she'd been living with since she'd shown up at her parents' house the week before flooded out of her. "Poppi, my entire court resigned. All the males in my First Circle—all twelve of them, including the Steward and Master of the Guard—informed me that they wanted to serve another Queen—a Queen who had served her apprenticeship in *my* court. *She* was their choice. For everything. For *everything,* Poppi."

She sobbed out all the hurt, the shock of betrayal. Only bad Queens were abandoned. Only abusive Queens had their First Circle walk away, breaking the court. Only . . .

She couldn't think about the man who had been her Consort. That hurt went too deep.

She wasn't pretty. Had never been pretty. She was tall, big-boned, and gawky. She had red hair and freckles, and a long, plain face. She didn't come from a wealthy family or an aristo family. Except for a distant cousin, Aaron, who was the Warlord Prince of Tajrana and was married to the Queen of Nharkhava, there was no social status connected with knowing her or being in her bed. And since she wore a Rose Jewel, she didn't have the kind of power that would intrigue anyone. There was no reason for anyone to look twice at her.

Except that she was a Queen, an oddity in a family that had rarely produced anyone who wore a dark Jewel, let alone someone who was in the most powerful caste—the *ruling* caste.

Now she was a Queen without a court. She felt as if something had been ripped out of her, and she didn't know how to stanch the emotional wound. Lady Kermilla had the First Circle who had served her, the Blood and landen villages she had ruled, the house she had lived in, and the gardens she had tended.

She hadn't wanted to be important, hadn't wanted to become a Province Queen and rule over District Queens. And she certainly had no ambitions to become the Queen of the whole Territory of Dharo. She'd been happy ruling Bhak and Woolskin. She had wanted to make her piece of Dharo a good place to live for Blood and landens alike.

But the males who had served her had seen her court as a stepping-stone to serving in more influential courts ruled by stronger Queens. When they realized she wasn't going to be a stepping-stone to anything, they grimly fulfilled their contracts—and walked away from her and straight into a contract with Kermilla, a pretty, vivacious Queen who was ready to establish her first court. Kermilla wore Summer-sky, which wasn't a dark enough Jewel to be a big lure, but she had some social connections, could dazzle stronger males without offending . . . and was twenty-one years old.

"There now, Kitten," Burle said as he patted her back. "Don't take on so. It's no shame on you that you ended up with a First Circle who has to drop their pants in order to use their brains."

The image that popped into Cassidy's head stopped the flow of tears. Made her hiccup. Ended with a watery giggle.

"That's better." Burle called in a neatly folded handkerchief. "Mop up or you'll end up on the sofa with bags of salad over your eyes."

"It's a slice of cucumber, Poppi. You put a slice of cucumber over your eyes." Cassidy mopped her face and blew her nose. "Mother swears by that remedy."

"Huh," Burle said. "Nothing wrong with the way your

mother looks. First thing in the morning, last thing at night, and every hour in between, she looks just fine."

He meant it. And because he meant it, and because she'd inherited the red hair and freckles from Devra, she'd thought the man who had been her Consort had also meant it when he said he thought she was lovely.

When he'd left, the bastard had told her what he really thought.

"Well," Cassidy said, vanishing the handkerchief, "we'd best get to the table before Mother comes out here, don't you think?"

"That we should." Slinging an arm around her shoulders, Burle aimed them for the house. "I'll say one more thing. I remember meeting Lady Kermilla when she was serving her apprenticeship in your court, and I'll tell you this, Kitten. If those fools chose her over you, then they deserve what they're going to get."

"Maybe." Probably. When she'd sent Kermilla's evaluation to the Province Queen, she'd tried to be kind, but there had been no denying that she'd had concerns about Kermilla's attitude toward anyone who wasn't strong enough to fight back.

"Their loss, my gain," Burle said. "I've got the two finest women in the whole Territory living in my house."

"For a little while," Cassidy said.

"What's that mean?"

"I'm just visiting, Poppi. Next week, I'll start looking for a place of my own." A very simple place, since there hadn't been much left of the tithes she received from Bhak and Woolskin, not after paying the court expenses and sending the Province Queen her share. That had been her income while she ruled, and the fact that there was any left was due to her careful upbringing and her mother's firm belief that a good life didn't have to be an expensive life.

And since it *was* her income and what she'd saved from the tithes was all she had, she would continue to tear up Kermilla's letters, which all asked the same thing: how much was the former Queen of Bhak going to "gift" the new Queen?

"What do you mean, you're getting your own place?" Burle said. "What for?"

"I'm thirty-one years old, Poppi. A grown woman doesn't live with her parents."

He stopped so fast he pulled her off-balance. "Why not? What can you do in your own place that you can't do—?" His face flushed as he came to an obvious—and incorrect—conclusion about what a woman wouldn't want to do in her parents' house.

"Well now," he muttered, lengthening his stride and pulling her with him. "We'll just see what your mother has to say about that. We'll just see."

She already knew what Devra would say, but this wasn't the time to tell her father he was outnumbered.

"Yes, Poppi," she said fondly. "We'll just see."

CHREE

"**W**hy am I doing this?"

Saetan Daemon SaDiablo, the former Warlord Prince of Dhemlan, glanced at Daemon Sadi, the current Warlord Prince of Dhemlan, and swallowed the urge to laugh. That tone of voice was more suited to a surly adolescent than a strong adult male in his prime, and being Hayllian, one of the long-lived races, Daemon had left adolescence behind several centuries ago.

But he'd noticed that there were times when Daemon and his brother, Lucivar Yaslana, set adulthood—and a good portion of their brains—aside and were just ... *boys*. They seemed to test the emotional waters of adolescence when they were alone with him. Maybe it was because he'd been denied the privilege of raising them and the three of them hadn't gone through the pissing contests they would have all endured if they'd lived with him. Maybe it was because they'd had to grow up too hard and too fast in order to survive the vicious slavery that had been used to control them. At least, that had attempted to control them. The slavery, the pain, the fear, and the cruelty had turned two young men, two Warlord Princes who were natural predators, into lethally honed weapons.

They were intelligent and vicious. Loyal and loving. Powerful and independent. Fiercely protective of those they loved to a sometimes annoying degree.

They were his sons, and he loved them both. But the one standing at the other end of the table, looking at him through long black eyelashes, was his mirror, his true heir. And since he was, among other things, the High Lord of

Hell, the fact that Daemon *was* a mirror was something he never forgot.

"Why am I doing this?" Daemon asked again.

"Because when you arrived at the Keep in Kaeleer and discovered I was here at the Keep in Terreille, you came through the Gate to this Realm in order to ask me something about the family estates. And when you saw me sorting reams of old papers, you asked if there was anything you could do to help."

"That was a polite offer, not a sincere one," Daemon grumbled.

"I know," Saetan replied dryly. "But I chose to take the words at face value."

Daemon snarled softly and went back to sorting papers.

Saetan hid a smile and concentrated on clearing out the stacks of papers at his end of the table.

"What are you planning to do with this?" Daemon asked several minutes later. "Bring it back to the Keep in Kaeleer?"

"Why in the name of Hell would I do that?"

"Marian says shredded parchment makes a good mulch for flower beds."

Marian was Lucivar's wife, a lovely woman and a talented hearth witch whose gentler nature balanced her husband's volatile one. But there were times, Saetan felt, when hearth-Craft practicality needed to be put aside for a more direct and simple solution.

"I'm planning to haul this out to one of the stone courtyards, put a shield around it to keep it contained, blast it with witchfire, and transform several wagonloads of useless paper into a barrel of ash."

"If you asked Marian to help, you'd get this done a lot faster. I bet she knows several 'tidy-up' spells," Daemon said. Then he paused. Considered. "Well, maybe you wouldn't get it done faster, but Marian would be thorough."

Damn the boy for knowing just where to apply the needle in order to prick and annoy.

He wasn't trying to *clean* the place; he was trying to eliminate reams of history so old it was no longer of any use to anyone—*including* the long-lived races.

Well, two could play the needle game. "If I wanted things to get interesting, I could ask Jaenelle to help."

Daemon looked at the parchment in his hand, tipped it a little closer to the ball of witchlight hovering over the table so he could read the faded script . . . and paled.

Saetan had no idea what was written on that parchment, but clearly the thought of Jaenelle Angelline, the former Queen of Ebon Askavi and now Daemon's darling wife, having that information was sufficient to scare a Black-Jeweled Warlord Prince.

Daemon put the paper on the discard pile and quietly cleared his throat. "I think the two of us can take care of this without mentioning it to the Ladies."

"A wise decision." And the same conclusion he'd come to when he'd decided to clear out some of this stuff.

They worked for another hour. Then Saetan said, "That's all that can be done today."

Daemon looked around. They'd thrown the discarded papers into a large crate, but the table and surrounding floor were still strewn with stacks that hadn't been touched.

"It's midday, Prince," Saetan said.

Daemon nodded. "I hadn't realized it had gotten so late."

The hours between sunset and sunrise were the part of the day that belonged to the demon-dead—and Guardians, the ones like Saetan who were the living dead, who straddled a line that extended their lifetimes beyond counting. During the years when Jaenelle had lived with him as his adopted daughter, his habits had changed and his waking hours had extended through the morning so that he would be available to the living. But even here at the Keep, the Sanctuary of Witch, he needed to rest when the sun was at its strongest.

"Let's go back to the Keep in Kaeleer," Saetan said. "We'll wash up, have something to eat before I retire, and you can ask me about whatever you'd originally come here to ask."

The library door opened before they reached it. A Warlord who served the Keep in Terreille nodded to them and said, "High Lord, a Warlord Prince has arrived."

"His name?" Saetan asked.

"He wouldn't offer it," the Warlord replied. "And he wouldn't say which Territory he's from. He says he's looking for someone, and he insists on talking to 'someone in authority.' "

"Does he?" Saetan said softly. "How foolish of him. Put

our guest in one of the receiving rooms. I'll be with him shortly."

"Yes, High Lord."

The Warlord's look of gleeful anticipation told Saetan how deeply the idiot had offended those who served the Keep by not following the basic courtesies. Fools who tried to withhold their names when asking to speak with someone here were usually given as much as they'd offered—which was nothing.

When the Warlord left, Saetan turned and touched Daemon's arm. "Why don't you go back to Kaeleer and ask for a meal. I'll talk to this unknown Prince and join you when I'm done. I doubt this will take more than a few minutes."

The air around them chilled—a warning that a violent temper was turning cold, cold, cold.

"If you're going to talk to anyone from Terreille, you should have someone watching your back," Daemon said too softly.

He wasn't sure if he should feel flattered or insulted by his son's desire to protect, but he decided it was best to keep his own temper out of this conversation—especially now that Daemon's temper had turned lethal. "Have you forgotten that I'm a Black-Jeweled Warlord Prince and do know how to defend myself?"

One sweep of those golden eyes that were now glazed and sleepy. One pointed look at his left hand—which was missing the little finger.

"I haven't forgotten anything," Daemon crooned.

A shiver went down Saetan's spine.

The boyish posturing was gone. Even their relationship as father and son was gone. The man before him was a Warlord Prince of equal rank, who was standing one step away from the killing edge. A Warlord Prince the Blood in Terreille had called the Sadist. A man who was capable of doing *anything* if provoked the wrong way.

And that, more than anything else, was reason enough to get Daemon out of Terreille.

"Would you have told Lucivar he had to have someone guarding his back?" Saetan asked.

"I wouldn't have needed to," Daemon replied. "He would have known I'd stand with him."

This isn't a fight, Saetan thought. But he caught, too late, the undercurrent that had been hiding beneath the boyish posturing.

For Daemon, simply being back in Terreille meant being prepared to fight. To kill.

"Prince, I'm asking you to return to Kaeleer. This is the Keep. It's a sanctuary. To treat someone as an enemy simply because they've come here requesting information would be a violation of everything this place stands for. Daemon, it isn't done." At least, not by another guest. What guarded the mountain called Ebon Askavi passed its own judgment on anyone entering the Keep. And people who entered did not always leave.

"I'm sorry I didn't realize how difficult it is for you to be in this Realm, even here at the Keep," Saetan said. "If I had, we would have left hours ago."

That keen mind assessed his words while those golden eyes assessed him.

"You'll shield?" Daemon finally asked.

"I will shield." Despite his efforts to hold on to his own temper, the words came out in a growl.

Daemon's lips twitched in a reluctant smile. "You would have made the same demand of me if I was the one staying."

"Of course I would, but that's different. I'm your father."

Daemon's smile—and the air around them—warmed. "Fine. I'll go back to Kaeleer and see about getting us a meal."

Saetan waited, tense, until he no longer felt the presence of the other Black Jewel—confirmation that Daemon had gone through the Gate and returned to Kaeleer. Then he sagged against the doorway until he heard the sound of Craft-enhanced footsteps announcing the Warlord's return.

"Is everything all right, High Lord?" the Warlord asked. "I felt ... We all felt ... Prince Sadi went cold for a minute."

"Yes, he did. Being in Terreille makes the Prince feel a little defensive."

The Warlord stared at him. "If that's how Prince Sadi reacts when he's feeling a *little* defensive, I wouldn't want to be around him when he's feeling *really* defensive."

"No," Saetan said quietly, "you wouldn't want to be around him."

*   *   *

Theran opened the glass doors that led out to a tiered garden, then closed them again until there was only a finger-width opening. Despite the spring season, it was cold up in the mountains. He would have preferred sitting in a comfortable chair by the fire, except . . .

This place chilled him a lot more than the cold air. The Black Mountain. Ebon Askavi. Repository of the Blood's history—and the lair of Witch, the living myth, dreams made flesh. Who was, he suspected, nothing more than a dream and myth. There had been rumors that there was, in fact, a Black-Jeweled Queen who ruled Ebon Askavi, but after the witch storm or war or whatever it was that had swept through Terreille and devastated the Blood, the rumors stopped.

The place didn't need a Queen. It was creepy enough without one, and he couldn't imagine anyone . . . normal . . . ruling this place. There were *things* flitting in the shadows, watching him. He was sure of it, even if he couldn't detect a psychic scent or *any* kind of presence.

Which didn't change the conviction that the things he couldn't feel or see could—and would—kill him before he realized anything was there.

When the door opened, he breathed a sigh of relief but stayed by the window. If something went wrong, he had a better chance of getting out and catching one of the Winds if he could reach open ground.

The man who entered the room was Hayllian or Dhemlan—the black hair, brown skin, and gold eyes were common to both long-lived races, and he'd never been able to distinguish between the two. An older man, whose black hair was heavily silvered at the temples, and whose face was beginning to show lines that indicated the weight of centuries. A Red Jewel hung from a gold chain. A Red Jewel flashed in the ring worn on a hand with slender fingers—and long, black-tinted nails.

"Who are you?" Theran demanded. The Territory of Hayll had been at the root of all the suffering his people had endured, and he didn't want to deal with *anyone* who came from that race. With one exception.

The man came to an abrupt halt.

A sharp-edged chill suddenly filled the room, a different kind of cold from the one coming from the open glass door.

"I am a Warlord Prince who outranks you," the man said too softly. "Now, puppy, you can brush off your manners and try again—or you can go back to wherever you came from."

He'd fixed on the man's race instead of paying attention to the Jewels that *did* outrank his own and the psychic scent that left no doubt the other man was a Warlord Prince.

"My apologies, sir," Theran said, trying to sound sincere. The sun would shine in Hell before he sincerely apologized to a Hayllian—for *any* reason. "I find this place a bit overwhelming."

"Many do. Let's see if we can't settle your business quickly so that you can be on your way."

"I'm not sure you can help me." *I don't want you to be the one helping me.*

"I'm the assistant historian/librarian here at the Keep. If I can't help you, no one can."

If I won't help you, no one will. That was the underlying message.

Pissy old cock, Theran thought.

He hadn't meant to send that thought along a psychic thread, and was almost certain he hadn't. But judging by the way those gold eyes were starting to glaze, something in his expression must have conveyed the sentiment clearly enough.

"Let's start with your name," the man said.

Because the man was Hayllian, Theran choked on the thought of giving the old bastard his family name.

"Let me put it this way," the man said. "You can offer the basic courtesy of your name and where you are from—or you can go to Hell."

Theran shivered, because there was something about the soft thunder in that deep voice that warned him his choices were very literal.

"Theran. From Dena Nehele."

"Since the mountain didn't fall down around us and your head didn't explode, I'm delighted that the consequences of revealing so much information were not, in fact, dire."

He wasn't used to being slapped down. Not by a stranger.

A response scalded his throat, but he choked it back. He didn't like the Hayllian on principle—and the Hayllian didn't seem to like him. But the man was the only way of getting the information he sought.

"There has been reason for secrecy," Theran muttered.

"Then your lack of manners can be understood—if not forgiven."

Cold voice, cold eyes, cold temper. If he'd ruined this chance . . .

"I understand you're looking for someone," the man said. "Who?"

Maybe there was still a chance.

"Daemon Sadi," Theran said.

The chill in the air gained a sharp edge. The man asked too softly, "Why?"

None of your business. Theran bit his tongue to keep from saying the words. "He owes my family a favor."

He wasn't sure that was an accurate assessment of the message that had been handed down to the males in his family, but it was sufficient explanation for this librarian.

"I see."

A long silence while those gold eyes stared at him.

"I'll have some refreshments brought in for you," the man said.

"I don't need anything." *Hell's fire! Remember some of the manners you were taught!* "Thank you. Something hot to drink would be most welcome."

"I'll have it brought in. And I'll see what I can find out about Prince Sadi."

The Hayllian walked out of the room—and Theran breathed a sigh of relief.

The control required to close the door and walk away, leaving that little whelp's mind intact, made Saetan's hand tremble.

I guess Daemon's not the only one who feels overprotective at times, he thought ruefully.

Feeling the other presence in the corridor, he made sure the door was firmly shut and stepped away from it as Geoffrey, the Keep's historian/librarian, dropped the sight shield that had kept him hidden.

"You heard?" Saetan asked.

"Since you left the door open, it was hard not to," Geoffrey replied.

"See to the refreshments, will you? I'll deal with the rest."

Geoffrey raised a white-skinned hand. "Just one question. Who *is* that jumping jackass?"

Saetan rocked back on his heels. "Jumping jackass? What have you been reading?"

The other Guardian wouldn't meet his eyes.

Saetan had seen over fifty thousand years. Geoffrey had been serving the Keep for much longer. The thought of discovering after all those years that Geoffrey's choice of recreational reading leaned toward ... Well, he wasn't sure what category of fiction would use such a phrase, and he was almost afraid to ask anyone in order to find out. But the whole thing tickled him enough to push aside temper.

Which, from the look in Geoffrey's black eyes, might have been the point.

"I'll look after our guest," Geoffrey said. "You look after your son."

The thought of Daemon owing *anyone* in Terreille was enough to prick his temper again, but out of courtesy to Geoffrey, he kept that temper leashed until he opened the Gate between the Realms and walked into the Keep that existed in Kaeleer.

Daemon studied the food on the table.

He could breathe again. He hadn't set foot in the thrice-cursed Realm of Terreille for two years—since he'd gone to Hayll to play out some savage games in order to give Jaenelle the time she'd needed to gather her strength and unleash all her dark power, cleansing the Realms of the Blood tainted by Dorothea and Hekatah SaDiablo.

Even here at the Keep, which *was* a protected sanctuary, he had felt the difference between Terreille and Kaeleer, had felt centuries of memories cling to him like cobwebby strands of pain and fear. When he'd lived in Terreille, he'd embraced the pain, and he'd met the fear by playing games that matched—or surpassed—the cruelty and viciousness that Dorothea had excelled in.

He'd survived seventeen centuries of slavery and

cruelty—but not without a price. His body was unmarked; the scars he bore he carried in his mind and heart.

When he found Saetan in the library, he should have admitted his discomfort instead of trying to push it aside. He should have realized he could no more be in Terreille with his father than he could with his brother, Lucivar. Too many memories—and the last memories of them being in Hayll together still crawled through his dreams on occasion.

His father in that Hayllian camp, being tortured. His brother in that camp, being tortured. And he, in order to keep them alive and get them out, had been the cruelest torturer.

Daemon scrubbed his face with his hands and focused on the table. While he waited for Saetan to come back to *this* Realm, he needed to fix his mind on something else.

"So what do we have?" Thick slices of rare roast beef. A vegetable casserole. Crusty bread and whipped butter. And . . .

He lifted the cover off the last dish, raising an eyebrow at the puff of cold air that was released.

Two bowls filled with . . .

Daemon picked one up, gave it a thoughtful study, then picked up a spoon. Since it wasn't anything he'd seen before, tasting it was the only way to figure out what it was.

He took a spoonful, then closed his eyes as the flavors melted on his tongue.

A sweetened cheese whipped into lightness. Little chunks of chocolate. Veins of raspberry sauce.

He opened his eyes and licked his lips. Then he studied the table once more. There were two bowls of the stuff, so one of them must be for him. What difference did it make if he ate it before the rest of the meal or after?

Pleased with the rationalization—in case one was needed—he dug in.

Whom was he going to have to bribe to get the recipe? And if he *did* get it, would he keep it to make himself, or would he offer to share it with Mrs. Beale, the large, rather terrifying witch who was his cook at SaDiablo Hall? Sharing a recipe like this might be a fair trade for her tolerating his putting in a small, additional kitchen for his personal use. So far the only reasons Mrs. Beale hadn't declared outright war on this affront to her domestic territory were (1) he owned the Hall; (2) his Black Jewels outranked her Yellow Jewels by a considerable degree; and (3) technically, she worked for him.

None of which meant a damn thing to Mrs. Beale unless it was convenient for her to remember them.

And in a way, having Mrs. Beale challenge his authority and power was convenient for him too. Now that he was ruling the Territory of Dhemlan, he understood why Saetan had been so passive within his own home and allowed himself to be dominated at times by the people who worked for him.

The people in Dhemlan—or more accurately the Queens and their courts, who were the ones who had to answer to him directly—feared him. They had reason to fear him. The Black Jewels were a reservoir for the power that lived within him, a warning of the depth and potency of strength that could be turned against anyone he considered an enemy. But at home ...

He'd been in places where everyone lived in constant, debilitating fear. He didn't want to live in a place like that. He didn't want to be the cause of that. Not in his home. Not with the people who worked for him.

And especially not with Jaenelle, the woman who was his life.

So he appreciated the game he played with Mrs. Beale, although, admittedly, she was a damn scary woman and his fear of her was not altogether feigned.

Rather like his father, come to think of it.

Lucivar was right. There was something cleansing—not to mention fun—about being able to throw yourself against a strong personality just to see what would happen, and to know you would come to no harm by doing it. It was a relief to be a son, to really be a son of a father who drew a firm line about some things and wouldn't bend but who also had a fine understanding of when to be indulgent—or look the other way altogether.

A father who truly understood him.

He was just scraping the last of the treat out of the second bowl when that father thundered into the room.

Mother Night, Daemon thought, hastily vanishing both bowls.

"If you truly owe a favor to that little prick's family, then we will pay the debt and be rid of him," Saetan snarled. "Or I can send him to the bowels of Hell here and now."

"What? Who?"

"The ill-mannered Warlord Prince who came to the Keep looking for someone? He's looking for you. He says you owe his family a favor."

Ice shivered in his veins, a prelude to his unsheathing the lethal blade of his temper. "Who?" he asked too softly.

"Theran. From Dena Nehele."

Dena Nehele. A place he wouldn't forget.

Daemon tightened the leash on his temper. "What does he look like?"

A light brush against the first of his inner barriers. When he opened that first level of his mind to his father, he saw the man. The same green eyes. The same sun-kissed skin. The same dark hair.

"Jared," Daemon whispered.

Saetan shook his head. "He said his name was Theran."

"The man I knew. Jared. This one has the look of him."

He could feel Saetan reevaluating, making an effort to rein in his own formidable temper. "Do you owe them a favor?"

"Not exactly."

Jared had left a written account of his journey with Lia while being pursued by Dorothea's Master of the Guard. Within that account, which Jared had left at the Keep for Daemon, Jaenelle had found the answer to cleansing the taint from the Blood without destroying *all* of the Blood.

So, in a way, he did owe Jared. Whether he owed anything to Jared's bloodline . . .

"I liked Jared," Daemon said. "He was a good man. So for his sake, I would be willing to talk to this Prince Theran and find out what he wants." He paused and considered. "But not here. I'd like Jaenelle to meet him."

"Why?"

"Because I would trust her instincts about him better than I'd trust mine."

Saetan considered that and nodded. "Then we'll arrange to have him brought to the Hall. How soon do you want me to discover your whereabouts?"

Daemon huffed out a laugh. "Since you're my father, you'd know where to find me."

"Oh, he doesn't know I'm your father. As far as Prince Theran is concerned, I'm just the assistant historian/librarian. Just a 'pissy old cock.' " Saetan's smile turned feral and sharp. "The boy doesn't shield his thoughts as well as he should."

Oh, shit. "Arrange to have him arrive at the Hall late this afternoon."

"Done." As if trying to shake off the mood—and the temper—Saetan looked at the table and raised an eyebrow. "I see you enjoyed the sweet-cheese confection."

Damn. He must not have vanished the bowls fast enough.

"Even so," Saetan continued, "you should eat some of the beef and vegetables."

An undercurrent of amusement. A *fatherly* kind of amusement.

Feeling like a boy wasn't as much fun when he didn't *choose* to feel like a boy. And feeling like an erring son was downright uncomfortable. "I just meant to taste it."

"Hmm." Saetan pulled out a chair and sat down. He took a spoonful of vegetable casserole and a slice of roast beef, and warmed his customary goblet of yarbarah, the blood wine that was all the sustenance the demon-dead—and Guardians—needed.

Not seeing any options, Daemon sat across from his father and filled his own plate.

"There's been very little of interest in those piles of papers," Saetan said. "Even with the preservation spells that were put on them, most are illegible or the parchment crumbles when it's touched. But I did find a few things—like the recipe for that sweet-cheese confection. Well, the basic idea for it at any rate. I had to fiddle with it a bit and embellished it after that."

Daemon chewed a mouthful of beef and swallowed carefully. "You made that?"

"Yes. Like you, I enjoy puttering in the kitchen on occasion."

"And you're the only one who has the recipe?"

"Yes."

They stared at each other.

Finally Daemon asked, "What are the chances of you sharing that recipe?"

His father, the too-knowing bastard, just smiled.

FOUR

Ebon Askavi

A room within the Keep held one of the thirteen Gates that connected the three Realms of Terreille, Kaeleer, and Hell. On the Dark Altar stood a four-branched candelabra. When the black candles were lit and the spell was invoked, a stone wall turned to mist and became a Gate between the Realms.

Following the assistant historian/librarian, Theran stepped out of that mist into a room that looked almost the same as the one he'd just left, but it felt different. It felt darker.

He had reached Kaeleer, the Shadow Realm. He was really here.

And home had never felt so far away.

Kaeleer

Stepping out of the Coach that had brought him from the Keep to this place, Theran stared at the massive structure of dark gray stone that rose up in front of him. It sprawled over the land, and its towers speared the sky. Its size intimidated, and the feel of age and dark power that surrounded it was sufficient warning to any visitor that a smart man walked softly around anything that lived behind those walls.

"Is that an enclosed community?" he asked. He could understand the feeling of that much power if several hundred Blood had lived in a place for many generations. There had been a few places "ruled" by covens in the Shalador reserves that had a similar feel. Or so he'd been told. Most of those places—and the strong witches who had lived in them—hadn't survived the purges that had been ordered a few years ago by Dorothea's pet Queens.

"Like a village, you mean?" the Coach driver said. Then he made a sound that might have been an effort not to laugh. "No. The village is that way." He pointed in the opposite direction. "This here is a private drive until you reach the bridge. After that, it becomes a public road to Halaway."

"Private . . ." He was looking at a *residence*? That feeling of dark power came from *one family*?

"That's SaDiablo Hall," the driver said. "Family seat of the SaDiablo family and home of the Warlord Prince of Dhemlan. I was told to bring you here."

SaDiablo. SaDiablo. Hell's fire, Mother Night, and may the Darkness be merciful.

But Dorothea SaDiablo was dead, wasn't she? Completely destroyed, body, mind, and Jewels. Wasn't she?

"Daemon Sadi lives here?" Theran asked.

"He does."

Was Sadi still controlled by the SaDiablo family? Was he still a slave? Was this branch of the SaDiablo family any better than the ones who had tried to destroy Terreille?

Have I just handed myself to the enemy? Damn that Hayllian bastard for sending me here.

"I'll take the Coach around to the stables, then wait around a bit to see if I'm needed," the driver said. "You should go on up to the Hall and state your business. Won't attract any atten—"

A solitary howl rose from the trees off to the right. Then another howl rose up from the left. The third came from behind him.

Theran turned in a circle, his heart hammering against his chest. Nothing he could see, but something was out there. He was picking up psychic scents, a feeling of power moving toward him from several directions. But those scents were just enough off-kilter that he couldn't identify *what* was out there.

"Well," the driver said, scratching his head. "Now that you've got *their* attention, you've got everyone's attention. So you might as well go on up."

"What are they?" Theran asked. "Guard dogs?"

"Wolves. The pack lives in the north woods that are part of this estate. They're protected by the Hall—and they protect the Hall."

Hell's fire. "Could be worse," Theran said.

"Could be," the driver agreed. He paused and gave Theran a considering look. "Don't know if any are here right now, but you don't want to be upsetting the cats. They're big, and they're mean."

Theran forced a smile. "It's not like they would eat me."

The driver just looked at him.

"Mother Night." Could it be any worse? He didn't ask because he didn't want the driver to tell him about whatever was worse than man-eating cats someone kept as pets.

The driver touched two fingers to his temple as a salute and went back into the Coach.

Theran quickly stepped off the landing web and hurried to the front door, which opened before he could knock, and showed him what could be worse than man-eating cats—a large, stern-faced man who was wearing a butler's uniform and was also a Red-Jeweled Warlord.

Outranked by a servant, Theran thought as he obeyed the silent invitation to step inside.

"Good afternoon," the butler said. "How may I be of service?"

"I'm looking for Daemon Sadi. I was told I could find him here." Of course, the Hayllian prick at the Keep hadn't mentioned he'd be looking for Sadi inside a SaDiablo fortress.

As the butler turned one hand, he suddenly held a small silver tray. The use of Craft was so smooth, Theran stared at the tray for a moment, feeling envious of the subtle training the butler must have received. Oh, Talon had given him the best training available, but their rough-and-ready life didn't require subtlety in anything except fighting.

"Your card?" the butler said.

Hell's fire. Did people still use such fussy things? Would the court he hoped to create have to use them?

"I don't have a card," Theran said, feeling like an awkward child who'd been caught out pretending to be an adult.

The butler's hand turned. The tray vanished. "Your name?"

Theran hesitated. His family had survived by hiding. But would anyone here in Kaeleer understand the significance of the name?

"Theran Grayhaven," he said reluctantly.

"Territory?" the butler prodded after a moment's silence.

"Dena Nehele."

The butler tipped his head in a tiny bow of acknowledgment. "I will inquire if the Warlord Prince of Dhemlan is available to receive you."

"I don't need to talk to . . ." He was talking to the butler's back, so there was no point continuing. Besides, the man didn't go far—just to the back of the great hall.

After a quick knock on the door, the butler stepped into an adjoining room and stepped back out a few moments later.

Nothing subtle about the snub if the butler now informed him that the Prince wasn't available.

"This way," the butler said.

Theran followed the man back to the half-open door. The butler stepped in and announced, "Prince Theran Grayhaven of the Territory of Dena Nehele."

"Thank you, Beale," a deep, cultured voice replied. "Show him in."

Beale stepped aside, allowing Theran to enter, then retreated, closing the door behind him.

The room was shaped like a reversed L. The long side was an informal sitting room, complete with tables, chairs, bookcases, and a leather sofa large enough for a full-grown man to sleep on. The short side of the room had floor-to-ceiling bookcases filling the back wall, red velvet covering the side walls, and a large blackwood desk with two chairs in front of it for visitors.

From behind the desk rose the most beautiful man Theran had ever seen. Hayllian coloring—the thick black hair, golden eyes, and light brown skin. But the man moved like something too graceful to be completely human, and as he came around the desk, Theran felt the punch of sexual heat.

"Prince Grayhaven."

The voice caressed him, a warm syrup over his skin, producing an unwelcome arousal.

"I'm Daemon Sadi."

Of course this was Sadi. Who else could it be?

He'd heard stories. Who hadn't heard stories? But now he had a glimpse of why Sadi had been called the Sadist. All Warlord Princes had that sexual heat to some degree, but he'd never met another Warlord Prince who could halfway seduce a normally uninterested man just by speaking, just by walking toward that person.

Then the door opened, Sadi looked around, and Theran felt the ground crumbling right out from under him.

He'd thought the sexual heat had been a deliberate ploy to throw him off-balance. It wasn't. The punch he'd experienced when he'd walked into the room was Sadi with his sexuality chained. One look at the woman who walked into the room, and Sadi . . .

Theran froze. Warlord Princes were territorial at the best of times, and lethally so when it came to a lover. A woman could end a relationship with a Warlord Prince without fear, but the only kind of male who could survive an attempt at poaching was a stronger Warlord Prince.

Based on what he was picking up from Sadi's psychic scent, this woman was definitely the lover, and since he was a stranger, just being in the same room with her might be enough to provoke Sadi into a kill.

Not pretty, Theran decided. Attractive in an uncommon way, but definitely not what he would call pretty. The golden hair looked shaggy and was too short for him to find personally appealing. And she looked too thin to have the kind of curves a man would find interesting.

And all those things that would have made Theran dismiss her as a potential partner didn't seem to matter to Sadi at all. The hunger in those gold eyes when he looked at her, the hunger that had sharpened his psychic scent . . .

She stopped, narrowed her blue eyes, and rocked back on her heels.

"Nighthawk and I are going for a ride," she said. "Beale said you wanted to see me before I went out."

"Wear a hat," Daemon said.

Her mouth primmed. "I don't like hats."

Daemon moved toward her.

Theran adjusted his coat to hide his reaction to the heat pouring off the other man.

The woman just narrowed her eyes a little more and seemed immune to the feel of seduction blanketing the room.

Daemon cupped her face in his hands. "You need to wear a hat when you go out in the sun," he purred.

"You don't wear a hat."

"My nose doesn't turn bright pink and peel."

She frowned at Daemon.

"And since I adore that nose," Daemon said, kissing the tip of the adored nose, "and the rest of your face, and the rest of you . . ."

Daemon's hands caressed her lightly but thoroughly as they traveled along her shoulders and down her back, his arms wrapping her tight against him as his mouth covered hers in a kiss that . . .

Theran felt his legs go weak. He should avert his eyes, give Sadi and the woman some token of privacy. But he couldn't look away.

He wanted that kind of heat and hunger. Hoped he'd find it with the new Queen who would rule Dena Nehele.

And hoped he could get out of this room very, very soon.

How in the name of Hell did anyone else manage to live here?

Sadi finally ended the kiss and loosened his hold. His lover braced her hands against his chest as if to push away but didn't move.

"Mother Night," she muttered. On her second try, she managed to push away from Sadi and stand on her own. Then she studied the warm golden eyes that were watching her. "Fine. I'll wear the damn hat."

"Thank you," Daemon purred.

"Pleased with yourself, aren't you?"

A flashing grin was her answer.

As she headed for the door, Daemon caught her and turned her around.

"There's someone I want you to meet," Daemon said.

Theran felt those blue eyes lock on to his face, and would have sworn they changed to a darker blue, a sapphire blue that became a doorway to something dangerous, something feral. Something he couldn't name but knew he didn't want to see.

"This is the Warlord Prince Theran Grayhaven, from Dena Nehele," Daemon said. "He hasn't said, but I believe he can trace his bloodline back to Jared, a Warlord I knew a few centuries ago."

"Jared," she said in a voice that made Theran shiver. "And Lia?"

Afraid to answer—and more afraid not to—Theran nodded.

He couldn't look away from those sapphire eyes.

Then her eyes were simply blue again. "Welcome to the Hall, Prince Grayhaven."

Maybe it was because he was getting used to the feel of being in a room with Sadi that he was finally getting some sense of the woman.

A Queen. He felt certain she was a Queen. That caste had a distinctive psychic scent. But he couldn't figure out if she wore a lighter Jewel or a dark one. She seemed to circle around his own Green, feeling lighter one moment and darker the next.

Your wits must still be addled, he thought. The Blood had a Birthright Jewel and a Jewel of rank, and each had a clear, separate feel. Since surviving could sometimes depend on knowing if the person you were facing wore a darker Jewel than your own, conflicting information like he was picking up from the woman could prove deadly.

"Prince Grayhaven," Daemon said, "this is my wife, the Lady Jaenelle Angelline."

"It is a pleasure, Lady."

A horse bugled, a sound full of annoyance, followed a moment later by hooves thundering down on a hard surface.

Jaenelle hitched a thumb over her shoulder. "My ride is getting impatient."

Theran wondered why anyone would bring a horse into the great hall—and wondered why the animal had sounded so loud—but he didn't get a chance to ask.

"Have a seat," Daemon said. "I'll be back in a minute."

Grateful to be alone, Theran scrubbed his hands over his face. After the past few minutes, he needed a long walk or a cold shower—or both.

*   *   *

As Daemon escorted Jaenelle into the great hall, he lightly touched the stallion's mind. *I need to talk to the Lady before you go riding.*

The stallion, wearing a hackamore and barely enough leather to be called a saddle, tossed his head, revealing the Gray Jewel that was usually hidden under his forelock.

Nighthawk was kindred—the name given to the Blood who were not human. A different body and a different race, but a Warlord Prince was still a Warlord Prince, and those who had chosen Jaenelle as their Queen had learned to work together and share their Lady. In most ways.

Theran Grayhaven, Daemon said on a psychic thread aimed exclusively at Jaenelle. *What do you think of him?*

Why does it matter?

He's come here to ask a favor. I can hear him out or show him the door.

When she looked at him, he saw who she was beneath the surface: Witch. The living myth. Dreams made flesh. *The* Queen, even though she no longer ruled.

I spun a tangled web this afternoon, she said. *That's why I want to go riding—to let my mind rest while I focus on something physical.* She paused. *He's part of it, Daemon. So is his connection to Jared and Lia. Hopefully a good gallop will clear my head and help me understand the vision.*

Then I'll hear him out and arrange to have him stay with us for the night.

Jaenelle nodded.

So, Daemon said. *You're riding Nighthawk this afternoon. Are you riding me tonight?*

"Daemon!"

The combination of shock and laughter in her voice told Beale, the footman Holt, and even the horse what they'd been talking about. The color blazing in her cheeks when she realized she'd said his name out loud in *that* tone of voice confirmed whatever assumptions the other males had.

"I was just asking," Daemon said, trying to sound meek instead of amused—or aroused.

He glanced at Beale, whose mouth had curved in a tiny smile despite the otherwise stern expression.

Mother Night, he was going to have to tell the butler *not* to arrange for an intimate dinner. Under the intimidating exterior, Beale was a romantic and wouldn't hesitate to exile Theran to a guest room and a dinner provided on a tray so that Lady Angelline could have a private dinner with her lover, who was also her adoring husband. And since he liked the idea of a private dinner much better than entertaining a man who had angered his father, he had to nip that idea before it took root. At least for tonight.

And apparently his thoughts had been a little too apparent, because Jaenelle was staring at him. Fortunately, she was still focused on his face.

As she turned away, she pointed at Beale. "Our guest will be joining us for dinner. I will expect him at the table."

Beale flicked a look at Daemon, who shrugged. "Very well, Lady."

She strode past Nighthawk and right out the door.

"Prince Nighthawk," Holt called softly.

Using Craft, the footman sailed a hat across the great hall. Nighthawk caught the brim of the hat with his teeth, bobbed his head, then turned and walked out the front door, which closed behind him.

Daemon stared at the door. Mother Night, Jaenelle was going to be *so* pissed when Nighthawk planted his feet and refused to move until she put on the hat.

"So," he said. "Which one of you told the horse about the hat?"

When neither Beale nor Holt answered him, he nodded. "Three out of three of us, then."

The Blood survived within a complex dance of power. There was caste, social rank, and Jewel rank, and an ever-changing pattern of who was dominant. Didn't matter which measuring stick was used, *he* was the dominant male here at the Hall. In the whole damn Realm, for that matter. But there were times, like this, when it tickled him to know that all the males who lived at the Hall were equal in one way: they all served, and they were very good at assessing one another's skills and letting the one most likely to succeed take the lead.

Of course, Jaenelle didn't always appreciate the fact that they worked together so well. Which also tickled him.

Until he remembered what waited for him in the study.

Daemon tipped his head toward the study door. "A pot of coffee and whatever Mrs. Beale might have handy."

"And then you'll be unavailable?" Beale asked.

Daemon considered Theran's claim that he owed the Grayhaven family a favor, and he considered Jaenelle's certainty that Theran was connected to the vision she had seen.

Jaenelle had been trained by the Arachnians, the golden spiders who were the weavers of dreams, to spin the tangled webs of dreams and visions. Even now, with her power diminished from what it had been, she was the most accomplished—and deadly—Black Widow in Kaeleer.

So he would listen to Theran's claim, and no matter what he heard, the other Warlord Prince would join him and his Lady for dinner.

Whether Theran Grayhaven would see another sunrise was a different consideration.

He looked at Beale and knew the butler understood the nature of the man who owned the Hall.

"Yes," Daemon said softly. "I'll be unavailable."

Something had changed, Theran thought as he watched Daemon walk back into the study and settle behind the blackwood desk. The sexuality was chained again, thank the Darkness, but the mood was both lighter and more grim than when Theran had first entered the room.

Sadi leaned back in his chair, steepled his slender fingers, and rested the black-tinted forefinger nails against his chin.

"I understand you think I owe you a favor," Daemon said.

Hell's fire.

"You *are* Jared's descendant, aren't you?"

"Yes," Theran replied. "The last of the bloodline that goes back to Jared and Lia, who was the last Gray-Jeweled Queen we had in Dena Nehele."

"Because of that bloodline, I'm willing to hear you out."

The words were courteously spoken, but there was a growing chill in the deep voice.

How to explain when it mattered so much, when so much was at stake?

He shrugged out of his coat and vanished it to give himself a little more time. He'd thought of little else during the journey between the Keep and here—what to say, how to explain. Now . . .

"We need a Queen."

Daemon raised one eyebrow. "I beg your pardon?"

Theran leaned forward, gripping the arms of the chair hard enough to make his hands ache. "You don't know what it's been like for my people. Two generations after Lia—just two!—the bloodline failed. The last Grayhaven Queen wore a *Yellow* Jewel. She wouldn't have been the Territory Queen at all if she hadn't been a Grayhaven. After that . . ." He swallowed hard.

"After that," Daemon said, "the Queens who were willing to sell themselves to Hayll in order to rise to a power they wouldn't have gained otherwise were the ones who ruled. Those who opposed Dorothea's bid to control the whole of Terreille were either broken so they had little or no power, or were killed outright so the males would have no one to serve except Dorothea's pets."

Theran stared at Daemon. "How did you know?"

"I was a pleasure slave for a lot of centuries, controlled by Dorothea and the Ladies she sold me to. I watched some Territories fall, village by village, court by court, until there was nothing left that was decent, no one left who was honorable." Daemon smiled bitterly. "Oh, I slaughtered the bitch's pets. Buried more of them than anyone will ever know. Hell's fire, there were times when Lucivar and I destroyed entire courts. But Dorothea was like a vile weed with a deep taproot. No matter how much you cut away, her poisonous influence would grow back. It always grew back—until the taint of her and the bitch who backed her was cleansed from the Blood for good."

Theran licked his lips. "The storm of power two years ago. You know about that?"

Something queer flickered in Daemon's eyes. "Yes," he said. "I know about that. I know what it did—and I know what it cost."

You know what it cost you, Theran thought, feeling hopeful that Daemon might be more sympathetic than he seemed. "We lost half the Blood in Dena Nehele to that storm. We lost half of the survivors while quelling the landen uprisings that followed that storm. There are one hundred Warlord Princes left in the whole of Dena Nehele. *One hundred.* My Green Jewel is the darkest we have." Not quite, but he didn't want to mention Talon.

"Theran . . ."

"We don't have any Queens." Theran rammed his fingers through his hair, then ended up fisting them and pulling until his scalp stung.

"Theran."

He let go of his hair and gripped the chair's arms again. "All right, we do have some Queens. But they're old women. Or they're little girls who are too young to deal with grown men, especially men as volatile as Warlord Princes. And there are a handful of adolescent Queens, but they're already starting to act like the Queens we're finally free of, and there's been some muttering that the Warlord Princes would rather kill them than let a bitch become old enough to rule. If those girls act like the previous Queens and we accept them, we've won nothing. All the blood that was shed and the people who were lost would have been for nothing."

When Daemon didn't respond, Theran plunged on with the shining coin of hope that Talon had given him. "When Jared was an old man, dying from the wounds of his last fight, he told a trusted friend this one thing. He said, 'If the need is great and nothing the family can do on its own will help Dena Nehele survive, find Daemon Sadi. Ask him for help. But only once.'" Theran closed his eyes for a moment. "Those were the last words Jared spoke. Well, we did all we could. We fought and we bled and we watched our people drown in the filth of Hayll. And now I'm the last one left. *The last one.* So I'm here, asking for help."

A long silence, interrupted by a knock on the door. All the items on the desk vanished, replaced by a woven mat as Beale brought in a large tray and set it in the center of the desk.

"Thank you, Beale," Daemon said.

After Beale left the room, Daemon poured coffee for both of them, then leaned back in his chair, ignoring the thin sandwiches and nutcakes that were also on the tray.

"You say you need a Queen," Daemon said. "What, exactly, are you looking for?"

Theran took a sip of coffee to wet his suddenly dry throat, then took a deep breath—and told him.

Dinner was over; the strained effort to be a courteous and entertaining host was finished—at least for tonight.

Daemon stood in front of the dresser in the Consort's suite and stared into the mirror.

"You've had worse days, old son," he told his reflection. "You know you've had worse days."

But being pummeled by Theran's words had made him feel soiled and weary, and listening to that particular blend of hope and despair had stirred up memories until they swelled and burst in his mind like pus coming out of a wound gone septic.

He'd heard it before. Heard it for centuries. He'd watched young men grow old and break under that blend of hope and despair.

It didn't help that Theran looked so much like Jared, as if all the generations in between had been erased. But Theran wasn't Jared, and there was some internal difference that Daemon recognized but couldn't name—and that difference was the reason he had considered Jared a friend and would never consider Theran as more than an acquaintance. Nothing indicated he wasn't a good man committed to helping his people, but . . .

A knock on the door that connected his bedroom with Jaenelle's. "Come," he said, turning away from the mirror.

She came in, wearing a silky sapphire robe.

His stomach clenched. He'd been the one who had hinted this afternoon—shit, more than hinted—that he was interested in sex tonight. But that was before he'd talked to Theran, before the barbs of memories had hooked into his mind and heart. Now he hoped she was too tired to want more than a cuddle.

"You didn't want to talk about it before dinner," Jaenelle said, "but I need to know what sort of favor Theran wants." She stretched out on the bed, propped her head in one hand, and studied him. "Daemon, do you feel all right?"

"I'm fine." He wasn't fine, he was nowhere close to fine, and he needed to tell her that instead of trying to hide it.

Talk. She wanted to talk. That, at least, he could do.

He removed his wallet from the inside pocket of his black jacket and dropped it on the dresser before he shrugged out of the jacket and hung it on the clothes stand so that his valet could decide if it needed to be cleaned, pressed, or simply aired. He'd done without a personal valet for a lot of years, and there were times when he missed the independence of having his wardrobe be *his*. On the other hand, Jazen managed to keep his favorite shirts hidden, leaving others out as bait when Jaenelle went foraging in his closet. For that reason alone he was willing to follow his valet's rules about where to leave the clothing that had been worn.

"Theran wants my help to convince a Queen from Kaeleer to go to Terreille and rule Dena Nehele," Daemon said, returning to the dresser. He positioned himself in the mirror so that he could see Jaenelle's face, but his own reflection hid the rest of her.

She'd sat on the bed dozens of times, talking to him while he got undressed, before they both retired to her bedroom. Their bedroom, since he used this room only when she wasn't home. But tonight it bothered him, scratched on his skin. Scratch, scratch, scratch. Scraping at those pus-filled wounds.

"Say that again," Jaenelle said.

"Dena Nehele needs a Queen who knows what it means to be a Queen, who knows Protocol and remembers the Blood's code of honor. Who knows how to live by the Old Ways."

"And if he doesn't find a Queen like that?"

Daemon sighed. "If he doesn't, I think what's left of two races—Dena Nehele *and* Shalador—will wither and die."

He slipped his hands in his trouser pockets, then called in some coins to provide an excuse for why he was still standing at the dresser, emptying his pockets, and delaying the moment when he had to tell her he was too churned up to be of use to her.

"What did you tell him?" Jaenelle asked.

"I told him I'd think about it."

"Will you?"

"No." When Jared had answered his summons that last time, Daemon had known Dena Nehele would fall under

Dorothea's relentless campaign to rule all of Terreille. Had he done the Shalador Warlord any favor by encouraging Jared to hold on to love for as long as possible? "The males in Kaeleer won't tolerate one of their Queens going to Terreille."

A hesitation. "I know a Queen who might be willing," Jaenelle said. "She knows Protocol, although she prefers to ignore it as much as the rest of us."

Daemon snorted softly as he fiddled with the coins, stacking and restacking them. The Territory Queens in Kaeleer belonged to Jaenelle's coven. They had been her First Circle and they were still her closest friends. Thanks to Saetan, every one of them knew all the nuances of Protocol and the give-and-take of power between males and females. Thanks to their own perversity, the Ladies ignored the formality of Protocol every chance they could. And it was that blend that made them so formidable—and made them such good Queens.

"She's a distant cousin of Aaron's," Jaenelle said. "She's a few years older than me. She's not a close friend, but I like her. As part of her own apprenticeship, she lived at the Hall with the rest of us for four months to get 'court polish.'"

Since Jaenelle's court had been the most informal gathering of power he'd ever seen, the humor of sending anyone there for training eased the tightness in his stomach a little. "Did she acquire any polish?"

"She got lessons in Protocol from Papa," Jaenelle replied. "Those will polish *anybody.*"

It was easier to talk to her reflection, so he kept his back to the room while he continued to fiddle with the items on the dresser. "What will her court say about relocating to Terreille?"

Jaenelle hesitated. "She doesn't have a court at the moment. That's why I think she would be willing to do this."

He looked at her exotically beautiful face, which only hinted at the wonderful and terrifying Self that lived beneath the human skin. She was capable of cruelty, but the cruelty was always entwined with justice.

What had she seen in her tangled web?

And why was the arm that had been covered by sapphire silk now bare?

"What happened to her court?" His stomach tightened again as the edge of his temper sharpened.

"Instead of renewing their contracts, her entire First Circle resigned, and that broke the court."

"Why?" he asked too softly. There were very few reasons why *all* the males would walk away from a Queen, and none of those reasons would help Theran or Dena Nehele.

"You won't like the answer."

He already didn't like any of this. "Tell me."

Jaenelle sighed. "She wears a Rose Jewel, which makes her a minor Queen in a Territory like Dharo; she doesn't come from an aristo family; and"—she winced—"she's not pretty."

Fury rose in him, a molten ice. "That's it? *That's all?*"

"She can't offer flash and glitter. It's not in her. But she's a good, solid Queen, and she's got the tenacity to dig in and work."

Daemon blew out a breath and rolled his shoulders to try to shake off some of the tension. Tried to shake off that terrible blend of hope and despair that was making it so hard to think clearly. But he'd done what he could, hadn't he? Even now he was doing what he could. "Well, Jared will have to give up some of what he wants in order to get the rest, but—"

"Jared?" Jaenelle asked.

Her voice sounded oddly sharp, and that pricked his temper, honed it to a lethal edge. But he was so tired tonight. So desperately tired. Still had to play the game, though. Dorothea couldn't prove he'd helped the Shalador Warlord, but lately the women she'd chosen to use him as a pleasure slave were an added barb of cruelty.

"Why are we talking about Jared?"

He turned toward the bed. "Because—"

He slammed back against the dresser hard enough to make everything rattle. His heart hammered against his chest, and his body was suddenly—and painfully—aroused.

There was a filthy bitch sprawled on *his* bed.

She lay on her side, her head propped up on one hand, one leg forward and bent at the knee to help her balance. Nothing blatantly provocative about the position, which meant only that she was smarter than the bitches who had tried before her. She was wearing sheer white stockings that came up to midthigh. No need for a garter belt when Craft could hold the stockings in place. Above that, she was wearing a simple white shift that ended just above the stockings and was sheer enough that it didn't hide the body beneath.

It also didn't hide the fact that she wasn't wearing anything else.

His cock strained against his trousers, wanting to be sheathed inside her and flood her with come.

Bitch. Filthy bitch.

"Daemon?"

She'd succeeded. Where all the others had failed, *this one had succeeded*. She made him want, made him need. And when the little bitch informed Dorothea that he *could* be aroused, the slavery he now endured would be *nothing* compared with what would be done to him to breed him with Dorothea's select bitches.

"Daemon? What's wrong?"

And the one untouched thing he had left to offer, the one clean thing he had given to no one else, would be taken from him. Like everything else had been taken from him.

Because of the little bitch now stinking up his bed.

She sat up. Shifted closer to the edge of the bed. *His* bed.

"I think I should leave."

Leave? No, no, no. Not until he'd purged himself of some of this anger, some of this hatred, some of this *need*.

He raised his right hand. The Black Jewel in his ring flashed. And he saw her tense as Black locks and shields surrounded the room, trapping her inside. With him.

This was his room, the one bit of peace and privacy he could claim. That was his bed, a place he shared with no one. And her body was his to do with as he pleased.

He took a step toward the bed, delighted by the way she shivered. Not with anticipation. The little bitch had finally figured out what she found in his bed wasn't going to be pleasure.

He took another step.

She tried to bolt, tried to launch herself off the bed.

Snarling viciously, he caught her, threw her back down on the bed, and came down on top of her, forcing her legs apart, pushing against her, taking dark pleasure in the knowledge that the moment he vanished his clothes, his cock would ram into her.

"*Daemon.*"

Go ahead, he thought. *Plead now that you can't control what's coming. Could never control what's coming.*

His hands tightened on her wrists. Tightened and tightened until just a little more pressure would break bone. Her pulse hammered under his fingers. Her heart thundered against his chest.

He smelled her fear. Reveled in the scent of it.

She turned her head, as if daring to deny him her mouth.

He clamped his teeth on the spot where her neck and right shoulder connected. . . .

And breathed in a scent that soothed and excited him. He licked that spot and tasted a flavor more heady than the best wine. And knew whose body trembled beneath his.

"Jaenelle," he whispered, nuzzling that spot, breathing in those scents that could belong to no other woman. "Jaenelle."

His hands relaxed, still cuffing her wrists but gently now. So gently.

"Jaenelle." He was safe. He was safe. She wouldn't hurt him for wanting her. She wouldn't punish him for needing her.

He could give her this because she was the one he had waited for.

As he raised his head to look at her beloved face, he realized something wasn't right about the room.

It didn't smell like her. Like them. It smelled only like him.

"Kiss me," he whispered before sinking into a kiss that was viciously gentle.

He needed her, couldn't survive without her. And he needed the scent of her arousal, the flood of her pleasure, to fill his bed.

His room. His bed. And . . .

He looked at the woman who meant more to him than anything else, and thought, *Mine.*

FIVE

Kaeleer

Theran looked at the man who walked into the breakfast room and thought, *Predator.*

Whatever mood was riding Daemon Sadi could have lethal repercussions for the rest of the males in this place. And judging by the way Beale held himself, as if a twitch at the wrong time could end with someone being gutted—or worse—the butler recognized the danger too. The difference between them was that Beale seemed to be offering something Sadi wanted, whereas he . . .

He dared give that cold, beautiful face a quick study before fixing his eyes on his plate.

In Dena Nehele, men had two ways to describe a man who had spent a vigorous night in bed: ridden hard or well used. A man who had been well used came to the breakfast table with a sated, lazy satisfaction. A man who had been ridden hard might have gotten *some* relief from the sex, but he was still edgy and looking for an excuse for a different kind of relief. And when a Warlord Prince went looking for *that* kind of relief, blood was spilled—and too many friends and families ended up grieving for the dead.

Sadi pulled out a chair and sat down across from him. Within moments Beale poured a cup of coffee for the Prince and, without asking, fixed a plate of food for the man.

"It will be ready in a few minutes," Beale said quietly.

Nodding, Sadi reached for the cup of black coffee.

Undercurrents. Any man who lived in Terreille learned to recognize them. Even someone who had spent his life in the rogue camps.

There was concern—and understanding—in Beale's voice. The same concern Theran had heard in older men's voices when they'd tried to offer support to a younger man who'd been twisted up by bedroom games. And there was a moment before Beale left the room when Theran thought the butler would actually lay a comforting hand on Sadi's shoulder.

He recognized all the signs and knew what they meant, but who in the name of Hell would be brave enough—or foolish enough—to twist up a Black-Jeweled Warlord Prince?

Sadi's wife.

That first exchange he'd witnessed between Lady Angelline and Sadi had left no doubt that Daemon's attention became focused exclusively on her whenever she entered a room. He'd figured it was because they were still in their first year of marriage—a time when a man's thoughts didn't stray too far from the bed.

Now he wondered. Who was Jaenelle Angelline? He'd heard of Sadi—who *hadn't* heard stories about the Sadist?—but the Prince's wife, the adopted daughter of the former Warlord Prince of Dhemlan, was a Queen who didn't have a court and didn't rule anywhere that he could tell, not even the little village just down the road from the Hall. She wore a Jewel so peculiar he'd never seen its like before. And everything about her outside of her life here at SaDiablo Hall was off-limits in terms of questions or conversation. Sadi had made that very clear when the three of them had dinner last night.

The other thing that was becoming clear was that no matter how they appeared for the servants and guests, no matter how Sadi was presented as the dominant power in Dhemlan, when the bedroom door closed at night, *she* had a Warlord Prince by the balls and wasn't afraid to squeeze.

Which brought him to the unpalatable conclusion that he was going to have to negotiate with *Lady* Angelline instead of Prince Sadi.

Then he looked up and realized those sleepy gold eyes were focused on him, had been focused on him all the time his thoughts had wandered—and he had the terrifying feeling that Sadi was analyzing him right down to the last drop of blood and the smallest sliver of bone.

A sudden chill hung over the table, along with an unspoken warning: *Keep your hands, and your thoughts, away from my wife.*

"Prince?"

Thank the Darkness, Theran thought as Daemon turned his head to look at the butler standing in the doorway.

Beale nodded once.

Daemon pushed his chair back, hesitated a moment, then called in a sheet of paper and dropped it on the table.

"Those are the terms for having a Kaeleer Queen go to Dena Nehele," Daemon said. "You can look them over and give me your decision later."

Theran waited until Daemon was out of the room before letting out a shuddering sigh of relief.

Maybe if he told the butler he was going to take a walk around the estate, he could catch the Winds and reach the Keep before anyone realized he was gone. Maybe he could persuade that Hayllian librarian to help him go through the Gate and get back to Terreille.

Maybe you can throw away the one chance you'll have of finding someone who might be able to help your people. If you run away now, you run away from everyone. Jared and Blaed wouldn't have run. They would have been scared— Hell's fire, they weren't stupid—but they wouldn't have run.

And neither would he.

Resigned to that much, Theran picked up the sheet of paper to look at the terms.

Carrying the loaded breakfast tray, Daemon paused outside the bedroom door.

Control it, damn you. Lock it away. Keep it leashed.

He was Daemon Sadi, Warlord Prince of Dhemlan, husband of Jaenelle Angelline. This morning, that was all he was. All he would allow himself to be.

Choked by that leash of self-control, he passed through the bedroom door and the shields still surrounding the room. When he'd crept out of the room at the first hint of dawn, he could have changed the locks and shields to Red, which would have kept Jazen out but allowed Jaenelle to leave. He hadn't. So she was still in his bed, tucked under the covers, just as he'd left her.

Not quite, he realized as he rounded the bed and saw her. She'd gotten up long enough to pull the shift on—and, most likely, to realize that he'd locked her in the Consort's suite.

Her eyes opened. He wasn't sure who stared at him—Jaenelle, his wife . . . or Witch.

"I'm still deciding if I should be very pleased with you or very pissed off at you," she said.

Cautiously hopeful, because he hadn't thought there would be *any* chance of her being pleased, he raised the tray to catch her attention. "I brought you some breakfast."

"Did you bring coffee?"

"Yes." Of course he'd brought coffee. He wouldn't have dared come back into the room if he hadn't.

He waited until she was sitting up and comfortably settled before he placed the tray across her lap.

A pointed look from her had him sitting gingerly on the edge of the bed. He didn't speak while she inspected the contents of the tray.

"Vegetable omelet and"—her eyebrows rose as she cut into the other one—"seafood omelet."

"Took a little persuading to convince Mrs. Beale to give up some of the shrimp and cold lobster she's using for the midday meal," he said.

She took a bite of the seafood—and didn't look at him. "Did you eat?"

"Wasn't hungry." He was so scared of what would happen now, even the thought of food made him queasy.

"I'd like an explanation," Jaenelle said quietly.

"Sweetheart, I'm sor—"

"An explanation, Daemon, not an apology."

He swallowed the words and closed his eyes. An apology would have been easier.

"Something snapped in you last night, in a way I've never seen before. I think I provoked it—or was the final shove. I'd like to know why."

"You didn't provoke anything," he snarled as he met those sapphire eyes. "It wasn't . . ." He wouldn't let her take the blame for this, not even a crumb of blame. But how to explain? Where to begin?

She sipped her coffee and waited.

"The Consort's room is a kind of sanctuary," he began, choosing each word with care. "A place for a man to let down his guard. A place where he doesn't have to perform."

She bit into a piece of toast and chewed slowly. "Do you feel like you have to perform, Daemon?"

He shook his head. "No. Never. Not with you. But . . . for most of my life I'd had to perform, had to be on my guard except for the few precious hours each day that I had to myself. So even though things are different now— so very different now—I like having this private space. I'll come up here sometimes in the afternoons, stretch out on the bed for an hour, and let my mind wander." And know he was safe when he did it.

She cut off a piece of the seafood omelet and held up the fork.

His stomach cramped, but he kept his eyes on hers as he leaned forward and accepted the offering.

"Nothing wrong with wanting a place for yourself," Jaenelle said. "The cabin in Ebon Rih is my private place and seldom shared even with the people I love. So I do understand."

"All those years in Terreille, I had to fight hard to have a private place," he said softly.

When he didn't say anything more, Jaenelle poked around the tray. "Ah. There is another fork." She handed it to him. "Eat in between the pauses."

He wasn't sure if being required to eat was a subtle punishment or confirmation that she was more shaken by last night than she wanted to admit. Otherwise, since she was a Healer, she would have known he couldn't eat.

He took a piece of toast, then a bite of the vegetable omelet. And swallowed hard to keep it down.

"I needed a private place," he said. "In order to stay sane, I needed a place. *My* room. *My* bed. Out of bounds to everyone."

She drank some coffee. Dabbed at her mouth with a napkin. "You could have asked me to leave."

"I didn't want you to leave." He kept his eyes fixed on the tray of food, no longer able to look at her. "In every court, there would always be one who wouldn't respect the boundaries, one who had to be the lesson to the others. Always one little bitch who thought I would bend in private in ways I wouldn't bend in public. And there she would be one night, dressed to arouse, rubbing her stink on *my* bed."

Jaenelle flinched.

"I hurt them, Jaenelle. Even when I let them live, I *hurt* them. They were violating what little peace I could make for myself, trying to create a need, a desire, a physical response that would have condemned me to a more savage kind of slavery once Dorothea found out I was capable of being aroused. And in a way those little bitches succeeded. They created a need to hurt them, a desire to inflict pain. As for physical response, they didn't get the one they wanted, but they got one—and they lived with the nightmares for the rest of their lives."

"Daemon," Jaenelle said gently.

He couldn't stop now. "Then last night, talking to Theran, remembering Jared and the last time I saw him—and the years that followed. Those weren't easy years for me."

"Those memories were riding you last night."

"Yes. And then I was here, in my room, my private space, trying to settle my feelings, talking to you but not paying attention to you. Listening to you, but not paying attention while I was getting undressed, still steeped in that other time in my life. And then I turned around...."

"And saw a memory."

"A thousand memories." Daemon swallowed hard. "I saw the body, but not the face. I saw the clothes, but not the person who wore them. And my own worst nightmare from those years happened. I was so completely aroused I couldn't turn away from what I wanted. What I *needed*. It was like being thrown into the rut without any warning. And then you moved as if you were going to leave, and—" He clamped his teeth together.

Jaenelle refilled the coffee cup, taking her time as she added cream and sugar. "You scared me last night."

He bowed his head. "I know."

"This was more than the rut, Daemon." She hesitated. "You know who I am when you're caught in the rut. Last night ... I wasn't sure you knew who was under you—or cared."

"I didn't know," he admitted. "Not until I touched you. And then ...." The smell of last night filled the room, and every thought encouraged his body to remember what he'd done while she was under him. Every thought encouraged the part of his nature he tried so hard to keep leashed to wake up again, play again, dance with her again.

After a long silence, Jaenelle said, "Say it."

"When I touched you, when I realized where we were and that I was aroused *because* it was you, I had one thought: This was my room, my bed, and you were . . . mine. And no one was going to stop me from having you. Nothing was going to stop me from satisfying every need."

He reached for the coffee cup, then reconsidered and took another bite of omelet.

"Once I knew it was you," he said softly, "all the things I had hated for so many years were the things I now wanted. I wanted your scent on my sheets. I wanted to lay in this bed on other nights and remember having you."

When she didn't comment, he poked at the food, eating to have something to do.

Finally she said with dry amusement, "You *were* pretty single-minded last night. Mine, mine, mine. I guess this really did jab at the possessive side of your nature, didn't it?"

He huffed out a laugh. "I guess it did."

She pinched a bit of the shift between thumb and forefinger. "As for this, I'm sorry it brought back bad memories. I'll—"

"Wear it again? Please?"

She looked wary.

He touched her hand briefly, the first contact he'd made since he'd walked back into the room. "Bad timing. If I'd seen you in those clothes in your bedroom or here on any other night . . . Well, I can't say the outcome would have been different, but the reasons I reacted to the clothes would have been."

Which made him wonder about something that hadn't occurred to him last night. "Why *were* you wearing that?"

She blushed. Shrugged. Fiddled with the coffee cup.

He waited, a patient predator.

"I was reading a story and when the woman wore something like this, the man . . ." Another shrug. More fiddling.

He tried to remember what she'd been reading lately, but couldn't recall a title. "Maybe I should read that book to get a few ideas."

"*You* don't need any ideas."

He was pretty sure that was a compliment.

Since he was feeling easier and the food was there in front of him, he ate some more.

"Will you wear it again?"

"To spend the night in this room or the other bedroom?" Jaenelle asked softly.

"Both," he answered, just as softly.

A slow, mischievous smile. "Instead of negotiating about which bed to use, maybe we should just flip a coin to see who gets to be on top."

Last night he'd dominated, possessed, kept her under his body and under his control. Now he had a sudden image of her riding him, her body a teasing shadow covered by the shift, her legs sheathed in those sheer white stockings, his fingers moving up her legs to the damp skin above the stockings, moving up to the wet heat that sheathed him.

That image stayed in his mind, but the tone changed, becoming a dark, spicy thrill when she realized she wasn't the one in control, that he was still . . .

He jerked back, snarling, as fingers snapped in front of his face.

Jaenelle stared at him. "I don't know where your brain went just now, but, Mother Night, Daemon, judging by the way your eyes glazed, we don't have time for whatever you were thinking."

They had all the time they wanted. Who would dare interrupt them?

"I'm going to Dharo today, remember?"

Leave? She was going to *leave*?

"Daemon. You have a guest, remember?"

Theran. Stranger. Male. *Rival.*

"Daemon."

Her hand clamped over his wrist. Physically, he could break the hold without effort. But her touch, her will, was the only chain strong enough to keep him leashed.

He shifted on the bed, trying to find a comfortable position, trying not to snarl at her for denying him the right to eliminate a rival.

She blew out a breath and kept her hand clamped on his wrist.

"You won't be able to settle if I stay here today, and if you don't settle, Prince Theran is going to end up dead."

She was right, and they both knew it.

"And you need to get out of this room until it's been cleaned and aired."

She was right about that too. But . . .

He wasn't Daemon anymore. Not completely. That other side of him was swimming close to the surface, wanting to dance, wanting to play, wanting to give her a little taste of fear while he aroused her body and produced a banquet of climaxes ranging from wild screams to soft, helpless moans.

He caught the back of her neck and pulled her forward gently, carefully, implacably. His mouth opened and hovered a breath away from hers.

"Kiss me." Not a request. A purring command.

She trembled a little as her mouth touched his. As her tongue touched his.

A soft kiss. A lingering kiss that soothed with the promise of fire at the end of the day.

He eased back and shoved his brain and libido—and the Sadist—away from all the thoughts of what his body wanted to do with hers.

"Am I forgiven?" he asked.

"For last night? Yes. For eating the last bite of the seafood omelet? I'll have to think about that."

He looked at the tray and realized they'd done a fair job of cleaning the plates. "I didn't drink any of the coffee," he muttered.

Jaenelle bared her teeth in a feral smile and lightly pinched his cheek. "That's why you still have all your fingers."

Daemon stepped out of the Consort's suite and felt the dark presence in the rooms across the corridor. He shivered as he stared at the door to his father's sitting room.

As much as he'd told Jaenelle in an effort to explain last night, there was so much more he hadn't said. Couldn't say. Not to her.

For one thing, he wasn't stable, wasn't sure he could be trusted around her—and that scared him to the bone.

He crossed the corridor, knocked on the door, and waited for his father's deep voice to give him permission to enter. Barely pausing to close the door, he hurried to the chair where Saetan was reading a book, and sank to his knees.

"Father."

Saetan closed the book, then removed and vanished his half-moon glasses. "What's wrong?"

Jaenelle's lack of anger and her willingness to understand had helped him maintain a crust of calm, a thin layer of control, that had hidden a seething ugliness for a little while.

But here, now, he faced a man who wouldn't hesitate to punish him if he needed to be punished, who wouldn't hesitate to hurt him if that was needed to pay the debt. Who would understand the depth of what he'd done wrong.

"Father," he said, his voice breaking. "I hurt Jaenelle. *I scared Jaenelle.*" Those words would mean little to most people, but Saetan would know what it would take to frighten Witch.

"Tell me," Saetan said.

He told Saetan everything. *Everything.* And when he was done, he pressed his face against his father's legs . . . and wept.

Hell's fire, Mother Night, and may the Darkness be merciful, Saetan thought as he stroked Daemon's hair, the movement of his hand weaving a soothing spell around his son.

It could have been worse. Could have been much worse. This was a painful reminder that Daemon's mind and sanity had been shattered twice—and no matter how strong the man, no matter how well he healed, there were always scars, always permanent damage. But he could help his boy deal with the fears stemming from last night.

"Are you ready to listen?" Saetan asked quietly.

What worried him was the certainty that if he told Daemon to strip and lie on the floor to be whipped until there wasn't any skin left on his back, Daemon wouldn't hesitate, wouldn't question—as long as the punishment came with the promise that Jaenelle would *truly* forgive him for last night.

Daemon nodded, his face still pressed against Saetan's legs.

"I'm here because Jaenelle asked me to come—not because she needed me, but because you did."

"She needs a Healer," Daemon whispered.

And you need more than a Healer. And the witch who had the skill to mend what had been broken was currently in the suite across the hall. "I'll see to it, and I will tell you what is needed. I'll also find something to do with your guest." *And wouldn't that be fun?*

"Now," he said, giving Daemon's hair a tweak, "you need some rest, so I want you to wash your face, strip down, and get into my bed."

He felt the jolt, recognized the reason. A Warlord Prince was what he was, and letting another male in his bed for any reason was an unspoken testimony of love. His bed had been forbidden ground, but every one of his boys had been allowed to have a nap there when they were feeling shaky or heartsore. Sometimes he had joined them, had held them while they whispered their little hurts and secrets; sometimes he sat in a chair by the bed, reading. Either way, his boys knew they were safe there, protected there. And sometimes knowing that was all they needed.

"Really?" Daemon asked, with just enough doubt to rip at Saetan's heart.

"Really. I'll even read you a story after I take care of a couple of things. Go on, now."

Daemon got to his feet, unable to hide how shaky he was physically and emotionally. He swallowed once, twice. Then he rushed to the bathroom and slammed the door shut.

A moment later, aural shields went up around the bathroom to hide the sounds of Daemon being violently sick.

Sighing, Saetan went across the hall and knocked on the door to Jaenelle's sitting room.

Fresh from a bath, she was bundled in a robe, her golden hair still damp. He saw no fear in the sapphire eyes that assessed him, but he did see worry.

Using Craft, he floated a footstool over to her chair and sat down in front of her.

"How is he?" Jaenelle asked.

"First things first. Was this rape?" *Am I going to have to execute my son?*

He saw the shock in her eyes, quickly followed by anger. "No."

"Are you saying that to protect him because he's your husband?"

"No." Her voice was icy and knife-edged. "I'm saying that because it wasn't. He gave me a choice, Saetan.

He asked me to stay, but he told me I could go. I chose to stay."

Sick relief washed through Saetan. Daemon hadn't remembered giving her a choice, and even though the word had remained unspoken, the fear that he'd crossed an unforgivable line had been in every word Daemon *had* said.

"You need to see a Healer, witch-child."

"I *am* a Healer."

And a Black Widow and a Queen. One of the three witches in all of Kaeleer who had a triple gift.

"Then I need an accurate list of your injuries." Jaenelle was his adopted daughter; Daemon was his son. More than that, he had been her Steward. This wouldn't be comfortable for either of them, but they *were* going to have this conversation. "Before you try to shrug this off because you'd rather not be frank with me, you should keep in mind that whatever broke in Daemon last night may stay broken unless it's fixed in a hurry, and if it stays broken, your husband may not be able to do more than imagine making love to you again."

"Does he really know what happened last night?"

Saetan frowned. "I had the impression he explained some of this to you."

"Yes, he did." Jaenelle studied him for a moment, then pushed back the sleeves of her robe and held out her wrists.

Ugly bruises. His own wrists ached in sympathy.

"That's the worst of it," Jaenelle said, smoothing the sleeves back down. "There are a few other bruises from love bites, but considering where they're located, I'm not going to show you."

On the basis of Daemon's fears, he'd been prepared for something far more serious, and he found himself comforted by Jaenelle's tone of amused snippiness.

"I'm a bit sore, but that has to do with quantity, not his temper, and at any other time, he'd be smugly sympathetic about that," Jaenelle continued. "And between the exercise I got with Nighthawk *and* Daemon, my thighs are sore enough that I'm not interested in riding anything for a couple of days."

Saetan gave in to the smile tugging his lips. "That's it?"

"That's it."

His smile faded. Couldn't be all of it. "He scared you. That's the sticking point for him. He scared *you*."

"Yes, he did," Jaenelle replied quietly. "He didn't know who I was, Saetan. He didn't know *where* he was. He was caught in some twisting memory, and when I realized that, I also realized that if he really tried to hurt me, I was going to have to hurt him, because he would be able to live with a physical injury much easier than he could live with the knowledge that he'd done more than give me a couple of unintentional bruises."

"Could you have hurt him?" Saetan asked. "Are you strong enough that you could have stopped him?"

She folded her right hand into a loose fist. When she opened her hand ...

Her fingers no longer had human nails. These were cat claws, the kind that could do serious damage with even a glancing blow.

"I see," Saetan said softly. A physical wound, even a permanently crippling one, would have been less destructive for Daemon. She had known that—and her choice of weapon would have shocked any man back into the present.

"Well." Jaenelle closed her right hand, then fluffed her hair with her normal fingers. "I'm heading out to Dharo. Aaron should be here by now."

"Oh?" He kept his voice carefully neutral, but he wondered if Jaenelle was being honest about her own emotional state. He understood her summoning him in the early-morning hours so that he would be here when Daemon most needed him, but summoning Aaron could indicate a need to escape.

"Oh." Those sapphire eyes looked through him—and understood everything he didn't say. "The purpose of the visit has changed, but the arrangements were made several days ago. I'm not hurt, Papa. I promise you. I'm ... shaky. I won't deny that. But I'm not hurt."

He nodded.

She laid her hand on his. "Will you stay over today? Be here for him? I think you can do more to help him heal right now than I can."

"Yes, I'll stay."

Her fingers curled around his. "Daemon can't go back

to Terreille. In memory of a friend, he'll try to do what's right, but he can't go back to Terreille."

"He has no defense against the memories anymore, does he?"

"No. His mind and his sanity are intact. He may feel broken right now, but that's a surface feeling, an emotion. Last night didn't actually break him. I did descend into the abyss during one of the times he fell asleep, and I made a thorough assessment of his mind, so I'm sure of that. But he's going to be fragile for a while. If it's needed, Lucivar can go to Dena Nehele."

"If Lucivar goes to Dena Nehele, he'll walk in ready to fight."

Jaenelle huffed. "That's not new. Lucivar walks into *every* place ready to fight."

Saetan laughed softly. Hard to deny the truth about his Eyrien son's temper. "All right." Raising her hand, he kissed her knuckles, then let her go. "You head out to Dharo. . . ."

"And you'll look after our guest?" Jaenelle asked knowingly.

"That I will. But first I'm going to read my boy a story. I had thought of reading him *Unicorn to the Rescue!* or *Sceltie Saves the Day*—"

Jaenelle's silvery, velvet-coated laugh eased his heart and vanished his concern about this child.

"—but I don't think he'd appreciate the humor of being read a story appropriate for his nephew," he finished. "At least, not today."

"No, I don't think he would. Not today."

When their laughter faded, Jaenelle called in a small wooden frame Black Widows used to hold their tangled webs. "That room needs to be cleaned and aired before Daemon can go back in. I think Helene will find this useful. Marian and I have been working on a way to cleanse a bedroom after a Warlord Prince goes through a rut. The vial is opened with a basic housekeeping spell. Once it's triggered, the web will absorb the psychic scents in the room, while the oil in the vial absorbs the physical odors. The whole thing takes a couple of hours. When it's done, the spider silk of the web will look thick and greasy. Same with the oil. We haven't figured out how to cleanse the frame or vial after it's been used, so the whole thing should be put in a shield and burned with witchfire, then buried so the ash doesn't drift on the Wind."

He had to marvel that no one else had ever thought of this. Of course, there probably hadn't been that many friendships between Black Widows and hearth witches, and until Marian and Jaenelle started working together to create specific spells, no one, to his knowledge, had thought to combine those two kinds of Craft.

"Yes," he said. "I'm sure Helene will find this useful." Setting it aside a moment, he asked about something that had troubled him in Daemon's story. "Witch-child, you must have known Daemon wasn't in the best frame of mind. Why did you wear something that . . . ?" If she weren't his daughter and his Queen, he wouldn't have any trouble in phrasing the question.

"Why did I wear an invitation?" she asked.

He nodded.

She fluffed her golden hair. The look she gave him was a little amused and embarrassed. "It's been said that when a man is feeling a bit broody about something, sometimes he wants sex as a comfort but doesn't feel secure enough to ask for it."

The thought of Jaenelle's coven exchanging confidences about their husbands and/or lovers made him want to run and hide, but he just sat there and nodded.

"I thought Daemon was feeling moody about Jared, about remembering a friend who was gone, but I hadn't realized it was more than that until it was too late. Anyway, I was reading a story, and the clothes the woman was wearing had caught the man's interest, so . . ." Jaenelle shrugged. "I knew if Daemon wasn't interested, he wouldn't notice the clothes and would be oblivious to the invitation."

"I beg your pardon?" Saetan blinked, sure he'd misheard. "Daemon wouldn't notice what you were wearing? *Daemon?*"

"Yes, Daemon."

"Witch-child . . ." He shook his head. "Maybe he pretends not to see, but he does notice."

"Before Surreal went back to Ebon Rih, we went shopping in Amdarh, and she picked out some things that she swore would make Daemon's tongue hit his toes and have his eyes roll back in his head."

"What a lovely picture," Saetan muttered.

"So I was trying the outfit on later that evening and wondering if I really had the nerve to wear it when Daemon walked into the bedroom. I don't remember what he'd been working on that day, but he looked exhausted. Before I could say anything, he stared at me for a moment, then told me I wasn't dressed warmly enough for the weather since a bad winter storm had hit a couple of hours before. He bundled me up in *his* winter robe, stuffed my feet in two pairs of socks—a pair of his over a pair of mine—made us both a hot drink, tucked us into bed, and promptly fell asleep."

Saetan pressed his lips together to hide his smile. Daemon's robe. Daemon's socks. The clues had been there, but neither Jaenelle nor Daemon had recognized the significance.

"That's not the only time it's happened," Jaenelle said. "It's a comfort."

"How so?"

So much understanding in those sapphire eyes. "I don't ever want him to feel like sex is a duty. The fact that he's sometimes blind to an invitation means he doesn't feel obliged to perform."

"Did you wear that outfit on another night?"

She hesitated a long time. "Yes."

"And did you get the response Surreal said you would?"

"Not exactly."

But judging by the sudden color flaming her cheeks, she had definitely gotten a response.

He stood up, kissed her forehead, picked up the frame with the web, and walked to the door. Then he turned back. "Are you sure there are no other injuries, witch-child?"

"I'm sure."

That assurance helped, especially when he walked out of Jaenelle's sitting room and found Beale, Helene, and Jazen standing in the doorway of the Consort's bedroom, a look of shock on their faces.

"Problem?" he asked softly. When they turned toward him, he raised a finger to his lips. "Prince Sadi is in my suite. It would be best not to disturb him."

Helene looked from him to the bedroom and back again. "Was anyone hurt?" she asked in a hushed voice.

They stepped aside for him, and when he stood in that doorway, he understood the question.

Nothing outwardly wrong with the room. Nothing broken or damaged. Even the bed didn't look unduly messy.

But the psychic scents in the room, combined with the muskiness of sex, made his own body tighten. Rage and fear filled the room, along with a hatred so deep it caught in the back of the throat like a bitter mist. If he'd walked into that room without already knowing both people were safe and unharmed, he would have been tearing the Hall apart to find Daemon and Jaenelle, certain one or both would be desperately hurt.

And there was something under all those other scents that he recognized, that he—and Daemon—would have to deal with.

But not yet. Not until his boy was feeling steady again.

He turned his back on the room and gave Helene the frame that held the cleansing web, and explained what it would do.

"Please give my thanks to the Ladies," Helene said. "This will help to clean the room." She looked at Beale and Jazen. "The fewer women in the room right now, the better."

"I'll help with the cleaning," Jazen said. "And I'll make sure the clothes don't need to be aired."

"I'll send up Holt to assist," Beale said.

Helene turned to Saetan. "We'll have the room done in a few hours."

"Good," Saetan replied. "Jazen, leave a complete change of clothes in my sitting room for the Prince."

"Yes, sir."

"Beale? Is there something else that needs my attention?"

"Prince Aaron is down in the breakfast room, waiting for Lady Angelline," Beale said. "The Prince's guest is pacing in the formal receiving room, muttering to himself."

"Inform Prince Theran that someone will be available in an hour if he wants to discuss anything."

"Very good, High Lord."

There was a look in Beale's eyes that told him plainly enough that the butler wasn't going to inform Theran about *who* would be available for that discussion.

What was it about the Dena Nehele Warlord Prince that raised the hackles of Kaeleer males?

Still wondering about that, he walked back into his bedroom and found Daemon tucked in his bed. The body belonged to a full-grown man, but the eyes that watched him, so full of despair, belonged to a boy.

He sat on the side of the bed. "She's all right," he said softly. "In better shape than you are, actually."

"There were bruises," Daemon whispered. "On her wrists. I saw them."

Saetan nodded. "Yes, there are. And there are a few love bites, which I didn't see. And her leg muscles are sore, but you and Nighthawk are being given equal blame for those."

"Oh."

The smallest twitch of lips; a hint of amusement in the golden eyes; the tight muscles in the shoulders beginning to relax one breath at a time.

He knew the signs, had watched this son struggle to repair himself once before when he'd believed Jaenelle had been lost forever.

"Now," he said, "you and Nighthawk may be equally to blame for the sore muscles, but you're the only one with hands, so I suggest that you be the one who offers to give Jaenelle a back rub this evening."

An unspoken question hung in the air. He waited.

Finally Daemon gave him the tiniest nod. The Steward of the Dark Court wouldn't tell the Consort to take care of the Queen if there was any doubt about the Consort's welcome.

Having done as much as could be done for the moment, Saetan called in a book, opened it to the table of contents, and pointed to the titles of two stories. "Which one would you like to hear?"

"Both?"

The answer made his heart ache—and also gave him hope that Jaenelle was right and Daemon was emotionally battered right now but not truly broken.

Daemon didn't remember giving the same answer so many times as a boy that it had become a ritual between them. But he did. And because he remembered, he called in his half-moon glasses, took his time settling them on his nose *just so,* and completed the ritual with the same words he'd always said. "Yes, I think we can read both this time."

SIX

Agitated and feeling reckless, Theran rapped on the
study door and walked in before he was invited.

"Hell's fire, Sadi. Are you serious about these conditions you've set?"

The man sitting behind the blackwood desk wasn't Daemon Sadi. It was the pissy old cock from the Keep. The
assistant historian/librarian—who no longer looked like a
somewhat benign clerk whose Red Jewels and caste could,
mostly, be ignored.

Now he saw the resemblance between Sadi and the
Hayllian Warlord Prince, who set a piece of paper on the
desk and removed the half-moon glasses, whose gold eyes
never left Theran's face.

Fear shuddered through Theran when he noticed the
Warlord Prince's right hand, with its long, black-tinted nails
and the Black-Jeweled ring.

"You managed to hone my temper before I walked into
that sitting room at the Keep, so we never did finish the
introductions. I'm Saetan Daemon SaDiablo, the former
Warlord Prince of Dhemlan—and still the High Lord of
Hell."

Theran's legs buckled. He hit the edge of the chair in
front of the desk and grabbed the arms to push himself
back in the seat.

"I—" What was he supposed to say to the High Lord?
Apologize for not being more courteous when he'd been
at the Keep?

"I'm assuming by the way you entered the room that

you want to discuss the terms Prince Sadi set for having a Kaeleer Queen rule Dena Nehele."

"Sadi . . ."

"Is indisposed this morning. You may discuss this with me."

May the Darkness have mercy. All he wanted right now was to get out of this room.

Jared wouldn't have run. Blaed wouldn't have run.

"The terms are . . ." Sadi had accepted the position of Warlord Prince of Dhemlan a few months after his father resigned. Theran remembered hearing that last night at dinner. How was he supposed to voice his objections to the terms without sounding like he was criticizing the son? Because this was one father he did *not* want to offend.

"Unreasonable? Insulting? Barbed?" Saetan offered with a hint of a sharp smile. "Everything has a price, Prince Grayhaven. The man who wrote up these terms has a good understanding of Terreille. A better understanding than you do, since yours, I suspect, is confined to your own Territory. Prince Sadi also has a fine understanding of how the males in Kaeleer, especially the Warlord Princes, respond to any threat to a female, let alone a Queen. You may feel hobbled by these terms, but they were thought through carefully and are designed to protect your people as well as the Queen who comes to rule."

Realizing he'd dropped the paper when he'd grabbed for the chair, Theran retrieved it and stared at the list of conditions.

"A year? She only stays *a year*?"

"A year is enough time for both of you to know if your people can accept an outsider ruling over them—and if your people really want to go back to following the Old Ways of the Blood."

"If we didn't want to go back to living the way we did when the Gray Lady ruled, we would have settled for . . ." *For one of the Queens we have—who would destroy what's left of us as surely as one of Dorothea's pet Queens would have done.*

Theran slumped in the chair, his hands dangling between his knees. "Grayhaven is my family's home—and my inheritance. What's left of it. She can have the use of it. As for a tithe . . . Hell's fire. We're just trying to get enough food planted and harvested so that everyone has enough to eat this winter. The Queens who ruled bled the land and the people dry. I told Sadi that last night."

"That doesn't change what is needed for a Queen's court," Saetan said quietly. "She deserves something for her effort, and the court needs some way to pay for its expenses."

"Couldn't the tithe be paid in goods and services?" Theran asked.

"If the Queen and the First Circle are agreeable to that condition, yes, a high percentage of the tithe could be done that way."

Hopeful that there might be more flexibility to these terms than he'd first thought, Theran looked at the sheet of paper again. "Inspections?"

"And weekly reports from the Queen."

"Why does she have to answer to anyone? And why should my people be treated like children who get surprise tests to see if we've learned our manners?"

Saetan leaned back, steepled his fingers, and rested his forefingers against his chin. "Because you don't have any manners. That's one of the reasons you're here. You want something you don't remember, something your people don't remember. The inspections aren't to test you; they're to appease the Warlord Princes from the Queen's home. Since you belong to that caste, you shouldn't be so dismissive of the power and temper that could land on your doorstep with the intention to kill. As for the Queen's weekly reports, those, too, are to offer reassurance and are in place of having armed escorts living with her in Dena Nehele." He paused. "I should say armed escorts from her home Territory. Providing sufficient escorts for her protection is your responsibility. Gathering the men and women who will form the First Circle is your responsibility. And assuring the Queen's physical and emotional well-being is also your responsibility."

Theran felt the blood drain from his face. He'd escaped all that. By living with Talon, by hiding in the mountains so the pet Queens couldn't control the last male in the Grayhaven bloodline, he'd escaped that kind of service.

"Assess your skills, Prince," Saetan said. "You will be one of the male triangle that serves the Queen most intimately."

"Consort?" Theran choked on the word. "You expect me to service—"

Saetan laughed, and the undercurrent of violence in the sound made Theran shiver.

"You're being presumptuous, puppy. No Kaeleer male is going to tolerate an assumption that any male in Terreille has a right to the Queen's bed."

"Then what . . . ?"

"First Escort," Saetan said. "Same duties for the most part, up until you reach the bedroom door. As First Escort, you don't cross the threshold. You don't serve in bed. However, if being First Escort isn't a service you can perform, you can stand as Master of the Guard or Steward—providing the other males in the First Circle will accept you in one of those positions."

Relief shuddered through him.

"But if a Queen does agree to go back with you and rule your people, you will be held responsible for her care, Theran. Make no mistake about that. And if that care is found wanting, you will answer to Kaeleer. Make no mistake about *that* either. The Warlord Princes here may sympathize with what you want to do for your Territory. They may even be willing to help. But if they think you're mistreating or endangering a Queen who comes from the Shadow Realm, they won't hesitate to destroy you and your people. They will wipe you out of existence more thoroughly than Dorothea ever could. Do we understand one another?"

He had to swallow to get his heart out of his throat. "Yes, High Lord. We understand one another."

"I'm delighted. Lady Angelline has gone to talk to a Queen who may be interested in helping your people. She'll be back for dinner. Since you have the time, I suggest—" Saetan frowned at the door.

Theran turned his head to catch the sound. Yes, there it was again. Something scratching at the door.

Saetan raised one hand. The study door swung open, and a small brown and white dog trotted into the room and stopped near Theran's chair.

He'd never had a dog. Always liked them, liked petting them when he was in a village, but the rogue camps in the mountains were hidden places, and while a dog might have alerted them to a stranger's presence, its barking could also have revealed the location of the camp to an enemy.

The dog didn't come quite close enough for a casual pat, but it did seem interested in him.

"Vae," Saetan said.

Wondering why the High Lord sounded cautious, Theran looked at the dog more carefully. A glint of something in the ruff. A gold chain and ...

His heart gave one hard bump before he recognized his mistake. For a moment, he thought someone had put a Purple Dusk Jewel on the dog, but it was just an amethyst, just someone thinking he was being clever by making it look like the dog wore a Jewel.

"Why don't you and Lady Vae walk down to the village?" Saetan said. "Since the people in Halaway live by the Old Ways, spending a few hours there would give you a good idea of what would be expected from your people."

Walkies? I like walkies!

The voice sounded like a young girl's, but he didn't actually *hear* it. It rang inside his head, just outside his inner barriers, as if someone had communicated on a psychic thread. But the only other being in the room besides him and the High Lord was ...

He does not talk? He is not trained?

"His training has just started." Saetan's mouth curved in a maliciously amused smile. "Lady Vae is a kindred Sceltie. A Purple Dusk witch."

Theran felt the blood draining out of his head. "Kindred? Witch?" That Jewel he'd seen was *real*? This dog was the same rank as his Birthright Jewel?

"Yes," Saetan crooned. "I think Vae will be the perfect escort for you."

He is male and foolish. I will protect him.

"You do that." A pause. "Is there anything else you wanted to discuss right now, Prince Theran?"

He knew a dismissal when he heard one, but his legs felt like overstretched taffy and it took him a couple of tries to get out of the chair. He vanished the paper with the conditions his people would have to agree to, and as he walked toward the door, he realized the dog was waiting for him.

I can pass through doors, Vae said. *I know my Craft.

But you are in training, so I will wait for you to open the door.*

As he stepped into the great hall and the study door closed behind him, he heard the High Lord of Hell laugh.

Cassidy stared at Jaenelle Angelline, then looked at her cousin Aaron, who was pacing the length of the sitting room in her parents' house.

"You're both teasing," Cassidy said. "This is a joke."

"I wish it were," Aaron growled. "But she's serious."

"You *can't* be serious!"

"Why not?" Jaenelle asked.

"I'm a *minor* Queen. I wear a Rose Jewel. I've never ruled anything larger than a small village." Which no one else had wanted until a new, young Queen needed a place to rule to gain credentials for something better. "Aaron, tell her!"

"I did," Aaron replied. "All the way here."

"My entire First Circle resigned and broke the court."

"They were idiots," Aaron growled.

"And because they were idiots, you're now available to help a people who need you," Jaenelle said calmly.

"They need a strong Queen," Cassidy argued.

"You are a strong Queen."

"They need a . . . a polished Queen."

"They need a Queen who knows the Old Ways, who lives by the Old Ways, who knows Protocol, and who knows how to rule fairly," Jaenelle said. "They need someone like you, Cassidy." She placed one hand over Cassidy's. "Look at me."

She didn't want to look into those sapphire eyes. They saw too much. Understood too much. But she obeyed because it didn't matter if Jaenelle officially ruled or not. She was still *the* Queen. And no one disobeyed Witch.

"They aren't going to understand you," Jaenelle said. "Most of them aren't going to see who you really are. They'll be disappointed by the surface."

Cassidy winced—and winced again when Aaron snarled his opinion of her former court.

"Most, Cassidy. But some will see who you are as a woman, and in time the others will appreciate who you are as a Queen. You can do this. I wouldn't be here if I had any doubts about that." Jaenelle patted her hand and sat back. "You'll have a few days to think about it."

Living in a strange Territory. In a different Realm. In Terreille. People didn't go to Terreille. They ran *from* Terreille.

But she could make a difference to these people. She could help them remember who they were, help them rebuild.

"How long would I be gone?" Cassidy asked. Would she ever see her family again? Could she go home to visit, to reassure her parents that she was all right?

"There would have to be terms, conditions," Aaron said as he continued to pace. "We are *not* letting her go to that damn Realm without *some* assurances."

"Who is 'we'?" Cassidy asked, bristling. "No one makes decisions about my life except me."

"Think again," Aaron snapped.

Cassidy blinked. "You're a distant cousin!"

Don't yank that leash, Jaenelle warned on a distaff thread.* When it comes to family, Warlord Princes are only as distant as they choose to be. He's already angry about your former court and didn't trust himself to come here on his own.*

Cassidy glanced at Aaron, then fixed her eyes on the carpet between her feet. She'd been curious when she'd received Aaron's note, requesting a visit at a specific day and time, but she'd thought he was going to give her a pat on the shoulder and a little sympathy about losing the court. Then, when Jaenelle showed up with him and began telling her about Dena Nehele, she hadn't been sure what to think about the visit. But it hadn't occurred to her that Aaron, who really was a distant cousin, would be angry enough to come to Dharo with the intention of going after the males from her former First Circle.

You weren't aware that Aaron has already had a "discussion" with Sabrina about your court breaking for the reasons it did? Jaenelle asked.

No. Thank the Darkness. *What kind of discussion?*

The kind that ended with them yelling at each other.

Aaron had yelled at the Queen of Dharo—who was a member of Jaenelle's coven and a longtime friend of his— because of her? Mother Night.

"I believe Daemon has already drafted a list of terms," Jaenelle said. "And the High Lord is reviewing it."

Aaron finally stopped pacing. "Daemon wrote the terms? The males will have to answer to him?"

Jaenelle nodded. "Or the High Lord. Or both."

Aaron sat in a chair, all his tension and temper gone. Cassidy, however, felt a lot more nervous. Knowing two Black-Jeweled Warlord Princes—the two most powerful males in the entire history of the Blood—were taking an interest in her life wasn't a pleasant feeling.

She looked up in time to see Jaenelle's lips twitch in a knowing smile.

Of course, long-distance interest would be easier than living in the same house with either man.

"I'd like to see a copy of those terms," Cassidy said.

"I'll arrange for that," Jaenelle replied. Then she slanted a look at Aaron. "And I'm sure your father—and the other males in your family—will want an opportunity to voice their opinions."

"Couldn't we skip that part?" Cassidy asked.

"Not a chance," Jaenelle said cheerfully. She stood up. "Well. You have plenty to think about. If you decide to accept the challenge, come to the Keep a week from today."

Cassidy rose to see them out. "Who else have you asked to consider this?"

Jaenelle just looked at her—and Cassidy felt a shiver run down her spine.

"I do not idly weave a tangled web of dreams and visions, Lady Cassidy," Jaenelle said with a hint of midnight and lightning in her voice. "Within the next year, Dena Nehele will begin to heal or it will break beyond all saving. You're my choice to stand as their Queen. Whether you will be their choice ... That is up to them. Whether you go ... That is up to you."

She was Witch's choice. Because of a web of dreams and visions. How could she not try?

"In that case, Lady," Cassidy said, "I'll see you in seven days."

SEVEN

Kaleer

⋆Theran? Theran! Wait! These are good smells!⋆

Theran hunched his shoulders and walked faster.

When he was ten years old, he'd spent a week sulking and pining because Talon wouldn't let him have a dog. Why in the name of Hell had he ever wanted one of the damn things?

⋆Theran!⋆

And how was he supposed to shake free of this one? Maybe, once he was in the village, she'd get distracted by another of those damn smells and he could slip away, and she'd lose the trail, the scent, whatever. Maybe she'd latch on to some other unsuspecting man.

Of course, there would be the little problem of going back to the Hall without her, but she'd find her way home, wouldn't she? Eventually?

⋆Theran!⋆

When *he* got home, he was going to apologize to Talon for being such a whiny little prick about not having a pet. Sure, that was seventeen years ago and something Talon had shrugged off, but the man had raised him and now with the wisdom of maturity—and less than an hour's worth of actual experience—he knew Talon's decision had been the correct one.

⋆Theran!⋆

He caught sight of the village of Halaway and forgot about the dog.

The road was the main street of a small, prosperous-looking village. Confident that he would go undetected at the depth of his Green Jewel, he sent out psychic tendrils to get a feel for the place. For a moment, he thought he detected a ripple of power under the strength of the Green, but it was gone before he could be certain.

The village smelled clean. There was no underlying psychic odor of fear that was typical in Dena Nehele's villages. These people were practically on the doorstep of SaDiablo Hall, but they weren't afraid of the power that lived there.

He wanted this for his own people, he thought as he strolled down the sidewalk, glancing into shop windows. He wanted this for the town of Grayhaven. He watched how the people moved, noticed the lack of wariness and tension when men and women passed one another on the sidewalks.

Then a door opened a couple of shops up. The woman who was leaving said, "Yes, I'll watch for that" to someone in the shop and didn't notice him until she stepped right in front of him.

He didn't particularly like the gold eyes that were typical of the long-lived races, but she would have been an attractive woman if she hadn't cropped her black hair so damn short. What was it about the women here that they tried to look unappealing? Sure, men served and women ruled the bed, but at least back home the women knew that arousing a man was the first step to their own pleasure.

"Prince," she said, sounding cautious—as she should when addressing a male of his caste, especially one who wore a dark Jewel.

He frowned at her, not bothering to hide his disapproval of her appearance.

Then he caught a whiff of her psychic scent and thought, *Oh, shit,* just before he was surrounded by hard-eyed, grim-faced men who seemed to come out of nowhere—including a Red-Jeweled Warlord who was holding a sledgehammer and was big enough to be a wall without any help.

"Gentlemen," the Queen said, tapping the Red-Jeweled wall on the shoulder.

No clean psychic scent in the village now. These men were pissed off, insulted that he'd *frowned* at their Queen.

"Gentlemen."

They didn't yield, didn't obey—and Theran recognized a fight he couldn't win.

Then . . .

Theran! Annoyance rang through a broad psychic thread, followed by a muttered, *Stubborn sheep.*

A vein of amusement suddenly flowed through the anger surrounding him. The circle shifted—and he didn't need to see the Queen peer around the large Warlord and smile to know that the dog was standing next to him.

"Lady Vae," the Queen said.

Lady Sylvia, Vae replied. *He is Theran. He is staying with Daemon and Jaenelle. I am taking him for walkies so he can see the village. We will get some food and he will sit and watch humans so he will learn how to behave.*

Sylvia's gold eyes sparkled. "Are you a stubborn sheep, Prince Theran?"

Sensing the amount of temper still focused on him, he decided not to answer, since he didn't think he could keep his voice sufficiently civil.

I am helping to train him, Vae said. *I am allowed to bite. But not hard. Not the first time.*

Hell's fire.

"I see." Sylvia ducked behind the Warlord. That didn't muffle the snorts and giggles.

He felt the anger break around him, and he had a feeling that whatever was coming was a harder punishment than a beating would have been.

"Well," Sylvia said, struggling to maintain some dignity as she stepped clear of the large Warlord. "We shouldn't delay your training any longer. Prince Theran, just tell any of the dining houses to put your meal on the Hall's tab."

Did he look like he didn't have marks to spare?

"It's customary," Sylvia added, showing more understanding than he liked.

The men opened up a space for him but not in a way that would allow him to get within reach of Lady Sylvia.

Accepting the dismissal and wanting to get away from the village, he started to turn back toward the Hall, then swore loudly when he got nipped.

This way, Theran. This way!

Not daring to do anything else, he let himself be herded down the main street with the Sceltie trotting a step behind him, ready to nip at his heels.

Mother Night, it was humiliating—and him a Warlord Prince!

⋆Sheep brains,⋆ Vae said, finally trotting alongside him.

"What?"

⋆You made those males angry. You act like you have sheep brains. Foolish.⋆

"I didn't do anything!" He kept his voice low, but he'd be damned if he'd swallow being scolded by a *dog*.

⋆You did. You made them angry. They do not fight for no reason.⋆

They didn't have a reason. Not really. Sure, he'd expressed an opinion of sorts, and he wouldn't have if he'd caught Sylvia's psychic scent first. But, Hell's fire, she didn't *look* like a Queen with that hair and the shirt and trousers and ...

He was making excuses for himself. He *hadn't* been careful, and if Vae hadn't amused them all, he wouldn't be strolling through the village. He'd be wounded—or dead.

He hadn't survived in Dena Nehele by being careless. He couldn't afford to set aside all the things Talon had taught him just because he didn't have a clear sense of the battlefield. And he couldn't afford to forget that the power that had devastated Terreille had come from Kaeleer.

So he walked and he watched. Children tensed at the sight of a stranger, then relaxed again when they saw Vae. Clearly the dog was a signal he didn't understand. He didn't approach, didn't talk to them, but he saw a pattern when he passed a group of children—the boys stepped forward, creating a shield between him and the girls.

"The men who were angry," Theran said. "Were they all members of the Queen's court?"

⋆They live in the village,⋆ Vae replied. ⋆They serve.⋆

"But were they court?"

⋆No, I do not think any of them were court.⋆

"Then why did they do that?"

Vae stopped walking and looked at him. ⋆It is their right to defend.⋆ She turned her head and sniffed the air. ⋆There is food.⋆

I guess one of us wants to eat.

Whatever the usual rule about animals being inside a dining house, the young witch who greeted them took one look at Vae, tipped her head as if in private conversation, then settled them at a table next to the windows.

He had a bowl of soup. Vae had a small plate of raw stew meat.

He ate slowly, watching, thinking.

The males considered it their *right* to defend, not their duty. So different from what he came from, what he knew.

Could his people do it? Could the males who would have to form the First Circle be able to make the transition from duty to desire?

He had no answers, so he watched and he thought—and he wondered.

Daemon buttoned the last button of his white silk shirt as Saetan walked into the bedroom.

"How do you feel?" Saetan asked.

"Better. Embarrassed." Daemon tucked the shirt into his trousers and gave more thought to the question. "Hungry." He'd slept for a few hours and didn't feel as shaky as he'd felt early that morning. But he still had to face that room, and that was better done on an empty stomach.

"Then I'll join you before I retire for the afternoon." Saetan opened the door.

Slipping into his black jacket, Daemon stepped into the corridor and stared at the door to the Consort's bedroom.

Saetan crossed the corridor, opened the door, and stepped into the room. Daemon hesitated, almost hoping for a command to stay out. When it didn't come, he followed his father into the room and looked toward the left wall that held the doors leading to the bathroom and closet.

It smelled clean, like it did when Helene gave the room its seasonal scrubbing. Almost too clean, he thought as he noticed the lack of psychic scent. A hint of his presence was still there under the scents of soap and polish, but less than usual. Less than a cleaning would account for.

"Well?" Saetan asked quietly.

Better this way. That lack of presence was better.

The room was safe again. Chaste again. And he wouldn't . . .

He looked at the bed.

Mine!

"Daemon, back away from whatever you're thinking. *Daemon.*"

The whiplash command and the power behind it was barely enough, but he leashed the desire—and felt disgust rising in its place.

He forced himself to say the words, to admit what he wanted to deny with all his heart. "The Sadist was in that bed with her last night."

"Yes, he was," Saetan said quietly. "And I imagine he enjoyed being there."

He studied his father, not sure how to interpret the words.

Saetan sighed and rubbed two fingers across his forehead as if trying to ease an ache. "It's unfortunate that this happened last night when you were churned up with memories of Terreille, but, Daemon, it would have happened. Because of who you are. Because of who Jaenelle is. This would have happened."

"No."

"Yes. You've twisted a part of yourself into a powerful weapon, honed it to the point people have given it a different name. *You've* given it a different name. But it's part of your nature, Daemon. It's part of your caste. It's in every one of us."

"What is?"

"There's no name for it. It's not like the rut, which is a kind of physical insanity that can be recognized by anyone who knows what to look for. This is emotional—and it's darker, more dangerous when it happens. It's the thrill of being feared while you seduce your lover to the point where she doesn't want to refuse. And at the same time it's the comfort of being able to reveal that side of your nature to a lover and know you're still trusted." Saetan lowered his hand and stared at the bed. "It's a potential for violence that is transformed into a kind of ruthless gentleness."

"If this is part of our caste, why isn't it recognized like the rut?" Daemon asked. *And why have I never heard about it?*

"Because it's something that shifts inside you for an hour, for a night—or sometimes for only as long as it takes you to feel that moment of possession, that moment when you look at a woman and think, *Mine,* and know it's true.

"The potential to possess. The *desire* to possess. Warlord Princes are dominating, territorial, and possessive. Most of the time those traits are seen in relation to other males, to possible rivals." Saetan looked him in the eyes. "But sometimes—especially for a Warlord Prince who is so strong, who stands so deep in the abyss—you look at the woman who pulls at you and the need to possess is overwhelming."

Saetan rubbed his hands together, then looked at the Black-Jeweled ring on his right hand. "We're guests most of the time and on our best behavior because of that. We come to our lover's bed, and even if we share that bed ninety-nine nights out of a hundred, it's still *her* bed. Our beds are for sleep, for rest, for solitude. But the rare times when we take a woman into our bed, it's different. It feels different. No matter how gentle you are, how careful, it isn't lovemaking. It's not even sex. It's possession. Her body belongs to you for that night, and you play with it. You bring her to a climax—or you deny her that completion. For a little while."

He was hearing a description of the Sadist in his mildest form. He was hearing a description of what he'd done last night. And he was hearing something else.

"You've felt that way," he said, looking at his father and seeing a man capable of playing those kinds of games. Seeing a man who *had* played those games. But not out of cruelty or rage. Saetan had played those games out of desire.

"I never looked at Hekatah and thought, *Mine,* which should have told me the truth about her feelings and my own."

Daemon hesitated, but curiosity pushed aside caution. "Sylvia?"

Saetan closed his eyes. "Yes, Sylvia. There were a few times while we were lovers when she came to my bed and . . ." He swallowed hard.

A feeling in the room. They both had to step away from it, shake it off. For now. But he would have to circle around the subject with Jaenelle and find out if she'd found the Sadist thrilling or frightening. If she'd found him thrilling . . .

Step back, fool, before you become a danger to everyone around you.

Since he could see Saetan trying to shake off the feeling as well, he cast around for something else to talk about.

"Where's Theran?"

A flash of amusement from Saetan. "I sent him down to the village. With Vae."

"Vae?" Daemon stared at his father. "You sent him to Halaway with *Vae*?"

"Yes."

"The young Sceltie who's such a managing little bitch that Khary used up every favor owed him in order to get her out of his own village for a month?"

"That's the one."

"You sent *her* with a man who doesn't know anything about Scelties or kindred?"

"Yes, I did."

Daemon swallowed the sudden tickle in his throat. "That was mean."

Saetan smiled. "I know."

As he thought about Theran trying to cope with any Sceltie, let alone Vae, Daemon staggered back a couple of steps, hit the wall—and filled the room with laughter.

By the time dinner was half-over, Theran missed being around Vae. At least with the nippy little bitch, he had a clear idea of where he stood. Sitting across from Jaenelle Angelline, with her husband and her father the only other people sitting at the table, he felt like he was walking on a knife's edge. Say too much or sound too flattering and he would be stepping on Sadi's territorial toes. Say too little and he would be condemned by the father for his lack of courtesy.

Either way, it wasn't making dinner sit easy. And Lady Angelline's refusal to say anything about her meeting wasn't helping his digestion. Neither was the way she looked at him, as if she knew something about him that amused her.

When the fruit and cheese arrived at the end of the meal, along with squares of thick chocolate and coffee, Saetan said, "All right, witch-child. Share the joke. What is it about Prince Theran that you find so funny?"

"Prince Theran has some traditional tastes," Jaenelle said with a sweetness that made Theran's palms sweat. "Apparently he has the same resistance toward women wearing short hair and trousers that you do."

Hell's fire, Mother Night, and may the Darkness be merciful.

Saetan gave Jaenelle a pointed look. "I don't recall making any comment about your hair."

Jaenelle pursed her lips. "That's true. You've never been *that* rigid in your preferences."

Two pairs of gold eyes fixed on Theran, and he was really hoping there was a house rule that guests were not executed at the dinner table.

"But like you," Jaenelle continued, "Theran will have to develop some flexibility and learn how to compromise."

"Is that what I did?" Saetan asked.

"Yes, Papa, that's what you did."

"I'm delighted to hear it."

She laughed, and Theran watched in a kind of wonder as the sound completely relaxed two violent and powerful men.

Then those sapphire eyes looked into his. "There is a Queen who may be willing to come to Dena Nehele and show your people how a Territory is ruled when the Old Ways are followed. If she decides to accept the offer, she will be at the Keep seven days from now. The terms Prince Sadi has set for her being in Terreille are acceptable to her. You need to talk to your people to see if the terms are acceptable to them. If they are, you'll meet us at the Keep, and she will return with you to Dena Nehele."

Theran's heart sank. "There's only one who might be willing? We're talking about a whole Territory, not some village."

"I'm sure there are others, and you're free to seek them if you choose. But you came here and asked for our help. This is our answer."

Your answer, Theran thought, knowing it was the only answer.

"I'd like to get back to Dena Nehele as soon as possible," he said. "There will be much to discuss before we make a decision."

"The Coach can take you back to the Keep this evening," Saetan said.

Theran nodded and said nothing more as the last course of the meal dragged on. As soon as he could, he left the table, offering the feeble excuse of needing to pack.

One choice. One chance. Would this Queen have enough dazzle to convince bitter men to serve?

One way or another, he'd have his answer in seven days.

"If you'll excuse me, I want to check the rest of the messages Beale has waiting for me," Jaenelle said. "I never got past Sylvia's note when I returned from Dharo."

"Probably because you were laughing so hard," Daemon said.

"True," she said, brushing a hand over his shoulder. "No, don't get up. You two enjoy your wine."

As soon as she walked out of the room, Daemon dismissed the footman who had served them at dinner.

For a few minutes, the two men simply drank wine—he finishing up the bottle of red, while Saetan drank yarbarah, the blood wine.

"You didn't tell me Sylvia cut her hair," Saetan said quietly.

"I wasn't sure you wanted to know about her personal life," Daemon replied.

"I don't. Can't. But . . . Is it that unattractive?"

"Not at all. It's sassy. It suits her."

"Then Grayhaven's an ass."

Daemon shrugged. "What he wants for his people shouldn't be dismissed. And it took balls to come here."

"Yes, it did." Saetan swirled the yarbarah in the raven-glass goblet. "He doesn't fit. His Jewels are dark enough and his personality is strong enough, but he doesn't fit in with us."

"He looks into Jaenelle's eyes and doesn't see who she is," Daemon said.

Saetan nodded. "Yes. That was always the test when it came to accepting someone into the Dark Court, even for an apprenticeship. If the person couldn't look into her eyes and *know*, he would rub the entire First Circle the wrong way and their tempers would start sharpening for an attack."

"Fortunately, Theran won't have to deal often with anyone who served in the Dark Court."

"Except his new Queen," Saetan said.

Daemon blew out a breath. "Except the new Queen."

"You and Jaenelle. Will you be all right this evening?"

"We'll be all right."

"Will *you* be all right?"

He smiled. "Yes, Father, I'll be all right."

"In that case, I'll return to the Keep and see Theran back to Terreille."

They found Jaenelle—and Vae—waiting for them in the great hall. Theran joined them a minute later.

"Thank you for your help and your hospitality," Theran said.

The words were properly spoken, but Daemon had the impression that Theran would have said anything if it got him out of the Hall.

"Witch-child," Saetan said, kissing Jaenelle's cheek.

Daemon felt more than saw a flash of understanding between them before Saetan shifted to him and put a hand against his face.

A different kind of understanding, an acknowledgment that the darkest feelings that lived inside him were not unique. He'd done something with those feelings no other male had done, but he knew now that he could temper those feelings when he chose to, could soften them to be an enticement rather than a weapon.

Massage, not sex tonight, Saetan said.

Right.

A pat on the shoulder and his father walked out the door with Grayhaven.

Bye, Theran! Vae said, bouncing in some kind of tail-wagging happy dance. *Bye!*

As soon as Beale closed the door, Vae looked at both of them. *He is male and foolish. He needs me. When he comes for the Queen, I will go live with him.*

She trotted out of the great hall, leaving him and Jaenelle staring at the door.

"We could make it part of the bargain," Daemon said.

"How so?" Jaenelle asked.

"If he wants the Queen, he has to take the Sceltie."

"Oh, Hell's fire."

It didn't occur to him until much later, when he was cuddled up with Jaenelle in her bed, that Beale hadn't thought there was anything odd about the Warlord Prince of Dhemlan and the former Queen of Ebon Askavi sitting on the floor of the great hall laughing like fools.

EIGHT

Theran stared at the ninety-nine Warlord Princes and wished one of them would sneeze, cough, fart—anything to break the stone-hard silence.

"That's it," he said. "That's the bargain."

"One choice," Ranon, the Shalador Warlord Prince, said. "And if she turns out to be a bad choice, she'll destroy what's left of us."

I know. "I don't believe Daemon Sadi would recommend a Queen who would be a danger to us."

"Sadi *hated* Terreille," Ranon said. "He might see this as an opportunity to crush a Territory completely."

"Sadi hated everything to do with Dorothea SaDiablo and what she was doing to the Realm," Theran said, raising his voice to be heard above the mutters.

"That may be true," Archerr said. "But you said it was his *wife* who went and talked to this Queen."

And you've said damn little about the wife, Talon said on a psychic thread aimed directly at him.

Nothing much to say, Theran replied.

Talon shifted in his chair. The mutters faded as the other Warlord Princes focused their attention on him.

"Here's the thing," Talon said. "Jared trusted Daemon Sadi. So did Blaed. They knew him. He gave them some training when they were slaves, and helped them survive. Yeah, that was a few centuries ago, and maybe he's changed—maybe he jumps now when his wife snaps her fingers. But the terms he set tell me he gave some thought to this request. They won't be all that easy for us to meet, and these 'inspections' don't sit well with me, I can tell you that. Even so, I think we have to take this chance."

"Forgive me, Prince Talon," Ranon said, his tone respectful, "but you're demon-dead. You have less to lose than the rest of us."

"I have less to lose physically," Talon agreed. "That doesn't mean I don't have anything to lose. But I'll offer to serve in this Queen's court—and that's an offer I didn't make to Grizelle or Lia when they ruled. I served them both in my own way, but I never chained myself to a contract."

Feet shuffled. Bodies shifted in chairs. They all understood how hard it would be for a man who had been rogue for so many years to hand over his life to a Queen.

"How do we decide who serves in the First Circle?" Ranon finally asked. "Any of us who leaves our piece of Dena Nehele for a year will leave those Blood open to landen attacks."

"I think we should all offer," Theran said. He'd thought about this on the way back to Grayhaven. "Let her choose whatever twelve of us appeal to her. I'm required to offer myself as one of the Queen's triangle. The rest of you can offer yourselves according to your skills."

"What about the rest of the Blood?" Archerr asked. "You're going to need other females in the court."

We're going to need a lot more than that, Theran thought. "A court is made by twelve males and a Queen. Everything else builds from that. Let's establish the First Circle and give the Queen a couple of days to settle in and get to know those males. Then we'll set up some audiences to let anyone else present themselves to her."

Ranon stood up. "In that case, I'm heading back to the Shalador reserves to inform the elders."

"Ranon . . . ," Theran began.

Ranon smiled bitterly. "I know we've never been welcome in a court, but we'll be ruled by this Queen too, Theran, so it's only polite to offer our Blood for the Lady's pleasure."

Ranon walked out. A few seconds later, the other Warlord Princes followed, leaving Talon and Theran alone.

Theran straddled a chair and braced his arms on the back. "Maybe it was a mistake to invite Ranon to be part of this. He's too bitter, too angry, although he hides that fairly well."

"I'll remind you that if you weren't who you are, you'd be living in the reserves with him," Talon said. "Half your bloodline came from the Shalador people. You've got the green eyes."

"Plenty of people in Dena Nehele have green eyes."

"Not that shade. You only find that shade of green in the reserves, and it's rare even there. You have Shalador eyes, Theran. Jared's eyes. He came from that race, and Dorothea SaDiablo went beyond the initial fighting there and destroyed that Territory and that race because Jared helped Lia. The Shalador people have had a harder time surviving than the rest of us, and you know it."

He did know it. That didn't erase his worry that the Blood living in the reserves would try to splinter Dena Nehele even more.

"I won't be going back to the rogue camps in the mountains," Theran said. "I'll be living here, at Grayhaven."

"I know that."

"If you're accepted in the court, you'll be here too."

"Yes. It's not likely she'll accept someone who's demon-dead, but if she does, I won't be going back to the mountains either." Talon sighed. "You have to tell Gray. You have to let him make his own choice."

"What choice? He can't survive on his own."

"There are plenty of rogues who will stay up in the mountains, not feeling easy enough to come down. They'll look after him."

"That's not the same as family."

"No, it's not," Talon said gently. "But he may not be able to do this. Most likely, he *can't* do this."

Theran stood up abruptly, no longer able to stay still. "Let's find out."

They were both twenty-seven years old. They both had dark hair and green eyes, although the shade of green came from different bloodlines, and one of them had fairer skin than the other. They were similar enough in body and face that they could easily be mistaken for each other at first glance.

But one of them had become a man only in terms of physical maturity and had retreated, mentally and emotionally, to being a docile boy, despite also being a Warlord Prince who wore Purple Dusk Jewels.

Jared Blaed Grayhaven. The young Warlord Prince who was supposed to be Theran's blade and shield in the same way that Blaed had backed Jared.

They were cousins through their mothers. Gray, as they called him, had no link to the Grayhaven bloodline, despite being given that family name, but he could trace his line back to Blaed and Thera, the Black Widow who had been Lia's closest friend.

Had their names been a deliberate attempt at deception or a way to honor the past? Theran had wondered about that a lot after what happened twelve years ago.

Theran's shield. Gray had been that. They had been making a rare visit to a village near the mountains and had separated to take care of their own business before returning to the camp they were currently calling home.

The Province Queen's guards, making a surprise inspection of the village, had spotted Gray and taken him to the Territory Queen, who had kept him to "serve" in her court. The guards had grabbed him and run, not wanting to tangle with the rogues who frequented the village when they had captured such a prize—and not realizing there had been a second boy.

They'd thought they had captured the Grayhaven bloodline, and Gray never told them anything different, never revealed that he wasn't the descendant of the Shalador Warlord who had been Lia's husband.

They worked him—and they tortured him—for two years before Talon was able to rescue him and get him back to the mountains.

Gray was fifteen when he was taken.

They didn't break his Jewels or castrate him—two common methods of diminishing a male who might be a threat. But they broke him in other ways, and now, as he sat across from Theran, his green eyes so full of fear, Theran wondered if taking Gray back to Grayhaven would be the ultimate act of betrayal.

"You're all right?" Gray asked. "You're not hurt?"

Didn't matter if Theran was returning from a fight or slipping into a village to spend a couple of needed hours with a woman; the questions were always the same because, for Gray, the last time he'd left the mountains, he'd lost everything he was.

"I'm fine, Gray. I'm fine," Theran said, leaning over to give his cousin's hand a friendly squeeze.

"But something bad has happened."

Too perceptive.

"Not bad, no." How to say this to cause the least harm? "We're getting a Queen, Gray. Do you remember me talking with Talon about that?"

"A Queen?" All the color drained out of Gray's face.

"From Kaeleer, the Shadow Realm. She's going to rule Dena Nehele."

"She's coming *here*?"

"Not to the mountains, no. She's going to be living at Grayhaven." Theran took a deep breath and let it out slowly. "And I'm going to be living there with her."

"You *can't*!" Gray leaped up, giving Talon a desperate look. "He can't! If she's at Grayhaven and knows who . . . who he . . ."

The keening started as Gray sank to his knees. That horrible keening of a boy in terrible pain.

"Gray." Dropping to his knees, Theran wrapped his arms around his cousin. "Gray, I have to do this. For all of us."

"She'll hurt you, she'll hurt you. I'm Grayhaven. *I'm Grayhaven!*"

The last words were said in a rising scream that echoed the pain remembered.

Theran looked at Talon, whose face was grim and sad. The old Warlord Prince had searched, and searched hard, to find the boy. But Talon didn't find Gray soon enough.

Talon went down on one knee and put a hand on Gray's shoulder. "You don't have to go down there. You can stay up here in the mountains. You know how to fend for yourself. I taught you that. And there will be others staying up here. You don't have to go back to Grayhaven."

"He can't go," Gray whispered as he sagged against Theran. "Theran can't go."

"He has to," Talon said. "That's part of the bargain."

Gray pulled away from both of them and walked over to a window.

What was he seeing? Theran wondered. The past? The present? Was he here with them in this cabin in the mountains or locked in some room in Grayhaven, waiting for the next bit of cruelty?

"I like growing things," Gray said quietly, more to himself than to them. "The land was good, parched of what it needed, but still good. I could work outside."

"Gray . . ."

"I wouldn't have to live inside, would I?"

Shock kept Theran silent for a moment. He hadn't expected Gray to consider leaving the mountains. Not really.

"No, you wouldn't have to live inside," Theran said. "There's an old stone gardening shed." He looked at Talon.

"Probably filled with broken tools and such," Talon said, "but someone could live rough out there."

"I could be a gardener," Gray said. "I could take care of the land. But I couldn't serve *her*."

"No, you wouldn't have to serve her," Theran said. But if the new Queen showed any inclination toward playing with a damaged male, he'd have to explain a few things to the Lady.

"Then I'll go."

"Gray . . ."

"I'll go." Gray turned and looked at him—and Theran had never seen anything as bleak as the look in his cousin's eyes. "I'm Theran's blade."

Oh, Gray.

Talon cleared his throat. "It's settled, then. Tomorrow we'll pack up and start getting Grayhaven ready for the new Queen."

Gray bolted out of the cabin.

Theran got to his feet, feeling more exhausted than if he'd been in a fight.

"Do you think he'll survive going back there?" he asked.

"I don't know, Theran," Talon replied. "I just don't know."

NINE

Kaeleer

Cassidy packed the last book and closed the lid of the small trunk. Just some favorites, things she read when she wanted the comfort of a familiar story.

She was as ready as she could be. Which wasn't saying much, since there was precious little information about Dena Nehele. What she did know was that Dharo was on the eastern side of a mountain range and Dena Nehele was on the western side of a mountain range. Dena Nehele had a variety of seasons, so she'd packed all her clothes, figuring most would be useful.

As for the rest . . .

"Second thoughts?"

Twisting around, Cassidy looked at her mother, who was standing in the doorway. "I'm on my fourth or fifth set of thoughts about doing this, but I haven't changed my mind."

"Didn't think you would." Devra came into the bedroom and sat on the floor beside her daughter. "I've got something for you. I know it's a bit more to carry, but you won't be straining to carry all of it yourself, so . . ." She called in an open-topped wooden box filled with glass jars. "A bit of home to take with you."

Cassidy lifted one jar and read the neat label. Then picked up another. "Mother, these are your seeds for the garden."

"I divided what I had between us," Devra said. "You'll need to be careful. Some of these might not be healthy to give to a different land. But most, I think, will be similar enough to what is there. So you can turn over a small patch of ground, plant a few seeds—and know we're with you in heart."

"Mother." Cassidy blinked back tears as she ran her fingers over the tops of the jars. "Thank you."

Devra brushed a hand lightly over Cassidy's hair. "You're still set on going after the midday meal?"

Cassidy nodded. "I'd like some time to settle before I meet the Warlord Prince from Dena Nehele. Prince Sadi and Lady Angelline arranged for us all to have dinner at the Keep so there would be an opportunity to talk with him a bit before making a final decision." A formality, really. Unless he was some kind of fearsome male, she would give his people a year of her life. Besides, she'd spent four months in the Dark Court and had slammed into Lucivar Yaslana on occasion, and there was *no* male more fearsome than Yaslana when he was in a mood.

Except Prince Sadi. Or so she'd heard.

"Is Poppi coming home to see me off?" Cassidy asked.

"Your father is in the sitting room, brooding. Has been for the past hour."

"He didn't have to leave his work so early."

"He hit his thumb with a hammer twice because he was busy brooding." Devra shook her head. "After that, old Lord Wittier tottered your father over to the Healer's to make sure nothing was broken, and refused to let him come back to finish the work until you were off."

She could picture old Lord Wittier clinging to Burle's arm to keep his balance while insisting that *he* was taking Burle to the Healer—and telling everyone *why* Burle needed a Healer.

Smacked himself with a hammer, the fool. Too busy thinking about his girl to tell the difference between a nail and a thumbnail. Gotta take him to the Healer's, make sure he didn't mash any bones. Who would have thought Burle would smack himself with a hammer?

"Oh, dear," she said, wishing she'd been in a shop where she could have watched that procession without being seen.

"Don't tease your father, Cassidy. He's already had a difficult day."

Taking the wooden box from her mother, Cassidy set

it next to the trunk of books. "Shall we go downstairs? There's nothing more to do."

"If you go down now, he'll have an extra hour to fuss about you leaving and to take you through the checklist he made in order to check the checklist he'd previously made."

Cassidy smiled. "I know. But he'll feel better for it, don't you think?"

Ebon Askavi

Despite the unmistakable psychic scent that identified his caste, the thing that had always amazed Cassidy was how a man as powerful as the High Lord of Hell could *feel* like a Steward—like a man who didn't find the tedium of paperwork tedious, like a benign clerk who simply wanted to be helpful. Like a strict and yet indulgent honorary uncle to the most powerful Queens and Warlord Princes in Kaeleer.

Kind. Courteous. Indulgent.

Unless you made him angry. Then there would be the lightning-fast change from benign clerk into predator. She'd never been the cause of that change in the few months she'd served in the Dark Court, but she'd seen it, felt the cold punch of temper that had flashed through the Hall, warning everyone that the High Lord was not pleased.

Right now she wasn't sure if his mood was benign clerk or honorary uncle, but after the past few days with her father, Cassidy recognized the look of a man who had his own checklist and wasn't about to let her walk away until they'd gone over every single item.

"Your trunks are all packed?" Saetan asked.

"Yes, and they've already been taken to the Keep in Terreille and stored in the Coach," Cassidy replied.

"You've brought some personal things with you? Books? Music?"

"Yes. They're also in the Coach."

"Winter clothes?"

"Yes," Cassidy huffed. "And I've brought a stack of clean handkerchiefs."

He stared at her, one eyebrow rising as his mouth curved in that dry, knowing smile.

She winced. *I don't believe I said that to the High Lord.*

"So," Saetan said, "was that on your mother's list or your father's list?"

"Both, actually."

"And which one tucked a few marks about two-thirds of the way down in the stack so you would find the gift about the time you might be feeling homesick?"

"No one ..." She remembered her father blushing and mumbling something when she'd walked into her room and found him poking around near her trunks. "How did you know?"

Saetan's smile warmed. "I'm a father." He leaned against a big stuffed chair and crossed his arms. "Do you want some advice?"

Since that wasn't actually a question, she nodded obediently.

"According to the conditions Prince Sadi set to have you go to Dena Nehele, you will send him a report once a week. That report is from the Queen of Dena Nehele to the Warlord Prince of Dhemlan and can be nothing more than information about your court and your official meetings for that week. That will tell him how the Queen is doing, but not how *you* are. He can accept that because you don't know him beyond a passing acquaintance. Therefore, you should also write a brief note to Jaenelle to let her know how you're doing. That's personal and equally important. Don't shrug it off. If you miss a report, there are Warlord Princes in Kaeleer who are already committed to finding out why, and they will descend on Dena Nehele ready to step onto a killing field. Is that clear?"

"Yes, sir." Cassidy hesitated. "Do you really think this will be that dangerous?"

"If I thought you'd be in danger, you wouldn't be going," Saetan replied softly. Then he shifted a little and continued in his usual voice. "You should also send a note to your mother when you send the report. We'll see that it reaches her. That should be a daughter-to-mother note. Tell her about your life. Between those reports and notes, send a note to your father. He won't be concerned about the court; he wants to know about you."

"Why don't I send them both at the same time?" Cassidy asked. "Then the messenger only has to make one trip to the Keep."

"It will be good exercise for the messenger," Saetan said dryly. "The point is to reassure. Staggering the notes will make both your parents feel better since they'll hear from you twice as often. And at least once a month, write a letter to your brother."

"Clayton?"

"Yes, Clayton. It doesn't matter if you've never sent him a letter before. It doesn't matter if he's always gotten news about you from your parents. You won't be in Dharo anymore, Cassidy. Getting a letter from you that's just for him will matter."

"I suppose I should send a note to cousin Aaron too."

"Not required, but definitely a good idea. This might help." Saetan called in a lap desk, which floated on air.

"Oh." Cassidy pulled it closer. The sides and back were decorated with carved flowers. The hinged top was smooth and silky. When she opened the lid, she discovered two sizes of stationery, both decorated with a *C* that had been made into a formal crest.

"There are drawers on the sides," Saetan said.

One drawer contained pens and ink. The other contained sticks of wax and three seals. One was a flower, one was the crest of her initial, and the other . . .

"Geoffrey and I did a little digging in the library and found the Grayhaven crest that had been used during the time when the Gray Ladies ruled. We had the seal made for you."

"But I'm not a Grayhaven," Cassidy protested.

"I was told it would be appropriate for you to use that crest for your formal correspondence."

Who told you? She didn't have to ask. There was only one person Saetan would obey without question. She didn't know why Jaenelle thought it was appropriate for her to use that particular crest, but she wouldn't argue.

"Thank you."

"A couple more things." He pointed to four large crates. "Two of those contain primers in basic Protocol. The other two crates contain the more advanced study of Protocol."

"Won't they be insulted if I bring those?"

"They'll be needed. Also, Prince Sadi has set aside some funds as a Queen's gift." He held up a hand, silencing her protest before it could form. "There are things that you will need that you may not be able to find in Terreille. Recognizing that you may hesitate to ask for those things from a people who will have little to spare, Daemon is willing to bear the cost."

"How much?" Cassidy asked. "It would help to know so that I'm not asking for anything unreasonable."

"If he feels you're overspending, I'm sure Daemon will let you know," Saetan replied mildly. "You don't have an easy task, Cassidy. You'll be the only one who knows the Old Ways and the Protocol that goes along with those ways. You'll be trying to help a people remember who they were. Accept the help we can give you."

She felt the blood draining out of her head. "I'll be the only one who knows Protocol?"

"Well." Saetan looked a little guilty. "You and Vae."

She frowned, puzzled. "Who is Vae?"

Hi, Theran! Hi!

Vae bounced in front of him, doing her happy dance.

I have my special brushes, so you can brush me properly. And the clippers for my nails. Do you have Healers for kindred? In Scelt we have Healers for kindred. They heal other animals too, but they trained to take care of us. Maybe one of them will have to come and teach your Healer how to properly clip nails.

He'd fought. He'd proved his worth as a leader. He wore a Green Jewel. He was the dominant living male in Dena Nehele.

And every time he was around these people, he seemed to stand there with his mouth hanging open while they ran right over him.

I will tell Jaenelle you are here, Vae said. *She and the new Queen are doing fussing things. You cannot eat until they are done doing the fussing things.*

He waited until he was sure the Sceltie was out of the room and out of hearing. Then he turned to Daemon and said, "No. The dog is not coming with us."

"Yes, she is," Daemon said in a voice that was pleasant in a way that liquefied the bones in Theran's legs—and not in a good way. "She knows Craft, which she will not hesitate to tell you, and she knows Protocol, which she will not hesitate to tell you. And she's decided to go with you."

"What will it take to keep her here?" Theran asked.

"A lot more than you can afford. Accept it, Prince. You're taking the Sceltie. Or you're leaving without a Queen."

"That's blackmail!"

"Oooooh, that's a harsh word." Daemon smiled. "But I won't quibble about it."

"I suppose you want a report on *her* too," Theran said, not bothering to hide the bitterness he and the other Warlord Princes felt about these reports. They were too close a reminder of the "reports" that had been sent to Dorothea SaDiablo—and the people who had disappeared one night after those reports were sent.

"No, that isn't required," Daemon said, "but Vae has worked out how you'll do it."

"How I'll—"

"You'll need to remember the basin of warm water so that you can clean the ink off her paw after she's told you what to write and puts her mark on the bottom of the page."

"After she—" He gave up trying to form words and just sputtered. He'd avoided capture, avoided being leashed, avoided every damn snare that had been set for him, only to find himself chained *to a dog*.

"Which side of the triangle are you taking?" Daemon asked.

As a change of topic, it wasn't any better. He felt some bitterness about that too. "First Escort." No one else had been willing to do it. A few of the Warlord Princes had offered to fill the position of Master of the Guard, but they still hadn't found anyone willing to be the Steward either. He'd considered it, but he would have hated being stuck behind a desk, and as Talon had pointed out, since he was being held personally responsible for this new Queen's well-being, First Escort was really the only choice.

Then Jaenelle Angelline walked into the room, followed by another woman, and Theran's first thought was, *Thank the Darkness I don't have to bed her.*

His second thought was he was mistaken—this large-boned, gawky female with the awful red hair and spots on her face must be a companion or servant for Lady Angelline. If it weren't for the Rose Jewel she was wearing and the fact that she was here, he would have thought she was a hefty farm girl, all right for a bit of relief—as long as the barn was dark enough—but no one he would consider otherwise.

Mother Night!

Her psychic scent, masked by the power all around him since the High Lord walked into the room behind the women, hit him a moment later.

Queen.

No!

"Prince Theran Grayhaven," Jaenelle said, "this is Lady Cassidy, the Queen who has consented to rule Dena Nehele. Cassidy, this is Theran Grayhaven"—she glanced at Daemon and her voice took on a strange, sharp edge—"who has offered to stand as First Escort, if he is acceptable to you."

"Prince Grayhaven honors me."

She sounded sincere enough, but he couldn't read any emotion on that plain face.

"Shall we go in to dinner?" Saetan asked, stepping to one side.

Lady Cassidy hurried out of the room with Jaenelle right behind her. When the High Lord walked out of the room, the door began to close.

Theran took a step forward, then pulled up short when Sadi's hand wrapped around his arm, the long nails pricking him through shirt and jacket.

"For a man who has lived in such a dangerous Territory, it's odd that you've never learned to hide what you think," Daemon said too softly.

"I didn't say anything improper," Theran snapped.

"You didn't have to. You've made your opinion very clear, Grayhaven. So. Are you still going to join us for dinner, or should I make your excuses for you?"

"What are you talking about?" Theran pulled away, unnerved by the chilling contempt he saw in Daemon's eyes.

"You rejected Lady Cassidy."

"I did no such thing!"

"Don't lie to me, boyo. You didn't even try to hide your opinion when you saw her."

"Well, what did you expect?" Theran let some of his own anger show. "Do you really think the other Warlord Princes will accept *her*?"

"That depends," Daemon said with vicious control, "on whether they're looking for someone to rule their people according to the Old Ways or trying to picture her riding their cocks."

"This isn't what I bargained for!"

"This is *exactly* what you bargained for," Daemon replied as he glided toward the door. Then he stopped and looked at Theran. "Being the last of Jared's bloodline got you this much and this far. But I'll tell you this now. If you had declared yourself Consort instead of First Escort, I'd kill you where you stand to spare her enduring one minute with you in bed."

Daemon didn't open the door. He used Craft to pass through the wood.

Theran stumbled over to a chair and sank into it.

No wonder this Queen had been available. No wonder she hadn't demanded more compensation for ruling a Territory. She was a Queen because she'd been born into that caste, just as he had been born a Warlord Prince.

But no one wanted her. Who in the name of Hell would want her?

They'd saddled him with a castoff, and he was stuck with her. Dena Nehele needed a Queen too desperately for him to go back home without her. So he would swallow his pride, go in to dinner, and bring Lady Cassidy to Dena Nehele to meet the rest of the Warlord Princes. And he would do the best he could for his people with what little she could offer.

TEN

A few steps away from the dining room, Jaenelle had linked arms with Cassidy and pulled her into another room.

"But," Cassidy had protested, "dinner—"

"Will wait." Jaenelle released her and stepped away. "What do you think of Grayhaven?"

Cassidy shrugged, not willing to voice her opinion.

Jaenelle pursed her lips. "As Lucivar would say, if you keep chewing on that gristle, sooner or later you're going to choke. So just spit it out."

Those last words were snapped out—and Cassidy snapped back.

"Did you see the look on his face when he realized I was the one who was supposed to go to Dena Nehele?"

"Explain 'supposed to.'"

"He doesn't want me in his precious Territory, doesn't want me ruling his people, and as sure as the sun doesn't shine in Hell, he doesn't want to serve me. So why am I doing this?"

"Because no matter what he wants—or thinks he wants—his land and his people need you," Jaenelle replied.

A truth lodged in her heart and throat, choking her. She tried to swallow it, because it shamed her, but the words tumbled out. "He feels like my old First Circle." Like the men who had turned their backs on her for a younger Queen they found more exciting.

Jaenelle gave her a sharp look. "Yes," she said slowly, "he would feel like your First Circle, since he has something in common with them. He doesn't belong to you."

"I don't want him as a pet," Cassidy snapped. Then added silently, *Or anything else.*

"Don't be obtuse."

Cassidy shivered at the hint of midnight in Jaenelle's voice and remembered to whom she spoke. "My apologies, Lady."

Jaenelle walked over to the windows and stared outside for a minute before turning back to Cassidy.

"A simple truth, Sister," Jaenelle said. "Theran Grayhaven doesn't belong to you. He never will. He doesn't understand that yet, but you need to accept it. As First Escort, consider him your personal guard and your companion at official functions. In time you might be able to be friends, and even if you're not, you may be able to work well together for the common goal of restoring Dena Nehele. But he'll never be a member of your court in the truest sense. Don't expect him to be."

An awkward silence filled the room. Awkward for her, Cassidy admitted. Witch simply studied her—and waited.

"Shall we join the men for dinner?" Jaenelle finally asked. "Or should I make your excuses and send Prince Theran back to Dena Nehele alone?"

Terreille

Remembering the previous evening, Cassidy gingerly pulled aside the curtains, looked out a grimy window, and thought, *It's only for a year.*

And if the rest of the days were anything like the journey to Dena Nehele, it would be a *long* year.

Of course, she probably wasn't the only one counting the days until Theran could take her back to Ebon Askavi. Especially after her rejection of the Queen's suite.

It had been obvious that people had worked hard to clean up the suite, but she could barely stand being in the rooms. She couldn't consider *living* there. She didn't know what could have been done in a Queen's bedroom to make the room feel like *that,* but an oppressive, gleeful cruelty seemed to pulse from the walls.

She had bolted. She'd stood in the hallway, trying not to be sick, trying to explain why she couldn't use the suite.

Theran had listened, tight-lipped and angry, as if her inability to use the suite that had been prepared for her was an insult to his people—or confirmed his own opinion of her inadequacy to be the Territory Queen. Finally he'd said, "The Lady must do as she pleases."

Close enough to Protocol. Avoiding the wing of the mansion that Theran had chosen as his family's residence, she quickly explored the rest of the available living quarters and found a suite of rooms that seemed to welcome her, even though the rooms were dusty and clearly hadn't been used in a long time.

The Blood who had been hired as servants scrambled to give the bedroom and bathroom enough of a cleaning so that she could move in. The mattress and bed linens in the other bedroom were new and hadn't absorbed the tainted psychic scent that filled the other suite. The look of relief on the servants' faces when she'd agreed to use them had been painful to see—and had told her more about the Queens who had ruled here than all the words Theran had grudgingly offered on the journey.

This morning he would introduce her to the other Warlord Princes. One hundred men, including Theran. All that was left of their caste after the Queens' purges had taken so many men who wouldn't bend to Dorothea's vision of the Blood. The landen uprisings that had started after Dorothea's taint had been cleansed from the Realms had taken even more. There must be boys in that caste who weren't included in that number, but she suspected they were hidden somewhere and were being trained in secret—and were not something she could ask about until she had gained the adult males' trust.

One hundred Warlord Princes. How was she supposed to choose the twelve males required to make a First Circle?

Jaenelle, thank the Darkness, had offered an answer.

"You don't choose the males who serve," Jaenelle had said. "They choose you. Cassie, the total failure of your First Circle was as much your fault as theirs. You accepted those men because they said they wanted to serve, but their reasons for wanting it had nothing to do with you. You chose with your head instead of letting your instincts as a Queen make the decisions."

"If I hadn't chosen with my head, there would have been no court, and that village wouldn't have had a Queen."

Jaenelle's sapphire eyes stared at her, into her. "They would have survived without a Queen living within their village borders. That village became available because the old District Queen no longer wanted to rule more than her home village. The other three Blood villages under her rule could have gone to one Queen instead of being divided."

"But that Queen wouldn't have been me."

"No, it wouldn't have been you. Dharo has a strong Territory Queen and strong Province Queens. The Blood there can be more indulgent in their choice of District Queens. They didn't need someone like you, Cassidy."

Jaenelle's words stung, more so because she'd expected a little sympathy to balance out their before-dinner "chat."

"They expect me to choose," Cassidy said. "How do I choose if I'm not supposed to choose?"

Jaenelle smiled. While the now-apparent sympathy was the tonic Cassidy needed to soothe her bruised feelings, the equally apparent amusement made her nervous.

"It's simple," Jaenelle said. "You stand in front of them and let them all get a look at you. Say something so they can hear your voice. Then you wait. Many are going to feel disappointed—and some will feel bitter about it because they don't realize it's part of forming a court. For most of them, you won't be the right Queen to serve—at least not in the First Circle. They'll need to look at the other Queens. But the ones who belong to you . . . You may not recognize it immediately, since you've never felt it, but they'll know. Some will approach you and look relaxed or relieved because they've finally found something they've needed. Others will be wary when they approach because they aren't sure if they can trust the instincts that are pushing them to hand over their lives and surrender to your rule. As each man approaches, look him in the eyes. If something inside you says, 'This one belongs to me,' then he does."

"I don't want a First Circle filled with Warlord Princes," Cassidy said.

"That's not your choice," Jaenelle replied. "And, really, they're sweet men once you get past the bossiness and temper. I wouldn't expect more than half the First Circle to be filled with Warlord Princes, but they get to offer themselves before the other castes of males."

"Warlords would be good," Cassidy muttered. Her four

months in the Dark Court had shown her the advantages— and disadvantages—of having so many dominating males working together. Warlords didn't tend to argue as much about everything. Of course, the Warlord Princes in the Dark Court didn't exactly argue. They just set their heels down and didn't budge from their opinion.

"Oh, one other thing about Warlord Princes," Jaenelle said just before they rejoined the men. "The ones that belong to you will want to sniff your neck. Don't make a fuss about it."

"Sniff my neck?" Cassidy muttered, turning away from the window when someone knocked on the door. "Come in."

Birdie, the maid assigned to clean her suite, entered with a hesitant smile and a breakfast tray.

"Good morning, Lady Cassidy," Birdie said. "The Warlord Princes are gathering to meet you, so Maydra—she's the cook—thought you might like to have your breakfast in peace. And thought you might be feeling a bit nervous in the stomach."

An undercurrent of fear beneath the words.

She'd been tired last night, and distressed by Theran's attitude toward her as well as by some of the things Jaenelle had said, but now that she thought about it, that same undercurrent had been in Dryden, the butler, and Elle, the housekeeper, as well. They had been hired because they had experience working around a Queen's court, but they, and the other servants, were all afraid.

What had those other Queens done to these people?

Hell's fire, Cassidy. Those Queens were killed by the storm Witch had unleashed. That should tell you something.

"Put the tray over there," Cassidy said. Following Birdie to the little table, she lifted the cover off the dish. Scrambled eggs and buttered toast. A little serving dish of fruit jam. A small pot of coffee, with cream and sugar on the side.

"Thank you," Cassidy said. "That looks lovely. And please thank Maydra as well. This is exactly the kind of breakfast I need this morning."

"She'll be relieved to hear it," Birdie said. "Elle says we'll be turning out your rooms for a proper cleaning while you're selecting the men for your court."

If Jaenelle was right about how a court usually formed

around a Queen, the selecting might not take as much time as everyone thought. Well, there would be plenty of other things to do that would keep her out of the servants' way for a few hours.

Suspecting this would be the last bit of solitude she would have for most of the day, Cassidy sat down to eat a quiet breakfast.

Then a thought made her snort. She clamped a hand over her mouth to keep from spraying toast crumbs all over the table.

Theran Grayhaven would never be hers, but *she* wasn't the one who would spend the next year on the receiving end of Vae's attention.

Theran? Theran! Those males are not herding properly. They are supposed to stay in this room to see the Queen. I will fetch them.

"You don't need—"

Why bother? Theran thought as Vae jumped off the platform that had been constructed for Lady Cassidy's audiences. The little bitch didn't listen to anything he said anyway, although she had plenty to say to *him*.

Of course, since the other men weren't being held responsible for the dog's welfare, they had no reason to pay attention to her.

But they were paying attention. Hard not to when a dog was standing on air so that she could bark in a man's face. And she wasn't floating at a height where she could nip at their heels, but *was* in a position to nip someone's ass.

Vae charged around the room, nipping and barking and issuing orders.

Come back here! It is time to meet the Queen! You there! Stop! Stubborn sheep.

The men in the room moved closer to the platform. The ones who had been wandering returned, curious about what was causing so much commotion. Some of the men looked amused; some looked a little pissed off and were, no doubt, wondering what kind of trick he might be playing.

No question Ranon was more pissed off than amused. The Shalador Warlord Prince worked his way closer to the platform, gave the dog, who was now floating in front of him, a pointed look, then said, "Grayhaven, what is this?"

I am Vae. I am a Sceltie. I am kindred. I am a witch. I know my Craft. You are male and foolish. And human.

Ranon blinked. "A witch? She's a *witch*? That's really a Purple Dusk *Jewel*?"

Yes, Vae replied before Theran could respond. *It is my Birthright Jewel. When I am older, I will make the Offering to the Darkness and get my other Jewel. I am going to help the Queen train her males. Especially Theran. It is time.*

Vae spun around and whapped Ranon in the face with her tail. *Theran? Theran! Go fetch the Queen.*

"Yeah, Theran," Ranon said, stepping back to avoid being whapped in the face again. "Go fetch."

Could be worse, Theran thought as he strode toward the previously unused wing of the mansion. At least Cassidy wasn't a yapper as far as he could tell. And by the time he escorted Cassidy to the audience room, and the other Warlord Princes had spent that time with Vae, maybe they'd all find the new Queen a lot more palatable.

Maybe eating breakfast hadn't been such a good idea, Cassidy thought as she and Theran walked down to the audience room.

He was ignoring Protocol by walking on her right to indicate his Jewels were dominant instead of walking on her left to indicate his power was in her service. He wasn't offering his hand in the traditional escort position so that she could rest her hand on top of his. Maybe he thought it wasn't necessary to follow those formalities until they were closer to the audience room, but the servants they had passed had noticed.

Prince Theran was sending a message that would trickle through the court and through the Blood who worked in the mansion: the new Queen wasn't worthy of courtesy or respect.

He was setting her up to fail before she had a chance to try.

He doesn't belong to you. Jaenelle recognized that the moment she saw the two of you in a room together.

But he was still Grayhaven. The Queen's residence was

his family's home. The town was named after the Gray-haven estate. Theran's opinion would matter far more than hers.

Theran opened a door and said, "The stairs to the plat-form are to your left."

As she walked into the room and climbed the platform's steps, she was aware of the silence that rippled from the front of the room to the back.

During the hours she'd spent at the Keep yesterday, Jaenelle had looked through her clothes and made suggestions for outfits appropriate for various functions. At first, she'd felt a spike of resentment. She wasn't a child who needed to be told what to wear. In fact, she was five years older than Jaenelle. Then she realized she was being given the confirmation of a Sister, a fellow Queen, that her choices were correct—and the reason for the exercise had been to give her that confirmation, since she wasn't likely to find any where she was going.

So she'd dressed with care for this first meeting, but she'd dressed for a working morning in a court—long skirt and matching jacket in a dark green that flattered her red hair and pale skin, along with a pale green shirt.

As she looked at the men who had made the decision to give their people a Queen from another Realm, she felt their disappointment roll over her like a heavy wave. She didn't dress like a Queen. She didn't look like what they had imagined.

Vae pushed her way to the platform, using shields to add heft to her small body to shove grown men out of her way.

These males are grumpy sheep, Vae said on a dis-taff thread, female to female. She floated on air above the platform to have the best view of the room. *You should choose the ones that belong to you so the rest can go out-side and run.*

I don't think they want to run, Cassidy replied.

I will chase them. They will run. They will be less grumpy when they are tired.

She doubted that the Warlord Princes would share Vae's opinion about what they needed, but the Sceltie wouldn't care about that. And she wouldn't care that these men were bigger and some of them were more powerful. She had a job to do, and she would do it.

And so do you, Cassie. So do you.

"Good morning, gentlemen," she said, using Craft to enhance her voice so that she could speak in a normal tone and still be heard at the back of the room. "I am Cassidy, from the Territory of Dharo in the Realm of Kaeleer. I'm here to help you restore Dena Nehele. I'm here to help your people."

Disappointment. Despair. Bitterness. She felt those things flow around her. More than other men, Warlord Princes needed a relationship with a Queen to keep them mentally and emotionally balanced. All that power and lethal temper craved a leash. That was one reason so many bad Queens had come into power in this Realm. Once the good Queens were destroyed, the Warlord Princes gave their allegiance to whatever Queens were available—and became corrupted in the process. Or they held out, held themselves back from the very thing they needed, and served an ideal instead of a woman.

Not many men could do that—and she needed to remember that, in one way or another, all these men had done just that.

Disappointment. Despair. Bitterness.

And then a flare of hope.

Wary. Almost angry. But still hope.

She watched the Opal-Jeweled Warlord Prince nudge other men aside in order to stand before her and stare into her eyes.

She couldn't tell if his skin was browned by the sun or if he had that coloring in common with Theran. Dark brown hair and dark brown eyes.

Mother Night.

She held the leash for this angry, wary man, and he knew it. Something about her called to him, and he couldn't turn away from her without paying a desperately high price.

"Who do you consider Dena Nehele's people?" the Warlord Prince asked.

The effort he was making to keep his voice neutral told her how important her answer was to him.

"Everyone who lives within the borders of this Territory," Cassidy replied. "Landens as well as Blood."

"What about the Shalador people?"

"Now is not the time for that, Ranon," Theran snapped.

"Then when is the time, Grayhaven?" Ranon snapped back.

"Who are the Shalador people?" Cassidy asked.

"What's left of a race who came from a Territory that no longer exists. We live on reserves in the southern part of Dena Nehele, land that was granted to us by the Gray Lady." Ranon gave Theran a hostile look. "Land that's been trimmed by the hand of every Queen who has ruled since Lia until there's barely enough farmland to feed us and not enough healthy woodland to supply the game we need."

"Now is not the time," Theran said again, shifting into a fighting stance.

"Prince Theran is right," Cassidy said as Ranon also shifted into a fighting stance. The odds were against Opal being able to win a fight with Green, but Warlord Princes who served in the same court could not be allowed to fight. "Now is not the time."

She saw bitterness in Ranon's eyes, but she pushed on. "What you have said deserves more thought and discussion than I can give it this morning. But we *will* discuss the concerns of your people, as well as the other people who live in Dena Nehele."

Hers. She saw it in his eyes as he relaxed a little and stepped back from the killing edge. Even if he'd hated her answer, he would have served in her court. It would have damaged something inside him, but he would have served.

Five more Warlord Princes made their way to the front of the room to stand before the platform. The connection, the *need* for what she was, wasn't as strong with them as she'd felt with Ranon, but it was there. For the first time, she felt the weight of being a Queen, of holding lives in her hands.

She stepped back to the center of the platform. As Theran announced each man, he came up on the platform, knelt before her, and said, "Your will is my life. Take what you need."

Surrender. Loyalty. At least for the next year.

Theran had knelt before her and said those words with Prince Sadi and the High Lord as witnesses. He hadn't meant them. They'd all known that last night.

But Ranon and the other five Warlord Princes *did* mean

the words—and the fact that they did mean the words terrified them.

Scared her too.

When the chosen stood at the back of the platform, Cassidy turned to Theran. "Who else is waiting to be considered for the First Circle?"

He looked at the remaining Warlord Princes, then at her. "You're dismissing the men who are here?"

"I don't think they're best suited for this First Circle," Cassidy replied quietly. "I would like to meet with the others before making further decisions. But I need some air and some time to think. We'll reconvene in two hours."

"May I remind you that you have seven males," Theran said, shifting so most of the men couldn't see that he was getting angry. "You need twelve to form a court. If you dismiss these men now, you may not get any of them back."

"I'm aware of that."

★Walkies!★ Vae shouted. ★You males will go for walkies now. You can mark the trees. Human males do that sometimes. And I will teach you how to play fetch.★

Vae leaped from the platform and sailed over the men's heads, landing in the middle of the room—an impossible thing to do without Craft. She disappeared for a moment, then popped up shoulder height, her tail smacking faces as she began herding the men out the door.

Theran was angry. This audience hadn't gone as he'd wanted, and by turning the Warlord Princes away, she was taking the risk of not being able to form a court. If she couldn't form a court, whatever favors he had called in would have been wasted, so she couldn't blame him for feeling upset.

Ranon, on the other hand, looked more relaxed as he came up to stand on her left side. Baffled, but more relaxed.

"She's a relentless little bitch, isn't she?" Ranon asked, tipping his head to indicate Vae.

The knot in Cassidy's stomach eased as she watched Warlord Princes obeying a dog because they couldn't figure out how *not* to obey the dog. That, at least, felt like home.

She smiled at Ranon. "Of course. She's a Sceltie."

ELEVEN

Terreille

Gray pressed himself against the big stone gardening shed, his limbs trembling, his heart racing, as if his body were still trying to outrun the nightmares that had filled his sleep last night.

There was a Queen at Grayhaven. He could *feel* her presence, even out here. She would be living in that suite of rooms, in *that* room, doing . . . things.

His back muscles, which had never fully healed on the left side, tightened in response to his fear, threatening to spasm and leave him helpless to run, to hide until she lost interest in looking for him.

I'm Grayhaven. I'm Grayhaven!

Theran's blade. He never betrayed his cousin, had protected Theran in the only way he could. Even when the bitch did those *things* to him.

He couldn't remember that. Couldn't. Theran was living in the mansion now. With *her*. No secrets. Not anymore. *She* knew Theran was the real Grayhaven.

He couldn't get near the house. He had tried because Theran was in there, but he couldn't get near the house. Talon had brought him food last night, and the men who worked in the stables had let him use their toilet and shower so he wouldn't have to go near the house.

Her presence tingled under the land, even here at the edge of what had been the formal gardens. He didn't remember that happening the last time. The gardens had been as close to a safe place as there had been when he'd been a prisoner here. The Queen had him shackled and staked to a long chain, like a pony being put out to graze. Let him stagger around the old gardens—or crawl when his tortured body couldn't do more. Left him where he could see the dead honey pear tree, the symbol of the Grayhaven Queens who had stood against Dorothea SaDiablo. Dead like their bloodline. Dead for so many years, but kept as a reminder that those Queens had not endured.

Jared had given that honey pear tree to Lia, who had tended it all her life.

Who could say if it was the same tree? But everyone believed it was, and that was all that really mattered.

Hope. Life. Love. All dead, like the tree.

That's what the last Queen had taught him.

Then Talon had found him, rescued him. And with Talon's help, Theran had done what he could to help Gray rebuild some kind of life.

He wasn't what he should have been. He knew that sometimes, could sense that something had been lost.

He would stay here because Theran was here, and Talon was here. But . . .

He felt her presence, felt her psychic scent as a heat against his skin.

But it was a pleasant heat, like beams of sunlight coming through a window on a day in early spring.

He peered around the corner of the shed and saw her walking toward him. But not looking for *him*. No, she was looking at the land.

Her scent said "Queen," but she didn't look like a Queen, wasn't dressed like a Queen. She looked . . . friendly. And her hair . . .

He watched as she pulled the pins from her hair and it tumbled around her shoulders and down her back.

He'd never seen red hair. He'd read stories where people had red hair, but he'd never seen anyone in real life. And she had spots on her face. Why did she have spots on her face? Such pale skin. What color were her eyes?

With his heart pounding, Gray stepped away from the stone shed and walked toward her slowly, fearfully. It wasn't safe. It *wasn't*. But he wanted, *needed*, to see the color of her eyes.

*   *   *

Cassidy watched him walk toward her. A good-looking man with a strong physical resemblance to Theran, right down to the dark hair and green eyes. Family, perhaps?

A well-toned body of a physically active adult male. But his psychic scent said "youth," even "boy," which was a sure sign of something wrong, and that wasn't good because inside that body . . .

Warlord Prince. Wild. Wounded.

Mine.

The thought startled her, made her heart pound because *it* seemed to recognize something about this man that her mind wasn't ready to acknowledge.

This wasn't the same feeling of recognition that she'd had with the Warlord Princes who were now in her First Circle. This was different. Personal.

So wounded inside. She could see it in his green eyes now that he was close enough. He looked like he was ready to run, and yet he kept moving toward her as if he couldn't help himself.

"Hello," she said quietly. "I'm Cassidy."

He stopped at the sound of her voice, shifting his weight from one foot to another, not sure if he should get closer or step back.

"I'm Gray," he finally said, taking another step toward her.

His eyes roamed her face. When he got close enough, he reached out, almost touching her cheek. Then he snatched his hand back, like a boy who had almost touched the forbidden.

Wondering what he saw that baffled and intrigued him so much, she touched her cheek to see if something was on her skin.

Oh. She wrinkled her nose. "You've never seen freckles?"

"Freckles." He said the word softly, as if it were a fragile gift. "Are they just on your face?"

She knew her cheeks flamed with color. She also knew that, despite the man's body, it was a boy asking out of curiosity. Still . . .

"I don't know you well enough to answer that."

He nodded, accepting.

He was half a head taller than she, if that. It would have

been easy enough to look him in the eyes if his own weren't so busy roaming over her face.

"Did you come out to look at the gardens?" she asked.

He cringed, as if she had scolded him for doing something wrong.

"I tend the gardens. It's my job now. I don't stay in the big house. I'm not in the way."

Who said you were in the way?

His voice had risen to a kind of desperate keening and he looked ready to bolt, so she turned toward what might have been a flower bed at one time. "Well, you've certainly got enough work. This land hasn't been loved in a long time."

Something changed so suddenly, she gasped in response to that flash of strong emotion. She couldn't decipher the look in Gray's eyes, couldn't get a feel for where he was now, mentally or emotionally. Which wasn't good because even if he was diminished in some way, he was still a Warlord Prince and he outranked her. She couldn't tell if the Purple Dusk power she was sensing was from his Birthright Jewel or his Jewel of rank, but either way, it was darker than her Rose.

And then, oddly, she had the feeling that some broken piece inside him suddenly settled back into its rightful place.

A moment after that, it was as if nothing had happened. Except that Gray seemed a little less like a boy.

"No, it hasn't been loved for a long time," he said.

Too many feelings. She'd come out here to walk and get away from all the feelings, to do something to settle herself before she went back to the next group of males who would be disappointed in the chosen Queen.

"Do you have a basket or a wheelbarrow?" she asked.

"We have both."

"Good. I have an hour before the next meeting, so that's enough time to clear a bit of ground."

"Clear ground?"

"Weed the flower bed."

His eyes widened. "You can't weed."

"Yes, I can."

"But . . . you're the Queen."

"Yes."

He rocked back on his heels, clearly at a loss.

"I'm the Queen who lives in this house now, so these are my gardens, right?"

"Yes," he said warily.

"So these are my weeds. And since I'm the Queen, I can pull weeds if I want to. Right?"

He wasn't quick to agree. Well, he *was* a Warlord Prince. They were never quick to agree about anything. Unless it was their idea in the first place.

Finally he said, "You'll get dirty. It rained last night."

"I know it rained. Which means the soil will be softer, and the weeds will be easier to pull."

"But you'll get dirty." He frowned at the hem of her skirt, which had already picked up some moisture from brushing the top of the grass.

"I can"—she looked toward the stone shed, saw him stiffen, and looked the other way—"change clothes behind those bushes while you get the wheelbarrow."

Not giving him time to argue, she hurried behind the bushes, vanished her good clothes, then called in the old shirt and trousers she usually wore for gardening. As she stuffed her legs into the trousers, she caught a heel of her shoe in the hem and hopped for a few steps, saying words her father pretended she didn't know.

"Should have used Craft, Cassie," she muttered as she finally got the heel clear of the hem. "Pass the shoe through the cloth and you're less likely to topple over and fall on your ass."

Once she got the trousers on, she buttoned up the long-sleeved shirt, and quickly braided her hair, using Craft to secure the end of the braid.

"Good enough," she muttered as she hurried back to the flower bed, returning at the same time Gray arrived with the rattling wheelbarrow.

"These are a bit rusty, but I found a couple of short-handled claws that are good for loosening soil and digging out weeds," he said. He hesitated, shifting his weight from one foot to the other as he kept glancing at her face and then looking away.

Finally he said, "Your skin is very pale."

Cassidy wrinkled her nose. "Pale skin goes with the red hair." Unlike her brother Clayton's, her skin never changed to that soft gold color when she spent time in the sun. It just went from milk to cooked lobster.

"Your eyes aren't brown, but they aren't green either."

"The color is called hazel. Doesn't anyone have eyes like that here?"

Gray shook his head. "Brown and blue mostly. Some green. None like yours. They're pretty."

A little flutter of feminine pleasure. The only man who had thought anything about her was pretty was her father, and fathers never saw daughters in the same way as other men, so Poppi's opinion didn't really count.

Which wasn't something she would *ever* say to Poppi.

Gray took a step back, as if he was leaving.

"I know you have other work to do," Cassidy said, "but could you stay a few minutes and point out some of the good plants?" She wanted him to stay. This place didn't feel as lonely now that she'd met him.

Another hesitation. "You want me to help?"

"If you wouldn't mind."

"No, I don't mind." He seemed to be mulling over a lot more than spending an hour weeding a flower bed. "You should wear a hat to protect your face."

"Oh, I . . ." He was right, of course. But somehow in the past few minutes he'd made some transition from scared younger boy to bossy older boy. Politely bossy, but she remembered a childhood afternoon visit with her cousin Aaron, which had been her first experience with being around a Warlord Prince of any age, and she still remembered that particular tone of bossiness that no one but a Warlord Prince could achieve.

"Don't you have a hat?"

"Yes, I have a hat, but . . . You'll laugh at my hat."

"I won't laugh," Gray said quickly, putting one hand over his heart. Then he thought for a moment and added, "I'll try not to laugh."

Good enough.

She called in her gardening hat and plunked it on her head. It was a simple straw hat with a wide brim that kept the sun off her face and neck.

Gray didn't laugh, but his smile kept getting wider and wider as he studied her hat.

"Why does it have a chunk missing from one side?" he asked.

"Because my brother was teasing me last summer and holding it behind his back—and didn't notice when the goat snuck up behind him and took a bite out of it."

His smile got even wider. "Shouldn't it have ribbons?"

"I use Craft to keep it in place."

Nodding, and still smiling, he handed her one of the short-handled claws. "I'll show you what doesn't belong in this garden."

Where in the name of Hell did she go? Theran scanned the weed-tangled mess of raised beds that framed a terrace before he headed for the rest of the formal gardens.

She'd *said* she wanted a little air and would be back shortly. That had been over an hour ago. A meal, and the men, were waiting for her return so they could get on with the rest of these meetings.

Considering how bad everything looked, what could *Lady* Cassidy find out here that would amuse her for so long?

The answer punched his heart. He lengthened his stride as he headed for the big stone shed. It had held the grounds-keeper's office at one time, but had become a catchall for unwanted tools. He'd helped Gray clear out the smaller room in the shed and put in a cot, a small chest of drawers, and a bookcase.

Gray was used to living rough. So was he. But here, with the mansion in sight, it seemed . . . meaner, coarser.

It was all Gray could tolerate.

If Cassidy thought she could play with a damaged man just because Gray wasn't able to fight back, she'd find out the truth quick enough. He, Theran, wasn't fifteen anymore, didn't—*wouldn't*—hide anymore. And Gray wasn't standing alone anymore, facing something that terrified him.

He spotted Gray and hurried toward his cousin, no longer caring if he found Cassidy. A wheelbarrow full of weeds was on Gray's left and someone—he caught a glimpse of a straw hat—was on the other side of the wheelbarrow.

"That's called pearl of wisdom," Gray said, pointing to a plant. "See? The flower has a sheen like the inside of a shell, and the seedpod looks like a pearl. The flower only blooms for a couple of weeks in the spring."

"Gray," Theran called, wondering what servant had be-friended his cousin.

Gray looked around, a queer wariness in his eyes before he spotted Theran.

"Theran!" he said happily.

From the other side of the wheelbarrow, a husky voice said, "Oh, shit. *Theran.*"

When she popped up, it took him a moment to recognize her. She was the only person in Dena Nehele who had red hair, but it still took him a moment to recognize her.

Not a Queen. Despite her caste, she was not a Queen.

"Has an hour gone by already?" Cassidy asked.

"And then some. We've held the midday meal, thinking you would be back soon." He couldn't keep the tightness out of his voice, couldn't even keep it on the right side of respectful.

"My apologies, Prince Theran." There was a tightness in her voice too as she stood up and vanished that stupid hat. "I'll wash up and join you as soon as I can. Please tell the men not to wait for me. They shouldn't have to eat cold food just because I lost track of the time."

"We live to serve," Theran said.

She winced and wouldn't meet his eyes as she hurried back to the mansion.

Theran watched her for a moment, then looked at Gray. "Are you all right?"

That queer wariness was back in Gray's eyes. "I'm fine."

What did she do to you? He couldn't ask, but he knew something wasn't quite right.

As he turned to go back to the mansion, Gray said, "Theran? She knows the land needs to be loved. The Queens who have been living here haven't cared about that."

A message there, but Gray had always had a sensitivity to the land, being more aware of it than the people around him were. That sensitivity had heightened after he'd been rescued.

I'm glad you're not afraid of her, Gray, Theran thought as he walked back to the mansion, *but what kind of Queen cares more about digging in the dirt than taking care of the people?*

*   *   *

It took most of the afternoon to meet the Warlords who wanted to be considered for the court. Three belonged to her and were suited to serve in her First Circle. The others wanted status, safety, something else. Whatever it was, they wouldn't find it with her.

Several Warlords who lived in the town of Grayhaven would be an asset in one of the other twelve circles that made up a court, and she hoped they would accept the offer when the Steward made it on her behalf.

Once she found a Steward. And a Master of the Guard.

And with every man who wasn't accepted, Theran tensed a little more.

Toward the end of the afternoon the first, and only, Prince arrived. A middle-aged man whose skin sagged as if he'd once been hefty but hadn't eaten well in quite some time and whose left hand had been broken and badly healed.

"What do you want, Powell?" Archerr asked in a challenging voice.

"I would like to be considered for a position in the court," Powell replied courteously, looking at Cassidy. "I'm good at organizing schedules and duties."

"You're also good at skimming off a percentage of the Queen's tithes," Archerr snapped.

"That was never proved," Ranon snapped in return.

Why would Ranon defend a man accused of stealing from a Queen? Unless the Warlord Prince knew, or suspected, something about Powell that the rest of the men didn't know.

"Did you steal from the Queen you served?" Cassidy asked.

"Yes," Powell replied.

Mutters from the Warlords and Warlord Princes who had remained in the room. Snarls from several of the Warlord Princes who were in her First Circle, but she couldn't tell if they were snarling at Powell or at one another.

"Why?" Cassidy asked.

"The Province Queen I served liked luxury," Powell said. "Well, they all did, didn't they? And it was the tithes from the District Queens that had to support those luxuries. It was hard to walk through the town where the Queen lived and see children who were hungry or who were wearing clothes and shoes too patched and torn to be useful. So sometimes a few coins would find their way back to a family for food or clothing."

"I see," Cassidy said. "Is that why your hand was broken?"

Powell nodded. "Most people were careful to spread out the spending. One man was not. I claimed to have given the man some coins from my own wages, and the Queen couldn't prove otherwise. That's why she had my left hand broken instead of maiming the right hand."

In Kaeleer, a tribunal of Queens would have known you were lying within minutes, Cassidy thought. *But their wrath would have been aimed at the Queen who had mistreated her people and not you.*

"I have to trust that the people who serve me will work for the good of Dena Nehele," Cassidy said to Powell. "I understand your reasons, and I can't say you were wrong. But everyone is going to be living lean for a while, and tithes will be necessary to support the court and take care of the expenses that come with the court. If you think someone is being tithed unfairly, I need to know. But the amount of the tithe, unfair or not, will be my decision. Is that understood?"

"Yes, Lady. That is understood," Powell said.

"In that case, are you willing to wear the Steward's ring?"

Silence. Disbelief from Theran that he didn't bother to hide. Surprise from the other men in her First Circle. Except for Ranon. He looked thoughtful.

"I would be honored to serve as your Steward," Powell said.

A commotion at the back of the room. Anger and resistance coming from the men nearest the door. Anger and a flash of worry coming from Ranon.

Vae launched herself into the men, using shields to plow a wide path that left several men staggering to keep their balance.

Bad males! Vae shouted. *Bad!*

The men glanced at the platform, then stepped away, since Cassidy wasn't calling Vae off.

A woman, a witch, approached the platform.

"Your kind shouldn't be here," Theran said at the same time Ranon said, "Shira."

He loves her, Cassidy thought, watching Ranon's effort to remain neutral. *But he didn't want her to come here. Why?*

"I have as much right to be here as you do, Theran Grayhaven," Shira said. Her omitting his title was a deliberate slap in the face. "You can trace your bloodline back to Jared. I can trace my bloodline back to Jared's cousin Shira. So if I don't belong here, neither do you."

Since that particular verbal slap left Theran speechless, Cassidy jumped in. "What can I do for you, Sister?"

Shira looked at her. "I want to offer my services. I'm a fully qualified Healer and—"

"That's not all you are," Theran snapped.

No, that wasn't all Shira was. The hourglass pendant she wore above her Summer-sky Jewel proclaimed her to be something more powerful—and more dangerous—than a Healer.

"I'm not ashamed of what I am," Shira said.

"Why should you be?" Cassidy asked. "You've completed your training in the Hourglass's Craft?" The question was a formality. The pendant Shira wore, with all the gold dust in the bottom half of the hourglass, indicated a Black Widow who had completed her training and could spin the tangled webs of dreams and visions, as well as help people caught in the Twisted Kingdom. The Black Widows were also the caste of witches who were well versed in the making and use of poisons.

"Her kind were outlawed generations ago," Theran said.

"You're a natural Black Widow?" Cassidy asked Shira.

"That's the only kind there are in Dena Nehele," Shira replied.

"The penalty for training anyone in that Craft is execution," Theran said.

Ranon snarled at Theran.

"Gentlemen," Cassidy said, using Craft to enhance her voice. She waited until they had all quieted down. Then waited until a couple of Warlords got done swearing after Vae nipped them because they didn't quiet fast enough to suit the Sceltie.

"I'm here because you wanted a Queen who knows the

Old Ways of the Blood, who *lives* by the Old Ways of the Blood, and who will require that *you* live by that Protocol and code of honor. That means a good many things that you knew no longer apply." Cassidy turned in her chair and looked at Theran. "You say Black Widows were outlawed. How many of the Queens who controlled Dena Nehele had Black Widows in their courts? My guess is all of them did. What was outlawed were the Black Widows who *wouldn't* serve in those courts. The ones whose skills would endanger a Queen who was hated.

"We're going back to the Old Ways, gentlemen, and in the Old Ways the Hourglass is an honored caste of witches. They are not outlaws. Their training is not outlawed." Cassidy turned to look at Shira. "If you accept the position of court Healer, you would have to reside here. Are you prepared to do that?"

"I am," Shira replied.

"Then welcome to the court, Sister."

You're forgetting something, Lady, Theran said. *We don't have a court. There are only eleven males.*

No, Cassidy said, *there's—* *Gray,* she finished silently.

He wasn't going to be part of her court. *Couldn't* be part of her court. Not as he was.

But he could have been—should have been—if he had been whole.

Ranon looked at the men on the platform, his expression grim. He too must have just realized they didn't have an official court.

"Is the other Warlord Prince still planning to present himself?" Ranon asked.

Theran shot him a hostile look. "He is." A glance at the windows. "He'll be here as soon as the sun sets."

And this Warlord Prince, whoever he is, is the reason the men who weren't selected have been waiting.

Folding her hands on the table, Cassidy looked at the windows at the other end of the room.

"He'll be here soon," her cousin Aaron had said, glancing out a window. *"The sun has almost set."*

She knew what it signified when someone wasn't usually available before sunset. So she knew *what* these men were waiting for.

He arrived within minutes after the sun had gone down, too soon to have taken care of his own needs. An older man, maimed by battles. Sapphire Jewel, which made him the dominant male. But it was more than that. As she watched him approach, she also watched the other men and had a flash of insight gleaned from her months in the Dark Court. She'd seen the men in that First Circle, including her cousin Aaron, step aside for Andulvar Yaslana with the same respect the men in this room were showing this demon-dead Warlord Prince. He had trained them, had been an honorary uncle or a surrogate father to many of them.

They had survived because of what he'd taught them.

He looked straight ahead while he walked the length of the room, finally looking at her when he reached the edge of the platform.

She felt the punch of that connection—and felt the same wariness she saw in his eyes. He hadn't expected to feel that pull. Neither had she. She would have accepted him into the First Circle because of the feelings she was sensing from her other males, but she hadn't expected him to belong to her.

She watched him climb the stairs, then rose when he approached the table.

Protocol. Her insides were quivering because he was, without question, the most dangerous man in the room. But she knew the words and the rituals, not just for dealing with a Warlord Prince, but for dealing with the demon-dead.

"Prince," she said.

"Lady." He tipped his head in a slight bow. "I am Talon." His eyes narrowed as he studied her face. "Do you know what I am?"

She smiled slightly. "My Master of the Guard."

He couldn't hide his surprise. "I am honored, Lady, but that wasn't what I meant."

"You're demon-dead. I'm aware of that."

"That doesn't bother you?"

"Why should it?" She saw a heat in Talon's eyes. A hunger. That was a danger with having one of the demon-dead walking among the living. "Prince Theran, would you bring in a bottle of yarbarah? I'm sure Prince Talon would appreciate a glass."

"A bottle of what?" Theran asked.

Cassidy frowned at Theran. "Yarbarah. The blood wine."

Blank expression. And Talon's expression was equally blank.

Hell's fire, Mother Night, and may the Darkness be merciful.

"You're unfamiliar with that particular vintage?" Cassidy asked Talon.

"Can't say I've heard of it," he replied warily.

"Well, then." What had he been consuming if he didn't know about yarbarah?

Best not to think about that because she was certain that whatever had been given had not been given according to the Protocol and rituals that had been created for transactions between the living and the demon-dead.

She called in the simple wooden box her father had made for the gift the High Lord had given her when she'd finished her apprenticeship in the Dark Court. Pressing the two spots on the sides to release the latches, she removed the cover, revealing the small silver cup and silver-handled knife. She set the cup on the table, pushed up her left sleeve, and, before anyone knew for certain what she intended, picked up the knife and opened a vein in her wrist.

A wash of sounds and protests was drowned out by the snarl of a Sceltie who knew her Craft.

Stay! Vae growled. *This is ceremony!*

Ceremony. Ritual. Sometimes formal, sometimes casual, but always, *always* precise in the intention.

As soon as the cup was filled, she turned the blade of the knife flat against her wrist, hiding the wound as she used the Healing Craft she'd been taught to seal this kind of cut.

Setting the knife on the table, she held out the cup to Talon. "Freely offered," she said, knowing every man in the room would remember the words. "Freely taken."

Talon hesitated, then took the cup, his hunger apparent in his face. "You honor me, Lady."

Two swallows. That was all the cup held. But blood freely offered had a different flavor from blood that was soured by fear.

Talon recognized the difference, even if he wasn't quite sure of the reason.

He set the cup on the table with great care.

"Is that dog going to bite me if I heal your wrist?" Shira asked.

In answer, Cassidy held out her wrist, all the permission her Healer needed.

As soon as Shira finished the healing, Cassidy vanished the cup, knife, and box, preferring to clean them in private.

She looked at Theran. Was he relieved a formal court was established? Upset about her offering her blood to Talon? She couldn't read him, couldn't tell what he was thinking.

And she suddenly felt too tired to care.

"Gentlemen, it's been a long day. Prince Powell, please send the Province Queens my regrets and ask them to meet me tomorrow morning."

Tense silence.

"Aren't the Province Queens aware that the Warlord Princes chose a Territory Queen?" Cassidy asked.

"There are no Province Queens," Talon said.

"All Territories are divided into Provinces and Districts," Cassidy said. "There must be Province Queens."

"They all died two years ago," Talon said. "The psychic storm that swept through Terreille took all of them."

Cassidy sank into the chair behind the table. "District Queens?"

"A few," Talon said. "The ones who are too old or weak to be a threat to anyone. Or the ones too young to form a court and rule anything."

Hell's fire, Mother Night, and may the Darkness be merciful. She'd thought the Warlord Princes of Dena Nehele had gone outside their own Territory because there wasn't a Queen they were willing to have rule over all of them. Theran hadn't said there weren't *any* Queens to help her.

She pressed both hands flat against the table and closed her eyes. What was she supposed to do?

Poppi laying out the pieces of wood, the nails and screws, the tools.

"When you're not sure of what you've got, Kitten, lay it all out and take a look," he said. "Then you decide if you can make something out of what you've got, even if it wasn't the thing you had in mind. Or you figure out what else you need in order to make what you want."

"Prince Powell," Cassidy said, keeping her eyes closed because it was easier to deal with them all when she imagined she was talking to Poppi or her brother, Clayton. "I need a map of Dena Nehele that will show me the whole of the Territory and the Provinces. Then I need maps of each Province that will show me all the towns, villages, and cities, both Blood and landen."

"I'll look in the Steward's office and see what I can find," Powell said.

"Then I need a list of all the Queens in Dena Nehele, where each one lives, and what Jewels she wears. That includes the girls who aren't yet old enough to rule. I also need a list of the Warlord Princes, where they live, and their rank. Prince Talon, you'll be in charge of obtaining that information."

"That won't be easy," Ranon said. "The Shalador Queens who are left survived by not making their whereabouts known. None of them are going to want to be on a hunting list."

Cassidy opened her eyes and looked at Ranon. "Then you'll have to convince them."

A flash of something in his dark eyes told her how deeply his loyalties were being challenged—and his choice would tell her whether she could trust him.

He looked in her eyes and said, "Your will is my life."

"Anything else?" Cassidy asked. When no one spoke, she pushed her chair back and stood up. "In that case, gentlemen, I would prefer to dine in my rooms this evening, so I'll bid you a good evening. Lady Shira, would you join me?"

Shira looked startled and stammered her answer. "It would be my pleasure, Lady."

Cassidy didn't give Theran time to protest or even think to offer himself as escort, which he should have done. She didn't care how it looked or what the men thought. She hustled Shira out of the room, and the only person who made an effort to catch up to them was Vae.

"You didn't want to dine with your court?" Shira asked.

"Not tonight," Cassidy replied.

"Are you feeling tired because of the blood loss?"

She is just tired of talking to males, Vae said, trotting

ahead of them. *You are female, so you are not yappy like males.*

Vae turned a corner, leading the way back to Cassidy's suite.

The two women walked in silence for a minute. Then Shira said, "Is she always so honest?"

Cassidy sighed. "She's a Sceltie."

TWELVE

Gray rolled the wheelbarrow to the edge of the partially weeded flower bed, just as he'd done for the past few days.

Cassie hadn't come back. She knew the land needed to be loved, and he'd thought she'd enjoyed working in the garden. So why didn't she come back?

He'd felt good working with her, listening to that husky voice as she asked him questions about the flowers. Smelling her, although he hadn't dared get close enough to get a good sniff.

He dreamed about her last night. Not a bad dream like he had sometimes about the *other* Queen. In this dream, Cassidy was helping him into a beautiful coat that had been made just for him. But it didn't quite fit. It frustrated him—and scared him—that it didn't quite fit. Then Cassie had smiled sadly and told him the coat couldn't be changed. If he wanted to wear it, *he* would have to change until it fit him the way it should.

He woke up with his heart pounding, on the verge of tears. He wanted to wear that coat. Had been born to wear that coat. But he didn't know how to change to make it fit.

Cassie knew. Cassie would help him change in the right way.

Why didn't she come back?

Maybe he could find Theran. Maybe he could go inside the house long enough to find Theran and ask why Cassie hadn't come back.

Shivering at the thought of being inside those walls

again, Gray turned to look at the house . . . and saw Cassie standing right there, holding a large tray.

He yelped. She jumped back, and the dishes on the tray rattled. He jumped forward to grab the tray—and his hands closed over hers. Touched her skin.

He stared at their hands and wanted to touch her skin forever.

"Gray? Are you all right?" she asked.

"What?"

"I'm sorry I startled you. I guess you didn't hear me calling."

"You called me on a psychic thread?" His heart pounded, but he wasn't sure if it was fear or happiness.

Cassie looked startled. "Oh. No. I didn't want to intrude."

"You wouldn't be intruding." He wanted to hear her inside his head, wanted to feel her inside him. But . . . maybe not too far inside him. Even if she already knew the secret the *other* Queen had tried to rip out of his mind, maybe it wasn't safe to let her inside too many of his inner barriers. But he wouldn't have to open any of his inner barriers in order to talk to her on a psychic thread.

"I brought some breakfast," Cassidy said. "I wasn't sure if you'd eaten yet, so I brought enough for two."

"I could eat." He'd gotten some food from the stable hands, but not enough to fill him.

Cassidy used Craft to balance the tray on air. Then she poured coffee for both of them. Splitting two rolls so they formed pockets, she handed one to Gray before spreading a thin layer of jam inside the other and filling it with scrambled eggs.

"Egg sandwich," Cassidy said, smiling. "My father would make these out of whatever eggs were left over from breakfast, and put them in a chill box to eat later in the morning when he took a break from his work. For all the years they've been married, I'm still not sure he knows that my mother cooks extra just so he can make his egg sandwich."

Gray stuffed the roll with scrambled eggs, then smeared a little jam on part of the roll. He took a bite and made a face.

"Too sweet?" Cassidy asked.

"Yes," he said, glad he hadn't smeared any more of the roll. "But it's good," he added quickly.

She laughed. She had a wonderful laugh, warm and earthy. Not the bright, brittle sound of cruelty.

"My mother and I like the jam with the eggs. My brother prefers this red sauce that's a little spicy."

"That sounds better."

She gave him an odd look—and an even odder smile. Not bad, just odd.

He ate his sandwich and drank his coffee, not sure what else to do.

"You didn't come back," he said quietly. "I brought the barrow out for you each day, but you didn't come back." He'd also watered that flower bed late each night so the ground would stay rain soft and be easier for her to dig.

"I wanted to come back, but there's been an awful lot of work to do. All these meetings and reports . . . Every time I've tried to take an hour in the garden, Theran has herded me to another meeting. I think he's spending too much time with Vae, and he's turning into a Sceltie."

Gray laughed. He'd met the Sceltie and was more than willing to play a short game of fetch with her, but she did spend more time with Theran.

Cassidy poured more coffee for both of them. "Last night I decided I can only work so long and so hard without taking some time for myself, and I can spend some time in the garden each morning before getting cleaned up for the business part of the day."

Gray felt light enough to float. "You're going to come every day?"

She nodded. "I need some time to be Cassidy before I have to be 'the Queen.' I know there's so much work to be done, but I need some time in the garden. I need this time."

Me too.

He set his cup back on the tray. "Then let's not waste the time you have to be Cassidy."

Smiling, Cassidy headed back to the house. Her arms and shoulders were a little tired and achy, but it was a good feeling to let her body work while her mind rested. Or while her mind focused on something besides maps and lists and persuading wary men to trust her enough to give her accurate information.

The Warlord Princes didn't trust Queens. They needed them for themselves and for the rest of Dena Nehele, but they didn't trust the caste of witches who had represented a brutal control for so long. Even the males who belonged to her were circling warily, and each action, each piece of information offered, was a way of testing the ground to find out what she would do, how she would respond.

Shira too was wary, but that had to do with her being a Black Widow and coming from the Shalador reserves. She wasn't used to being accepted.

Were Shira and Ranon lovers? Or were they still dancing around each other?

Not her problem—she hoped. But wouldn't it be lovely to watch two people fall in love?

About the only person here whom she could simply talk to was Gray, but even Gray was struggling with something whenever he was around her. At least they could talk about plants. At least there was the companionship and satisfaction of working together and seeing results.

Hours spent poring over maps might accomplish something in the long run, but an hour spent weeding a flower bed provided results she could see.

And Gray had provided her with something else this morning. She'd already sent her first report to Prince Sadi and a note to her mother, but now she had a reason to write to Clayton—and wouldn't her brother be surprised at her request to send her a jar of the red sauce he liked so much?

Her smile widened to a grin as she pictured Clayton's face when he read the note. Yes, this morning—

"Lady."

—*had been* a good morning. "Prince Theran."

"Prince Powell has been waiting to go over the reports with you."

"The Steward has plenty to do," Cassidy said with stiff politeness. "Talking to me an hour ago or an hour from now won't make any difference. And if I was truly needed for something immediately, I wasn't hard to find."

Theran's lips tightened, as if he was struggling to hold back words that shouldn't be said.

"Now if you'll excuse me, Prince, I need to get ready for the day's work."

He stepped aside, letting her pass.

She wanted to like him, if for no better reason than he was her First Escort and that required them to work closely. But as she walked to her suite, she wondered if it was worth the effort to try to like a man who was making it more clear every day that he didn't like her.

Bitch.

Theran stared at the gardens, at the plot of ground that was noticeably cleaner, and at his cousin who was still out there, sweating too hard over some damn patch of dirt. A wrong move when the back muscles were tight and tired and Gray would be down for days, sedated to quiet the pain.

But Cassidy had to have her ground cleared instead of focusing on what needed to be done, so Gray was out there working too long and too hard.

Damn her. Why couldn't she leave the boy alone?

He'd done his best to keep her occupied, to pile up the work until she didn't have a minute to think about playing with Gray and pushing the boy to tidy up the posies. But he hadn't gotten to her room fast enough this morning to stop her, hadn't even known she'd left her rooms until he'd knocked on her door to find out when she planned to get to work and Birdie had told him she was already gone.

Gone. Yeah, she was gone. And how long would it be before she got tired of watching Gray dig up weeds and figured out something else she could do with him?

Not going to happen, Theran thought as he went back into the house. He and Gray were the same height, the same build. They both had dark hair and green eyes. The women he'd bedded had considered him a good-looking man and skilled enough to be welcomed back for a second night.

He didn't want Cassidy. Who would? But her voice was the kind that could heat a man's blood—as long as he didn't have to look at her face.

So he'd do his duty to court and family—and give Lady Cassidy enough reasons not to give Gray another thought.

*   *   *

Theran couldn't put off the unpalatable duty any longer. Cassidy had retired to her suite, and the First Circle was ready to have an hour or two without dancing for the Queen's pleasure. Not that there had been any dancing. Or much of anything else once they had gathered in this sitting room after dinner.

Picking up the shawl Cassidy had left behind, he smiled at the other men and started to open the sitting room door. "Guess this is my signal."

Startled silence.

"Meaning what?" Ranon asked, sitting up straighter in his chair.

"You know."

"I thought that duty wasn't required of a First Escort," Talon said.

Theran shrugged. "Not required, but it can be requested."

He wasn't sure about that. Wasn't sure if offering wasn't crossing some line according to those books of Protocol Cassidy had brought with her. But he figured a woman who hadn't gotten a ride for a few days wasn't going to turn down an offer, even if it wasn't strictly following the damn rules.

"Theran," Ranon said, sounding concerned. "Are you sure about this?"

He wasn't sure about anything except that he had to do something to keep Gray safe. He smiled again. "I can fulfill my duties to the Queen. When it comes right down to it, all women look the same in the dark."

A rustle of material outside the room, but no one was there when he opened the door.

Hell's fire. Had a maid been standing there eavesdropping? Didn't matter.

He took his time walking up to that wing of the house, but he still arrived at Cassidy's door much too soon. He knocked twice, and when she finally opened the door, he noticed that the spots on her face seemed to be popping out of her pale skin more than usual.

"Is something wrong?" he asked.

She just stared at him.

"You left your shawl down in the sitting room."

No response.

"May I come in?"

"No." Hoarsely spoken, as if she was fighting back some strong emotion.

"Lady?"

"All women may look the same in the dark, but all men don't feel the same. In fact, a woman will find out more about a man's true nature in the dark than she'll ever see in the light of day."

Hell's fire. *She* was the one who had been standing outside the door. "Look, I just—"

"I don't need your penis, and I don't need your pity."

She slammed the door in his face, and a moment later he felt a Rose lock on the door.

"Shit," Theran muttered. He folded the shawl and left it outside her door—and wondered how much groveling he would have to do in the morning.

THIRTEEN

Terreille

A ll women look the same in the dark.
 Did you really think I was excited about being with you? I worked damn hard in your bed, Cassidy, and thank the Darkness you never wanted a ride in daylight.

All women look the same in the dark.

Five years when you were all I could have. At least with Lady Kermilla I won't need a drug to keep myself hard in order to fulfill my duties.

All women look the same in the dark. All women. All women.

Dreams. Memories. Lashed by words spoken by her previous Consort on the day he left her court and by Theran last night, Cassidy headed for the gardens as soon as there was enough light. She couldn't stay in the house, couldn't breathe in the house.

It hurt to think, hurt to feel, hurt to remember.

Theran didn't want her, wasn't even supposed to make that kind of offer. A First Escort wasn't a Consort. She didn't want a Consort. Didn't want another man telling her she wasn't good enough, pretty enough, hot enough, arousing enough, whatever enough she wasn't, because she could only be who she was, and she didn't want to be hurt like that. Not ever again.

And even now, when she should have been free of that kind of pain because no man here was required to warm her bed, Theran had shoved that truth in her face.

She was good enough when bedding her could be used

to feed ambition or provide relief, but she would never be wanted for herself.

"No tools," she muttered. "Need tools."

She entered the big stone shed as quietly as possible, but the *clunk* of shovels was enough to have Gray pulling aside the old blanket that served as a door to his room.

"Cassidy?"

Couldn't talk to him now. Couldn't talk to anyone. "Go back to sleep, Gray. It's early. I just needed to get some tools." Shovel, hoe, rake, short-handled claw.

"You're going to start weeding now?"

"Yes." Hard to hold all of them. Easier to vanish them and call them back in when she got to the bed where she planned to work. But she didn't want easier. Not today. Easier wouldn't help her run from the words.

"Okay," Gray said. "I'll just—"

"No." Cassidy tried to hold back anger, hurt, all the feelings that wanted to lash out at someone, anyone. "I need to work alone. You need to leave me alone."

She ran from the shed and stopped at a part of the garden that looked like it hadn't been touched in years. The ground here wasn't soft like the bed she'd been working on with Gray. This ground would require muscle, sweat, even pain.

Nothing easy. Not here.

All women look the same in the dark.

Did you really think I was excited about being with you?

She had to move. Had to. Work. Move. Keep moving. *Don't think.* Because if she let the words keep ripping at her heart, she'd simply lie down and not get up again.

Ebon Askavi

Lucivar closed the door of the sitting room, took a moment to get a feel for what kind of temper he was about to meet, and didn't like the answer. Didn't like it at all.

"Draca told me you were here," he said.

Daemon turned away from the windows. "I received the first report from Cassidy."

"Is she doing all right?"

Daemon smiled dryly. "Hard to say. I think she was nervous about writing the report and was trying hard not to say anything negative, so it's a bit lean on information. However, she did say that her Master of the Guard is a Sapphire-Jeweled Warlord Prince who is demon-dead. Since yarbarah isn't a vintage known in Dena Nehele, she requested that some bottles be sent to her, paid for by the Queen's gift."

"You're taking care of those bills, aren't you?"

"I am. And since at least half of the yarbarah made in Kaeleer comes from our family's vineyards, I decided to deliver a couple of cases personally."

"You mean deliver them personally as far as the Keep here in Kaeleer. You can't go to Terreille."

Daemon stiffened. His eyes began to glaze. "Are you giving me orders, Prick?" he asked too softly.

"I'm telling you I'll help you follow our Queen's command, even if that means we'll both need a Healer by the time the discussion is done."

Daemon looked away. "Did Father tell you what happened?"

"He told me dealing with Theran Grayhaven opened up some old wounds," Lucivar replied. Saetan had told him more than that, and what their father hadn't said he could guess.

"Did he tell you I attacked Jaenelle?"

Mother Night. Lucivar blew out a breath, not sure how to answer that.

"Did he tell you the Sadist was in bed with her?"

Oh, now. *That* he knew how to deal with. "The way I heard it, *Daemon* attacked Jaenelle while caught in an old, bad memory, and the Sadist enjoyed a snuggle that included a lot of moaning and several climaxes."

"What?"

Hell's fire, he's fragile.

"The Sadist uses sex as a weapon," Lucivar said, "but the Sadist rises out of temper, not desire. Usually."

Daemon swayed—and Lucivar had the queer sense of circling around a memory . . . about another time and place when Daemon had come to him, already mentally fragile, and he had lashed out with words that had created a wound that would never fully heal. Even now.

"Old son, Daemon makes love to Jaenelle, but the Sadist dances with Witch," Lucivar said gently. "Not out of hate or temper; he dances with her out of desire. But this time, for whatever reason, she didn't make that transition with you—and it scared you."

"Wouldn't it scare you?"

"*Tch.* You scare the shit out of me when you're the Sadist. But you don't scare her. You don't scare Jaenelle."

"I did scare her."

"Yeah, well, not as much as you think. And I figure scaring her once in a while helps her remember what you're feeling when she does something that scares you. Which, you have to admit, she does on a regular basis."

Daemon's response was a brief, reluctant smile to acknowledge that particular truth. Then the smile faded. "Have you ever . . . ?"

Pain there. Fear there. And too damn close to one of those emotional scars that created a line Daemon couldn't cross anymore. Not without paying too high a price.

"Just say it," Lucivar said.

"Do you ever feel possessive about Marian?"

Lucivar sat back on air, as if he were sitting on a stool. "Most of the time, I think of myself as Marian's husband, or I think of her as an independent woman who lives with me and is the mother of my son. But when Marian and I first became lovers, she moved into my bedroom—and into my bed. So there's not a night that goes by that I'm not saying 'Mine.' "

Daemon turned to look at him. Lucivar couldn't tell what was going on in his brother's mind or heart, but he knew what he said here and now would matter. Really matter. So he took a moment to choose his words.

"Marian comes to my bed every night, but some nights it feels different. Occasionally I'm in bed before her, and when I see her walking toward the bed, watch her get into bed, I feel . . . different. I don't have the words for it, Daemon. I just feel different. More . . . dangerous. It's not like the rut. When this happens, I'm still there. My brain is still there. But something changes inside me, and I don't see her the same way.

"I don't know what she sees in my face, in my eyes. Sometimes when she gets into bed, she's nervous but excited. Aroused. And sometimes she's scared. Of me. Of whatever I am when that feeling fills me."

Their eyes met. Held.

"What do you do?" Daemon asked softly.

"On the nights when she's nervous and excited, the sex is . . . *more*. It has a flavor it doesn't have any other time."

"And on the other nights?"

"I'll kiss her once, because I need to. And I'll hold her while she sleeps. But I won't have sex with her. Even if I'm ready to burst and she says she's willing, I won't have sex with her when I can smell her fear."

Lucivar took a breath and blew it out. Not an easy thing to talk about, even with a brother he loved.

Not something he'd ever admitted to anyone before.

"Want some advice?" he asked.

"Yes."

"Some night soon, when nothing is riding you, when you're feeling easy, invite Jaenelle to your bed. To the bed that's yours, not hers."

"To prove that the Sadist won't always be there?"

"Oh, no. No, Daemon, the Sadist will rise in a heartbeat to defend your most private bit of territory. But I don't think he'll hurt Jaenelle. He'll play games. That's what he does. But he won't hurt her."

He felt a change inside Daemon, pieces that would never be completely whole settling back into place.

"I'll take the yarbarah to Dena Nehele," he said. "I'd like to get a look around, and this is a good excuse. And I'd like to get a look at this demon-dead Warlord Prince."

"Which means you won't be back until later tonight."

"I'll let you know when I get back to the Keep."

"All right. Anything I can do here?"

Lucivar gave Daemon a lazy, arrogant smile. "You feeling brave?"

Daemon groaned.

"It's market day. I was going to entertain the little beast for a couple of hours so Marian could go down to Riada alone."

Daemon groaned louder, but this groan sounded less sincere.

"Fine. All right," Daemon said. "For Marian."

"Of course."

Daemon laughed, and the sound had Lucivar breathing easy again.

"Will you be all right going to Terreille?" Daemon asked.

"I'll be fine."

Daemon hesitated. "You'll shield?"

Lucivar vanished the two boxes of yarbarah. "Of course. I have to set a good example." Slipping the hunting knife out of its sheath, he studied the blade for a moment before deciding it was a sufficient weapon to wear openly. "Is Surreal still pissed off at me for chewing on her because she didn't shield before she went into that spooky house?"

"She doesn't automatically swear anymore when she hears your name, so I think she's getting over it."

Lucivar grinned. "In that case, it's time to get some other woman riled up."

Terreille

She had to move. Had to work. Move. Work. Keep moving.

Whenever she stopped for a moment, her hands throbbed in time with her heart, and she knew that wasn't good. But the words were there, waiting to cut, jab, tear. The pain in her back, arms, shoulders, and hands kept the words at bay. Formed a wall that the other hurt couldn't breach.

So she kept working, kept moving, kept the words at bay.

"How long can she keep that up?" Ranon asked, sounding worried.

Theran shook his head as he watched Cassidy. As they *all* watched Cassidy. Since early this morning, the First Circle had been gathering on the terrace to watch their Queen tear into the gardens.

So she got up feeling pissy. If she hadn't been eavesdropping, she would have had a good ride last night and would have been feeling just fine this morning.

But she was out there digging in that damn garden so *everyone* would know little Cassidy was feeling pouty.

She'd snapped at Ranon when he'd gone out to talk to her, told him flat out to leave her alone. And when he, Theran, had approached her, she had screamed at him. *Screamed.* Scared Gray so much the boy had been hovering around the terrace ever since.

She'll stop when she gets tired of playing the wounded party, Theran thought. *Hell's fire, it's not like I actually did anything.*

"What in the name of Hell is going on here?"

Theran spun around and stared at the Red-Jeweled Eyrien standing in the doorway. A Warlord Prince whose glazed gold eyes were a warning that the man was standing close to the killing edge, if he wasn't already dancing on it.

Ranon shifted into a fighting stance.

The Eyrien stepped out on the terrace, ignoring Ranon, his eyes fixed on Cassidy.

"You don't want to start a pissing contest with me," the Eyrien said to Ranon. "You really don't." He turned his head, and Theran felt the punch of power as those gold eyes stared at him.

He was looking at death. This man was a stranger who had walked into his home and should be challenged, but he knew, with absolute certainty, that he was looking at death.

Then the Eyrien fixed his eyes on Gray. "You do anything to piss her off?" he asked mildly.

Gray shook his head.

"Then get me two large buckets of cold water, and put them over there." He pointed to a spot near the stairs leading down to the lawn. "Do it now."

Gray bolted.

"What are you going to do?" Theran asked.

"What you should have done," the Eyrien replied. "Take care of your Queen."

"She ordered us to leave her alone," Ranon said.

The Eyrien snorted. "And you let her get away with that? Well, she knows better than to say that to me."

As soon as Gray returned with the buckets of water, the Eyrien headed for Cassidy. When he got close to her, he whistled sharply.

Her head came up—and the hoe came up like a weapon. The Eyrien simply grabbed the wood between her hands and tugged. She yanked back. He tugged. Then he yanked, lifting her off her feet for a moment before he turned and walked back to the terrace, dragging her with him.

Her feet kept trying to find purchase, but she skimmed along the top of the grass while the Eyrien ignored her increasingly shrill demands.

"It's my hoe!" Cassidy yelled, still fighting the Eyrien as he yanked her up high enough to clear the terrace steps. "Let go! It's mine!"

"Uh-huh." The Eyrien set her down in front of the buckets.

"Mine!"

A fast twist of his wrist, and the length of the hoe handle between Cassidy's hands snapped off cleanly. He tossed it off the terrace.

"You broke my hoe!" Cassidy wailed. *"You broke my hoe!"*

As she threw down the broken pieces, the buckets rose up behind her and doused her with cold water.

Her shriek had all of them jumping back. Except the Eyrien.

"Have I got your attention now, witchling?" the Eyrien asked.

"You—" Cassidy blinked. Stared at the man.

"Yeah. Remember me?"

"Oh, shit." Her eyes skipped over Theran and settled on Ranon and the others before coming back to the Eyrien.

"Listen up, Cassie, because I'll only tell you this once," the Eyrien said. "If you have a problem with your court, you deal with your court. And if they end up with a few bruises because of it, so be it."

"A Queen doesn't do that to her court," Cassidy said.

The Eyrien grabbed her wrists and turned her hands palms up. "And a woman doesn't do *this* to herself."

Theran looked at Cassidy's hands and felt his stomach roll. How could she have done that? Why didn't she stop?

She looked at her hands—and grew pale.

"You ever do anything like this again, I'll haul you back to Kaeleer," the Eyrien said. "And I'll bury anyone who tries to stop me."

"You have no right to—"

"You do anything like this again, I will haul you back to

Kaeleer, and *you* can explain to your father why you did this to his daughter."

Kick in the gut. Her lower lip quivered. Her eyes filled with tears. The damn Eyrien knew right where to hit her to take all the fight out of her.

Bastard.

"Do you have a Healer?" the Eyrien asked.

"Yes," Cassidy said.

"Then you call her, and you get those hands fixed. I'll look in on you in a little while. We've got some things to talk about."

She stumbled a little when she headed for the door, and she flinched away from him when Theran reached out to give her a little support through the doorway.

He waited until he was sure she was out of sight and hearing before he looked at the Eyrien. "Who do you—"

His back slammed into the house. The Eyrien's forearm pressed against his chest, holding him in place.

Hell's fire. He hadn't even seen the man move.

"The only reason a woman does that to herself is because she's running from pain that hurts a lot more," the Eyrien snarled. "And in my experience, the source of that kind of pain is usually attached to a cock. I'm guessing you're the reason she was out there this morning. Whatever the problem is, you'd better fix it. Because if I ever find her in that shape again, boyo, I will skin you alive."

The Eyrien stepped back. Theran sagged against the wall.

The Eyrien looked at Ranon, who stiffened but offered no challenge. "Does the Master of the Guard live in this house?"

"Yes," Ranon replied. "But he's not available until sundown."

"I'm aware of that. I have a delivery for him. And a few things to discuss."

The Eyrien walked into the house. No one asked him where he was going.

"Mother Night," Ranon said. Then he looked at Theran. "You all right?"

"Bruises. Nothing more." Except he had looked at death.

The Eyrien wasn't bluffing about skinning him alive.

Cassidy walked into the healing room Shira had set up in the wing that held the working rooms for the court.

"What's going on?" Shira said. "Ranon keeps calling me on a psychic thread, telling me to get to the healing room as fast as I can, and I've never heard him sound so nervous. What's . . . ?"

Cassidy held out her hands.

"Mother Night!"

Shira hurried around the table where she mixed her tonics and healing brews. Her hands hovered around Cassidy's but didn't touch.

Cassidy kept her eyes fixed on a spot over Shira's left shoulder. "Can you fix them?"

Shira let out a quivering sigh. "I think so. It's going to take a while just to clean them out and see how bad it really is, but I think so." She led Cassidy to a chair at one end of the table.

Cassidy sat quietly, cocooned in pain. She didn't pay attention as Shira hustled around the healing room, gathering supplies and starting a series of different brews to cleanse and heal. But she did look over when Shira placed a basin on the table.

"What's that for?" she asked.

Shira gave her a long look. "This isn't going to be easy, and I'm thinking one or both of us is going to need to puke in that basin before this is done."

Gray followed the Eyrien who had *dared* to dump cold water over Cassie. Who had *yelled* at Cassie.

Bastard.

Why didn't Theran or Ranon say anything? Why did they let him *do that*?

The bastard had no right. He—"had no right!"

The Eyrien stopped and turned his head just enough to indicate he knew someone was behind him. Had probably known all along.

The man was power and temper like he'd never felt before, but he would have his say.

"She's our Queen!" Gray shouted. "Ours! You had no right to be scolding her or getting her wet."

The Eyrien turned to look at him. "Your Queen," he said quietly. "Why didn't you stop her?"

His eyes filled with frustrated tears. "She wouldn't let me. She *ordered* me to stay away, to leave her alone. And she got hurt." His shoulders sagged. "She got hurt."

The Eyrien took a step closer. "The first law is not obedience. The first law is to honor, cherish, and protect. The second is to serve. The third is to obey."

"But if you don't obey, you get punished."

The Eyrien studied him. "Everything has a price. You take a chance of being punished, even killed, for challenging a Queen even if you're doing it to protect her, but you accept that risk and do what you should. If the Queen is truly worthy of your loyalty, she'll understand the reason for the challenge and back down. Doesn't mean she'll like it or be happy with the man, but she'll back down."

"She told everyone to leave her alone." It had been so painful to watch her, to know she was hurting and not be able to stop her.

"Someone hurt her and—"

"Who?" Gray felt something in him stir. "Who hurt Cassie?"

"I don't know, and that's healthier for everyone," the Eyrien said. "I do know she was hurting before she went out into the garden, and she was trying to sweat out some of the hurt and temper. Her First Escort should have given her an hour; then he should have used Protocol to stop her. And if that didn't work, he should have fought her into the ground."

Gray frowned. "Protocol? But those are just words."

"Yeah. And one sentence that used the right words could have stopped this."

He'd gotten a glimpse of Cassie's hands. One sentence could have stopped that?

The Eyrien made a sound. Annoyance? Disgust? "This court is supposed to be learning the Old Ways. I know Lady Cassidy brought books of Protocol with her. Haven't any of you looked at them?"

"Don't know." Gray rubbed his nose with the back of his hand. "If I had said the sentence, she would have stopped before she got hurt?"

It was the way the Eyrien looked at him that made Gray wonder what the man saw.

"A Queen doesn't like having a man set his heels down and get ready to fight her about something, so if you use Protocol to stop her, she'll probably swear at you. A lot."

"That's it? She'll swear at me?" He wouldn't like it, but that didn't sound so bad. "Will she hit?"

"Depends on the woman. I've gotten slugged in the arm more than once because I annoyed a witch who needed to be protected from herself." The Eyrien shrugged. "I can take a bruised muscle a lot easier than I can take watching someone I care about get hurt."

If he learned the Protocol, then . . .

Gray looked around and realized where he was. He'd been so focused on catching up to the Eyrien and yelling at the man for dumping water on Cassie, he hadn't paid attention.

"Nothing is going to come at you," the Eyrien said, "because there is nothing here that can get past me."

He knew. Somehow this stranger knew.

"Who are you?" Gray whispered. He wanted to curl up and hide, wanted to run.

"Lucivar. And you?"

"Gray." His body shook with the effort to stand there and not run, not hide, not scream out the old fear until his voice was gone.

The *other* Queen never stopped the pain until his voice was gone.

"I'm not . . . right," Gray said. That was the reason he couldn't serve in the court. Talon and Theran had both told him that. Not that he'd wanted to serve in the court. At least, not until he'd met Cassie.

"No, you're not," Lucivar said quietly. "You have scars, Gray, and they run deep. I can feel them in you. When a man has scars like that, there are boundaries he can't cross, lines he has to draw to keep himself whole. But those boundaries aren't as small as you might think, and a man can choose to live safe or he can choose to live right up to those lines. He might slip over a line every now and then, and that will hurt like a wicked bitch, but he might decide that what he gains will be worth the price."

"Do you have scars?" Gray asked.

Lucivar nodded. "I have scars. And sometimes they still bleed."

Gray studied Lucivar. This man didn't know him, didn't know about the times when he was so scared he couldn't take care of himself, when his body seized up so badly he couldn't move. And yet there was a message underneath the words, a message that had been there since Lucivar had first turned and looked at him.

"I'm not a warrior," Gray said.

"Yes, you are." Lucivar smiled grimly. "Just because you fought on a different kind of battlefield doesn't make you less a warrior."

Something stirred, shifted, fit into place.

"You get a copy of those books of Protocol and you study them," Lucivar said. "Next time you won't have to stand back if Cassidy does something foolish."

"The first law is not obedience," Gray said.

Lucivar grinned. "That was the best rule I ever learned."

Gray grinned in reply. Then the grin faded as he looked at the walls that seemed to be closing in around him.

"Do you want me to walk you out of here?" Lucivar asked.

Gray hesitated. "Can those boundaries you talked about change?"

"Up to a point. The challenge is to learn which ones are still fluid and which ones are made of stone. I'm guessing you entered what had been the enemy's lair. That's pushing the boundaries plenty for one day."

Gray nodded. Then he pointed to a door on the right. "That room has the fastest way out from here. Not a door, just a window, but there's nothing in the way under it."

"Let's go."

When Gray had the window open and one leg over the sill, he realized what was missing from Lucivar's psychic scent that was there in all the other Warlord Princes' scents. Even Theran's and Talon's.

"You don't pity me," Gray said.

Lucivar gave him one of those long, assessing looks. "A lot of us have scars, boyo. The biggest difference between you and the rest of us is you haven't learned to live with yours yet."

FOURTEEN

Terreille

Talon waited in the small meeting room. As Master of
the Guard, he didn't have an office like the Steward—
and didn't want one—but this small room was becoming
his place to talk with one or two of the men when he had
specific instructions or one of them wanted to report something in private. Not that there had been much to report.

He had a bad feeling that was about to change.

Didn't need to be told they were in trouble. He'd felt
that dark presence the moment he woke; known a strong
predator had come to the estate. And Powell had knocked
on his door a minute after sunset to tell him an Eyrien was
waiting to see him. A Red-Jeweled Warlord Prince.

"Red-Jeweled, my ass," Talon muttered. He wore Sapphire. He knew the feel of Red. And he was willing to bet
that if the Eyrien wore the Red, it wasn't his Jewel of rank.
Which meant the Eyrien had to be . . .

The door opened and controlled fury walked into the
room.

"Lucivar Yaslana," Talon whispered, feeling his legs go
weak. He'd never met the man before, thank the Darkness, but there was no mistaking the Ebon-gray Jewel that
gleamed against Lucivar's brown skin. "I'm Talon, Master
of the Guard."

"You know what I am?" Lucivar asked.

Talon nodded. He'd heard enough stories to know exactly what was standing in this room.

Lucivar raised one hand. Two boxes appeared on the
table. He approached the table and pulled the top off one

box. "Official business first. This is yarbarah, the blood wine."

With no wasted movement, Lucivar opened a bottle of yarbarah, called in a wineglass, filled it, and began warming the blood wine over a tongue of witchfire.

"Since you're going to need to keep replenishing your power, you should drink a glass of this three times a day. More if you want, but three glasses will provide enough blood to maintain someone who is demon-dead. Every ten days, you should add some fresh human blood. How much depends on the strength of the person who is giving it, but a couple of spoonfuls is usually enough. And once a month you should drink an offering cup of undiluted human blood." Lucivar handed the glass to Talon. "Yarbarah is best drunk warm. It tastes a little thick otherwise. And it's best to keep a bottle chilled once you open it."

Talon took the wineglass but didn't drink. "The court can't afford the expense of—"

"Queen's gift. Won't cost the court anything to keep you supplied with what you need to serve as Master."

Someone's paying for it, Talon thought, but he didn't argue. And he didn't try to resist any longer when the smell of blood was sharpening his hunger and need.

He took a sip, got the taste of it, then gulped down the rest of the glass. Not as rich or potent as human blood, but there wasn't any shame in drinking it.

"There are specific rituals for the giving and taking of blood," Lucivar said. "You should learn them."

Talon hesitated, then filled the glass again and warmed it with witchfire the way Lucivar had done.

"Why do you know so much about yarbarah?" he asked.

"My uncle, cousin, and older brother were demon-dead. My father is a Guardian. Yarbarah is standard fare with the family."

Talon took another swallow of yarbarah and frowned. "They *were* demon-dead?"

"They're gone now."

"And your father is . . . ?" According to some stories, Yaslana was a half-breed bastard whose bloodlines were unknown. According to other stories, Daemon Sadi shared that unknown paternal bloodline, making Sadi and Yaslana half brothers.

"A Guardian," Lucivar said. "One of the living dead. And the High Lord of Hell."

Ice twined around Talon's spine. *Saetan* had sired Sadi and Yaslana? Hell's fire, Mother Night, and may the Darkness be merciful!

That explained some things about the two of them. And it made Talon wonder if going to Sadi for a favor hadn't been a serious mistake if his brother was also going to take an interest in Dena Nehele.

And his father as well? That wasn't a thought Talon wanted to entertain.

"What's your unofficial business?" Talon asked.

Lucivar's gold eyes glazed. "I don't like what I see here, Talon. I don't like what I *feel* here. If it doesn't change, I'm taking Cassidy back to Kaeleer, and I'll leave nothing but corpses behind me."

"You have no right to make that decision."

"I say I do. Your Queen got hurt today, and not one of her court did a damn thing to stop it."

"Hurt? How? What happened?"

"Ask the First Circle. Ask the First Escort, who's lucky to still be alive."

"What happened?" Talon asked again.

"I figured it was better for everyone if I didn't ask for the details."

Hell's fire.

Something wasn't right. Even if Yaslana was here because Sadi had asked his brother to play messenger, Lucivar's interest in Cassidy seemed a bit too proprietary.

"What's your interest in a Rose-Jeweled Queen?" Talon asked. He'd tried to put it aside because Cassidy seemed a likable enough girl—and because there was something about her that pulled at him and pulled hard—but the truth was they needed strength and had gotten weakness.

Lucivar tipped his head, and his expression changed to cold amusement. "You don't know? Your boy Grayhaven didn't tell you?"

"Tell me what?"

"The Jewels a Queen wears are not the only kind of

power she wields. You should know that well enough. How many of the Queens you endured over these past few decades would have ruled at all if they hadn't been backed by that bitch Dorothea SaDiablo?"

"None," Talon said bitterly. "What's that got to do with the here and now?"

"Connections, Prince. You looked at Cassidy's Jewels and forgot to consider the connections."

"What connections?"

"Do you know why Cassidy is here?" Lucivar asked.

"Because Sadi's wife is a friend of hers, and Theran's choice was to take Cassidy or walk away without a Queen," Talon snapped, frustrated enough to be imprudent.

"Sadi's wife."

"A Queen who doesn't seem able to form a court of her own, even with Sadi's backing."

The room suddenly turned cold enough to bite.

"Your boy left out a few things," Lucivar said too softly. "Because of that, I'll overlook your lack of courtesy. This time. Since Grayhaven has chosen to leave out a few details—or didn't care enough to ask—you would do well to ask Cassidy a few questions. Like who really sent her to Dena Nehele."

The cold was turning his muscles to stone. He wouldn't be able to move fast enough to avoid an attack. Wouldn't survive an attack even if he *could* move.

Killing field. Battlefield. Didn't matter. Any man who fought knew that no one on the opposing side survived when Yaslana stepped into a fight.

"I'll be back, Talon," Lucivar said as he turned toward the door. "You can count on it. And the next time I won't be as forgiving. You can count on that too."

Lucivar opened the door, then stopped and looked back. "The Warlord Prince Gray."

Talon swallowed hard. Mother Night! How would a defenseless boy like Gray handle crossing paths with something like Yaslana? "What about him?"

"How old was he when he was tortured?"

Talon rocked back on his heels, not sure what to think. "How did you know?"

Lucivar snorted. "I've lived seventeen hundred years. I've seen a lot of courts and a lot of men during that time.

I know the look, and I know the feel, of a man who's been tortured."

"Fifteen," Talon said. "He was fifteen years old and the most promising Warlord Prince to come along in a couple generations or more. Not as good with weapons as Theran, but stronger in other ways. He could have been stronger." He sighed, feeling the old regrets. "Wasn't much left of that promising boy two years later when I finally found him and got him away from the bitch."

Lucivar just looked at him for a long time. "Ask the questions, Prince," he said softly. "Ask the questions before it's too late."

Talon waited until Lucivar left the room before he drained the second glass of yarbarah. Then he corked the bottle and put a cooling spell on it. He wanted more, needed more blood, since he'd resisted asking for any— or demanding any—from the Warlord Princes in the court since the night Cassidy had freely given her blood.

"Too many warnings and not enough information," Talon growled.

When he opened the door, he found Ranon on the other side.

"I came to tell you the Eyrien is gone," Ranon said.

"In here," Talon snapped.

Ranon came into the room, wary.

"What in the name of Hell happened today?"

"I don't know," Ranon said.

"You have no idea how much trouble we're in, so don't be playing games with me."

"I don't know!"

Frustration. Worry. Ranon wasn't trying to hide those things.

"Then tell me what you do know."

"I respectfully refuse to give you a shovel. Or a hoe. Or a rake. Or any of the tools. I Craft-locked the shed."

Cassidy slanted a look at Gray, who had crept up to the flower bed and now stood a long step away from her.

Her hands throbbed whenever she lowered them. Her arms ached when she held her hands up. She shouldn't even be out there. She should be in her room, resting. She'd slept for a little while after Shira finished the healing and helped her to her suite, but she didn't feel easy about being inside the house. At least out here, there was the illusion of comfort.

Then the phrasing Gray used sank in and had her looking at him more closely—and had her eyeing the book he clutched to his chest like a shield.

"Is that one of the books of Protocol I brought?"

Gray nodded. "If I'd studied the book before, I could have stopped you from getting hurt."

"I told you to stay away," Cassidy said. "You obeyed my orders."

"The first law is not obedience. Lucivar said so."

Thank you very much, Lucivar. Even if he was an adult, Gray was still an impressionable young man, and Lucivar Yaslana could certainly leave an impression.

"How much time did you spend with Lucivar?" Cassidy asked.

"Not long."

Long enough. There was a look in Gray's eyes that hadn't been there yesterday.

"You can swear at me if you want," Gray said with complete sincerity. "You can swear at me because I won't let you have any tools."

For the first time, Cassidy appreciated the lessons in maintaining a dignified expression and a steady voice.

"Thank you, Gray, but I don't feel like swearing right now. I'll take you up on that offer another time."

"Okay." He sidled up until he was standing right next to her. Until his shoulder brushed against hers.

Not wanting to wonder why he was standing that close, she stared at the flower bed. And frowned.

"You cleaned it up, didn't you?" she asked.

He nodded. "You kept digging them up, but you stopped tossing the weeds out. Stopped picking up the rocks and tossing them out too." He paused, then added softly, "Some of the rocks have your blood smeared on them."

She felt sick. She hadn't noticed the blood.

"So," Gray said, giving her a light nudge as he pointed to the boulder she'd been digging around when Lucivar hauled her out of the garden. "What do you think? Should the rock stay, or should it go?"

*   *   *

Talon walked toward the back of the garden as fast as his limping gait allowed.

Connections. Yes, he knew about connections. But he hadn't read the signs right this time. Hadn't made the effort he should have over these past few days to find out more about the Queen who now ruled Dena Nehele. He had been disappointed by Cassidy's lack of strength, hadn't questioned Theran's unhappiness that the one favor he could use hadn't netted something better.

Until today, he'd thought the connection had been between Sadi and Theran, because of Jared. Now he understood: Jared's bloodline had gotten Theran an audience and nothing more. The only reason they had a Queen at all was Cassidy's connection to Sadi and Yaslana.

And he'd damn well better find out why two of the darkest-Jeweled males in the history of the Blood were taking such a keen interest in a Rose-Jeweled Queen they didn't serve.

Gray noticed him first, and even in the dusky light, Talon saw the queer look in the boy's eyes. In another Warlord Prince, he would have called that look a challenge. Then it was gone, and he pushed aside the thought.

"Lady," Talon said.

"Prince Talon," Cassidy replied.

"Gray, you should go on and get some supper," Talon said.

Gray didn't move.

"That was Prince Talon's subtle way of telling you he wants to talk to me alone," Cassidy said.

"Do you want to talk to him?" Gray asked.

Talon felt as if he'd stepped on ice but didn't quite lose his footing.

What in the name of Hell happened to Gray today?

"I'll see you tomorrow," Cassidy said, nudging Gray with an elbow. "I should go back inside before Vae comes out to find me."

"You'll wear your hat tomorrow," Gray said.

"I'll wear my hat."

"You won't pick up tools."

"I won't pick up tools."

"You'll—"

"*Gray.*"

"Are you going to swear at me?"

"I'm thinking about it."

Gray grinned, nothing more than a boy again. Then he headed for the stables, where the men would have some food for him.

Alone with her, Talon wondered how to ask the questions that needed asking.

It's been a long time since I've been around a Queen. Maybe too long.

"I heard there was some trouble today," Talon said, looking at her hands. They were bandaged so thickly he wondered if she had any use of them.

Cassidy shrugged and stared at the dug-up flower bed she could barely see.

"Are your hands going to be all right?" Talon asked.

"Yes," Cassidy replied. "Shira says I didn't do any permanent damage. I'll just have to be careful for a while because they'll be tender."

Talon nodded. "You want to tell me what happened?"

"No."

He tapped a finger against his chest. "Master of the Guard, remember?"

"It's . . . personal."

Personal. Theran wasn't stupid. He wouldn't have gone up to her room last night without an invitation. Would he?

"Did Theran . . . ?" He looked away. He didn't want to say the words, but he couldn't dismiss the depth of Yaslana's fury—especially when that fury seemed mostly aimed at Theran. "Did he do something he shouldn't have?"

"No."

He heard the lie, but he couldn't call her on it. Even as her Master of the Guard, he couldn't call her on the lie. But he could—and would—talk to Shira and find out if Cassidy had any other injuries.

He didn't think Shira would tell him anything ugly—mostly because he was certain Yaslana wouldn't have let Theran live if the harm the boy had done to Cassidy had been physical.

"I heard Yaslana dumped a couple buckets of water on you," Talon said. "Not exactly a courteous thing to do."

Cassidy looked at him, clearly surprised—and relieved—that he wasn't demanding an explanation of what had ridden her so hard she hadn't noticed the damage she was doing to herself. "Oh. Well. That's Lucivar. He used to do that to everyone. When he was annoyed with his sister, he used to toss her into the pond, and *she* was the Queen he served."

"How did you get to know someone like Yaslana?"

"My cousin Aaron served in the Dark Court's First Circle, and Lucivar was the First Escort. Before the court formed officially, apprenticeships were offered to give some people an opportunity to work with darker-Jeweled witches and Warlord Princes and to study Protocol with the High Lord."

Talon's jaw dropped. "You learned Protocol from the High Lord of Hell?"

"Training in Protocol starts after a child's Birthright Ceremony and continues all through schooling. The High Lord's lessons were more about dealing with darker-Jeweled males and also the Protocols used when the living had contact with the demon-dead. And Jaenelle said trying to deal with Lucivar was an experience a Queen should have at least once."

So Sadi's wife had been there too.

"Where was this dark court located?"

Cassidy looked puzzled. "Where?"

"Seemed like there was at least one court in every Territory that was referring to itself as a dark court," Talon said. "I was just wondering where the one you mentioned was located."

"In Kaeleer, there was only one that was referred to as the Dark Court," Cassidy said slowly. "That was the court at Ebon Askavi."

Mother Night.

"With that kind of credentials, why doesn't Sadi's wife have a court?" Talon asked, but he was more wondering out loud than expecting an answer.

"After she recovered from her injuries, she didn't want to rule anymore," Cassidy said, "and everyone was so glad she survived, they didn't care if there was an official court."

"She was injured?"

"Two years ago. It was several months before anyone knew for sure that she survived, and several more before she was fully healed."

Two years ago. *Two years ago.*

"She got caught in that storm of power the Kaeleer army unleashed?"

Cassidy frowned at him. "There wasn't an army. That was Jaenelle. She unleashed her full strength and cleansed all three Realms of the Blood tainted by that bad High Priestess."

Talon swayed. He had felt that power when it screamed through Terreille two years ago. Had felt the bite of it before it let him go, passed him by.

One witch had unleashed that much power? *One?*

He stared at Cassidy.

"Didn't Theran tell you?" Cassidy asked.

"Tell me what?"

"Before she was injured, Jaenelle was the Queen of Ebon Askavi."

Theran paced the length of the larger meeting room, shooting looks at Ranon every time he passed that end of the table.

"You're sure Talon said to meet him here?"

Ranon gave him a cold stare. "I'm sure. He said to give him an hour, and then he wanted to meet with the whole First Circle. Guess he got delayed."

By what? Theran wondered.

When Talon walked in a few minutes later, he knew something was terribly wrong, because he'd never seen the older man look so shaken—or scared.

"You young fool," Talon said, heading right for him. "What did you do? *What did you do?*"

Talon grabbed Theran by the shirt and shook him before giving him a shove that had him half falling on the men sitting around the table.

"I didn't do anything," Theran snapped.

"You want to think for a minute and try the answer again?" Talon roared.

"I didn't. Do. Anything."

"You forgot a few details, boy. The kind of details that could destroy all of us—and Dena Nehele as well."

"What details?"

"Connections, Theran. Connections."

Talon sagged suddenly, and that was more frightening than his anger.

"I'm just as much to blame," Talon said quietly. "Didn't look closely enough. Didn't think to ask until it was shoved in my face that I hadn't asked."

"Talon," Powell said. "It would help the rest of us understand the danger if you could be a little less vague."

Theran eased around to the other side of the table but didn't take a seat. What sort of tale was Cassidy telling that would get Talon that pissed off at him?

"We've got Lucivar Yaslana—yes, *that's* who that Eyrien was—honing his weapons and looking in our direction. Which means Sadi is also going to be looking in our direction and honing his own brand of weapons. And don't think for a minute that Yaslana isn't going to report to his father—who happens to be the High Lord of Hell."

Some of the men sucked in a breath. Others groaned.

"And worst of all," Talon said grimly, "I don't think Lady Cassidy's friend is going to be looking kindly at us."

"Friend?" Ranon said, glancing at Theran. "You mean Sadi's wife?"

Talon looked at Theran, and there was a bleakness in the older man's eyes that made Theran shudder.

"Sadi's wife," Talon said softly. "Who was the Queen of Ebon Askavi."

Shocked silence.

"Witch," Talon continued, "chose Cassidy to be our Queen. So we'd all better start looking beyond a Rose Jewel to figure out why. Gentlemen, we've already made one bad mistake. We can't afford to make another. So we're going to study those books of Protocol, and we're going to learn what we said we wanted to learn. And if the Darkness is merciful, the next time Lucivar Yaslana shows up here, he won't invite all of us to step onto a killing field."

Ebon Askavi

Lucivar stepped into the sitting room and stopped. He'd expected to find his father waiting for him, but . . .

"What are you still doing here?" he asked Daemon as

he approached a low table filled with different kinds of edibles.

"Waiting for you." Daemon put a thin slice of cheese on top of a triangle of toast and added a spoonful of chopped spicy beef.

"Wine?" Saetan asked, indicating the open bottle.

"I'd rather have ale," Lucivar said as he took the remaining seat around the table.

Saetan smiled dryly. "I thought as much. That's why there's some on the way."

Lucivar filled a plate while he considered the other two men. Saetan was ... Amused was the politest word that came to mind. Daemon was definitely grumpy.

"How was your day?" Lucivar asked, watching his brother.

"Fine."

"And you're still here because you were waiting for me?"

Daemon made an inarticulate sound.

Saetan said, "He's trying to figure out how to explain a certain bit of Craft to his wife."

"Oh?" Lucivar said.

Daemon was paying an awful lot of attention to making little sandwiches he wasn't eating.

"Marian is pretty sure she can clean the paint off the floor," Daemon muttered. "Eventually."

"Oh?"

Daemon huffed out a sigh. "Doesn't that little beast ever get tired?"

Saetan had an arm wrapped around his belly and his other fist pressed against his lips.

"Oh, shit, Bastard. What did you do?"

"He made the mistake of falling asleep," Saetan said.

Daemon growled. "I just thought ... Something quiet. Just for a little while. We were sitting on the floor with sheets of sketching paper. They were big sheets. Why couldn't he keep the paint on the paper?"

"It would have been better if Daemon had thought to provide watercolors instead of a different kind of paint," Saetan said.

"And who in the name of Hell taught that boy about shields at his age?" Daemon snarled.

Probably the wolf pups. "Wasn't me." Lucivar looked at both of them. "So Daemonar managed to put some kind of shield *into* the paint so the standard ways of removing it aren't working? At least, not completely?"

Saetan was going to strain a muscle trying not to laugh, and Daemon . . .

"Besides the floor, what else did he paint?" Lucivar asked.

A beat of silence. Then Saetan said, "He painted Unka Daemon."

Lucivar ended up on the floor, roaring with laughter, which might have pissed off his brother if their father hadn't ended up on the floor too.

"Oh, my," Lucivar said, crawling back up on the chair. He looked at Daemon's face, which, outside of looking unnaturally flushed, didn't seem any different. "Where?"

Saetan propped himself up against a chair. "Let's just say Daemon needs to explain this to Jaenelle *before* he takes his shirt off."

Oh, shit.

The pitcher of ale arrived at that moment, making Lucivar wonder if that was luck or his father's exquisite sense of timing.

For a few minutes they ate, drank, and generally avoided looking at one another.

Then Saetan said, "So. Would you like to tell us why you were still pissed off when you walked in the room?"

Should have known he couldn't keep it leashed enough to hide it from those two.

"Is there a problem?" Daemon asked.

"Maybe." Lucivar drained his glass and refilled it. "Cassidy got hurt. She was so focused on running from one kind of pain, she worked until she ripped up her hands." He hesitated, then looked at Daemon. "I think Grayhaven was the cause of that pain, but I don't know that for sure."

Daemon's eyes looked glazed and a little sleepy—and the chill that was filling the room came from two sources.

"Why didn't you bring her back with you?" Saetan asked too softly.

"There's another Warlord Prince at the house. About the same age as Grayhaven. Calls himself Gray. He was tortured when he was fifteen and hasn't recovered from it mentally or emotionally. It's safe for him to be a boy, to be nothing that would be considered a threat." Lucivar took a long swallow of ale. "And yet he's the one who stepped up to the line. He's the one who told me flat out I had no right to take his Queen anywhere. He called her Cassie."

"Jewels?" Saetan asked.

"Didn't see them, but he felt like Purple Dusk. And he felt like he should have been more."

"Your impression?" Daemon asked.

"They're not a court yet. The males are resisting, and damned if I could figure out why. So I left some instructions with Vae. I'll be there for Cassidy's first moontime to make sure things get sorted out. And if I don't trust the males in her First Circle the next time I see them, I'll bring her back."

"Fair enough," Saetan said.

"What about Gray?" Daemon asked. "Anything we can do to help him?"

Lucivar thought for a moment, then shook his head. "Not yet. But I'll tell you this: if that boy decides to wake up, the Master of the Guard is going to have his hands full."

FIFTEEN

Terreille

As the last bandage came off, Shira studied Cassidy's hands, then sighed in relief.

So did Cassidy.

"You'll need to work them gently," Shira said, "and I do mean *gently*. There's still healing going on under the skin. And the skin itself is still fragile. Pulling on a tough blade of grass could be enough to slice it open."

"Are you telling me not to work in the garden?"

"I'm telling you to be very careful about how much you do for the next few days," Shira said. "And you should put a tight shield over your hands to protect them. And wear gloves."

Cassidy rolled her eyes. "Now you sound like my father."

"Maybe you should have listened to him."

They glared at each other. Then Shira looked away, as if suddenly realizing she'd crossed some line.

And she had.

"I guess we've become friends," Cassidy said, noting the look of surprise and pleasure in Shira's eyes.

"I guess we have," Shira replied a little cautiously. "So, what are you going to do first now that you *can* do things again?"

"It's not the first thing I'll do, but tonight I'm going to take a long, hot bath and soak until all of me wrinkles." To her way of thinking, being given sponge baths because she couldn't wash herself had been sufficient punishment for ripping up both hands. And needing someone's help with even more personal needs . . .

Which made her think of the other thing she needed to discuss with Shira.

"Do you know a brew to delay a moontime?" Cassidy asked.

Shira frowned. "Why would you want to do that? It will only make the next one a lot worse."

Cassidy wasn't sure how to explain without sounding insulting. Because wanting to delay this *was* insulting.

"You don't trust them, do you?" Shira asked.

"Trust who?"

"Your First Circle. You don't trust them to protect you. You don't trust them not to turn on you."

She didn't want to admit it, but she wasn't going to deny the truth. A witch was vulnerable during the first three days of her moon cycle because she couldn't use her own power to protect herself. And she felt far more vulnerable here in Dena Nehele than she had back home in Dharo.

Shira gave her a considering look. "You can trust Ranon. He won't hurt you."

"He's not sure he wants to serve me."

"No," Shira said thoughtfully, "he's sure of that. He's . . . puzzled . . . by his response to you."

A flash of understanding, especially when she realized Shira was acting more like a woman trying to brace herself for a truth that would wound.

"He wants to sniff my neck," Cassidy said.

Shira hesitated, then nodded.

"And he's not sure if that means something sexual."

Another reluctant nod.

"It doesn't."

Shira's eyes widened. "It *doesn't*?"

"No. I'm not sure what the attraction is. *I* can't see or feel anything. And I'm not sure what this impulse means to the males, except it's not sexual." She was pretty sure it wasn't sexual. Maybe she should write to Jaenelle soon and ask. "When I was preparing to come here, Jaenelle told me any Warlord Prince who truly belongs to me will want to sniff my neck and I wasn't to make a fuss about it."

Shira's mouth hung open. "Jaenelle? *Witch* told you that?"

Obviously the rest of the court knew what she'd told Talon about Jaenelle Angelline. Maybe that was why

Theran had been so stiffly polite these past few days. "Yes. When I thought about it later, I realized I'd seen all the males in her First Circle stand behind her and a little to the right so that they could ... Well, they weren't *obvious* about it, but basically they were standing there in order to sniff her. But there wasn't anything sexual about it. I suppose it *was* sexual with her Consort, but he arrived years after I had served my apprenticeship in the Dark Court, so Jaenelle's brother Lucivar was the only one I saw kiss her on that spot, and it was friendly. Like when my brother, Clayton, gives me a kiss on the head."

"It's not sexual," Shira said, not quite believing.

Cassidy shook her head and smiled. "Ranon is in love with you. I figured that out the first day when you offered your services to the court. So if the two of you want to find a suite of rooms in this place so you can live together, I have no objection. If you want to handfast, we'll all ignore Theran's mutters about expenses and have a party." She frowned. "There are still Priestesses here, aren't there?"

Looking a bit dazed, Shira nodded. "But I'm a Black Widow."

"And judging by the reaction when you first came here, that's not going to be an easy thing to be openly. But it shouldn't stop you from being with someone you love."

Shira walked over to the window and stared out. Since she kept wiping her cheeks, Cassidy went to the door, intending to slip out and give the other woman a little time to shed happy tears in private.

"How close are you?" Shira asked, turning her head a little. "To your moontime."

"It will start in a few days. Maybe any day now, actually."

"I can make up a brew that will delay it. Since you're so close, I'm not sure it will delay it for a full cycle, but it will give you a little more time to get used to the males here."

"Thank you."

Cassidy left the room and paused outside the door. In Dharo, she had made few decisions that had meant much. Here, every decision she made, no matter how small, could ripple through the entire Territory.

Be what you are. That had been Jaenelle's last bit of advice.

Maybe she wouldn't accomplish much. Maybe her court

would decide among themselves to keep her for a year as a token while they actually ruled. The Darkness knew they were all stronger than she, so there wasn't anything she could do if they opposed her.

But she *had* done something of value today, and if she did nothing else while she was here, at least she'd made it possible for two people to love each other openly.

As she headed for the door that opened onto the terrace, Cassidy couldn't stop smiling.

Gray pretended to rake the softened earth in front of him while he watched Cassie. The sun shone on that braid of fire as she walked across the lawn, and her strides were long and easy. Like the rest of her.

Every morning since the hurting she had come out to sit in the chair he set out for her. They talked about plants while he dug and weeded, reclaiming another piece of the gardens. And she talked to him about Protocol, since he studied a little more of the books each night and asked her questions.

He enjoyed the simple easiness of being around her, and looked forward to the hour or so they could spend together before she had to go inside to do her Queen work.

He hoped *she* would enjoy the surprise he had hidden in the wheelbarrow.

"Look," Cassidy said, giving him a wide smile as she held up her hands. "No more bandages."

Setting the rake aside, Gray scrubbed his hands on his pants to clean off a bit of the dirt before taking careful hold of her hands.

Healed. Not even a small scar to show the damage she had done to her hands.

Healed but not whole. Not yet. Maybe never. Maybe never as strong as before the hurting.

He had learned that painful lesson years ago.

"They're not strong enough for digging," Gray said. "Not yet."

"I won't know that until I—"

"No," he said, his voice sharpened by a certainty he couldn't explain. "They're not strong enough yet, Cassie. Not for digging in ground that hasn't been tended for too many years."

She looked bewildered—and hurt—that he would snap at her like that.

He couldn't stand to see her hurting, so he added quickly, "But you could plant."

"Plant?"

Gray stepped to one side so that Cassie could see inside the wheelbarrow.

"Oh," Cassie said, picking up one seed pot. "What are they?"

No longer sounding hurt. Now she sounded curious and excited—the seedlings of happiness.

"Don't know the fancy name for it, but the common name is blue river," Gray said. "It's a delicate trailing plant that has small blue flowers. Starts blooming in late spring and into summer. If you cut it back some at that point, it will have a second blooming season. I was thinking about that boulder you weren't sure of."

Still looking at the plant, Cassie nodded. "It has that funny hole in it."

"I figure that hole is about the size of a good-size pot. So if you plant one blue river in that hole and the others in front of the boulder . . ."

"It will look like a waterfall tumbling down rocks into a river. Gray, that's a *wonderful* idea." She gave him a quick kiss, right on the mouth, before she turned back to the wheelbarrow and began crooning to the little plants.

Gray stood frozen. She had *kissed* him. But not in a mean way. Not in a way that meant he was going to be tied down and hurt. Not the way the *other* Queen had done.

And not quite like a man-and-woman kiss. At least, he didn't think so. It was done before he'd known it had started.

He wouldn't mind trying a man-and-woman kiss if the woman was Cassie.

Would she want to try that kind of kissing with him?

"Gray?"

"Huh?"

"Where did you go?"

"Huh?"

Cassie stood in front of him, holding two of the seed pots, smiling at him, and looking a little puzzled.

"You have the strangest expression on your face," Cassie said. "What are you thinking about?"

Oh, no. He knew better than to answer *that* question. "Did you ask me something before?"

Cassie studied him for a moment, then shook her head. "Males are very strange."

Not half as strange as females, Gray thought.

"I asked where you got the plants."

"Oh. There are a couple of women in town who grow plants for sale. They have greenhouses and everything. And there are two sisters who grow a lot of the plants Healers need for their brews and salves. So when Shira and Ranon went to look at plants yesterday, I went with them. And I found these."

"I'd like to take a look at what's available," Cassidy said. "Maybe we could go back to those places tomorrow morning or the day after." She wrinkled her nose. "I haven't been in the town yet; things have been so busy here."

"We?" Gray asked, wondering why his heart was feeling funny all of a sudden.

"You and me. Oh, and I suppose I'll need an official escort as well just to keep everything proper."

"Protocol," Gray said, nodding. "You have to set a good example."

Cassie rolled her eyes. "I know you've lived here all your life, but you *sound* like you're from Kaeleer."

The words made him feel strange—and good. And stronger in a way he couldn't describe.

"I thought you could go with me," Cassie said. "If you want to," she added.

"I want to."

Her smile when she was happy was bright enough to dazzle the sun.

"Daylight's wasting," Cassie said. She set the seed pots aside and held up her hands. "Look. A double shield over the skin and then heavy gardening gloves." Which she called in and slipped over her hands.

"And your hat," Gray said.

She wrinkled her nose at him but obeyed and called in her hat.

"Are you going to swear at me?" Gray asked.

"I'm thinking about it."

He just grinned.

*   *   *

Cassie? Cassie!

Gray paused to watch the Sceltie's dance of indecision. Vae clearly had an opinion about Cassie working in the garden—Hell's fire, the dog had an opinion about *everything*—but she wasn't sure if her "permission to nip" applied to the Queen.

"She's all right," Gray told Vae, glad for the excuse to take a break. Not that he needed an excuse. Not with Cassie. But he didn't want to admit about himself what he'd been so quick to point out to her—sometimes damage couldn't be healed all the way if you weren't careful during the healing.

He didn't want her to know. Wasn't ready to tell her. Not yet. But he knew the warning signs and knew he needed to take some care or he'd be helpless and hurting.

"Yes, I'm all right," Cassie said. She stripped off her gloves and held up her hands so Vae could see them. "See? Nothing hurt." Then she looked at Gray. "But the hands have had enough work for the day."

He shrugged and smiled. "Nothing more to plant anyway."

"Was that deliberate?"

"Maybe."

She studied him for a moment as a thread of awareness grew between them. Then she looked at the Sceltie. "Did you come out for walkies?"

Theran said I am underfoot and should go outside for a while, Vae replied.

"Nipped him, didn't you?" Cassie said.

Many times he will not listen until I nip him. But he is learning.

"I'll bet he is." Cassie vanished her gloves and got to her feet. "I want to take a look at the rest of the garden, get a feel for the whole thing."

"I'll warn you now," Gray said. "This is the best of it. At the far end, the ground is overrun with some kind of weed. Can't dig it out. It just grows right back. Can't even burn it out."

"I'll take a look." Cassie turned toward the house. "What about that dead tree? Why didn't anyone take down what's left of it?"

"Can't." Gray rubbed his nose with the back of his hand.

"That honey pear tree is a symbol of the Grayhaven line. That's why the Queens let it stand. At least, that's partly why."

"But it's dead, Gray."

"Yes."

He saw the moment when she understood.

"Bitches," she said softly.

"It's dead, but it still taunted them," Gray said. "I've been talking to some of the men who used to work here and some whose fathers worked here. They said some of the Queens tried to pull the tree down, but there's something about it, about what's left of it. Saws won't cut the wood. Axes can't do more than chip at the outside. And the roots are still so chained to the ground, the tree can't be pulled out either. The soil all around it is so hard it can break a shovel, and Craft can't touch it at all. So all that time, *they* said they left the tree to remind everyone that the Grayhaven line was gone, but in truth they left it because they couldn't get rid of it."

"Maybe because the line isn't completely gone," Cassie said.

"Maybe."

"I hear the names Jared and Lia, Thera and Blaed. They must have been so important to this land, but I know so little. Does anyone know stories about them? Or were those lost too when the other Queens took over Dena Nehele?"

"Sure, there are stories," Gray said. "I know some. So does Theran. Talon would know more because he knew the four of them. They were friends."

"Do you think Talon would share some of those stories with me?"

"He'll tell you. So will I."

She stared at the tree and looked a little sad. Then she smiled at him. "I'd better take a look at the rest of the garden before someone comes looking for me."

He watched her walk away, with Vae trotting beside her.

As he shifted his weight from one foot to the other, he felt a warning twinge in his back.

"Enough," he said.

It surprised him how bitter his voice sounded that he couldn't work anymore today. He'd never minded before when he had to stop.

But that was before it mattered that someone might think he was weak.

One last thing, he thought as he vanished the tools. He'd get a bucket of water to wet down the new plants, and he'd use Craft to take the weight of the full bucket instead of forcing his body to do more than it should. Then he'd get something to eat and sit in the shade while he studied the next part of the book on—

*Gray? *Gray!**

His body stiffened in response to the panic in Vae's voice. He saw Cassie at the far end of the garden, backing away from that weedy spot, one hand clamped over her mouth.

Something wrong. Something terribly wrong.

Gray!

He ran.

The moment Vae saw him running toward Cassie, she ran toward the house. He had no idea who the Sceltie was calling for help, but he was certain she'd do her best to rouse everyone she could.

He slowed to avoid running Cassie down. "Cassie!" Maybe it was nothing worse than a snake or a dead mouse. Maybe . . .

She turned to look at him. Her freckles were the only color in her face.

"It's witchblood," she whispered. Then she threw her arms around him and held on as if her life depended on it. "It's *witchblood.*"

Her legs buckled, and he went down with her, wincing when his knees hit the ground.

"So many," Cassie sobbed. "So many."

He didn't know what to ask, didn't know what to do, didn't understand why those black-edged red flowers upset her so much.

Cassie? Cassie!

Not alone, Gray thought as the Sceltie returned, whining anxiously.

Voices. Shouts. He couldn't twist around to see, but moments later Theran and Ranon were there, asking questions he couldn't answer while Cassie sobbed.

Then Shira was there, on her knees beside him. "What's wrong? What happened? Is she hurt?"

"I don't know," Gray said, so shaken he began to stammer. "She looked at those weeds and got upset."

"Not w-weeds," Cassie gasped before she started crying harder.

"Mother Night," Shira muttered. She called in a bottle Healers used to store tonics, yanked out the stopper, then grabbed a hunk of red braid and pulled Cassie's head up. "Here. Drink this. *Drink!*"

Cassie drank. Gasped. Gulped air.

But she settled. When she rested her head on Gray's shoulder, she was still shaking but no longer crying.

Shira sat back, took a swig from the bottle, then held it out to Gray. "You too."

He obeyed and took a long swallow.

"What is that?" Theran asked.

"Brandy," Shira replied.

By now the rest of the First Circle except Talon had reached the spot—even Powell, who was still puffing from the run.

Gray looked up at Theran. "I don't know what happened."

"Not your fault, Gray," Theran replied softly.

"So many," Cassie whispered. "So many."

"So many what?" Shira asked with that quiet voice Healers used when they were asking about something painful.

"One for each," Cassie said. "That's how it grows. That's how you know. One plant for each. Living memento mori. Can't be killed once it takes root, can't be hidden. Ground soaked in blood nourishes the seed."

Gray saw the shock on the men's faces. Saw Shira pale.

"Cassidy . . . ," Shira said.

"It grows where a witch was killed," Cassidy said. "It grows where her blood was spilled in violence. So many died in that spot."

"Mother Night," Ranon said.

Gray wasn't sure which of them was still shaking—he or Cassie—until she pulled away from him to sit up on her own.

It was him.

"Can I have more of that?" Cassie asked, reaching for the tonic bottle.

Shira handed it over without a word.

"Do you know who might have died here, Theran?" Ranon asked.

Theran looked sick. "I'm not sure. Thera, I think. And Talon's wife."

"I've seen so much of this stuff growing in Dena Nehele—and in the Shalador reserves," Ranon said. "Was told it was just a weed, an invasive weed. Mother Night."

Feeling timid, Gray touched Cassie's shoulder. "What do we do now?"

"It's overgrown with weeds and hasn't been tended for too long," Cassie said. "So we'll tend that ground and the witchblood that grows there." She paused. "The Black Widows in the Dark Court told me that witchblood knows the name of the one who has gone, and if you know how, the plant can tell you whose blood nourished the seed."

Mutters. Murmurs. Shira shuddered.

"I can ask how it's done—if you want to know," Cassie said, looking at Shira.

"I— Grayhaven?" Shira said, looking at Theran.

"I don't know," he said. "I don't know if . . . I don't know."

Cassie nodded. When she shifted position, Theran offered a hand to help her stand up.

Gray got to his feet, wincing a little and pretending he didn't see the way Shira was studying him before Ranon pulled her up.

"We're going to clean up that ground," Cassie said.

Gray and Cassie need to rest, Vae said.

"Yes, they do," Shira said. "Lady Cassidy's hands are still fragile, and if she's going to stay out here and supervise, I want Gray to stay close by and keep her company. But I'd like to help clean up that part of the garden."

"So would I," Ranon said.

"Gray?" Theran said. "Do you have tools we could use?"

Gray called in the tools he'd vanished, handing them out as Theran, Ranon, and Archerr came up to claim them.

"The short-handled claws would work better for the tight places," he said. "They're still in the shed."

"I'll get them," Ranon said, handing the hoe to Shira.

They worked in the garden the rest of the morning, moving carefully between plants that now held a different meaning.

Gray watched them, frustrated because all he *could* do was watch. There was an odd comfort in knowing Cassie was just as frustrated that she couldn't help.

And there was no comfort at all in the way Theran kept looking at Cassie when he thought no one was watching.

SIXTEEN

Terreille

"I don't know which one is harder to get through," Cassidy muttered a couple of days later as she stomped to the garden to work off a little frustration. "A man's head or ground as solid as rock."

The day they'd all worked together to clean up the part of the garden filled with witchblood, she'd *thought* she and Theran had finally settled into some kind of understanding, that he might actually *listen* to what she was saying instead of telling her it couldn't be done "that way." Hell's fire! Anyone with a pebble's worth of brain could figure out Dena Nehele couldn't be ruled in "the ordinary way." They didn't have enough Queens to rule in "the ordinary way." That had been the point! And there was nothing unusual about males ruling on a Queen's behalf. It was done all the time in Kaeleer. Her cousin Aaron ruled Tajrana, the capital city of Nharkhava, on his Queen's behalf. And Prince Yaslana ruled Ebon Rih. And she *knew* there were Warlords assigned to be a Queen's representative who, in essence, ruled their home villages.

How in the name of Hell was she supposed to decide which available Queens might be able—and willing—to rule more than their little villages if she couldn't talk to them? But *Prince* Grayhaven kept finding reasons for her not to travel and see other parts of Dena Nehele, and he was just as quick with the excuses for why the other Queens—even with an escort of Warlord Princes—couldn't come to Grayhaven to talk to her.

And none of the other Warlord Princes challenged his asinine statements because he was *Grayhaven*.

"The man farts every time he opens his mouth," Cassidy muttered as she reached the big stone shed.

She closed her eyes, took a deep breath, and blew it out. "And Poppi would whack your butt if he heard you say that," she scolded herself.

"I'm Grayhaven."

Cassidy took a step closer to the shed's open door. Nobody in the part of the shed she could see. Most of the tools were stored neatly now, except for that jumble of things in the back left corner.

She looked at the old blanket that separated Gray's room from the rest of the shed.

"I'm Grayhaven."

"Gray?" she called softly. Theran was still in the house, so who was talking to Gray? The voice sounded familiar, but it was muffled too much for her to be sure, except it sounded male—and young.

Then Gray's voice rose in a kind of desperate keening. "I'm Grayhaven! *I'm Grayhaven!*"

"Gray!"

She rushed to the doorway and pulled the blanket aside—and saw him shivering on a pathetic excuse of a bed, caught in some kind of nightmare. He was wearing trousers and nothing else, and she felt her knees grow weak as she stared at the scars on his back.

"Mother Night, Gray," she whispered. "What did they do to you?"

"I'm Grayhaven!"

She wanted to touch him, wanted to shake him out of the nightmare—or the memory—but she was afraid touching him might frighten him even more.

She braced herself and said in a firm voice, "Prince Gray, your presence is requested."

He jerked, whimpered. But she thought her use of Protocol had pulled him out of the dream-memory, because the next thing he said was, "Cassie?"

It took him a couple of tries to turn himself so he was facing the doorway. "Cassie?"

His dark hair was matted with sweat, and his face had the drawn, exhausted look of a man who had endured too much.

"What's your name?" Cassidy asked, keeping her voice Queen firm. "What's your full name? Your real name?"

He hesitated, then said, "Jared Blaed Grayhaven."

She looked at the room—at the straight-backed chair that had a flat stone under one leg to keep it from wobbling, at the broken-down chest of drawers that had a single lamp, at the bookcase that had only one unbroken shelf.

"This is the best he could do?" she asked too softly as she looked at the room, piece by piece. "You're his family, and this is the best he would do?"

She backed out of the room, letting the blanket fall across the opening.

"Cassie?" Gray called.

She walked out of the shed, her stride lengthening with every step she took toward the house.

"Cassie!"

She couldn't stop, couldn't answer. Because every step stoked her fury just a little more.

***

"This was your idea to begin with," Ranon said, dogging Theran's footsteps with as much persistence as that damn Sceltie. "Why are you so determined now to stand in the way?"

"I'm not standing in the way," Theran tossed over his shoulder.

"You won't even give Cassidy the courtesy of listening to what she has to say."

He turned on Ranon. "If Warlord Princes are going to rule Dena Nehele, what was the point of trying to get a Queen?"

"And what's the point of having a Queen if you won't let her do anything?" Ranon snapped. "I can understand not wanting her to travel around the Territory right now, but why are you so determined not to have the few Queens who are left come to Grayhaven to meet her? After all, she *rules* them now."

"And how many of those Queens that we passed over are going to be impressed with a witch who wears a Rose Jewel?" Theran asked, feeling bitter again. He had to hide that bitterness from Talon, but he'd be damned if he'd hide it from the rest of the First Circle. Especially Ranon.

"The Shalador Queens might be willing to come and talk to her—*and* listen to what she has to say," Ranon said.

"Shalador. *Shalador.* That's all you harp about, isn't it? Every meeting of the First Circle, you bring up something about the reserves."

"Someone has to remember our people," Ranon said with his own touch of bitterness.

"Just because our Queen has given her consent for you to mount a Black Widow—"

"Watch your tongue, Grayhaven," Ranon snarled.

Theran caught a movement out of the corner of his eye and turned to see Cassidy coming toward him, her hands clenched and a look on her face. . . .

"You coldhearted son of a whoring *bitch!*"

She rammed him with a force that knocked him into the wall.

Instinct and temper took over, and he shoved her hard enough that she would have fallen if Ranon hadn't caught her. She shook off the Opal-Jeweled Warlord Prince, and the expression on Ranon's face would have been amusing if the woman didn't look ready to kill someone.

"You made such a point of *family*, you bastard," Cassidy snarled. "The *family* wing was to be off-limits to the court because this had been the Grayhaven *family* home."

"Why are you so pissed about that now?" Theran shouted.

"Because he's *family!*" she shouted back. "But you stick him in a damn gardening shed, don't even let him come in for meals, all because someone hurt him, scarred him so he isn't perfect anymore, and you won't accept anyone or anything that isn't perfect, will you? Well, you're not perfect either, *Grayhaven.* Far from it."

Theran looked at her in disbelief. "This is about Gray?"

"YES, THIS IS ABOUT GRAY!"

She used Craft to enhance her voice, and that shout rattled the windows. And brought everyone running.

"Shit," Ranon said softly, turning and raising a hand to stop the men who rushed into the room from the other door.

"Jared Blaed Grayhaven," Cassidy said with a kind of cold anger that put a chill down Theran's spine. "Family, isn't he?"

"We're cousins," Theran replied cautiously. He wore Green. She wore Rose. He wasn't in any danger. Not from her. But he couldn't forget right now that she had the backing of the kind of power that could wipe Dena Nehele and its people out of existence.

"Cousins," Cassidy said. "But he's not good enough to be *family*, is he? Not good enough to stay in your precious house."

"He can't stay here."

"Why?"

Something snapped inside him. Something that had festered for a lot of years. Something that cut him every time he'd heard that desperate keening.

"Because he was tortured here," Theran shouted. "*Here*, in this house. For *two years* they beat him and hurt him and did things he only remembers in nightmares. And do you know why they did that? Because they thought he was me! Because that bitch thought she had captured the last of the Grayhaven line, and she savored every wound she inflicted.

"And he never told them they'd caught the wrong boy. Never told them he wasn't Grayhaven. Jared Blaed. That was his name then. Cousins through our mothers, who could trace their line back to Thera and Blaed. He protected me in the only way he could for *two years*."

Theran turned, paced, circled. Wanted to beat her with words.

"Do you think I want him out in that damn shed? No, *Lady*, I don't." He blinked back the tears stinging his eyes—and refused to see the tears in hers. "But he's terrified to come into this house. He won't even come to the kitchen door to get food. We bring it out to the stables for him. He had to come with us. We couldn't leave him in the mountain camp, even though the other rogues up there were willing to look after him. But he's in that shed because it's the best *he* can do. All he can tolerate."

Cassidy squared her shoulders and raised her chin. "I'm sorry for that. I didn't know. But that doesn't change anything, Theran. He is your family, and he will have a room in the family wing."

"Haven't you been listening?"

"I don't care if he never sets foot in this house or never

sets foot in that room, but he will have a proper room in the family wing, just like you and Talon. He will know it is there if he wants it. And if he's more comfortable staying in the shed, then it will be fixed up."

"We can't afford to be—" Theran began.

"This isn't a suggestion, and it's not a request," Cassidy snapped. "This is an order, *Prince*. Get it done."

She started to turn away, then turned back. "And I think we should agree on a division of labor from here on in, Grayhaven. You do what you can—and I'll do what's important."

She turned to leave the room—and Ranon skipped out of her way, raising his hands in a gesture of surrender. The other men who had come in scrambled to give her a clear path to the door.

"Hell's fire, Theran," Ranon said softly. "That woman is *pissed*."

"Yeah," Theran said. "I guess she is." He felt shaky, as if he'd clashed with an enemy far more deadly than he'd expected.

"Theran?"

Mother Night. Gray.

Theran turned to find Gray standing in the other doorway—the doorway Cassidy had originally come in by. He watched, not sure if offering assistance would help or harm, as Gray walked into the room, shaking more and more with every step.

Unable to stand it any longer, Theran covered the distance between them, oddly grateful that Ranon came with him as additional support.

As he put his hands on Gray's shoulders, he saw Ranon's face tighten as the man got a look at Gray's back.

"She doesn't understand," Gray said. "That's why she's so mad at you."

"It doesn't matter," Theran said.

"Yes, it does. Family is important to Cassie. Family matters. That's why she's mad at you. She doesn't know that it matters to you too."

"Gray . . ."

"I'll take the room, Theran. Then she won't be mad at you anymore."

"You don't have to do this. Not for her."

Gray gave him an odd smile. "That's exactly why I have to do it. For her."

Theran stiffened at the sound of someone running. Footsteps too light to be a man's, so who . . . ?

Shira barreled into the room, pulled up short, and stared at Gray's back for a long moment before she whispered, "Mother Night."

Theran felt a reluctant admiration for her when she quickly regained her composure and her professional attitude.

"Would it hurt you if I touch your back?" Shira asked Gray.

"No." But his voice was becoming a tight whisper, a prelude to the pain that usually left him helpless.

Gray shook, shuddered—and Theran saw the shame in his cousin's eyes when Gray couldn't stop himself from whimpering. Not because Shira's light, gentle touch was hurting him, but because he was afraid of being touched by a female. Because that touch brought back too many memories.

"We'll start simple," Shira finally said after her examination. "I've got a good, strong liniment that will help relax those tight muscles and ease the pain. And I'm recommending you take a mild sedative that will let you sleep."

"I have work," Gray said, sounding too close to desperate.

Damn the work! Theran thought.

"Not today," Shira said. "Today your only work is to rest and heal. If you do that, by tomorrow you and Lady Cassidy can go back to digging in the garden for an hour or so—under Vae's supervision."

Despite the fact that he was still shaking, Gray tried to smile. "Vae bites."

"Which makes her the perfect choice for watching over the two of you," Shira replied tartly. Then her voice softened. "Come on, now. Let's get you settled wherever you feel comfortable. Then I can do something about the pain."

Gray didn't argue when Shira led him away, his expression once more that of a docile boy.

Theran watched Gray and Shira, ignoring the sounds of the other men leaving the room.

"It took a lot of courage for him to walk into this house," Ranon said.

Theran continued to stare at that doorway, even though Shira and Gray were gone. Then he swallowed hard and said, "He's always had courage."

The door of the Steward's office was open, but Talon knocked on the wood anyway before entering.

"You wanted to see me?"

Powell's smile of greeting wobbled for a moment, then failed altogether. "Yes. Please close the door."

Not good, Talon thought as he closed the door and settled himself in the visitor's chair. This was not good.

Powell lifted the corners of a few papers on his desk, removed an envelope, and handed it to Talon. "This needs to go to the Keep."

Talon stared at the name on the front of the envelope, then studied the seal on the back. "When did the Queen give this to you?"

"Shortly after the midday meal."

"It's marked 'urgent.' "

"It was . . . misplaced . . . for a few hours," Powell said. "I wanted to discuss the situation with you before I sent this message . . . *there.*"

"Situation." He hadn't needed a message slipped under his door, asking him to meet with Powell, to know something had happened today. He'd felt the tension the moment he left the family wing.

"Lady Cassidy and Prince Theran had an altercation this morning. Sharp words were exchanged—and a few shoves."

"Hell's fire," Talon muttered.

"Afterward, Lady Cassidy retired to her rooms and hasn't come down since."

"She's not hurt?" Talon asked, making it more of a demand for the right answer than a question.

"No, no. Neither of them were hurt." Powell hesitated. "But that—and the order to get it to the Keep as soon as possible—was the only communication any of us have had from her since then."

Telling tales, Cassidy? Talon wondered. It was tempting to toss it into the fire, but someone would have to shoulder the blame for failing to deliver the message—and sometimes the first break in trust was the one that could never be fully repaired.

"I'll take it," Talon said. "I can ride the Sapphire Winds, so I'll be able to get it there faster than anyone else." *And I want a chance to tell our side of it.*

Powell nodded. "If anyone asks where you've gone?"

Talon vanished the envelope. "Tell them I had a meeting."

He returned to his room long enough to warm and drink a glass of yarbarah. He hadn't ridden the Winds outside Dena Nehele since he'd become demon-dead, and he had no idea how much power might be drained by riding those psychic roadways through the Darkness over a long distance.

Had no idea what he would face once he got to the Keep.

And he had no idea if the High Lord of Hell would allow him to return to Dena Nehele—and the people there who were still among the living.

Ebon Askavi

The Black Mountain. Ebon Askavi. Warrens of rooms carved out of the living stone to house a court, a library that was, supposedly, the repository of the Blood's history—and Witch.

No paneling or plaster on the walls to soften the weight of stone. No illusion to help someone forget that the weight of a mountain rested above a man's head.

The feeling of age pressed down on Talon as much as the feeling of stone. And even though the sitting room where he had been taken to wait was as finely furnished as any he'd ever seen, he wondered how anyone could stand living in this place.

Then the sitting room door opened.

Talon didn't need to see the Black Jewels to know that the Warlord Prince who walked into the room was dangerous. Just looking into those gold eyes would tell anyone with any sense that you walked softly in this man's presence.

Especially if you were demon-dead.

"I'm the High Lord," the man said, a croon in his deep voice.

A shudder went through Talon at the sound of that voice. Nothing threatening, not in and of itself, but he wondered how many men hadn't survived a meeting when the High Lord's voice had held that particular tone.

"I'm Talon."

"What brings Dena Nehele's Master of the Guard to the Keep?"

Apparently Prince Sadi was sharing Cassidy's reports with his father. Why else would the High Lord know who he was?

Hell's fire, Mother Night, and may the Darkness be merciful.

Talon called in the envelope and held it out. "Message from Lady Cassidy."

Saetan closed the distance between them and took the envelope just as a chime sounded and a tray with a decanter and two ravenglass goblets appeared on a table.

"Would you join me in a glass of yarbarah, Prince Talon?" Saetan asked. "Then we can sit comfortably while you tell me whatever it is you came to say."

"I'm just delivering Lady Cassidy's message," Talon said. "I wear Sapphire and could ride a Wind darker and faster than anyone else in the court could ride."

"Give me some credit, boyo," Saetan said dryly. "I've been a Steward. I *know* a Master of the Guard doesn't deliver messages, no matter how urgent, unless there's more than one message. Sit down."

He sat.

"Guess no one gives you much argument," Talon said, feeling a little stunned that he had obeyed before he'd consciously decided to obey.

Setting the envelope aside, Saetan warmed two glasses of yarbarah, then handed one to Talon. "A man uses the tools he has available, and he learns to use them well. The males in the court seldom argued with a direct order. The coven . . ." He shrugged, and his smile was as affectionate as it was reluctant. "That tone of voice usually stopped them long enough to give me a chance to argue about what they were—or weren't—going to do."

Settling into a chair, Saetan put his goblet on the tray,

picked up the envelope, and called in his half-moon glasses. "So let's see what has Cassidy so riled up she wasn't willing to wait to send this with her regular report."

Talon almost choked as he swallowed a mouthful of yarbarah. "It's addressed to Prince Sadi."

Saetan broke the seal and removed the sheets of paper. "Prince Sadi gave me the authority to open any messages from Dena Nehele that I felt needed to be considered immediately. I think something marked 'urgent' qualifies as such a message, don't you?"

"Look," Talon said, setting his glass aside. "I don't know what Cassidy and Theran wrangled about today or why it got her so riled, but they seem to butt heads more often than not."

"Which is not good for Queen or court," Saetan said mildly as he read the first page and went on to the second. "But we both know Theran wasn't chosen to be First Escort because he was qualified for the position."

Talon felt his jaw drop.

Saetan finished reading the second page. He glanced at Talon as he vanished the papers and envelope. "Oh, don't look so surprised. Theran had decided he didn't like her before they left the Keep to go to Dena Nehele, and by now Cassie's dislike for him is probably just as strong."

"He's . . . disappointed."

"I don't give a damn about his disappointment," Saetan snarled. "If he can't honor the Queen he chose to serve and do his duties, he should ask to be released from the contract."

"There's only the twelve of us," Talon protested. "If any man steps aside, we lose the court!"

"Then maybe you should explain to your boy that he should help build the court instead of trying to break it."

"What did she say about him in that letter?"

"Nothing."

Talon sat back, feeling as if he'd been kicked in the chest.

"She said nothing about him," Saetan said. "If you hadn't mentioned Theran, I wouldn't have known he was involved."

"But I was told they'd had words today, and after that, she wrote that letter. I thought—"

"No, Talon. You haven't thought."

There was an angry heat in Saetan's eyes, but it was the ice in his voice that made Talon sit very still.

"So I'll give you something to think about," Saetan said too softly. "Your boy doesn't like the Queen he accepted, and whether you agree with him or not, you've let him set the tone. You've let his disrespect set the flavor of the court. You've seen enough to know better, but you're letting it happen."

"I'm not letting anything—"

"You're the Master of the Guard. Stand up for your Queen. Even if it means standing *against* Theran."

Talon said nothing. What could he say?

"Do you want to know who would have liked Cassidy?" Saetan asked. "Jared would have liked her. Thera would have liked her. Lia would have understood her. I can't say how Blaed would have responded, since he never made it to the Dark Realm."

"You saw them?" Talon whispered.

"I saw them, briefly, and got a feel for the kind of people they were. Lia stayed the longest because she waited for Jared. Once he arrived, they had a little time together. Then their power faded and they became a whisper in the Darkness. Thera's power was almost burned out by the time she made the transition to demon-dead, so she didn't stay in the Dark Realm for long."

"My wife?"

A hesitation.

"There are some things that are said at the end that would never be said otherwise," Saetan said softly, "and I don't break the confidences of the dead. But I can tell you this. She loved you, Talon, and she understood why you felt you had to stay. She hoped you understood why she couldn't."

Talon closed his eyes and nodded.

"Tell Cassie it will take a couple of days, but we'll take care of her request."

There was nothing in the High Lord's tone that invited him to ask about the request, so he didn't. He just thanked the man for his time and gladly followed the servant who responded to the High Lord's summons and escorted him to one of the landing webs.

He didn't feel easy until he was riding the Sapphire Winds and heading home.

Jared would have liked her. Thera would have liked her. Lia would have understood her.

Yes, he had a lot to think about.

SaetaN walked into a sitting room similar to the one he'd left at the Keep in Terreille, but this one held a golden-haired treasure.

"Before we were interrupted, I believe you were going to tell me why you're spending a few days with me here," he said as he settled on the sofa next to Jaenelle.

"Because my moontime was supposed to start this evening, and Daemon politely requested that I spend the three days when I'm vulnerable here instead of remaining at the Hall."

"With him."

"With him." She looked tired and sad.

"Was he right? Did it start?"

She gave him a sour look. "You know it did."

Of course he knew. He smelled the change in her scent the moment he walked in the room.

"Give him time, witch-child. He's running scared. He loves you with everything that's in him—and he's just beginning to understand that it really is *everything* that's in him."

"I miss him."

Saetan drew her closer and put an arm around her shoulders. "Not half as much as he's missing you. And right about now, he's wondering why he'd been such a fool as to ask you to come here."

"How do you know?"

"Because he's a mirror." He kissed her head. "So tomorrow when he shows up, don't tell him he looks like he hasn't slept, because he *hasn't* slept. And don't bristle over whatever paltry excuse he makes about you needing a nap. Just tuck in with him so he can get some sleep—and let him heal his wounds in his own way."

Those sapphire eyes looked at him, looked through him.

"Will he heal, Papa?"

"In order to be with you, Daemon needs to heal. So he'll heal," Saetan replied.

They sat quietly for a couple of minutes. Then Jaenelle said, "So why were you called to the Keep in Terreille?"

"For this." He called in Cassidy's note and handed the pages to her.

About halfway through the first page, Jaenelle began to chuckle. Wasn't his reaction to the words, but he had suspected it would be hers.

"Oh, my," Jaenelle said. "Cassie is *really* pissed."

"And showing a fair amount of backbone," Saetan said.

"She always had that, but she never had to fight for anything enough for it to show."

"Looks like she's fighting now."

"And may the Darkness help whoever is dumb enough to get in her way." Jaenelle folded the pages and handed them back to him. "She didn't provide any dimensions. Hard to really know what she wants, isn't it?"

He knew a leading question when he heard one. "Yes, it is. Any suggestions?" As if he hadn't guessed.

Jaenelle smiled at him. "I think we know a good carpenter who could be persuaded to work in Dena Nehele for a few days."

He returned her smile. "Yes, I think we do."

SEVENTEEN

Kaeleer

Daemon walked into his closet and pulled a white silk shirt off its hanger. As he stuffed one arm into a sleeve, he muttered, "It's your own fault, you brainless fool. So do something about it." And he damn well *was* going to do something about it just as soon as he got this miserable rag of a shirt over his shoul—

"Stop it," Jazen snapped, rushing into the closet. "Stop! You'll rip the seams."

Daemon bared his teeth and snarled at his valet. "What's wrong with Lord Aldric that he couldn't get the measurements right? I give him enough business."

The valet stripped the shirt off him and hung it back up with a fussy care that honed Daemon's temper—and also made him wary.

"It doesn't fit because it's not your shirt," Jazen said, examining the shoulder seams for rips.

"Then why is it in my closet?"

"Because it's Lady Angelline's shirt."

"Then why is it in my closet?"

Jazen huffed out a breath, and Daemon got the impression the valet had hoped never to have this conversation.

"It has to stay in your closet with the rest of your clothes in order to absorb your scent," Jazen said.

"Are you saying I *smell*?"

"If you want to pick a fight, look elsewhere," Jazen said with a rigid courtesy. "You asked a question; I'm trying to give you an answer."

Daemon closed his eyes and struggled to leash his temper. "My apologies, Jazen," he finally said. "I'm a bit . . . cranky."

"Prince, you passed cranky halfway through breakfast—which is when Beale suggested I pack a bag for you so that you could leave the moment you decided to go to the Keep."

He'd always been so good at hiding feelings he didn't want anyone to see. When had he stopped being good at hiding?

He opened his eyes and looked at Jazen. "The shirt."

Jazen selected another white silk shirt and handed it to him. It didn't look any different from the other one—except it fit him perfectly.

"Servants are discreet," Jazen said. "Especially personal servants. And while they won't discuss things that go on in the household with anyone outside their house, they do talk among themselves. So I began to see a pattern with the laundry. Lady Angelline would borrow one of your shirts, and when it was laundered, it would be returned to her closet. But the second time she wore it, she would seem dissatisfied—and go browsing in your closet again. That's when I realized the shirt itself wasn't the attraction. The appeal was your scent—physical and psychic—that was absorbed by the material.

"I also realized from the things the maids said that your shirts were a little *too* big to be comfortably big, and it was easy enough to learn that the High Lord's shirts had been a better fit. So the last time I was in Amdarh to place an order for your shirts, I took the liberty of talking to Lord Aldric, and he made a couple of shirts that were just a little smaller than your measurements for shoulders and sleeves. I put a little bead on the hanger so that those shirts are easy to identify, and I position them so that Lady Angelline is more likely to choose one of them than any other."

"I see," Daemon said. He hadn't considered why Jaenelle chose to wear one of his shirts. The way she looked always aroused him, even when it was clear she had no interest in him doing anything with that arousal. "Do you know why she does that?"

Jazen hesitated. "I wouldn't presume to know what the Lady thinks."

"I asked, Jazen. I'm not going to hold your opinion against you."

Jazen hesitated a moment longer. "The servants at the Hall are very discreet," he said again, emphasizing that point, "but they've told me a little about things that happened before the Lady came to live with the High Lord. So I would understand why she responds to some things the way she does.

"I'm guessing that she first started wearing the High Lord's shirts when she felt nervous or vulnerable because she needed the reminder that she was safe, that he would stand as her sword and shield. Later on, since Helene and the laundry maids didn't remember Lady Angelline abandoning his shirts after a couple of washings and she only occasionally borrowed a different one, I think she was at an age when she simply liked wearing one of his shirts—and she enjoyed a small rebellion against a father who liked women to dress for dinner."

"So she arrived at the table well dressed but in a man's shirt," Daemon said—and wondered if Saetan had been amused or annoyed by that maneuver.

He missed her so much he ached. Missed her so much the loneliness gnawed at his gut. He hadn't been able to sleep last night because her absence was too much of a reminder of all the nights of misery when he'd thought she was dead.

But this he had done to himself. He had sent her away to keep her safe from a potentially dangerous adversary.

Him.

But he had to go to the Keep. Had to be with her. And had to believe that Saetan would do whatever needed to be done if he crossed some line that shouldn't be crossed.

"So the High Lord's scent represents safety," Daemon said. "What does she get from me?"

Jazen studied him for a long moment before saying quietly, "If I've understood correctly, you're the only man Lady Angelline has ever welcomed as a lover. Considering her past, I would say, Prince, that your scent represents pleasure and love—and trust."

Terreille

"You brainless, pigheaded ass."

Theran stopped at the edge of the terrace and faced Cassidy, choking on the words that razored his throat. He wanted to fight, wanted to spew out his own opinions and disappointments, but he didn't dare. Not after Talon returned from an unexplained visit to the Keep and told him flat out that from now on, the Master of the Guard would back the Queen in any dispute, no questions asked.

So no matter what Lady Cassidy did or said, if she complained about him, *he* would be in the wrong.

The only good thing about Cassidy snapping at him this morning was the look on Gray's face. Maybe his cousin would start to realize Cassidy wasn't so wonderful after all.

"No need to be pointing the way," a rough voice said. "When her temper is on the boil, the girl sounds just like her mother."

Cassidy's eyes widened with a strange kind of apprehension.

"Poppi?" she said as she turned toward the terrace doors and looked at the burly stranger. "Poppi?"

"Hello, Kitten."

The look on her face as she launched herself at the man, who hugged her hard enough to lift her off her feet.

I've never seen her happy, Theran thought, feeling uncomfortable about that realization because he might be partly to blame.

Who is he? Gray asked as he joined Theran on the edge of the terrace.

The psychic communication startled Theran since Gray used it so rarely.

I don't know, Theran replied. *But he seems to know her well.*

A flash of *something* from Gray, gone too fast to identify.

The man set Cassidy down, then smiled broadly as he ran his hands down her arms. But his smile faded as he held her hands, his thumbs brushing her palms. Sadness clouded his face as he looked at her hands.

"Poppi . . . ," Cassidy began.

"No," he said firmly. "It's best if we not have words

about this." He nodded as if he'd made some decision. "Yes, I think it's best."

Theran caught sight of Ranon coming up behind the stranger and figured it was time to do his duty as First Escort before Ranon did it for him. So he said, "Lady?" in a tone that politely demanded information.

"Oh." Looking flustered, Cassidy linked her arm with the stranger's and turned to face him. "Poppi, this is Prince Theran Grayhaven, my First Escort. And that's his cousin, Gray." She looked over her shoulder. "And that's Prince Ranon."

"Gentlemen," the man said, touching two fingers to the brim of an old brown hat.

Certainly doesn't look worried about facing Warlord Princes, Theran thought.

"Prince Theran, gentlemen, this is my father, Lord Burle."

Theran saw Gray's eyes widen.

"Your father's come to visit?" Gray asked.

"Yes," Cassidy said.

"Not exactly," Burle said. Letting go of Cassidy, he pulled a piece of paper from the inside pocket of his jacket and handed it to Cassidy.

She opened it, read it—and just stared at it until Theran wanted to rip it out of her hands and find out what in the name of Hell was going on.

"I don't understand," Cassidy finally said.

"Seems clear enough," Burle said.

"I asked Prince Sadi to send a bed, a dresser, and a bookcase," Cassidy said.

"You left out a few details, Kitten. Instead of sending something that may not be what you wanted, the Prince sent me. Four days of my time to cobble together the furniture you wanted. If it takes longer than that to get it all done, I might have some pieces already made that will do, or we can negotiate for more time. I brought tools and lumber and other things. Was brought down by Coach, courtesy of Prince Sadi. The driver says he can leave the Coach as a supply shed while I'm here, but it's still sitting on the landing web beyond the gates and needs to be moved out of the way, so he'll set it wherever you want before he heads back to Kaeleer."

"I can take care of that," Ranon said, looking at Cassidy. "You want it near the house?"

"Actually . . ." Cassidy looked flustered. "The furniture is for Gray, so somewhere near the back of the gardens would probably be more convenient."

"For me?" Gray said, looking stunned.

"In that case," Burle said, "perhaps Prince Gray could give me a few minutes of his time and show me the space and give me some thoughts about what might suit him."

"But you just got here," Cassidy protested.

"And I'll be here for the next few days," Burle replied. "But when I'm paid for a full day's work, I give a full day's work. So you get on with your work, and I'll get on with mine, and I'll see you at dinner. Go on, now. Git."

"Are you allowed to talk to a Queen like that?" Gray asked.

"Hell's fire, no," Burle said, laughing. "But I'm not talking to a Queen now, am I? I'm talking to my daughter." He gave Cassidy a comically fierce look. "You still here?"

"Fine," Cassidy grumbled as a smile tugged her lips. "I'm going."

Didn't take much brainpower to figure out Lord Burle was going to be reporting personally to Prince Sadi when he went home, so Theran extended his right hand and said politely, "Lady, if you're ready, the Steward is waiting to review some information about the Provinces."

His conduct as he escorted her into the house was absolutely correct.

Too bad she looked so stunned by it.

Cassie's father. This man is Cassie's father.

Gray couldn't keep his mind on anything but the big man walking beside him—including where he put his feet—so he kept tripping over nothing.

"I guess you've known Cassie for a long time," Gray said.

"All her life," Burle replied with an odd smile and a twinkle in his eyes.

Fool. Idiot. Gray wanted to smack himself. Now he was tripping over his tongue as well as his feet. Could he sound any dumber? Why couldn't he sound like Theran or Ranon or any other grown man?

And why did it suddenly matter so much that *this* man didn't look at him and see a boy easily dismissed?

"I guess Cassie was upset about the stuff in the shed," Gray said.

"I didn't see the note myself, but I gathered she was pretty riled about it," Burle replied.

"She didn't need to get riled. It's not important."

Burle stopped walking. "You didn't tell her that, did you?"

"No, sir." And considering the way Burle looked and sounded right now, he was very glad he hadn't said anything.

"Smart man. When a woman's riled up about something, the biggest mistake a man can make is telling her it's not important. She won't hear it the way the words are meant, and sometimes it can take a long time to mend things between a man and a woman—if they can be mended at all. If she thinks something is important, it's best for the man to treat it as such."

Gray thought about that. "Because treating the thing that's got her riled as important tells her that *she's* important?"

"That's the way of it," Burle agreed, continuing on to the shed.

When they entered the shed, Gray wished he had straightened the tools, swept the floor. Something. But, Hell's fire, he hadn't expected Cassie's father to show up!

Burle pushed the old blanket aside and pursed his lips. "You gonna get a new chair to put in that corner? With a better lamp, that would give you a place to read. I'm figuring you like books, since a bookcase is one of the pieces requested."

"I like books, stories and such," Gray said. "And I'm studying the Protocol books."

"Protocol is a good thing to know," Burle said, nodding.

But Gray's thoughts had followed a different path. "You would know stories about when Cassie was little."

"I know stories," Burle agreed. "Might even share a few."

Gray smiled. He wanted to hear those stories, wanted to share more than the *now* of Cassie's life. "When I have a daughter, can I call her Kitten?"

Burle made a strange sound. "You're skipping a few steps in the dance, aren't you?"

"Huh?"

Burle studied him a bit too long before saying, "You know how to use a hammer?"

"Not to build things."

"You want to learn?"

Gray hesitated. He *did* want to learn, and he wanted to spend time with Burle, who understood an important difference between a daughter and a Queen—and had shown him, and everyone else, that *Cassie* understood the difference. That was something the Queens who had controlled Dena Nehele before the witch storm killed them all *hadn't* understood. But he didn't want to risk what might happen if he wasn't honest before they began.

"I can't work a full day," Gray said, feeling bitter because he didn't want to be seen as someone *less*. "Not yet. I was . . . tortured . . . when I was younger, and sometimes my body doesn't work right."

"Your body's not working right because you over-worked it recently?" Burle asked. "That's what you're telling me?"

Gray nodded, unable to look the older man in the eyes. "Shira says I can work a few hours a day, but not more than that, not yet, and Vae will get yappy about it if I try to do more. And not just yappy. Vae *bites.*"

"And who might Vae be?"

"She's a Sceltie."

"Ah." Burle nodded. "Heard of them. Haven't met one."

"You will," Gray said darkly. "Vae has opinions about *everything*."

Burle looked at the room. "Tell you what. I'll trade you. You help me for two hours and learn a bit in the process, and I'll give you two hours of labor to help take care of your work. And we'll see how it goes."

"Okay."

Burle didn't think less of him for not being able to work a full day. Didn't say anything about the torture. Was just as matter-of-fact about it all as Lucivar had been.

Something inside Gray relaxed.

"Let's start by taking some measurements," Burle said.

"Then, while we're taking care of some of your work, we can talk about how to make some furniture that will suit you and still make my girl happy."

Later that evening, after a meal when no one seemed able to relax enough to just *talk*, Cassidy and Burle went out walking, heading toward open fields that were away from the house—and the people.

"You want to tell me what's wrong?" Burle asked.

Cassidy linked her arm with her father's and said nothing.

"All right," Burle said after a minute. "Let me put it this way: what's wrong?"

"Theran is a pigheaded ass."

"You're entitled to your opinion, Kitten, but I'm *not* sure you're entitled to shame him in front of the people he has to work with."

"Why not? He does it to me."

Burle stopped walking, and Cassidy felt an odd chill in the air.

Mother Night. Her father was a Warlord who wore Tiger Eye, and under most circumstances, Burle wouldn't think of going up against a Warlord Prince. But fathers weren't always careful when they stepped up to defend a daughter.

"He blocks everything I try to do," Cassidy said hurriedly. "He won't let me go out to the Provinces to meet the remaining Queens and see who might be willing—and capable—of doing more than they're doing now. Hell's fire! He doesn't tell the housekeeper how to do her work, but he's trying to make every decision for me!"

Burle hesitated—and the air around them changed back to evening cool.

"From what I've gathered, going out and about just yet may not be the wisest—or safest—thing for a Queen to do," he said.

"But Theran won't let those Queens come to Grayhaven either. He even got his back up when I wanted to go into town with Gray and look at plants for the garden."

"He might have his reasons."

"I'm not pretty enough to impress anyone," Cassidy muttered.

"That's foolish talk, and you know it."

Is it really that foolish? she wondered. Since she didn't want her father challenging Theran—and getting killed because of it—she held her tongue.

"Time for plain talk, Kitten," Burle said. "Queens do important work, and they are as necessary to a land as they are to its people. They can make or break a Territory. Hell's fire, they can make or break a Province or a village. But you've missed something along the way, my girl. What you do is *work*, and when you accepted this contract, you were hired for a particular job."

"No one seems to want me to do that job," Cassidy said, her voice roughened by frustration.

"Including you?"

Barely enough light to see his face, but enough to know it was a serious question.

"Sometimes I have an idea for a piece of furniture," Burle said, "and I build it just the way I see it in my mind, exactly the way it suits me to build it out of particular materials. I take pride in the work. Some people will like it and some won't, but it's all mine. And then there are other times when I'm hired to help someone build a piece of furniture the way *they* want it built. Their vision, their design. I'll make suggestions if I foresee a problem in the design or materials, but I'm not the designer, Kitten. I'm the skilled laborer who's helping someone else create something that matters to them. And even if I think it could have been done differently—or better—I respect what they're trying to do and give them the best work I can.

"You've been here a few weeks. Prince Theran's been here his whole life, watching what bad Queens did to his land and his people. I've been working with Gray this afternoon, and he's told me a fair amount about his cousin. Enough for me to figure out that Theran wants to do right by his people and do right by Dena Nehele. The name Grayhaven means something here, and it's a weight as well as a privilege to carry the name."

"So I should help him build a new foundation the way he thinks it should be built?" Which reminded her of one of Burle's sayings: *Don't go knocking down a wall because you think the room will look better when all you were asked to do was paint.*

"A year from now, you can walk away from these people and their problems. He can't. Won't. Is he pigheaded?" Burle shrugged. "Probably couldn't have survived if he wasn't."

Nothing to say when Poppi put it like that.

"I'll tell you what else I figured out in these few hours. You and Theran might not be as far apart as you both seem to think." Burle smiled and patted her hand. "You're looking to prove something to yourself. He's looking to prove something to his people. Maybe, Kitten, the reason you're scrapping instead of working together is that you both want too much too fast, and you're getting in your own way."

EIGHTEEN

Terreille

Cassidy pulled her nightgown over her head, then pressed a hand against her abdomen. A heaviness, settling low. A dull ache that got more pronounced every time she stood up this evening.

Well, Shira warned her that it would hurt more if she delayed her moontime. Looked like she was going to find out how much more.

She called in her supplies and tucked them in a bathroom drawer where they would be handy, then got into bed, feeling chilled despite the mild night. She plumped up pillows and opened the book she was reading. But she didn't feel like reading.

When she first arrived in Dena Nehele, it felt like an adventure, like a chance to do something *good*. Since then, she felt like she was constantly slogging through emotional mud that was knee-deep and getting deeper. She could see the value of looking at this like a contract job, but that didn't seem to be working either, because every time she'd asked Theran what he would like to do about *anything*, he danced away from giving her a straight answer. He opposed her suggestions but wouldn't make any of his own because that wasn't a First Escort's duty.

And why not? If his reason for opposing her suggestions was superior knowledge of what was happening in the Provinces and villages, why didn't he share the information?

Sweet Darkness, she missed her father, and he'd left only yesterday.

Cassidy snorted. "Left out a few details in my letter, my

eye." The dresser had already been made, and the wood had been cut for a small bookcase. Since he'd brought a mattress as part of the supplies, her father had had a good idea of how big the bed could be.

It had been an excuse to come visit, but she wasn't sure whose idea it had been—her father's, Prince Sadi's, or the High Lord's. Didn't matter. Besides her own time with Poppi, her father's visit had done so much good for Gray. One of Burle's sayings was "Work hard, but work smart," and his practical balance of when to use muscle and when to use Craft—and when to rest—helped Gray feel less wounded.

And the occasional silly smile on Gray's face, combined with a twinkle in Burle's eyes, meant her father had been telling tales about her. She might have wondered more about what was said if Gray hadn't found the courage to enter the house and join them for meals the last day Burle was there.

That had been her father's finest piece of work.

The only person who hadn't warmed to Burle was Theran, who had remained freezingly polite. Even Talon, after he'd realized Burle wasn't uneasy about being around someone who was demon-dead, joined them in the evenings to play cards or just talk.

Only Theran had viewed her less-than-aristo background as further proof that she wasn't worthy of ruling Dena Nehele.

"Let him take a piss in the wind," Cassidy muttered, putting the book aside, since even reading seemed too much effort tonight.

As she pulled the covers up and tried to find a comfortable position, she heard Craft-enhanced scratching on her suite's door.

Cassie? Cassie!

To avoid getting out of bed, she used Craft to open the door to the suite and the glass doors that led into her bedroom.

You are not downstairs with the males, Vae said as soon as she entered the bedroom.

"Needed some quiet time tonight," Cassidy replied. And needed some time to think about what she was going to do in the morning when every male around her would react to the scent of moon's blood—and to the fact that she would be vulnerable, unable to use her own power during the first three days without causing herself debilitating pain.

You are not well? Vae asked.

An odd hesitation in the question, and the same phrasing a human would use to ask about such a personal subject. But why would the Sceltie know, or care, about her moontime?

"Want to keep me company?" Cassidy asked.

Vae jumped up on the bed and lay down next to her. Cassidy put her arm around the dog and cuddled closer, the warmth of that furry body soon easing the ache in her lower belly as her muscles relaxed.

Sighing, she shifted her head to a more comfortable spot on the pillows, and fell sleep.

Vae dozed on and off throughout the night, waiting for the change in scent that would tell her for certain if Cassie was moody because her sire had gone home or if it was the blood time that meant Cassie wasn't safe around males. Even the males who were supposed to protect her.

It wasn't sensible for human females to come into heat so often, but there were many things about humans that were not sensible. That was why Scelties had been looking after humans for such a long time.

Cassie was a Queen, and her court should protect her. *Theran* should protect her.

But Yas did not trust Cassie's court, did not think the males would defend her properly. Ladvarian said Yas knew how to protect a Queen. Ladvarian said Yas was a human the kindred could trust.

Ladvarian had learned his Craft from Jaenelle, who was the *special* Queen, even for kindred, and Ladvarian had taught other kindred what he had learned. So Vae knew her Craft, and she knew Yas understood things about the males here that she did not. Even Theran.

Well before dawn, Cassie's scent changed.

Vae wiggled backward until her head was level with Cassie's female place. Then she sniffed to confirm the scent.

Human females did not like to be sniffed there by anyone but their mates, so it was good that Cassie was still sleeping.

Jumping off the bed, Vae padded out of the bedroom and used Craft to pull aside a curtain on one window in the living area.

Early. No one awake yet. But when the first birds woke up and began to chirp, Cook and her helpers would wake up too and start making food for the day. Then the Blood who took care of the house would wake up.

But not yet. No one but Talon would be awake now, and he did not come to Cassie's rooms, so he wouldn't know about the change in her scent. Not yet.

She wore Purple Dusk. Since she couldn't ride a faster, darker Wind than the Purple Dusk, the Keep was far away.

Cassie needed protection now. Cassie needed Yas.

Cassie would be safe enough until the males smelled the blood.

Vae leaped through the window, using Craft to pass through the curtain and glass. She landed lightly on air, two stories above the ground, and floated there for a minute.

Going up was faster than going down and around, so still floating on air, she trotted up one side of the roof and down the other before leaping away from the house and gliding over the ground and locked gates.

Landing lightly, she trotted over to the landing web and took a moment to make sure of her direction. Then she caught the Purple Dusk Wind and rode to Ebon Askavi.

Ebon Askavi

Wanting nothing more than to spend an hour with the novel currently intriguing him before he retired earlier than usual, Saetan turned away from his suite and retraced his steps to one of the Keep's private sitting rooms, where Lucivar was doing a slow prowl.

"Is there a reason why you're showing up here every morning?" Saetan asked.

"I can count," Lucivar replied.

"And that's significant because . . . ?" He could think of one reason for the edgy prowling. "Is Marian pregnant?"

"What?" Lucivar jumped as if he'd gotten jabbed in the ass. "Hell's fire, no! Although she's working on it," he added in a mutter.

"*She's* working on it?"

Lucivar gave him a dark look. "She hasn't talked me into putting aside the contraceptive brew. Not yet."

Thank the Darkness for that. He loved his grandson, Daemonar. He really did. But he suspected everyone in the family would be grateful for a little more time before they had to deal with another miniature Lucivar.

Including Lucivar.

"Did Lord Burle say anything to you about Cassidy?" Lucivar asked.

"A few things. Are you interested in something in particular?"

"Did she have her moontime while he was there?"

"I didn't ask."

"Why not?"

Saetan pressed his lips together, not sure if he was amused or appalled. He had known Andulvar Yaslana for over fifty thousand years, and even having all those years of experience with the straightforward way Eyriens had of looking at things didn't always prepare him for Lucivar's bluntness.

"That's a delicate subject." He studied his son. "You would have asked him."

"Damn right I would have. Even if she'd had her last moontime right before she went to Dena Nehele, she's late."

"It does happen."

"Especially with some help."

Apparently Lucivar had kept a few things to himself about his last visit to Dena Nehele. Like the fact that Cassidy might feel too uneasy about being vulnerable around the males who were supposed to serve her.

"Her court," Saetan said quietly. "You don't trust them."

"No, I don't," Lucivar replied. "But I'm sure I can get things settled enough that she won't have to worry for the rest of the time she's there."

Preferring to have only a vague idea of how Lucivar might settle things "enough," Saetan said, "If you don't trust them, who is supposed to send a mes—"

Yas? Yas!

Of course, he thought as he turned toward the door just as the Sceltie barreled into the room.

It's Cassie's bleeding time!

He felt his temper shift, sharpen. Recognized that same shift by the look in Lucivar's eyes.

No, Cassidy wasn't their Queen, and she wasn't family. But she was connected to them because of Jaenelle—and Daemon—so they would respond in a way that was in keeping with their nature.

"I'll be back in four days," Lucivar said.

Saetan nodded. "I'll go to your eyrie and inform Marian. Anything I need to know?"

"No, there's nothing that needs particular care at the moment." As Lucivar headed for the door, he added, "Come on, Vae. You'll ride the Ebon-gray Wind with me."

Saetan stared at the empty doorway a long time before saying softly, "May the Darkness have mercy on you, Theran, if you do anything in the next few days that pisses off Lucivar."

Terreille

You can't hide in your room for the next three days, Cassie thought as she pulled a long, moss green sweater over her head. *There's work to be done, and how can you prove to Theran and the others that you're capable of going out among the people if you can't even move among your own First Circle?*

She couldn't hide in her room. But she wanted to. She knew what to expect from the males back home, but not here. Would they work together, or would the personalities that rubbed against one another turn savage?

No way to tell. Not from her bedroom.

Pressing a hand to her abdomen, she took a deep breath, blew it out, and left her suite.

Maybe it wouldn't be so bad, she thought a few minutes later. The male servants she had passed on the way to her office had given her a sharp glance, but that was the only change in their behavior.

As she rounded a corner, she thought, *I guess I was worried over noth—*

Theran drew in a breath, no doubt getting ready to "ask" why it had taken her so long to come down when the Steward and others were waiting for her.

Then his nostrils flared. His eyes glazed. And the look in those eyes was predatory, not protective.

"Cassidy," Theran growled.

She took a step back. Took another. "I need some air. I'll join you in the Steward's office in a few minutes."

"Cassidy."

"I need some air!"

She turned and headed for the nearest door that would take her out of the house. She almost made it, almost got the outside door open, when Ranon stormed into the room, moving with an intent that made it plain he had caught the scent and come after her.

The glazed eyes. The power and savagery. Warlord Princes rising to the killing edge and honing their tempers to lethal intensity because of a blood scent.

She knew she should direct that savagery, turn it into a fierce kind of service. She was a Queen, and dealing with a Warlord Prince when he rode the killing edge was part of her training.

"Lady," Ranon snarled, taking a step toward her.

If she trusted him, trusted any of them, she could stand her ground and find a way to keep things from turning deadly. But she looked into Ranon's eyes and realized he had taken advantage of those vulnerable days to kill witches he had hated, and right now, he was struggling not to see her as prey, not to see her as he'd seen most other Queens.

One hundred Warlord Princes in Dena Nehele. For the first time, she understood what they must have done to survive, how much blood they must have spilled to keep the failing heart of their people from being destroyed completely.

"I need some air," Cassidy said, easing herself out the door. "Take care of your duties, Prince. I'll join you shortly."

Did he sense the lie?

Fool. You should have gone to the Keep last night when you suspected this would start.

But she hadn't been frightened last night. Not really frightened. She'd had a false confidence, based on her experience with the Warlord Princes in Jaenelle's court. She'd never felt threatened by those men, even the most powerful among them. Hell's fire, Lucivar didn't waste time discussing anything with a witch during her moontime. He'd simply pick her up and haul her to wherever he wanted her to be, and that was the end of it. If she was lucky—and he was feeling generous in a snarly kind of way—the witch would have a choice of what she was going to eat and whether she had one blanket tucked around her or two.

Despite his power and temper, despite what she'd heard he could do when he rode the killing edge, she had never had a moment when she'd thought Lucivar would hurt her.

Her thoughts fled in every direction. She kept her head down and her eyes focused on the ground as she hurried without considering where she was going. When strong hands grabbed her upper arms, she let out a breathless shriek.

"Cassie?" Gray asked. "What's wrong?"

"Gray," she gasped. "Nothing's wrong. I was just . . ."

His nostrils flared. His eyes glazed. And a friend was replaced by a stranger whose hands tightened on her arms when she tried to step back.

"You're hurt," Gray said, his voice roughened by a temper turned unpredictable. "You need the Healer."

He started to pull her toward the house. She dug her heels into the ground, resisting.

"I don't need a Healer, Gray. I'm not hurt."

"You're bleeding. I can smell it."

Mother Night. "It's moon's blood, Gray. You know about moon's blood. Don't you?"

Did he? Boys didn't notice the smell of moon's blood until they began to mature sexually. When she'd first met him, Gray's psychic scent had said "boy" despite his physical maturity.

"I know about it," Gray finally said.

There was just enough hesitation in his voice for her to wonder if she could believe him.

"You shouldn't be out here," Gray said. "You should be inside. Someone should be looking after you."

Well, he knew that much.

She thought of going back inside, thought of the look in Theran's eyes—and Ranon's eyes—and shuddered.

"Too many people in the house."

"You mean too many males."

"Yes."

His hands gentled. His voice gentled. "You need to rest, Cassie."

"I—" She couldn't deny it without lying, so she said nothing.

Gray released her, then slid a hand down her arm until he could take her hand. "Come on. You can take a nap in my bed. You'll be safe there."

Gray's little room in the shed. A quiet, private place where she could gather her wits and her courage.

She didn't argue with him when he coaxed her to lie down on the bed her father had built. She didn't argue when he removed her shoes.

She didn't resist when he tucked himself in beside her.

"Get some rest, Cassie," he said quietly. "You can rest."

His fingertips gently stroked her forehead, stroked her hair. Such a soothing motion. When he told her to close her eyes, she obeyed.

Cradled by the warmth of him, she fell asleep.

Gray watched her sleep. That sunset hair, with its streaks of honey, was spread over his pillow. He studied that wonderful face with its crop of freckles. An honest face. A face he could trust.

Just like she trusted him. She hadn't stayed in the house with Theran or Ranon. She'd come to him, trusted him to keep her safe.

And he would keep her safe. He'd put a Purple Dusk shield around the gardening shed, as strong a shield as he could make. It wouldn't keep the other males out if they were determined to get in, but it would give him the precious moments he'd need to prepare for a fight.

Gray?

Leave me be, Theran.

Are you all right? Why have you put a shield around the shed?

I'm fine. More than fine. His blood was singing in his veins, potent and ripe.

Have you seen Cassidy?

Leave me alone.

When a minute passed without another call from Theran, Gray relaxed again. Turned his attention to the woman.

Cassie. His eyes focused on her neck. He bent his head as he carefully pulled her sweater away from the spot that intrigued him so much. Then he breathed in the scent of her. His lips pressed against her skin, and his tongue got the taste of her.

He raised his head and looked at her, seeing something different. Something wonderful.

Mine.

In response to the thought, a strange feeling flooded him, body, heart, and mind. A feeling fierce and powerful. A feeling that shattered the husk he'd lived inside for so long—and no longer wanted.

"Cassie," Gray whispered. "Cassie."

He pressed his lips once more to that sweet spot, feeling a hunger stirring his body, arousing much more than his cock.

Smiling, he looked at her, asleep in his bed, and whispered, "Mine."

Theran watched Gray and Cassidy walking toward the house, hand in hand.

"That little prick," Theran growled. "He *was* hiding her in the shed."

"At least we know where she was," Ranon said, rubbing the back of his neck to ease some tension.

"He could have said something," Theran snapped.

The whole household had been in a state of quiet panic since Cassidy walked out the door.

A vulnerable Queen is a dead Queen.

Even if you couldn't get the Queen the first time, you could start picking off her protectors, could get a feel for who was loyal—and, therefore, a traitor to his own people—and who wouldn't get in the way of the fighters trying to hold on to the little in Dena Nehele that hadn't been corrupted.

He hadn't been out in the open—not like Ranon or some of the others—but he'd done his share of fighting. And he knew there were plenty of men out there—including some of the Warlord Princes who had presented themselves for consideration—who wouldn't hesitate to attack a Queen because that's what they'd spent a lifetime doing.

"Is she all right?" Shira asked, rushing up to them.

Theran glanced over his shoulder and swore silently. With the exception of Talon, who would surely have a few things to say when he joined them at sundown, the whole damn First Circle was there, waiting for Gray and Cassidy to take the last few steps across the terrace and enter the house.

He didn't give anyone else time to voice an opinion. As soon as Gray crossed the threshold, Theran stepped forward.

"Gray, what in the name of Hell—"

Gray snarled at him, and the glazed green eyes that stared at him held no recognition.

"It's all right, Gray," Cassidy said quietly, trying to slip her hand out of Gray's grasp. "It's all right."

Gray tightened his grip and snarled, "Mine."

Before Theran could respond, a sharp whistle from the back of the room caught their attention. Power and temper formed a wedge that had the rest of the men scrambling to get out of the way as Lucivar crossed the room and stopped when no one stood between him and Gray.

"Mine," Gray snarled again.

"I don't hear anyone challenging your claim, boyo," Lucivar said, "but there are things that need to be done, and we're going to take them in order. First." He pointed to Gray's Jewel, then his own. "Purple Dusk. Ebon-gray. I have no quarrel with you. In fact, I'm here to help. But if you start a pissing contest with me, I will rip you apart. Are we clear on that?"

Gray nodded once, sharply.

"Second, ease up on her hand before you crack a bone."

Theran saw Gray's hand jerk open, then close again. But not as tight.

And he noticed how intensely Cassidy watched Lucivar.

"Third," Lucivar said, "is the Healer present?"

Since Shira was standing beside Ranon, it was obvious she was present, but she stepped forward and said, "I'm here."

"Do you know how to make moontime brews?" Lucivar asked.

"Of course I—"

A small sound from Cassidy.

Shira pulled back. "Yes, Prince," she said courteously. "I'm well versed in brews that can ease moontime discomfort."

Lucivar nodded, his gold eyes fixed on Gray. "The Healer will go with Lady Cassidy up to the Lady's suite. The Healer will make the brew and Lady Cassidy will have some private time to take care of personal needs. Vae will go with them. If there's anything that needs our attention, Vae will let us know. We clear so far?"

Gray nodded.

"Let go, Gray," Cassidy said. "It's all right. I need to go with Shira now."

Reluctance. Resistance. Theran watched Gray struggle with conflicting instincts—and knew the only reason things hadn't turned bloody was Lucivar's overpowering presence.

The moment Cassidy eased her hand out of Gray's grasp, Shira hustled her out of the room, followed by Vae.

"Now," Lucivar said to Gray. "You're going to go outside and clear your head of the blood scent enough to have your brain working again. Then you come back in, and we'll all work out an agreement for taking care of Cassidy during her moontime."

"Mine!"

"She's a Queen," Lucivar said firmly. "She has a court. You have to share."

Gray bared his teeth and snarled at Lucivar.

Lucivar just looked at him until Gray subsided, yielding to the dominant power.

"Even the sweetest-tempered witch turns bitchy during the first three days of her moontime," Lucivar said. "Why should you be the only one on the receiving end of her temper? Let her court shoulder some of it. That's part of what it means to be First Circle."

Gray, don't be a fool, Theran thought. *He's giving you a chance to back down. Take it!*

"How much sharing?" Gray asked, sounding wary.

"That's what we're going to decide. Go on," Lucivar added gently. "Get some air. The first time it matters always hits a man hard."

Theran didn't take a full breath until Gray retreated.

"Hell's fire," Ranon said. "What got into him?"

"His temper and his balls woke up," Lucivar replied. "Since they woke up about ten years late, you all need to be very careful with him."

"Gray wouldn't hurt anyone," Theran said.

"A week ago, I'd say you were right," Lucivar said, giving Theran a long look. "But he's a Warlord Prince who has staked a claim. Until Cassidy accepts him or rejects him according to Protocol, he won't see you as a cousin when you're in the same room with her. He'll see you as a rival. And Grayhaven, if he believes you're trespassing, don't think for a moment he won't do his damnedest to rip your throat out."

NINETEEN

Ebon Askavi

Lucivar walked into the sitting room at the Keep and wasn't surprised to find Daemon there as well as Saetan. His brother's presence wasn't a lack of confidence in his ability to handle himself in a potentially hostile place; it was a need for firsthand assurance that he had returned home safely.

Or maybe it was Daemon's way of letting him see that the emotional fragility had passed—or, at least, had mended enough not to be the first thing he sensed about his brother. In fact, he'd say Daemon had the contented feel of a man who had been well stroked last night—a condition he hoped to find himself in tonight if he and Marian had enough energy left after they put the little beast to bed.

There was food on the table, so he filled a plate, accepted the coffee Daemon poured for him, and said, "Young Warlord Princes are a pain in the ass."

His father, the coldhearted bastard, laughed.

"I could have told you that," Saetan said.

"Did Theran give you trouble?" Daemon asked.

"Not Theran. Gray." Seeing the same narrowing of their gold eyes, Lucivar nodded. "Yeah. The one who didn't leave boyhood behind after he was tortured. He's making up for it now."

"In what way?" Saetan asked.

"He staked a claim on the Queen."

"What?"

Two voices. The same disbelief swiftly followed by

thoughtful consideration. He could have used some of that thoughtful consideration over the past three days.

Comfortable with the silence, Lucivar ate the first relaxed meal he'd had since he walked into the Grayhaven estate and found a situation a lot more potentially explosive than he'd anticipated.

"Gray is twenty-seven?" Saetan asked.

Lucivar nodded. "He's a couple months older than Theran."

"This is the first time he's caught the scent of moon's blood?" Daemon asked.

"Apparently. Combine that with the fact that I'm pretty sure he's falling in love with Cassidy. . . ."

Saetan sighed. "No training, no control, no one prepared for his reaction. He and Cassidy must have been alone when he caught the scent. He could have killed one of her First Circle before anyone realized he was dangerous."

"I arrived at the same time he was bringing her back to the house. The First Circle was there, waiting for them."

"Talk about drawing a line," Daemon murmured.

"I drew quite a few lines while I was there," Lucivar said. "And I convinced Gray I would hammer his cock into the ground if he crossed any of those lines."

"Cassidy has a court," Saetan said.

"I know," Lucivar replied. "Since Gray is studying the Protocol books, it wouldn't hurt if he received a note calling his attention to the parts that deal with the proper way for a Warlord Prince to stake a claim and what is considered acceptable behavior."

"I can do that," Saetan said.

"Getting a note from the High Lord should impress him enough to take the studying seriously," Lucivar said.

"Killing his rivals isn't acceptable because it can destroy an entire community, but it isn't unexpected behavior," Daemon said. "If Gray is that aroused and attracted to Cassidy, maintaining self-control is going to be difficult if he's pushed in any way."

"I divided her," Lucivar said. "Gray is courting Cassidy the woman. The First Circle serves Cassidy the Queen. Steward, Master of the Guard, and First Escort form the triangle around the Queen and always have access to her. The fact that two out of three are family made it easier.

The only other male Gray could accept being around Cassidy in an informal way was a Warlord Prince of Shalador descent."

"Why him?" Daemon asked.

Lucivar smiled. "Because he's in love with the court's Healer and isn't interested in warming anyone else's bed."

"Ah."

Lucivar set his empty plate on the table. "Maybe it would be a good idea to invite Cassidy to the Keep for dinner sometime soon, along with Theran and Gray."

Saetan raised an eyebrow. "Theran because he's her First Escort, and Gray because . . . ?"

"Because I think Gray would benefit in seeing how he should conduct himself. And I'm guessing right now he has questions he doesn't really want to ask anyone back home."

"So this is dinner and sex primer?" Daemon asked dryly.

Well, at least Daemon understood who was going to be answering most of those questions.

"All right," Saetan said. "I'll extend the invitation for a week from today. Will that suit both of you?"

"I'll check with Marian," Lucivar said.

"I'll be back by then," Daemon said. "So will Jaenelle."

Lucivar let his expression ask the question.

"Visits to a couple of Provinces," Daemon said. "Seems my presence is required to sort out some things. Jaenelle left this morning for Dea al Mon to visit Surreal, who is feeling crowded by the amount of trees in the Territory."

"The Dea al Mon are called the Children of the Wood," Lucivar said. "Isn't hard to figure their Territory would have trees."

"Isn't hard to figure that the Dea al Mon's idea of a city is vastly different from Surreal's," Saetan said.

"She doesn't have to stay there," Lucivar said. "She can come back to the town house in Amdarh if she's happier living there."

"She's not quite ready to leave. Apparently she and Grandmammy Teele are getting along extremely well."

It took a minute before Lucivar remembered to breathe. Grandmammy Teele, as she was called, was the matriarch of a Dea al Mon clan and had adopted Jaenelle into her family before Saetan had formally adopted Witch. She wore the role of cranky old woman because she enjoyed it, but she was a force to be reckoned with—not to mention a very skilled Black Widow. "That's a terrifying thought."

Saetan's gold eyes twinkled as he said dryly, "Isn't it?"

Terreille

"Cassie."

Cassidy sat back on her heels, looked over her shoulder, and wondered whom she was dealing with—Gray the boy, or Gray as the man he was becoming. Since she wasn't sure, she said warily, "Yes?"

"Do you think you've had enough for today?"

Asking, not telling. But not a long step away from telling, and a much shorter step away from that bossy, fussy state of mind that was impossible to deal with when a Warlord Prince got stubborn.

"I've got one more annual to plant. Then I'll get cleaned up and meet with the Steward for Queen's work," Cassidy said. Which meant she would be sitting quietly for the next several hours, an activity that didn't make Warlord Princes as temperamental as physical activity did.

"All right," Gray replied.

Satisfied with each other's answers, they went back to their respective work.

Cassidy took her time planting the last annual just to stay outside a little while longer and take in how much had been done over the past three days.

Lucivar had been a lesson in how one man could shake up a court. By the time she and Shira had joined the men, Lucivar had set down rules and boundaries that everyone had agreed to. All right, to be accurate, no one had dared to argue. Even Gray, who was clearly trying to deal with a side of his nature he'd never dealt with before.

But Lucivar had done more than set boundaries. He'd knocked down boundaries the other men hadn't been aware of building.

"You have a problem with sweating?" Lucivar asked Ranon.

"No," Ranon replied.

"Then get your ass out in the garden and help Gray. There's no danger of frost anymore, plants need to be planted, and nothing will happen until that ground is cleared. Besides, the Healer probably would like to have a little garden of her own to grow at least some of the herbs she uses for her healing brews. And since she's also a Black Widow, she'd appreciate some ground to grow the plants the Hourglass finds useful. If you're going to warm the woman's bed, it's time to give her use of more than your cock."

Ranon might have been resentful about having any man say that to him if Lucivar hadn't turned around and done a lot of the work himself, using a combination of muscle and Craft to clear out the old flower beds with ruthless efficiency. He'd shown the others that a Warlord Prince wasn't just a warrior—and that serving meant taking care of small things that mattered and not just the big things other people thought were important.

More than that, Lucivar had been both teacher and leash for Gray, calmly meeting Gray's flashes of temper while demanding that Gray remain within the boundaries of Protocol when dealing with her or with her court. Three days with Lucivar had taught Gray a lot.

Maybe more than she would have wanted him to learn.

Cassidy patted the soil around the last little plant, put her tools in the basket Gray had bought for her when he and Lucivar had gone to town, then frowned as she picked up the watering can.

Empty.

Easy enough to walk over to the pump and fill the can.

She glanced over her shoulder at Gray.

Better to ask for help.

"Gray? I need to get back to the house now. Could you fill the watering can and water this last plant for me?"

"Sure, Cassie," he replied, almost glowing with happy enthusiasm.

Was that happy, boyish enthusiasm at the core of Jared Blaed Grayhaven, or would it be lost during this maturing process of becoming the Warlord Prince he should have been?

She put her basket of tools away in the shed. When she turned around, Gray was blocking the doorway, and there was nothing boyish about the look in his eyes.

She walked up to him, not sure of his intentions, but certain he wouldn't hurt her.

"You kissed me," Gray said. "The day I brought you the blue river plants. Today it's my turn."

A light kiss on the lips, soft and lingering. The lightest touch of his fingers on her hair.

Delicious flutters in her belly.

He stepped back and smiled. "Lucivar said since we're courting, I'm allowed to kiss you. But only above the shoulders. For now."

There was a different kind of flutter in her belly. "Did he give you a timetable for when you can do things without him coming down on you like an avalanche?"

"Yes."

Mother Night.

"Cassie? If you don't want me to kiss you, I'll understand."

Understand what?

He was younger than she, and his mind was still healing. Those were two reasons to tell him not to kiss her.

But her Consort had never given her that delicious flutter in the belly. So she gave Gray a light kiss in reply and walked out of the shed, wondering if she was asking to have her heart broken when he started seeing her the way other men did.

She stopped walking when she reached the dead honey pear tree. More than a symbol of the Grayhaven line, it had been a symbol of love.

Wondering if she would ever experience that kind of love, and remembering how Gray's kiss made her feel, she pressed her palm against the tree.

A violent *snapping* beneath her feet. Sharp *cracks* of something breaking.

She grabbed the tree for support.

It wobbled.

"Cassie!"

"Be careful!" Cassie said as Gray ran up to her. "Look!" Putting both hands on the trunk, she pushed a little, and they both watched the tree wobble.

"The roots must have cracked," Gray said, going to the opposite side of the tree and placing his hands on it.

More *snaps* and *cracks* on his side of the tree.

"It's going to fall," Gray said. "After all this time, it's going to fall."

"Gray," Cassidy breathed, hardly daring to believe what was rising up from the ground around them and through the dead wood. A message that had been masked all these years. "Gray, there's something under the tree."

He stared at her, his eyes filling with excitement. "Do you think it's the treasure?"

"What?"

"There's supposed to be a treasure buried somewhere at Grayhaven. Lia buried it, and even Jared didn't know where, but he told his grandsons that there was a treasure that would help restore Dena Nehele when it was found. People have been searching ever since, but no one has found it."

"You said they couldn't cut down what was left of the tree," Cassidy said.

"And the ground was too hard to dig it up."

Treasure? Why would she feel it?

She eyed Gray and decided he'd get too upset if she didn't tell him first. Releasing the tree, she said, "I'm going to do something you won't like, but it's necessary."

Now he eyed *her*.

She kept her nails short, since it was more practical for gardening, so she called in a pocketknife, opened the blade, and sliced the tip of her little finger deep enough to have blood welling before Gray could snarl an objection.

She closed the knife and vanished it. As she pressed her hand against the tree, she said, "And the Blood shall sing to the Blood."

Spells releasing. Realigning. Triggering other spells.

The complexity of what was under their feet staggered her.

Or maybe the staggering was simply because the texture of the ground was changing. Or because of what she sensed.

"Cassie?"

"It's alive," she said. "Whatever is under this tree is still alive."

They looked at each other.

"It's your family, Gray," she said. "It should be your choice."

*   *   *

"Theran," Ranon said, making a "come here" motion with his hand as he continued staring out an upstairs window. "You need to see this."

Joining the other Warlord Prince, Theran watched Gray and Cassidy rock the dead honey pear tree. Then he swore. "What in the name of Hell are those two doing now?"

Wood that had been impervious to ax or Craft crumbled under their hands as she and Gray used Craft to float the remains of the tree out of the way. When they set it on the ground, its own weight broke it up even more.

We'll have a nice pile of wood chips for mulch, Cassidy thought as she and Gray hurried to the shed for picks and shovels.

"You wash off that slice," Gray said. "You don't want dirt getting into it."

She didn't argue, since he was right. It stung when she washed it at the pump, but she made sure the slice was clean before she called in her own little jar of healing ointment and slathered some ointment on her finger before running back to the spot.

She had to put two shields around her hands and then gloves, as well as promise to let Shira see her finger, before Gray handed her one of the shovels.

"The ground has changed," Cassidy said as she started shoveling.

"Good potting soil," Gray said, working swiftly but carefully.

She was so focused on the ground in front of her, she didn't notice Theran until he was almost on top of them.

"What are you doing?" he roared.

"Digging," Gray snapped. "Theran, you take the other shovel. Cassie's already done enough."

"There's something buried under the tree," Cassidy said, seeing Theran's eyes blaze with fury as he looked at the crumbling tree that had been his family's symbol. "Something is alive down there."

His face was wiped clean of everything but his fury. Then he seemed to absorb the words. "Alive?"

She nodded.

Gray hadn't stopped digging. Now Theran threw himself into it.

Cassidy looked toward the terrace and sighed when she saw Shira, Ranon, Powell, and a few others, including several servants, heading toward her to find out what was happening now.

More often than not these days, she felt like a one-woman drama society. It seemed like she never did anything without an audience.

"Can't they use Craft to move the dirt?" Shira asked.

Gray and Theran both stopped digging and looked at her.

Cassidy stared at the hole for a moment, then closed her eyes. Blood to blood. But this didn't start when she sliced her finger just now. This started when she had worked her hands bloody trying to run from the pain caused by Theran's words.

Her blood had smeared on rocks, had mixed with the soil.

A Queen's power connecting with the land.

If they tried to do this without sweat, without toil, they would find nothing worth having.

"We can't use Craft," she said.

Theran and Gray went back to digging. The ground kept crumbling, so they had to widen the hole. Ranon got the wheelbarrow and another shovel in order to shift the dirt. Other members of the court joined them, along with servants and men from the stables.

But it was Theran and Gray who dug.

And it was Theran and Gray who found the old locked chest and dragged it out of the hole.

One blow of a shovel broke the lock. Theran opened the chest, then sat back on his heels, his face filled with disappointment.

Cassidy picked up one of the pieces and felt the preservation spells begin to break.

"Why would anyone go to this much trouble to preserve some pieces of fruit?" Theran said.

Because they'll grow, Cassidy thought.

"Those are honey pears," Gray said, one hand hovering over the other pieces in the chest.

"Not like any I've seen," Shira said. "There are a few orchards left on the Shalador reserves, but the trees are dying off, and the fruit is small and hard."

What grows from these will have the taste of memories.

The preservation spell suddenly broke, and the fruit in her hand felt pulpy, already decaying.

"We have to plant these now," Cassidy said. "Give them soil, give them care, and new orchards will come from what's in this chest."

"Mother Night," Gray said as he picked up a handful of soil. "This is perfect."

Cassidy looked at Gray. "Hurry. I don't think there's much time to get them into soil once the preservation spells break."

"Pots," Gray said. "We'll start them in pots so we can put them on the terrace, where they'll be more protected." He sprang to his feet. "There are pots in the shed."

The pear she held turned to lifeless mush.

Theran stared at it for a moment, then swore and raced to catch up to Gray, followed by Ranon and Shira.

They each ran back hugging a pot.

Cassidy stripped off her gloves and dropped the shields around her hands. She needed a connection to the soil and the pears, without barriers.

"Gray, you and Cassidy should do the planting," Theran said. "You both seem to have a feel for this."

What was in his voice? Cassidy wondered. Annoyance? Bitterness? It would take years for these trees to grow and bear fruit, but wasn't a living symbol better than a dead one?

She didn't ask. Didn't really care. What mattered was not wasting what someone had gone to great lengths to preserve.

Gray filled pots with soil as Cassidy held each pear at the right depth, releasing the fruits gently one by one until there was only one left in the chest that hadn't turned to mush.

"One more," she said.

"No more pots," Theran said.

"There has to be something."

"We got twelve planted."

But there's still one left.

She ran to the shed, probably pissing him off because she didn't take his word for it, but she couldn't care about that.

Something, she thought as she searched under the potting bench and then the rest of the shed. Anything.

The jumble of broken tools in the back left corner looked like it had been rummaged through already, but she pushed things aside for another look.

And found a pot with some bad chips around the rim.

Old, she thought as she shifted it to get a better look. And smaller than the others because it was divided into two sections, but still big enough.

As she picked it up, she felt something give way at the bottom of the pot.

Damn. If it was broken at the bottom, it wouldn't be of any use.

She set it on the potting bench to get a better look at it. Then she just stared.

The small piece that broke off revealed a compartment under the pot—and the corner of a yellowed piece of paper that had been placed inside.

Time was running out. She had to get this pot to Gray before the pear decayed. But even though she was certain she would feel foolish about wasting time when she saw what it was, she took those moments needed to pinch the corner of the paper and use Craft to pass the paper through the pot.

The paper had been folded to fit the compartment and bore the Grayhaven seal. And on the front, in faded ink, was written, *"For the Queen."*

Cassidy looked at that corner of the shed and struggled to breathe.

Spells releasing. Realigning. A jumble of old tools that never seemed to get straightened out. Had this been there all along, waiting?

For the Queen.

"Mother Night," Cassidy whispered.

Then she heard voices shouting. She vanished the paper, grabbed the pot, and ran back to where the others waited.

No time, she thought. *Or just enough.*

"Found this," she said, dropping to her knees next to Gray. As he started filling one-half of the pot with soil, she cradled the last honey pear before it sank into the mush of the ones that hadn't survived.

This is the one that will stay at Grayhaven, she thought as she held it gently while Gray added soil. *Maybe the others will be planted in an orchard here on the estate, but this one will grow near the house.*

When the last honey pear was safely planted, she sat back, tired and aching, and certain she looked like she'd been rolling in the dirt. Of course, Theran and Gray looked just as dirty.

"Well," she said, "should we put these pots on the terrace and then get on with our day?"

"They all need water," Gray said. "We'll put them on the terrace, and then give them a good soaking." He grinned at all the people around him. "Looks like we found the treasure after all."

"Where did you get that?" Theran said. He turned pale as he pointed to the bottom of the pot, where the broken piece revealed the compartment.

"It was in that jumble of old stuff," Cassidy replied.

He shook his head. "I looked there. I didn't find anything."

You weren't supposed to find it.

"It's a wishing pot," Theran said. "I remember that from the stories. The pots came from Jared's family. The compartment held written messages, wishes."

"Did you find a message?" Gray asked her, his eyes gleaming with excitement.

A message preserved for centuries. Hidden for centuries. A message for the Queen.

She shook her head. After she read the message, she would decide whether to share it with the others.

Gray helped her to her feet, and the twinges in various muscles changed her mind from taking a fast shower to taking a long, hot bath. The court could wait. The paperwork could wait.

As she reached for the old pot, Theran said, "I'll take that one."

Several people gave him wary looks, since his voice sounded sharp, but she looked at his eyes and ignored the voice.

That old pot matters to him. Its history. Its connection.

Until the first two leaves break the soil, the pears won't be valued. But the pot matters to him.

She stepped back and smiled. "Of course."

Theran took the old pot and walked back to the house. One by one the other men picked up a pot and followed him.

"Do you think there's anything left in there?" Shira asked as she looked into the chest and made a face.

"Not likely," Cassidy replied. "The men can turn it over later just to be sure, but I think we found what we were meant to find."

Shira gave her a long, odd look. "Theran's part of the family wasn't the only part that had stories handed down."

Black Widow.

This wasn't idle conversation, but she had the feeling Shira wasn't willing to share her thoughts right now.

"I'd better get cleaned up, and get this cleaned up before Gray starts fretting." She held up her hand.

Still giving Cassidy an odd look, Shira nodded. "And you'll come by the healing room so I can take a look at that slice in your finger. Since you must have used Craft to keep it bleeding while you planted those pears, I imagine the wound is clean, but we shouldn't get careless about such things. Not now."

"What's different about now?" Cassidy asked.

Shira smiled gently. "I think you're right. Maybe we have found what we were meant to find."

TWENTY

Welcome, Sister.
Because you found this message, you have set the spells in motion that eventually will reveal a treasure that will help the people of Dena Nehele restore their land. There are no clues, as such. There is no map to lead you to a specific spot as there is in stories. But there are rules. Break the rules, and you break the spells, and what we have hidden remains hidden.

The First Rule: Tell no one you found this message. Tell no one you hold the key to finding the treasure.

The Second Rule: Don't search for the treasure. Rule the people. Live your life. If you're meant to find the next piece of the puzzle, you will find it as easily as you found the pot—when the time is right, and not before.

Thera is a gifted Black Widow and wove her spells extremely well. She cannot tell me for certain that the treasure will be found, only that there will be a time when it might be found—a time when Dena Nehele will need it the most. Since you are reading this, that time is now.

I wish you luck, Sister.
Arabella Ardelia, Queen of Dena Nehele
P.S. Most people call me Lia.

Cassidy folded the message carefully and vanished it before picking up the small gold key that had been inside the paper when she'd first opened it yesterday.

Thank the Darkness she hadn't told anyone about finding the message in the compartment. The possibility of finding the treasure would have ended before it began.

"I have a message that has to remain a secret, and a gold key that fits an unknown lock," Cassidy said. "Lia, could you have made it any harder?"

The search wasn't meant to be hard, because she wasn't meant to search.

Rule the people. Live your life.

"Neither is as easy as you might think," Cassidy muttered as she put the key in a trinket box her father had made for her years ago. "Your descendant is a very stubborn, pigheaded man."

Live your life.

Her life. Not the same thing as her duties as a Queen.

She might have to allow Theran to restrict her actions as a Queen, but it was time to reclaim her life.

When she reached the breakfast room, Ranon looked like he was about to be backed into a corner, Shira looked amused, and Theran looked wary. Powell was clearly lingering over his breakfast, and Cassidy didn't think her Steward was waiting because he needed to discuss some business with her that couldn't wait for an hour. He probably didn't want to miss today's chapter of the Grayhaven drama.

"Where is Gray?" she asked. He'd relaxed enough about being in the house to come in and eat with the rest of them, so she felt worry scratching her heart when he wasn't there.

"He's on the terrace, explaining the facts of life to the honey pears," Theran said.

Cassidy clamped her lips together and didn't dare ask what that meant.

Shira carefully spread some jam on a piece of toast. Since it was the second one on her plate, Cassidy figured Shira was doing it simply to have something to do.

"Do you play an instrument, Lady Cassidy?" Shira asked.

Ranon growled in response, so the question clearly wasn't as innocent as it sounded.

"That depends on how you define 'play,' " Cassidy replied, quickly filling a plate and pulling out a chair next to Shira. "I can read music, and I can pick out a tune on a piano. Why?"

"Gray thinks the honey pears would enjoy having someone play music to them for a little while each day, and I think you're the only one he hasn't questioned yet about your proficiency with an instrument."

Ranon seemed to be giving his scrambled eggs a lot more attention than they required. Or deserved.

"Do you play?" Cassidy asked Shira.

"Drums," Shira replied as Cassidy took one of her pieces of toast. "Too much sound for tender seedlings-to-be."

Theran snorted.

Powell fiddled with his coffee cup but didn't try to drink—and didn't look at anyone else around the table.

"Ranon plays the Shalador flute," Shira said brightly.

"I am not going to stand out there and play music for thirteen pots of dirt," Ranon growled.

"I've never heard a Shalador flute," Cassidy said—and watched the color drain from his face as he realized playing for the pear trees really wasn't his choice to make.

"Whenever it gives the Lady pleasure," Ranon said.

Either that phrase had remained in the training, or Ranon had been studying the books of Protocol.

Live your life.

"Speaking of music, Theran," Cassidy began, noticing the way his body jerked and the wary look he gave her, "I'm planning to attend the outdoor concert. I heard this was a weekly event in the town. You and the Master of the Guard may take whatever precautions you feel necessary, but this isn't a formal visit by the Queen, so discretion is preferred."

"No," Theran said. "It isn't safe."

Cassidy pushed her plate away and locked her fingers together. "Prince, I'm not talking about visiting a Province that is still recovering from all the things that have caused upheaval in this Territory. I'm talking about spending a few hours in what amounts to the home village. Grayhaven is the town connected with this estate. It grew up *around* this estate. This is the place where I'll do my personal shopping, attend the theater and concerts. This is the town where I live. If I'm not safe here, I'm not safe anywhere. If you can't relent enough for me to informally meet the people in this one town, then my being here is nothing more than a fool's dream. On both our parts," she finished softly.

Theran looked shaken—and even more wary.

She intended to visit the town. She couldn't spend the rest of the year confined to this estate.

Now there was a bitterness in his face—a look that was, sadly, becoming too familiar.

He called in an envelope and slid it across the table. "That came for you this morning."

She wasn't sure she recognized the writing until she turned the envelope over and saw the SaDiablo seal pressed into the black wax. Feeling a flash of concern that the High Lord might be writing to tell her bad news about her family, she relaxed when she opened the envelope and realized what she held.

"It's an invitation," she said, smiling in anticipation. As she absorbed the significance of the phrasing, a trickle of worry began to seep in. "You, Gray, and I are invited to dine at the Keep."

Theran clenched his hands. The muscles in his tightened jaw twitched. "Invitation."

"More or less." She held out the invitation so he could read it.

He hesitated, then took the invitation and read it. And relaxed. "It isn't convenient to go."

He's afraid, she thought. *And if he's afraid of spending an evening with those men, how will Gray react?*

Unfortunately, it wasn't as simple as Theran seemed to think.

"Look at the phrasing, Theran," Cassidy said.

He read it again, and she saw no understanding in his eyes.

"There is only one correct response to an invitation like this when it is made by someone like the High Lord," she said.

He understood her then. "But . . . Gray."

She nodded. "That has been taken into account. Lady Angelline being the kind of Healer she is . . . Believe me, that has been taken into account."

"No choice, then," Theran said.

"None."

"Then going to the town and hearing some of our music would be a good idea," Shira said, her voice sounding far more confident than the look in her eyes. "It will give you all something to talk about."

ᴛᴡᴇɴᴛʏ-ᴏɴᴇ

Kaeleer

Daemon glided through the Hall's corridors, a vessel for the cold, silent fury that held a single thought: how many of these bitches would he need to kill before the rest of them finally learned to *leave him alone*?

The silence held until he reached his suite. Then he slammed the door, letting temper and Craft enhance the sound until it thundered through the Hall, warning everyone of what they faced if anyone dared disturb him.

Moments after that came the knock on the door between his bedroom and Jaenelle's.

He ignored it, so moments after that, Jaenelle opened the door just enough to stick her head in the room.

"Are you all right?" she asked.

"You do not want to step into this room," he snarled, knowing his eyes were glazed and his temper was lethal.

It didn't matter if she wanted to enter his room or not. *He* didn't want her there. Not now.

"That doesn't answer the question," she said.

She pushed the door all the way open but stayed on her side of the threshold, which infuriated him even more. Especially because she was wearing one of his white silk shirts over a pair of slim black trousers—and her feet were deliciously bare, revealing toenails painted an enticing rose color.

The only reason she painted her toenails was that he enjoyed seeing them that way—and since she did it rarely, it never failed to catch his attention.

She must have painted them as a "welcome home" surprise for him, which only stoked his fury. Warlord Princes were passionately violent and violently passionate. Trouble was, he was spinning between violence and passion too fast to know which emotion would dominate if *anyone* gave him the slightest push.

He wanted to pounce on her. He just didn't know which kind of pouncing he wanted to do. Which was her fault, actually, because she'd painted her damn toenails, but it was clearly Jaenelle the Healer rather than Jaenelle the Wife who was studying him.

And because he knew why the *Healer* would be asking the question, he let his temper slip the leash for a moment.

"I'm not sick, I'm not damaged, and as sure as the sun doesn't shine in Hell, I'm not feeling fragile in any damn way," he roared. "What I am feeling is *angry*. So leave. Me. Alone."

Those sapphire eyes stared at him. Stared through him. She stepped into the room.

Not sure if he was acting on temper or sheer possessiveness, he slapped a Black shield around the room, sealing her in with him.

If she noticed, she didn't react. She just took another step toward him.

"You're riding a lot of temper, Prince," Jaenelle said. "But something was the cause of that temper, and that something is going to be dealt with one way or the other. If we have to work through all the temper first, so be it."

Hot. Cold. One moment he was Daemon, feeling furious and cornered; the next he was the Sadist, wanting to step up for this dance. And, oh, how he wanted to dance!

That particular truth scared him enough to be furious with *her*, so he dropped the Black shield and punched up his temper for the kind of fight that would get her angry enough to storm out of the room. Which would be the safest thing for both of them.

Turning his back on her, he removed his black jacket.

"You don't want to be in this room right now," he said in the cold, brutally dismissive voice that used to flay women's feelings so successfully.

"Why not?"

Her tone was so snippy, he saw the room through a red haze and stopped thinking.

"Because you can't defend yourself against what I am!" As he said the words, he swung the jacket at her, intending to smack her with it and *prove* that she shouldn't be in a room with him when his temper was barely chained.

Her right hand lashed out.

Hell's fire.

Daemon stared at the slices that went all the way through the back of the jacket. He flicked a look at her right hand. Had he really seen claws instead of fingernails for just that moment when she lashed out?

"Tell me again I can't defend myself," she said too softly.

Not while he still wanted to live.

His temper fizzled and a giddy joy filled him as he acknowledged that truth.

It was completely ruined, but he hung the jacket on the clothes stand to have something to do.

Mother Night, those claws were impressive. *She* was impressive. And such a vital, *needed* part of his life.

How could some bitch think a few superficial tricks could make her a substitute for Jaenelle?

That thought brought his temper roaring back to a cold, deadly edge.

Which his Lady recognized—and chose to ignore.

"You went to visit two of the Province Queens," Jaenelle said. "You came home a day early and furious. What happened?"

He vented some of his temper in sheer volume. "This evening when I walked into my room at Lady Rhea's house, that bitch Vulchera was wearing one of my shirts!"

There was a look in her eyes he'd never seen before, a kind of pissed-off incredulity.

"When in the name of Hell did you get so damn possessive about a shirt?" she yelled. "If you don't want me wearing one of your precious shirts, *say so*. Or have Jazen tell me, since he seems to be just as possessive of anything that resides in your closet."

"That's not—"

She ripped open the shirt, sending the buttons flying. Stripping it off, she scrunched it up and threw it behind her.

He wasn't sure what she was wearing under the shirt,

except that it was a combination of sheer fabric and lace that veiled her nipples without hiding them.

His mouth watered, and his mind went wonderfully blank of everything that didn't concern having their two bodies come together in particularly delicious ways.

"Daemon."

Which was a problem, since he'd finally managed to get her well and truly angry with him.

You started this fight, old son, so pay attention.

Besides, the sooner he figured out a way to end the fight, the sooner he could apologize for being an ass and they could put all that energy and emotion to better use.

"Let's start with some basic truths, Prince," Jaenelle said.

He winced at her tone of voice.

"You're a beautiful man, Daemon. It's more than your face. It's the way you move, and the timbre of your voice, and the sexual heat that comes off you even when you've got it leashed. All of those things are part of what you are. And women are going to be drawn to you because of it. Hell's fire, *I* was drawn to you because of those things. I still am, you ass."

His lips twitched, trying to smile.

"And you can't deny that the times when you walk into the bedroom wearing leather pants and nothing else, you aren't looking for the reaction you get."

Just remembering her reaction was making him hard. Harder.

"No, I can't deny it." His voice turned husky, almost a purr.

"A lot of women are going to want the body they see. Some of those women will also want the man who lives inside it."

"The man they think lives inside it."

"Point taken." She sighed, and the sound made him hopeful she was shaking off the anger. "Aaron runs into the same problem on occasion when he's an overnight guest, especially when Kalush isn't with him. I don't know what to tell him either, except to make his refusal so embarrassingly public the woman won't dare go near him again."

"It wasn't that," Daemon said, looking away. "Not all of it anyway." His fury returned, but he worked to keep it leashed. "Vulchera is a woman, not a girl, and can't use the excuse of being young for being stupid. She's a trusted friend of Rhea's, so she was among the aristos Rhea had invited to provide conversation and company after she and I reviewed the business I was there to review."

"Was there any business?" Jaenelle asked.

"Some. Anyway, Vulchera's flirting was too pointed and obvious from the moment we were introduced—and not the friendly kind of flirting your coven indulges in that's meant to be nothing more than fun. Your friends taught me that there are ways a woman can flirt with a man that lets him know he's safe." He slipped his hands in his pockets. "This woman wasn't interested in doing anything that was safe, and she certainly wasn't interested in my reputation or my feelings. She used the same scented soap that you had purchased the last time we visited Lady Rhea's court."

"It's not an exclusive soap or an exclusive scent. It's not even exclusive to the shops in that Province."

"Vulchera wasn't wearing that scent the first day," Daemon said softly. "Since we were at Rhea's country home, there was only one shop that carried items suited for an aristo purse. She paid one of the clerks to find out what scent you used." And he intended to have a little chat with that fool very, very soon.

"And then she put on one of your shirts," Jaenelle said, nodding as if she understood.

But she didn't. "Do you know how I feel when I see you wearing one of my shirts?" he asked. "Do you understand how aroused it makes me, how much possessive pleasure it gives me? Because of who you are, when you wear one of my shirts, you're telling the whole household that you're mine. And more than that, that I'm yours."

"I feel surrounded by you," she said quietly. "Comfortable. Safe. Loved."

"And aroused?" he asked just as quietly.

"Only if I picture you wearing it," she muttered.

Her answer made him smile—and smoothed some of the jagged edges inside him.

"Well, this bitch did understand. Before we got through dinner that first evening, she realized I wouldn't invite her to my bed or accept an invitation to hers. So she used a scent I associated with you, put on a piece of clothing that would carry my own scent. She wanted me to pretend she was you. She wanted me to believe she could be a substitute for you."

Jaenelle studied him. "So you were insulted on my behalf?"

Rage flashed through him before he got it back under control. "Of course."

For the first time since she walked into the room, she looked wary. With good reason. He might overlook an insult aimed at himself, but he would never tolerate an insult aimed at her.

"Is she still alive?" Jaenelle asked.

"She's alive." The Sadist smiled a cold, cruel smile. "But I did inform her that the next time she tried to seduce a married man, she would lose all feeling between her legs, guaranteeing a total lack of pleasure and no possibility of climax until the spell ran its course."

Jaenelle swallowed hard. "How long?"

"Six months for every married man she had tried to seduce, and a year for every one she had successfully seduced."

"Can . . . can you do that?"

"The spell is already in place."

She looked stunned. "Mother Night."

He stepped closer. Slipped a finger under a strap of that *whatever* she was wearing.

"I don't want to talk about Vulchera anymore," he crooned. "I don't want to think about her. Not her."

He knew his eyes were glazed, knew which side of himself wanted to play.

And so did Jaenelle.

"Stay with me tonight," the Sadist purred. "Here. In this room. Let me play with you."

"What . . . wh-what does that mean?"

The stutter pleased him. So did the nerves.

"Leave this on. I find it intriguing. With it, I want you to wear one of my shirts and those sheer white stockings. Nothing else."

She made a small sound. Might have been a whimper.

"I'm going to plump up the pillows and make myself comfortable. You're going to straddle me. Sheathe me. And then, my darling, I am going to make you stay perfectly still.

I'm not going to let you touch me in any way except to give me sweet kisses while I enjoy touching you. I'm going to play with you, lover. I promise I'll be very, very gentle, and by the time I'm through, I'll make you very, very happy."

Her eyes were glassy, and she looked dazed by the force of sexual heat now surrounding her.

"Why don't you go into the bathroom and get ready?" he said, taking a step back.

He hardly dared to breathe until she closed the bathroom door.

He wanted her desperately at that moment, but he knew what he was asking, knew what he was going to do. He had to give her enough time to think clearly and decide if she was willing to play.

He took off his shoes and socks, removed his belt. He pulled back the covers, plumped the pillows into a mound, and reclined against them, waiting.

The Sadist as lover.

Oh, yes. He wanted to play.

When she came out of the bathroom dressed exactly as he'd requested, he knew in a way he hadn't before that there was no part of him she feared—and that was the most arousing thing about her.

He was pleasure and trust—even as the Sadist.

When she climbed onto the bed and straddled him, he caught the scents of nerves and excitement. By the time he allowed her to sheathe him, she whimpered out of need.

And hours later, while he watched her sleep, he knew he had made her very, very happy.

TWENTY-TWO

Terreille

Theran walked out on the terrace and crouched beside Gray and the honey pear pots.

"Anything poking out of the dirt yet?" he asked, even though he could see perfectly well there were no seedlings.

"Too early," Gray said, sounding distant and distracted. And sad. "Won't know for a while yet if anything will want to grow."

You didn't sound this discouraged when you found the things. And what does "if anything will want to grow" mean?

"Something wrong?" Theran asked. "Are you worried about going to the Keep for dinner tonight?"

Why wouldn't Gray be worried? *He* was worried. They wouldn't be dealing with either the High Lord *or* Yaslana *or* Sadi; they'd be dealing with all three. As far as he was concerned, those were three good reasons for having nightmares.

At least this dinner had been the leverage he'd needed to stop Cassidy from going into town for the outdoor concert. She'd been disappointed—and unhappy with him—but she had accepted his "request" that she remain at the estate and not take risks.

The Darkness only knew what sort of excuse he could find the next time she wanted to expose herself to the Dena Nehele people.

"Cassie doesn't want to plant the seeds she brought from Dharo," Gray said quietly, keeping his eyes fixed on the pot in front of him. "When I asked her this morning why she hadn't picked out a spot in the garden for them, she said maybe it would be a mistake to plant them, that maybe things that aren't from Dena Nehele shouldn't be trying to put down roots here."

"Makes sense," Theran said. "We don't want our own plants pushed out because something else was brought into our land."

"She wasn't talking about the plants," Gray said. "Not really." He sighed and looked at Theran. "I love you, Theran, and I am grateful for the way you've taken care of me these past years."

"There's nothing to be grateful for," Theran grumbled. "We're family." *And you wouldn't have needed that care if you hadn't been protecting me.*

"When Cassie goes back to Dharo, I'm going with her."

The words shocked him. Chilled him. Showed him a potential loss that wasn't about a physical distance separating them.

"Gray," he breathed. "Gray, this is your home. Here. In Dena Nehele."

"She doesn't think there's anything here for her. She doesn't think she can put down roots and make a life."

"You're talking about going to Dharo," Theran argued. "About going to *Kaeleer.*"

Gray nodded. "I've been thinking about it all morning, after she said that about not putting down roots." He shifted so he was sitting on the flagstones. "If Cassie doesn't belong here because her bloodlines began in a different place, do we belong here, Theran?"

"What?"

"I guess you belong here because you have the Grayhaven bloodline, but I'm wondering about me."

"Hell's fire, Gray. Do I need to show you a map and point out the village where you were born? A village that's *in* Dena Nehele?"

"I didn't begin there," Gray said. "I can trace my bloodline to Thera and Blaed on my mother's side."

"So can I," Theran snapped. "Our mothers were sisters, remember?"

"Thera and Blaed came over the Tamanara Mountains with Lia and settled in Dena Nehele."

"To serve Lia."

"They put down roots, made a life for themselves here, but they didn't come from Dena Nehele. Neither did Jared. He came from Shalador. And his people, the ones who came over the mountains to escape the destruction of their Territory . . . Did enough Shalador blood get spilled defending Dena Nehele to entitle the survivors to put down roots?"

"Gray . . ." The thought staggered him—and made him wonder how Ranon would respond to that question.

"I'll be going with her," Gray said. "If she'll have me."

He'd never heard his cousin talk like this. "What would you do in Dharo?"

Gray shrugged. "I'll find work. Maybe I could work for Cassie's father."

A Purple Dusk Warlord Prince working for a Warlord who wore Tiger Eye? What was Gray thinking?

If he was thinking.

If any part of this was actually Gray's idea.

Was Cassidy using Gray as a pawn in some kind of game? Wouldn't be the first time a Queen had used one man in order to chain another.

"Well," Theran said, rising, "there's plenty of time to think about all this. Right now, we both need to get cleaned up and properly dressed. For Cassidy's sake, we want to make a good impression."

Gray's eyes flashed with temper, turning a familiar face into a stranger's. Then the temper faded, and the man looking at him was more like the boy Theran had known during these ten years since Talon rescued Gray.

"Yes," Gray said, "we want to make a good impression."

Ebon Askavi

Settling on the arm of the sofa, Saetan crossed his arms as he studied his daughter.

"I'm not sure what you're looking for, witch-child," he said. He'd listened to Jaenelle's account of Daemon's return from the visit to Lady Rhea's country house, and he heard the concern in her voice. Since he'd already heard

Daemon's report about the incident, he didn't understand *why* she was concerned.

"I wasn't hurt, and Daemon wasn't hurt," Jaenelle said. "Don't you think his . . . punishment . . . is a bit harsh?"

"On the contrary, I think it showed a remarkable amount of self-control." *Maybe too much self-control.*

She frowned at him, and he suppressed a sigh of annoyance.

"What do you want me to say?" Saetan asked. "Do I think Daemon is entitled to his fury? I certainly do. Do I think his punishment was just? I've already said so. In fact, his solution probably will do nothing more than buy a little time for him to confirm what he already suspects about Rhea's friend. I doubt she'll live all that much longer. If Daemon doesn't kill her, another Warlord Prince will."

"I understand that he's uneasy about another woman being so attracted to him that she acts foolishly, but—"

"Take off the blinders, Jaenelle," Saetan snapped. "You're being obtuse about this because it's you and Daemon, and because of how he responded last spring when that witch tried to eliminate you in order to have him. But if Lucivar had found another woman in his bed, trying to play this particular game, and had shrugged the incident off instead of doing something about her, you would have pinned him to a wall, either as his Queen—"

"Former Queen," Jaenelle said.

"—or as his sister. And before you use 'former' in front of 'Queen' again, Lady, I suggest you review what the term 'lifetime contract' means."

She blinked. Shifted her weight from one hip to the other. Frowned at him. "You're really feeling pissy about this."

Insulted because the word "pissy" dismissed his feelings in a way he wouldn't tolerate, he let his temper slip from its sheath, sharp and lethal. He pushed away from the sofa, allowing himself one slash of power to relieve some of the rage.

Jaenelle pressed her lips together and studied the pile of ash that, moments before, had been a sofa.

"My apologies, High Lord," she said quietly. "Please tell me what I'm not seeing."

The formality of the words no longer made this discussion personal. He appreciated that. He didn't want to fight with his daughter, but he was more than willing to enlighten his Queen.

"First," he said as he prowled in front of the destroyed sofa, "you're forgetting that when Daemon was a pleasure slave, the kind of gathering Rhea had arranged at her country house had been his hunting ground. Better than anyone else there, he would have recognized another hunter."

"Hunter." She didn't make it a question, which could be interpreted as doubt, but her tone asked for confirmation.

"Indulge me for a moment in a possible scenario." Saetan waited for her nod of consent. "Daemon walks into his room at the Province Queen's country house and finds a woman waiting for him, a woman who has been openly flirting with him and now indicates that she wants the kind of attention a married man reserves for his wife. He demands that she leave, and she does, wearing his shirt. A month later, a package arrives at the Hall, addressed in such a way that you're the most likely person to open it, even though it's not blatantly aimed at you. And inside the package is your husband's shirt, smelling of another woman's perfume. Smelling of another woman. And there's a note, carefully phrased, that says something like 'Hope your wife didn't notice that a shirt was missing.' What would you do?"

"Since she was clearly trying to hurt my husband by sending that package, I would find her, and we would have a little chat."

A razored chill in her voice. A look in her sapphire eyes.

Yes, she and the woman who sent that package would have a little chat—and the webs Jaenelle would weave around the bitch would be a far more terrifying punishment than the physical penalty Daemon had devised.

And that, Saetan realized, was the reason Jaenelle didn't understand. She *knew* the depth of Daemon's loyalty, so she would react as though he was under attack and move to defend her husband—in the same way she had always responded whenever she thought her father was under attack.

Remembering *how* she responded to attacks on her family, he pulled back. Chained his own temper as he considered the best way to explain.

"Although," Jaenelle added thoughtfully, "I suppose another woman would either file a complaint with the Province Queen or the District Queen who ruled her hometown."

"And some of the men would have filed a complaint as soon as they got home, especially if they felt vulnerable because they had young children, and a charge of infidelity could end with paternity being denied at their children's Birthright Ceremony." Saetan shook his head. "I think once Daemon begins making discreet inquiries about that Lady's activities, he'll find that a number of complaints *had* been submitted—but were somehow lost before they reached someone with enough power or authority to make the woman's activities public."

"You don't think this was about Daemon?"

"It wasn't about Daemon—and it wasn't about you. Not this time. Oh, I think she would have enjoyed the opportunity to bed him—which only proves she's an arrogant fool—but I think she was more interested in having the Warlord Prince of Dhemlan owing her for her silence."

"I see. Blackmail."

Saetan nodded. "She's not the first to play this game. She won't be the last."

"You didn't know about her?"

"Things can always be hidden, witch-child. The ruler of a Territory depends on the integrity of the Province Queens and District Queens to keep the land and the people in balance. If I'd known about this bitch, she wouldn't still be among the living."

A memory. A flash of thought that made him wonder if he had known about her.

He locked that thought away until he could consider it in private.

"What happens now?" Jaenelle asked.

"That will be for Daemon to decide," Saetan replied. "The real question now isn't about the witch who likes to play this game. The real question is whether Lady Rhea was aware of the game. Did she know what her friend was doing at these house parties? If she did, her silence was tacit approval. Even if she didn't know, even if she disposed of the complaints because she didn't believe they could be true ... Well, everything has a price."

As he came abreast of her, he stopped his prowling.

"Daemon is going to ask Rhea to dissolve her court and step down," Jaenelle said.

"Yes."

"Won't the rest of the Queens and their courts wonder why she's stepping down?"

"He rules Dhemlan, witch-child, and he wears a Black Jewel," Saetan replied dryly. "I doubt anyone is going to ask."

Obviously there were a few things Daemon left out when he'd told Jaenelle about this incident. Like the fact that Rhea had pissed herself when Daemon exploded into the drawing room. His rage and his opinion of her friend left no doubt in anyone's mind that Prince Sadi now viewed Lady Rhea and her friend as enemies.

"I imagine Daemon was quite upset when he arrived home," Saetan said.

"You could say that," Jaenelle replied, sounding vague.

"Is everything all right between you?" He hadn't seen any signs of distress or sensed any distance between Daemon and Jaenelle when they arrived at the Keep. But Daemon had sidestepped questions about what had happened after he told Jaenelle about this incident. Not that it was any of his business, but . . . Hell's fire. They were his children, so he was damn well going to make it his business. "Did you work things out?"

Jaenelle's face blazed with color, and she looked everywhere but at him.

"Oh," she said. "Yeah. We worked things out pretty well."

"I see," he said faintly. Maybe he wouldn't make it his business after all.

He cleared his throat to find his voice. "In that case, why don't we join the rest of the family? Our guests should be arriving anytime now."

"Won't that be fun?"

Not sure how to judge the words, he simply guided her to the door, and said, "I don't know about fun, but it should be interesting."

Lucivar was waiting for them when they stepped through the Gate that brought them from the Keep in Terreille to the Keep in Kaeleer.

Theran wasn't sure if that was because Lucivar knew all of them or because he was probably considered the least dangerous of the three men who were waiting to pass judgment on him and Gray and, possibly, all of Dena Nehele.

"Lady Cassidy," Lucivar said, tipping his head in the slight bow that indicated respect from someone of his rank.

"Prince Yaslana," Cassidy replied. "It's a pleasure to be here."

For you, maybe, Theran thought. He expected to dance around questions that were no one's business, and since he wasn't there by choice, he didn't expect any part of this evening to be a pleasure.

Lucivar gave Theran and Gray a nod of greeting, then said, "Why don't we join the others and take care of all the introductions?"

Cassidy smiled as she placed her left hand on top of Lucivar's right, accepting his offer of escort. "I'm looking forward to seeing Jaenelle again. There are a couple of things I'd like to talk to her about."

Jaenelle, Theran thought as he and Gray followed Lucivar and Cassidy. *Not Lady Angelline. Jaenelle.*

An unintentional reminder that Cassidy knew the Queen who had ruled Ebon Askavi well enough to address her casually. Should he warn Gray about who—and what—Jaenelle Angelline had been?

When Lucivar opened the sitting room door, Theran still hadn't decided how much to tell Gray about the people they were going to see. Then it was too late to decide because as the people in the room turned to greet the newcomers, Gray rushed toward the golden-haired woman standing next to Daemon Sadi and stopped when he got close enough to touch her. His face was filled with awed delight, and he looked at her as if he'd spent his life in a desert and she was the pool of water he'd searched for.

"Ladies, this is Prince Jared Blaed Grayhaven and Prince Theran Grayhaven," Lucivar said. "Gentlemen, this is—"

"The Queen," Gray said, sounding a little breathless as he stared at Jaenelle.

Jaenelle smiled. "I was the Queen. Now—"

"She's still the Queen."

Three male voices, each sounding equally annoyed.

"—I'm Daemon's wife."

"The Lady honors me," Daemon purred.

Oh, the look on Gray's face. The look in his eyes as he gave Daemon, Lucivar, and the High Lord an assessing glance before focusing on Jaenelle.

"Of course you are," Gray said. The words sounded sincere. The tone said he was siding with the other males.

Jaenelle studied Gray through narrowed eyes. Then she shook her head and sighed. "Why do I bother arguing with any male from your caste?"

"Because it's entertaining?" Lucivar replied.

"Before we throw our guests into the family game of 'snap and snarl,' why doesn't someone finish the introductions?" Saetan said.

The Eyrien woman standing near the High Lord clapped a hand over her mouth to try to muffle her laughter.

"I'm sorry," she said. "But it's a perfect description of some of these discussions."

"The woman who finds me amusing is my wife, Marian," Lucivar said.

This Purple Dusk–Jeweled witch was married to *Yaslana*? How did she survive?

As soon as the introductions were made, Jaenelle said, "If you gentlemen will excuse us, Marian and I would like some time for a private chat with Cassidy before dinner."

Leaving him and Gray alone with Lucivar, Daemon, and the High Lord. Could the evening get any worse?

Of course it could. If Cassidy complained about him, Marian and Jaenelle would tell their husbands, and the odds of his surviving long enough to get home . . .

Who was he kidding? If either Yaslana or Sadi turned on him, he had no chance of surviving.

A bottle of wine was opened and glasses were filled. As everyone else settled comfortably, Theran braced himself for the interrogation about Dena Nehele and Cassidy's court.

If they intended to question him, they never got the chance because Gray blurted out, "Cassie doesn't want to put down roots."

Something quiet, terrible, and predatory filled the room. Something he'd never felt anyplace else or in anyone else—not even Talon, who was the darkest-Jeweled male back home.

"Explain," Saetan said softly.

"She brought seeds from her mother's garden," Gray said, "but she doesn't want to plant them, doesn't want them to grow in Dena Nehele soil."

A moment's silence as that terrible feeling faded from the room. Then Daemon said, "That's a prudent decision, Gray. Windblown seeds could spread for miles."

Gray looked stricken, and Theran wanted to erase Daemon's words, even though he'd basically said the same thing earlier that day.

"What about bulbs?" Lucivar said. "Something that could be contained in pots? Marian does that in her garden when she wants a particular plant but wants to control where it grows."

"So does Jaenelle," Daemon said.

"That's certainly a possibility," Saetan agreed. "But perhaps finding common ground would be a better idea for this first year."

"Common ground?" Gray asked.

"For example, some form of daisy grows in most of the Territories in Kaeleer," Saetan said. "If you put them all together, you'll notice differences, but if someone saw one growing in its own soil, it would be recognized as 'daisy.' Maybe you should see what plants are native to Dena Nehele that would look similar to the seeds Cassie brought with her."

"A flower bed like that would remind her of Dharo but still belong to the place she now calls home," Daemon said.

"I don't know what the plants look like," Gray said.

"Write to Lord Burle," Daemon replied. "Ask him for descriptions of the plants that come from the seeds Cassie brought with her."

"But he doesn't know about gardens," Gray protested. "He told me that when he was in Dena Nehele."

"He has a wife who knows about gardens," Saetan replied. "A wife who will remember exactly what seeds she gave her daughter. But you send your request to Lord Burle whether he knows about gardens or not."

Gray nodded. "Because a male doesn't interact directly with a Lady unless he's been formally introduced, especially when he knows a male who *is* connected to the Lady."

"You've studied your Protocol," Saetan said, his voice warm with approval.

"Yes, sir. Cassie is helping me."

I don't know him, Theran thought, feeling a pang of loss as he watched Gray. *I don't know this man who is sitting there chatting with the High Lord of Hell as if he did it every week.*

"Add your note to the next batch of reports that are sent to me," Daemon said. "I'll see that it gets to Lord Burle in Dharo."

Gray smiled. "Thank you. I'll write it tomorrow."

Theran cast about for something to say, but he wasn't comfortable around those men, didn't want to share anything with them that he didn't have to share.

"I have scars," Gray said quietly, his eyes fixed on the carpet between his feet.

Another of those strange silences, as if Saetan, Daemon, and Lucivar were hearing more than words.

"Has Cassie seen them?" Saetan asked gently.

"Some of them," Gray mumbled.

"Do any of them interfere with your ability to have sex?"

Gray blushed and shook his head.

"Well, then . . ."

"I have *scars.*"

The pain in those words ripped at Theran's heart.

Another beat of silence.

"If you kiss a girl the right way, she won't notice the scars," Daemon said.

"The right way?" Gray slowly lifted his head. "There's a right way?"

Daemon smiled.

Gray stared at Lucivar, and there was a hint of challenge in his voice. "You didn't tell me there was a right way."

"You're in the first stage of courtship," Lucivar said. "Beginner kisses. As long as you don't drool on the girl or chew her face, you're doing fine."

Saetan and Daemon made pained sounds.

"What?" Lucivar said. "Let him figure it out for himself. He's not kissing her below the neck—or he shouldn't be."

"I'm not," Gray said hotly. "But—"

"We'll discuss technique later," Daemon said quietly.

Gray swallowed whatever he'd been about to say and sat back.

"Oh, the joy of dealing with young men," Saetan said dryly as he looked toward the sitting room door. "Thank the Darkness, I think the Ladies are returning."

Theran rose to his feet with the rest of the men, feeling awkward, exposed. Gray had been the one dumping intimate worries in front of men he barely knew, but Theran felt as if *he* had been stripped naked as well.

Then Cassidy walked into the room between Jaenelle and Marian—and Gray gasped and rushed over to her, knocking Theran out of the way.

Gray clamped his hands on either side of Cassidy's face, his expression horrified.

"What happened to her face?" His voice began rising to that desperate keening. "Where is her face?"

"Gray," Cassidy said, "what's wrong?"

"WHERE IS HER FACE?"

Saetan and Daemon grabbed Gray's wrists, trying to pull his hands away from Cassidy's face.

Theran leaped toward them, wanting to stop them before Gray got hurt, but Lucivar grabbed his arm and yanked him back.

"Easy, Gray," Daemon said.

"WHERE IS HER FACE?"

Saetan snapped out a sentence that sounded like a command. Theran didn't recognize the language Saetan spoke, but the tone was sharp, commanding, and angry—and Jaenelle jerked back as if she'd been slapped.

A moment later, Gray's keening changed to gasping sobs as he smiled and said, "There it is. There's her face."

"Gray," Saetan said. "Come with me now. We need to talk."

Seeing naked fear on Gray's face, Theran tried to shake off Lucivar's hold on his arm—and almost got yanked off his feet.

"*Jared.*"

Green eyes stared into gold. Gray's hands relaxed and were gently drawn away from Cassidy's face.

"Come with me," Saetan said, still holding one of Gray's wrists while wrapping his other arm around Gray's shoulders. "We won't leave the room. We'll just go over there so we can talk for a minute."

At first there was that audible hitch in Gray's breathing, the prelude to one of his bouts of mindless terror. Then the breathing evened out. Looking beaten, he let Saetan lead him to another part of the room.

This time when Theran tried to shake Lucivar off, the Eyrien let him go. Sadi was between him and where the High Lord was talking to Gray, and he wasn't foolish enough to think Daemon would let him interfere with the discussion.

"It was just an illusion spell," Cassidy said, sounding shaken. "To hide the freckles."

He hadn't noticed, hadn't seen anything different about her. The room wasn't brightly lit. How in the name of Hell had Gray seen the difference halfway across the room?

"I'm sorry," Jaenelle said, looking at Daemon. "It never occurred to me that it would upset him."

"Not your fault," Daemon replied. "But I think Gray does better with changes when he has plenty of warning."

The movements looked casual, as if they were drifting from one position in the room to another without any real reason, but when they stopped, Daemon and Lucivar were flanking the women. Theran had the impression that no matter what they personally thought about what had just happened, they would support and defend their wives—and Cassidy.

Gray looked anxious and uncertain when he and Saetan rejoined their tense little group, and he stared at Cassidy's face for so long all three women squirmed.

"Now," Saetan said, his voice a velvet-coated whip.

Theran felt his shoulders tighten in response to that sound. This was a voice that allowed no challenge, no discussion, no defiance.

"Every relationship requires compromises," Saetan said. "So those compromises are going to be established here and now."

A moment of silence, as if the High Lord was giving all of them an opportunity to be dumb enough to argue.

"Since Lady Cassidy's freckles are important to Gray, they will not be altered in any way," Saetan said.

"But . . . ," Cassidy began.

"In. Any. Way."

Cassidy hunched her shoulders. "Yes, sir."

"In return, Gray, you must accept that women like to paint their faces, adding color to eyes, lips, and cheeks."

"Why do they want to do that?" Gray asked, his eyes still fixed on Cassidy's face as if something might disappear the moment he looked away.

"Boyo," Saetan said, "I've been observing females for over fifty thousand years, and I can't tell you *why* they do what they do. Don't expect to understand how they think; just understand that some things are important to them that are incomprehensible to us, and learn to work with their way of thinking when you have to."

"Like putting color on her face?" Gray asked.

"Exactly," Saetan replied. "Although . . . a woman using face paints to enhance her beauty can be intriguing."

Theran watched Gray's face change, watched anxiety shift to curiosity.

"Darkening the lashes, for instance, to draw more attention to her eyes," Saetan said.

"Cassie has pretty eyes," Gray said.

"Putting a little gold dust on the cheeks—and other places—so the skin glitters in candlelight," Daemon purred. "But that's usually reserved for romantic dinners."

"Daemon."

Watching Jaenelle blush gave Theran a good idea of how those romantic dinners ended—and the room suddenly got much too warm.

"Now, the hair," Saetan said.

Gray whimpered.

"Changing the color would be an insult to every man who admires beauty, so it will not be changed."

Now Cassidy whimpered.

"However, you, Gray, have to accept that, like their faces, women like to play with their hair, putting it up in different styles or even cutting it."

"Cut?" Gray sounded alarmed.

"Compromise, Prince," Saetan said in that voice that allowed no challenge.

After a moment, Gray nodded. "Okay. I won't get upset if she cuts her hair."

"Then we're agreed."

Theran hadn't heard anyone but Gray agree to anything, but judging by the look on everyone's face, that wasn't going to be mentioned.

Daemon looked at Gray. "There's still a few minutes before dinner. Why don't we get some fresh air and discuss that other matter?" And he winked.

Gray's eyes widened. He started to move, then stopped and looked at the High Lord. "Sir?"

"We're done here, so you two go on."

When Daemon and Gray left, Saetan fixed his attention on Cassidy, and Theran felt sorry for her. After all, she'd just wanted to get rid of those awful spots and look a little better. It wasn't her fault Gray had gotten fixated on the damn things.

"I didn't know," Cassidy said in a small voice.

"Now you do," Saetan said in that implacable voice.

Cassidy brushed her fingers against one cheek. "Maybe . . ."

"Witchling, if you really think that boy isn't going to notice if a single freckle is missing, then you have *not* been paying attention."

The whiplash without the velvet coating.

Theran winced.

Jaenelle squared her shoulders. "If you gentlemen will excuse us, my Sisters and I need a few minutes to settle before dinner."

Saetan tipped his head in a bow and walked out of the room.

Lucivar kissed his wife's head and left the room, giving Theran no choice but to follow him to another sitting room.

"I need some air," Lucivar said. "How about you?"

Theran shook his head.

As Lucivar opened a glass door that led to some kind of courtyard, Theran said, "I guess the High Lord wouldn't have lashed at them like that if Lady Angelline had still been the Queen of Ebon Askavi."

Lucivar gave him an odd look. "Then you would have guessed wrong."

TWENTY-THREE

Kaeleer

No sex tonight, Daemon thought as he took off his robe and slipped into bed. Propped up on one elbow, he studied Jaenelle's face. She'd been broody and unhappy all the way home, and it didn't look like her mood had changed.

"Well, things didn't go too badly," he said.

Jaenelle made a sound that was one part laugh and two parts disbelief. "What dinner party were you at tonight?"

"The point of the evening was to give Gray a foundation for interacting with a Kaeleer Queen, and in that, I think we did quite well."

Her eyes widened. "I created an illusion spell to give Cassie more confidence about her looks and ended up scaring Gray out of half his wits, and also managed to stomp on Papa's toes hard enough to have him angry with me *twice*, and you think we did well?"

Daemon raised a shoulder in a half shrug. "Gray got to ask about things that were bothering him, he now has a measuring stick for how to react the next time Cassidy does something that upsets him, and he learned that he doesn't have to give up the things that are most important to him if he's willing to yield about other things." Gauging her mood—unchanged—he added, "And I learned that Lucivar's idea of a romantic kiss is not drooling on the girl or chewing her face."

Jaenelle popped up so fast she almost clobbered his chin.

"No," she said. "You're making that up. He is *not* that . . . that . . ."

"Eyrien?"

"Mother Night." Jaenelle looked a little stunned, but when her sapphire eyes focused on him, he wished he had the width of the bed between them. And he was beginning to think that teasing her about Lucivar's sexual skills hadn't been the best idea. Especially since he *knew* Lucivar had said that for Gray's benefit.

"You have to do something," Jaenelle said.

"Like what?"

"No woman should have to put up with that. And certainly *Marian* shouldn't have to put up with that. If that's Lucivar's idea of romance, you need to teach him how to kiss properly."

"If a man is doing it right, there's nothing proper about a romantic kiss," Daemon murmured.

"Daemon." She poked his chest with a finger. *"Do something."*

So he did. He kissed her. And when he was done, one of her hands was fisted in his hair, encouraging him not to go too far away.

"I gave Gray some tips about romantic kissing," he said as his lips drifted across her face, leaving a trail of delicate kisses.

"You did?" She sounded breathless, and her scent had shifted toward arousal enough to warm his blood very nicely.

"Hmm. I don't think he had his mind on much else through the whole of dinner."

"That explains why he was so cheerful," Jaenelle murmured, tipping her head to one side so that he could nibble on his favorite part of her neck.

"Lucivar is a more difficult challenge." He slipped one hand under her nightgown and his fingertips whispered up and down the insides of her thighs.

Nothing in her eyes now but desire. Nothing in her touch but love as she slipped a hand under the covers and stroked him.

"I should practice my technique," he said as he licked the valley between her breasts.

"Daemon," she gasped when his fingers found other interesting bits of her to play with. "How much practice do you need?"

He settled over her, enjoying, for the moment, the thin barrier of fabric between them. "I'll let you know in the morning," he purred.

Her reply was a moan of pleasure.

Terreille

Theran walked into the parlor in the family wing and flopped on the sofa.

"Want some brandy?" Talon asked.

"Sure."

He accepted the glass Talon poured for him, then slugged back half the liquor.

"How did it go tonight?" Talon asked, settling into a chair near the sofa.

"Well enough."

"Is Gray all right?"

Theran made a sound that might have been a laugh. "Better than I am."

"You hurt?"

He shook his head. He didn't want Talon to be alarmed; he just didn't know if he should repeat what he'd been told. Wasn't sure he wanted Talon to agree with the High Lord's assessment.

"Gray is like them," he said, swirling the brandy so he wouldn't have to look at Talon. "He fit in like he was just another piece of an intricate pattern. The way he talked with them, listened to them. If he decides to emigrate to Dharo, they'll help him."

"If he decides *what*?"

Theran winced. Of course Talon didn't know about it. Gray hadn't mentioned it until this morning.

"I didn't know him tonight," Theran said. "He had one of his . . . scares . . ."

"Damn," Talon muttered.

". . . and they handled it, Sadi and the High Lord. Soothing spells and power. They got him settled in minutes."

"Did you think to ask about the spell?" Talon asked. "Sounds like a handy thing to know. Hell's fire, I've tried everything I know and couldn't get him settled when he was having a bad night."

"The High Lord took me aside after dinner and taught me the soothing spell he'd used. He considered it a basic spell and was surprised that it wasn't part of our usual training."

Talon studied him, then sat back in his chair. "You're circling around something."

"Theran's blade," Theran said quietly. "Gray and I used to joke about him being my great protector. But Jewels only measure one kind of power, don't they? Two men can wear the same Jewel, even have the exact same depth of power, and one might be a dominant male, while the other is better as a follower. If Gray hadn't been captured twelve years ago, if we'd both grown up as we should have, he would have been my defender. He would have stood in front of me. Overshadowed me. Because he's a Warlord Prince like they are—like Sadi and Yaslana—or he would have been. I could almost see him changing, hour by hour, as he talked with them. The High Lord said that even with his emotional scars, Gray won't have any trouble settling in Kaeleer if that's what he decides to do."

Theran drained his glass and poured himself another. "Gray remained a child all these years, so I had to become a man."

"You would have become a man no matter what," Talon said. He shifted in his chair, a restless movement that wasn't like him. "So you don't fit in with Sadi and Yaslana. There aren't many who could."

"Guess not."

"Go to bed," Talon said. "Things will look different after some sleep."

Theran rose and lifted his glass in a salute. "I'll do that."

Talon waited until Theran left the room before he got up to pour and warm a glass of yarbarah.

...Jewels only measure one kind of power.... would have stood in front of me ... Overshadowed me ... he's a Warlord Prince like they are....

Talon raised the glass and studied the blood wine. "Theran, my boy, I'll never say this to your face, but you're right about Gray. He would have overshadowed you. Not deliberately. He'd been taught from the cradle on up that he was your sword and your shield. Had been raised to believe it was his duty to protect and defend the Grayhaven line. Men have followed you because of your name, but being a leader is still an ill-fitting coat on you. For Gray, being the dominant Warlord Prince of Dena Nehele would have been as natural as breathing."

He took a swallow of yarbarah. "You might have ended up hating him for being what everyone expected you to be. And as much as my heart aches to say it, and as much as I wish he'd never been harmed, maybe it's just as well he's waking up now when you're old enough to hold your own."

Talon drank the rest of the yarbarah and sighed. "Maybe it's just as well."

Gray leaned against the outside wall of the stone shed and studied the glow of witchlight coming from his window. Soft light, Daemon had said. Enough so nobody was stumbling around in the dark, but not so much to spotlight desire. It was easier to yield just a little more in the dark.

And wasn't that a wonder? he thought as he waited for Cassie. Talking to Daemon was like having an older friend who not only knew things about women but was willing to *tell* you things.

Was willing to do more than tell.

"Put your hands on her waist. Like this. She'll be so concerned with apologizing for that damn illusion spell, she won't even notice your hands until the warmth seeps through her clothes. That moment when she becomes aware is when the romance needs to begin. She's feeling vulnerable tonight. She'll try to shy away. This is the moment when you offer just enough to make her want more. Let her lose a few hours' sleep because you've given her a reason to think about you. To wonder about you. To dream about you."

Then Daemon had shown him. . . .

"Gray?" Cassie called softly. "Gray, are you in there?"

"Back here," he called.

Realizing a tactical error, he shifted so his back was against the shed. That way, once she was standing in front of him, it would be easy to shift so she was in the soft light and he was in the shadows.

She came around the corner, hesitated a moment, then hurried to reach him.

"Is something wrong?" she asked, sounding like she was braced for bad news.

"Why would something be wrong?"

"You're outside."

"It's a soft night in early summer," he replied, smiling. "The air is deliciously scented with all the things that are growing." *And I was waiting for you.*

"Gray, I'm sorry about the illusion spell. I didn't know it would upset you. I just wanted to look . . ." She pressed her lips together.

He shifted away from the wall and put his hands on her waist, holding her lightly. "How did you want to look?"

"Pretty. Or as pretty as someone like me can look."

He heard pain and bitterness in her voice, and he suspected someone had inflicted a deep wound at some time in her life, but he didn't understand what that wound had to do with her using that stupid illusion spell. "Why do you want to be pretty when you're already beautiful?"

So vulnerable.

She didn't believe him. *Couldn't* believe him.

She drew in a breath, probably to deny what he'd said. Instead, she looked at him, and he saw the moment she realized his hands were on her, realized how close they were standing, realized what the brush of her body was doing to his.

"Cassie," Gray whispered.

He placed the first feather kiss at the corner of her mouth and worked his way along a cheekbone up to her temple. "Cassie."

"She doesn't understand yet how you see her, boyo," Dae-mon had said, "so don't waste your breath on words that will cause her to pay attention to the wrong things."

He didn't waste his breath. He diligently practiced the things he'd been taught that evening and felt her melt against him, caught the intoxicating scent of her arousal, both physical and psychic. When she pressed her lips to his and slipped her tongue in his mouth, he wrapped his arms around her and *almost* ignored the last instruction.

His self-preservation kicked in when he remembered

who would demand an explanation if he ignored that last instruction.

He waited until she broke the kiss before he eased back—and added the footnote to the evening.

"Everything has a price, Lady," Gray said, smiling. "You owe me a little something for that illusion spell."

A jumble of emotions in her hazel eyes, wariness and arousal being dominant. "What do I owe you?"

"The answer to a question."

She relaxed a little.

"Are the freckles only on your face?"

Her face colored. She swallowed hard and eventually said, "No, they're not just on my face."

"I'm looking forward to seeing the rest of them." He stepped back, not sure if he wanted to snarl or whimper about that particular instruction. "Come on. It's late. I'll walk you back to the house."

She looked a little dazed during the walk back to the house. She looked more than a little confused as he nudged her inside and closed the door.

And he thought the light would be burning in her bedroom for a while longer that night.

Returning to his little room in the shed, he stripped and got into bed. He wanted to write the letter to Lord Burle and ask about the plants, but he didn't feel quite ballsy enough to write a polite letter to Burle when he was having *these* kinds of feelings about the man's daughter—and wanting to do things with that daughter that were less than polite.

So he turned off the lamp and lay in the dark, thinking about the evening. He'd made friends tonight. He was damaged, and they didn't dismiss that, but even though nothing had been said, the High Lord, Lucivar, and Daemon had made it plain that they expected him to live up to his potential. And if he asked, they would show him how.

"Daemon? Have you kissed men before?"

"I have." Sadi's mouth curved in a predatory smile. "Some even survived the experience."

"Have you taught other boys to kiss the way you just taught me?"

The smile softened, and there was an odd expression in Daemon's gold eyes. "I taught Jared. And Blaed."

Ebon Askavi

Saetan swirled the brandy in the snifter.

"If I'd known about this bitch, she wouldn't still be among the living."

He should have known about her. Daemon had said the witch wasn't a girl, and it was hard to believe this incident was the first time she'd flirted that way with a married man—especially because the detail of taking a shirt as a trophy kept tugging at him, making him think the scenario he'd told Jaenelle wasn't just a scenario. It was also hard to believe she waited decades between her victims, which meant she'd been playing this game while he'd actively ruled Dhemlan.

And no one had told him. Even if the Queens, for some inexplicable reason, had chosen to remain ignorant of the bitch's activities, at least *one* Warlord Prince should have had balls enough to come to the Hall and inform him.

His conclusion? Some of her prey had helped cover her tracks and hide her games.

He wasn't interested in the men. Not yet, anyway. But the witch who had dared try to tangle up his son in her petty little game . . .

A flicker of memory, there and gone. A man's anguish. A child's face.

Or what was left of the child's face.

There and gone.

Taking the brandy with him, he went out to one of the courtyards.

"When I stepped away from the living Realms, and Dhemlan," he told the night sky, "I thought I'd given Daemon a healthy Territory and a clean slate to begin his rule. But it looks like I have some unfinished business after all."

TWENTY-FOUR

Terreille

Several days after the dinner party at the Keep, Theran walked into Powell's office so soon after breakfast, the Steward wasn't settled behind his desk yet.

"Did the letter arrive?" he asked.

"The messenger just returned from the Keep with the sack," Powell replied. "I haven't even opened it yet."

"Well, get on with it."

Before Powell could say what he looked like he wanted to say, Ranon and Shira walked into the office, with Archerr following right behind them.

"Did the letter arrive?" Ranon asked.

"Hell's fire," Powell muttered. "The last time this many men were interested in a single letter, it was because all the young men in my village were waiting to see who the prettiest girl had asked to be her escort to the harvest dance."

"It's been enough time," Theran muttered. "How long can it take to write down the names of a few plants?"

Shira rolled her eyes. "Men are so dim about some things. The more it matters, the more time it takes."

Theran gave Ranon a sharp smile. "So what's Ranon hurrying that he shouldn't be?"

Ranon snarled at Theran.

"I wasn't talking about *him*," Shira said.

"If anyone is interested," Powell said, "Lady Cassidy has two letters here—no, three. And there's a box for Gray. Looks like Prince Sadi's writing on the label, and that's definitely the SaDiablo seal."

"Damn," Theran and Ranon said.

Theran sighed, then raked his fingers through his dark hair. "Give it to me. I'll take it out to Gray." *And try to figure out what to say today when that look of disappointment fills his eyes.*

Powell handed over the box.

Breakfast felt like a cold, heavy lump in Theran's stomach, and it got heavier and colder with every step he took toward the ground Gray was breaking for this new planting.

He's working too hard, hoping for too much, Theran thought. These past few days, he had the feeling that Gray had made a blind leap and had broken the life he'd cobbled together, but wasn't sure of what kind of life he would have in its place. What kind of life he could build.

If he could build anything at all.

"Gray?"

Gray set aside the spade and reached for the water jug. He glanced at the box Theran carried, but he didn't ask about it. He drank, then pulled a scrap of towel out of the waistband of his trousers and wiped his face.

"No letter," he said.

There was a flatness in Gray's voice, a lack of light in his eyes, that worried Theran.

"No letter," Theran said. "But this box came from Prince Sadi. Gray, it hasn't been that long since you sent the letter."

"Long enough for a mother to decide that she doesn't want a particular man showing interest in her daughter."

Mother Night, Gray, what are you thinking?

The hurt in Gray's voice made it clear *exactly* what his cousin was thinking: he wasn't good enough to be more than a friend.

"Open the box," Theran said. "Maybe there's an explanation."

Gray wiped his hands on his trousers to clean off some of the dirt. Then he took the box and set it on the freshly turned earth, which made Theran wonder why he'd bothered to wipe off his hands.

The box had a simple hook closure, so whatever was inside couldn't be valuable. Or it meant that no one would be foolish enough to take anything from a box that had the SaDiablo seal.

Gray opened the box. He sat back on his heels. He lifted one Craft-preserved flower out of the box. Then another—and another until he was holding a bouquet.

"There's a note and a book in there," Theran said, looking into the box. "And something else."

Handing the bouquet to Theran, Gray opened the note.

" 'Prince Gray,' " Gray read.

"A common-ground planting is a wonderful idea. The seeds I gave Cassie were meant to span the seasons, so there aren't many yet that I can show you. I've sent flowers from the late-spring and early-summer plants, but hopefully you'll be able to match the others from the sketches in the book. The bulbs can go in pots. Those, too, span the seasons—a reminder of family as she makes a new home. Burle spoke highly of you. I'm beginning to see why. I hope we can meet one day. Devra."

Gray set aside the note, picked up the book, and riffled the pages. "Plants from Dharo. There are drawings and information about planting, and . . ." He closed the book and studied the cover. "Cassie's mother wrote this book. Cassie said her mother knew a lot about gardening, but I didn't realize. . . . No wonder she understands the land so well."

"So this is good?"

"Better than good. It's—" Gray's eyes widened and his face paled. He grabbed the bouquet from Theran and shoved it in the box. "Cassie's coming. You have to distract her. She'll notice I'm breaking new ground, and she'll ask about it, and I can't lie to her. I *can't.* And she can't see what her mother sent. She'll know then, and it will spoil the surprise."

"What am I supposed to do?"

"Theran."

Step up to the line, Grayhaven, and be his shield. What he feels for Cassidy is something you've never felt for anyone. Not even in passing.

"Get that stuff tucked away," Theran said as he rose and turned toward the house.

"Thanks, Theran."

He watched Gray bolt for the stone shed, then hurried to intercept Cassidy.

"Is something wrong with Gray?" Cassidy asked as soon as he got close enough to hear her.

"He's fine," Theran replied, taking her arm and turning her back toward the house. "He's got a bundle of work he wants to get done today."

She wasn't dressed for spending time in the garden this morning. Was that good or bad, since she *always* spent time in the garden after breakfast?

"Maybe I should give him a hand?"

Cassidy sounded doubtful. Was she trying to back away from Gray? She *had* been acting a bit skittish about being around him. At first Gray had been pleased about that, but that had changed more and more as the hoped-for letter didn't arrive.

"I was going to come out and work in the garden, but Ranon is going back to his home village for a couple of days, and he and Powell said there was something urgent I needed to do before Ranon left, but they weren't clear about what that was, and said I should talk to you."

Theran tossed a psychic thread toward Ranon. *Next time you decide to be helpful, give me some warning.*

We gave her a reason to come looking for you instead of Gray, so figure out why she's supposed to be stuck at a desk for the next few hours.

Go piss yourself. He didn't say it, but the feeling traveled through the link between them—and the feeling was quite mutual.

What could he ask her to do that had to be done before Ranon left?

They were on the terrace and almost to the door before he had an answer.

"The Shalador Queens," Theran said. "You need to write a letter inviting the Queens on the Shalador reserves to meet you. Ranon will take the letter when he goes back to his village. That's why it's urgent."

"You don't want me to contact the Queens in Dena Nehele," Cassidy said. "You've opposed that suggestion every time I've made it."

"Seemed more important for the court to adjust to working with each other. Now . . ." He shrugged.

"You really want me to contact the Queens on the reserves?"

"Yes, I do." *Besides,* he added silently, *it's not likely any of them will come.*

He opened the door for her. "Come on. Once you wade through the paperwork Powell seems to create overnight, you'll be free the rest of the day to save the posies from the nasty weeds."

She stopped in the doorway and looked at him as if she suddenly saw a different man.

"You don't have a feel for the land, do you?" she asked. "It's just dirt and boundaries to you."

"I don't fuss over it like you and Gray seem to," he said dismissively. "It's the people that matter. It's the people that need tending."

"How do you take care of one without taking care of the other?"

Since she didn't wait for him to answer, he guessed she didn't expect one.

Gray set the items in the box on the potting bench, one by one, and marveled at this gift.

Cassie's mother had written this book. Cassie's mother had sent this box. No hasty reply to his letter, but a bundle of information from a woman who seemed to understand that he was hoping to put down roots in her daughter's heart.

And the flowers, preserved in shields so he could study them at his leisure.

His own mother had given him a fierce kind of love. He didn't know if it was because she was unable to be soft, or if because he'd been destined for the killing fields, she hadn't wanted to give him anything a warrior wouldn't need.

He could still see her face, filled with hard pride, on the evening when Talon came to take him to the mountain camps. He'd been seven years old, but there had been no tears, no hugs. To her, he was already a warrior. To her, he always had been.

He didn't think Cassie's mother was a fierce woman. Didn't mean she couldn't be dangerous if there was need, but he thought, maybe, she'd be the kind of woman who wouldn't be afraid to hug a boy.

Was his mother still alive? Did she know how to find him—if she wanted to find him?

He hadn't wondered until now. Maybe Powell, being the Steward of the court, would know how to find out.

A knock on the shed's door. He used Craft to vanish the box before the door opened and Ranon walked in.

The Shalador Warlord Prince glanced at the empty potting bench.

"None of my business," Ranon said, "but I saw the box this morning. Well, a few of us did, and we wondered...."

Gray called in the box and showed Ranon what Devra had sent to him.

"Look at this one," Ranon said, picking up one of the cuttings. "It's got one flower open and one still in the bud. Maybe that's why it took her a few days to send a reply. She must have waited for some of these flowers to bloom so she could send them to you."

"I hadn't thought of that."

Ranon set the cutting down. "Look, Gray, planting this bed is going to be a lot of work."

"I know."

"When are you planning to do this?"

"I'll need a few days to study the book and select the plants that will work best in the place I've cleared. Then I'll need to see what I can find."

Ranon nodded. "I'm heading to my village, but I'll be back in a couple of days. Three at the most. When you're ready to plant, I'd like to help. Shira said she'd help too. And I think there are a couple of other men in the First Circle who would be willing to help."

Gray studied Ranon, seeing more than a Warlord Prince who seemed to rub against Theran the wrong way.

"You liked Yaslana, didn't you?"

Ranon gave him a considering look. "That one scares the shit out of me, but I'd follow him into battle without a doubt or second thought."

And you'd have both if it was Theran who was leading.

"Thanks for the offer," Gray said. "I'll figure out the planting day and let you know."

Ranon smiled and walked to the shed door. Then he paused. "Shira wanted me to ask. Are you the reason Cassidy isn't sleeping well?"

Gray grinned.

After a moment Ranon laughed. "Good for you, Gray. Good for you."

※※※

Cassidy sat on the edge of her bed, fingering the key she'd found in the old wish pot—something she'd done every day, hoping the key would provide some clue to the treasure that was supposed to exist on the estate. Of course, her mind wasn't on treasure. Not tonight. Her mind was on . . .

"Lia and Thera, your male descendants are a pain in the ass."

At least Theran and Gray could share the blame for her being unable to sleep tonight. Theran had run hot and cold all morning—wanting her to write to the Shalador Queens and then being opposed to her writing to any of the other Queens who must have heard by now that there was a Territory Queen to whom they owed allegiance. Then this evening, Gray had just run . . . hot. But not hot enough to do more than kissing and petting. Not hot enough to go to his room and make use of his bed.

But that could be Lucivar's fault because at one point this evening, when Gray pulled away because what he really needed was *more*, he had snarled something about writing to Daemon to find out if he *really* had to follow that stupid schedule.

She hadn't met Daemon before the dinner party, but she'd spent enough time around Lucivar to know the Eyrien wouldn't hesitate to give Gray a few bruises if Gray didn't stay within the boundaries Lucivar had set. So until Daemon convinced Lucivar to alter the rules, she wasn't going to ask Gray for more.

Wasn't sure she'd have the courage to ask for more anyway.

Doesn't matter who decided what, she thought sourly as she turned the key over and over. *It still means another sleepless night.*

A scratching on her suite's door. She got up to let Vae in, mostly because the sofa in her sitting room was a comfortable place to brood.

*Cassie? Cassie! You are not sleeping. Why aren't you

sleeping? It is sleep time. Everyone is sleeping. Except Talon. But it is not his sleep time.*

Cassidy barely had time to settle into a corner of the sofa before Vae was beside her, pressing close.

"You need to be brushed," Cassidy said, noticing how much loose fur was now coating her trousers.

I will nip Theran tomorrow, Vae said. *Then he will brush me.*

Oh, good. Serves you right, Grayhaven, for being a brainless ass.

You have smells, Vae said happily.

Cassidy was about to remind Vae that it wasn't polite to talk about human smells—especially the female kind. Then she realized the Sceltie was focused on the key in her hand.

"It's a key, Vae. It's made of metal. It doesn't have smells."

Vae sniffed the key again, jumped off the sofa, and trotted into the bedroom. *I will find the smells.*

"You do that." If the dog was hunting for nonexistent smells, at least she'd stay out of trouble. Maybe.

Keeping one ear cocked toward the bedroom in case Vae began rummaging where she shouldn't, Cassidy slumped in the corner of the sofa, feeling frustrated and wrung out.

Sometimes when Gray kissed her, she knew she was being kissed—and held—by a grown man. But other times, she felt like she was kissing a fifteen-year-old boy who was fumbling through his first exploration of a female body. And in some ways she wasn't fifteen anymore, and those times when he seemed more boy than man made her uncomfortable.

And yet she couldn't back away from the intimacy or end the relationship altogether, because her heart recognized something in Gray that she had never felt with or for any other man.

Cassie?

Maybe it was for the best that Lucivar had set such firm boundaries around what Gray could—and couldn't—do in terms of sex. Physically she was ready—more than ready—for *more*. Emotionally . . .

Cassie!

"What?" She felt frustrated and snappish, and her voice proclaimed her mood.

I found the smells.

"What smells?"

The smells that match the key.

Cassidy tangled her legs and almost fell off the sofa in her haste to get to the bedroom.

She didn't see anything messed up or displaced. She also didn't see a Sceltie.

"Vae?"

Here! The smells are here!

"Where?"

The tip of Vae's tail suddenly stuck out from under her bed, wagged at her, then disappeared again.

Cassidy hurried to the bed, dropped to the floor, and lifted the bedcovers. "Get out of there before you get stuck."

Won't get stuck, Vae said. *Smells are here.*

Under the bed. The treasure had been hidden for centuries. Wouldn't *someone* have looked under the bed?

That wish pot had been in the shed for centuries too and hadn't been found.

"Get out of there, Vae," Cassidy said. "I have to move the bed, and I can't do that while you're under it."

She waited impatiently while Vae wiggled out from under the bed. Then she used Craft to lift and shift the bed as far as she could.

Vae went back to sniffing the carpet, then began scratching.

"Wait," Cassidy said firmly. She moved the night tables and rolled up the carpet.

No trapdoor. No visible sign that there was anything different about that part of the floor. No lock embedded in the wood.

Here, Vae said, placing a small white paw near the spot that held the smells.

Cassidy ran her fingers over and over that spot. And found nothing until she held the key over that part of the floor.

A shadow so subtle she wasn't sure she was seeing anything. But the key slipped into that shadow like a well-oiled lock, and when she turned it, a rectangle of floor as long as her arm popped up. When she moved it aside ...

Vae sniffed. Sneezed.

Ignoring the box in the secret compartment, Cassidy took out one of the books and opened it to a random page.

Like the letter in the wish pot, the ink had faded, although not as badly.

"A journal," she said softly.

Paper? Vae asked, sounding disappointed.

"Yes, paper. But valuable." It didn't take more than reading a few lines to realize this was Lia's journal—and a few lines more to realize the entries were made near the end of her life.

Cassidy riffled the pages until she found the last entry. Which was written by a different hand.

> *Lia is dead. And Dena Nehele grieves.*
>
> *Without the Gray Lady, Dena Nehele will fall to the twisted ideas Dorothea SaDiablo spews. It won't happen next year, or the year after that. The dreams and visions I see in my tangled webs all show me the same thing—Lia's granddaughter will hold the land for a while. Long enough to keep the bloodline from dying out with so much else that will die in the years ahead. And Jared and his grandsons will continue fighting to keep the shadows at bay.*
>
> *I will die before the seasons change, slaughtered here at Grayhaven, which should have been the safest place, while Jared, Blaed, and Talon are fighting elsewhere. I will not tell them because if they are here, they will not survive—and they must survive a few years longer. They must.*
>
> *Lia is dead. Tomorrow I will grieve. Tonight I will set in motion all the spells we created to keep the treasure safe—and the hope that is hidden with it.*
>
> *Thera*

Cassidy closed the journal and started to put it back. Then she hesitated. If she left it all where it had been safely hidden for so long, would the key work a second time? Or was this part of the spell done, and this was the only opportunity to retrieve these items?

Not willing to take that chance, she pulled all the journals out of the compartment and set them aside before she removed the last item—the trinket box.

During all this, Vae stayed with her, not really interested or curious, but still watchful.

Cassidy opened the trinket box and smiled as she lifted a few pieces from the jumble of jewelry.

No expensive pieces here, no precious stones. She imagined that, during Lia's lifetime, the pieces weren't jumbled to deceive someone into thinking they weren't important. Because these trinkets were important. When she went through the journals, she'd find each piece recorded. Gifts from Lia's children. Sentimental presents from her husband. Not expensive, but priceless nonetheless.

She spent an hour wiping the journals and trinket box clean of dust before hiding them in the bottom of a trunk of her own belongings.

Then she put the piece of floor back in place.

The smells are gone, Vae said.

The key was embedded in the wood, and when she tried to remove it, it broke cleanly, becoming nothing more than an odd gold glint in the wood.

She put the rest of the key in her own trinket box, then finished putting the room in order.

Time had made its shift from late night to early morning before she finally climbed into bed with Vae stretched out beside her.

Just before she fell asleep, she realized why the servants had acted so oddly when she'd chosen these rooms over the fancy Queen's suite.

This must have been the suite that had belonged to Lia.

TWENTY-FIVE

Kaeleer

Vulchera slipped into the bedroom and looked around. The maid had turned down the bedcovers and plumped the pillows. Everything was ready for the Warlord when he bade the other guests good night and came up here to his chaste bed.

Damn Sadi for his lack of discretion. Why in the name of Hell did he have to *explode* like that? She hadn't been aiming for him at that house party. Not initially. But when he wouldn't even *flirt* with her, when he looked at her with those cold yellow eyes like she was some kind of scabby street whore, when every remark he did make to her had been blandly worded but so heavily laced with contempt everyone knew he wouldn't consider soiling himself by being with her . . .

Well, she had her pride, didn't she? She'd wanted only to give him a twinge of discomfort, a little payback because the other men who had been present at Rhea's country house had taken a good measure of Sadi's feelings and avoided her.

She'd wanted only to make him uneasy. She certainly hadn't intended to do anything that would upset Jaenelle Angelline. Anyone who had heard about what Sadi had done to Lady Lektra last spring knew better than to aim *anything*, even a barbed comment, at Sadi's wife.

But he had exploded when he found her in his room, had heaped his rage on Rhea's head to the point where the Province Queen had "suggested" she leave their little house party—and had made it clear there would never be another invitation.

They had been friends, and she'd truly liked Rhea. Besides, having a Province Queen as a friend had put her in contact with the kind of men who could be most useful, and it had provided her with some clout she wouldn't have had otherwise when she'd asked for favors from those men, even if Rhea hadn't been aware of providing that clout. Now it was all spoiled because she had miscalculated the depth of Sadi's rage.

None of that mattered now. Rhea still wanted to believe that she had intended to meet a lover who *was* an available male and had gotten the rooms mixed up. But they both knew Rhea's court was going to break under the weight of Sadi's temper, and that the friendship was just the first thing to break because of her mistake.

It wasn't prudent to play this game again so soon, especially at this particular friend's house. His wife didn't like her. *He* didn't like her, but he was an aristo Warlord who had wanted a bit of spice instead of what he usually found in his marriage bed. The shirt she'd kept as a memento of that evening gave her a standing invitation to his house— at least until his youngest son went through the Birthright Ceremony and he was granted paternity.

But she had to know—*had to*—if Sadi's threat had been an empty one. She'd gone to her Healer and was assured there was nothing wrong. She'd gone to a Black Widow, who assured her there was no sign of any kind of spell around her.

Assurances. But not enough assurance, not when the person aiming a spell at her was a Black-Jeweled Warlord Prince. She had to know if Sadi really could strip her of the ability to get any pleasure out of sex.

She'd picked the Warlord at this house party because he was married and he'd made it clear he wanted to romp. At any other time, she wouldn't have done more than flirt with him, because he wasn't wealthy enough or influential enough to do her favors. But he would help her prove that nothing would happen to her—as long as she avoided crossing paths with Sadi.

The candle-light in the lamp on the table beside the bed was on a low setting and, oddly, lit only one side of the room, leaving the other side midnight dark. She shrugged off that detail even quicker than she stripped off her clothes until she was down to high-heeled shoes and sheer panties.

And wasn't that considerate of him? she thought when she noticed the shirt draped over a chair.

Heavy silk, lovely to touch. She hadn't seen him wear anything like this, wouldn't have guessed he could afford a shirt like this.

Unless this was the shirt he offered women for a romp.

The thought wasn't appealing, and even less appealing was the possibility that he might not think her being here was anything special.

But there was a hint of spice rising up from the shirt where her hands had warmed the silk. Not cologne, just a spicy male scent that made her feel fluid and female.

She slipped on the shirt, loving the way it settled over her skin. She buttoned the cuffs, then buttoned half the buttons down the front.

She twirled once, twice. The shirt caressed her skin as it settled around her.

A bead of sweat tickled her as it followed the channel of her spine.

Damn, damn, damn. She didn't want to *sweat*. At least, not before she and the Warlord were heavily into the romp part of the evening.

Then she caught sight of herself in the mirror over the dressing table.

Dark specks on the shirt, growing bigger by the moment.

More sweat trickling down her spine.

What in the name of Hell was going on?

She walked over to the mirror to get a better look. The shirt was clinging to her shoulders. As she reached the mirror, she pressed her fingers on a patch of now-dark silk.

When she raised her fingers, they were wet—and red.

She was sweating blood. *How could she be sweating blood?*

The shirt. Had to be something in the shirt.

She grabbed the fabric with both hands, intending to tear the shirt off.

Blood gushed from her hands.

She released the fabric and stumbled toward the door.

Help. She needed help.

The door wouldn't open.

She pounded on the door, leaving bloody handprints.

"Help me! Somebody, help me!"

No response from the other side of the door.

"They can't hear you," a deep voice said in a singsong croon. "They won't help you."

She turned toward the voice coming from the dark side of the room. "My lover will be coming up to bed at any moment."

Movement. Then a man appeared on the edge of the dark side of the room. Most of his face was still in shadow, but his smile was viciously gentle. "The Warlord? No, my dear, he won't be coming up here. He was encouraged to leave and is, by now, on his way home."

"What do you want?" she cried.

The shirt got wetter and heavier, clinging to her skin. Her legs trembled with the effort to remain standing.

"Odd how much terror can be produced by a piece of cloth," he said in that singsong croon. "Don't you think it's odd? A simple shirt can destroy a person's life. How does it feel to be on the receiving end of that fear?"

She heard the *splat* of blood dripping off the shirt and hitting the carpet.

"I've learned my lesson. Do you hear me? I won't play with married men ever again."

"I know you won't." There was nothing gentle about the gentleness in that deep voice.

"Why are you doing this?" she screamed. "I never played with you!"

He took a step closer. Got a good look at her face.

And felt something inside him snap.

A man's anguish. What was left of a child's face. A ceremony. A betrayal. *Rage*.

Memories collided, spun, became a twisting storm that hurled him over the border and into the Twisted Kingdom—where a terrible, and familiar, clarity waited for him.

"Who are you?"

She knew. How could she not know? But he would play her game a little longer, since it would be the last time.

"I'm the Prince of the Darkness, the High Lord of Hell. And Daemon Sadi's father."

The storm inside him gathered speed, gathered power, gathered the cold, deadly rage. The sweet, cleansing rage.

"You took my boy."

She shook her head.

Lying bitch.

"You tried to hurt my son."

"I wouldn't have done anything," she cried. "It was just a game!"

"It's always just a game, isn't it?" he said too softly. "You like playing games, shattering lives."

"I—" She sank to the floor, too weak to stand.

He breathed in the exciting scent of blood but had no desire to taste it. Not hers. Not that disgusting, foul brew that flowed in her veins.

But after this first payment was made . . .

She was . . . but she wasn't. It didn't matter. She and the other were enough alike.

She tried to hurt his son—and everything has a price.

He smiled a cold, vicious smile. "Dorothea, my darling, it's finally time to pay the debt."

TWENTY-SIX

Kaeleer

Someone tapped lightly on the first of Daemon's inner barriers, waking him from a sound sleep.

Prince Sadi?

Beale? The butler wasn't in the bedroom, but Daemon still pulled the covers up around Jaenelle's delightfully naked body before he shifted far enough to turn over without disturbing her. *Beale?*

You're needed downstairs, Prince, Beale said.

He took a moment to sift through the messages coming from the controlled tone of Beale's voice on the psychic thread as well as the butler's psychic scent. Whatever brought Beale up here to wake him required his immediate attention but didn't require a Warlord Prince rising from sleep primed to fight.

Understanding the careful line the man needed to walk in order to get the desired response rather than the instinctive one, Daemon realized just how skilled Beale was at his job. *What time is it?*

A little after three in the morning.

Daemon slipped out of bed, pulled on his robe, and went into the Consort's bedroom, where Beale waited. After putting an aural shield around the room so Jaenelle wouldn't be disturbed, he said, "What's wrong?"

"A Warlord arrived a few minutes ago," Beale said, keeping his voice quiet despite the shield. "From the Province Queen's court."

Dhemlan had several Provinces, each ruled by a Queen.

But there was an edge in Beale's voice that told Daemon *exactly* which Province Queen was asking for help.

Something must have happened to make Rhea desperate enough to ask for *his* help.

"Apparently there has been some trouble," Beale said. "Under other circumstances, I would have assigned the Warlord to a guest room and had him wait to speak with you at a more convenient hour."

"But?"

"He's very frightened, Prince. Whatever he heard, whatever he saw . . . He's very frightened."

"All right. I'll see him."

"Mrs. Beale is making coffee and will have a plate ready for you. Just a little something until she can make you a proper breakfast."

"Thank you. I'll be down in a few minutes."

Beale hesitated, and Daemon noticed a curious kind of tension in the other man.

"Something else?" Daemon asked.

"You'll be going to that Province to talk to the Queen?"

The thought of going back to that damn Province and being a guest of Rhea's again made his chest muscles tighten so much it was hard to breathe. "Probably."

"One of the SaDiablo estates is in the neighboring Province, almost at the border of the two," Beale said, sounding as if he was feeling his way over very shaky ground. "It's a short distance to travel when a person is riding one of the darker Winds. I could send a messenger and let the staff there know you'll be staying for a day or two."

He hadn't thought that far ahead, but now that Beale mentioned the ease of staying somewhere else, he realized it would be some time before he viewed any Queen's residence as anything but a potential battleground.

Which was exactly how he had viewed the Queens' courts when he was a pleasure slave in Terreille.

"Thank you, Beale."

Why *had* Beale mentioned it?

Look at his eyes, old son. When he did, Daemon felt the ground shift under him just a little.

"It is not always a pleasure to work in an aristo house,"

Beale said. "Even among the Blood, sometimes the employer forgets that the servant is also a person."

What are you driving at, Beale?

"The High Lord was an excellent employer. No man who worked on any of his estates or in any of his houses needed to fear that he would be cornered into doing something that would smear his reputation, perhaps irreparably. No woman needed to fear the males around her during the days when she was vulnerable. The High Lord took care of his own. Always." Beale paused. "And so do you. The small courtesies have not gone unnoticed by those who work for you, and the feeling of safety is still here."

"I appreciate you telling me." But they hadn't gotten to the point of this conversation.

"You take care of your own, Prince." Beale tapped a finger against his own chest. "So do we. Which is why, when you need to visit the Provinces from now on, the nearest residence that belongs to the SaDiablo family will be ready to accommodate you."

"The residences are always ready...." No, Daemon realized. It wasn't about the houses. It was about *him.* It was about staying in a place where he wouldn't have to be on guard all the time. It was about having servants around him that he could trust.

It was about other people—one Lady in particular—being safe around him because *he* felt safe.

"I should give you a raise," Daemon said, not sure if he felt grateful or embarrassed.

"You already pay me quite well," Beale said with a little smile as he left the room.

A few minutes later, dressed in trousers and a dressing gown, Daemon was down in his study listening to the barely coherent report of a murder. When he left the study, he found Jaenelle waiting for him in the great hall, with Beale and the footman Holt in watchful attendance.

"Have one of the Coaches brought round to the landing web," Daemon told Beale.

"I'll do that," Holt said, looking at Beale.

Beale nodded. "I'll ask Mrs. Beale to prepare something you can eat on the way."

When the two men headed for their assigned tasks, Daemon led Jaenelle into the informal receiving room.

"Problem?" Jaenelle asked.

"The bitch who tried to play with me has been murdered," Daemon replied.

"That didn't take long," she muttered.

"Apparently it's how she died that's causing alarm. The host's wife has also been injured, but I don't have a clear idea of how or how badly. I have to go there." He could keep his pride or he could ask for what he needed. "Come with me."

Her smile was gentle and teasing. "You want me to come as your escort and protect you from all the nasty witchlings?"

"Yes, I do."

Her smile faded.

Did she understand what it cost him to ask?

Of course she did. She was Witch. In some ways, she knew him better than he knew himself.

She placed a hand against his cheek, a touch full of comfort. "I'll make a bargain with you, Prince. I'll stand as your sword and shield when you need it if you'll do the same for me."

He pressed a kiss into her palm. "I'll take that bargain. Gladly."

She stepped back. "Find out as much as you can, then ask Beale to slip that Warlord the sedative I prepared. I don't think either of us wants to ride in a Coach with a hysterical man, and I could feel him losing control even before I came downstairs. I'll pack some clothes and ask Jazen to pack a bag for you."

She was about to open the door when Daemon said, "Jaenelle, they think it was me." She didn't turn to look at him. She froze in place, listening. "Rhea sent her man here to ask for help because everyone in that aristo Warlord's house is more than scared. The Warlord who brought the message is afraid to say as much as he knows, but I got the impression that there's something about the way Vulchera died that . . . They think they're asking for help from the same man who killed her."

"It wasn't you," Jaenelle said, finally turning to look at him. "May the Darkness have mercy on her, because it wasn't you."

She looked pale, and that confirmed his own suspicion. And the worry that went hand in hand with that suspicion.

"I'll get packed," she said.

He went back to his study and reviewed the information with the Warlord again but didn't learn more than he had gleaned the first time. Leaving the man in Beale's care, he returned to his suite and took a quick shower before getting dressed.

The sun—that lazy bastard—was just beginning to think about dawdling its way to the eastern horizon when he tucked the lightly sedated Warlord into the back of the Coach with Holt and took a seat in the driver's compartment.

Jaenelle hovered in the doorway between the two compartments, frowning at the large urn of coffee Beale had put in the Coach, along with a variety of foods to provide them with a cold but substantial breakfast.

Daemon lifted the Coach off the landing web, then caught the Black Wind and headed for the house of the aristo Warlord and his wife.

"An urn of coffee?" Jaenelle said. "Riding on the Black, it won't take *that* long to reach Rhea's Province and that Warlord's house. Why would Beale give us that much coffee?"

He knew better. He really did. But he tucked his tongue firmly in one cheek and said as casually as possible, "I guess he wanted to make sure I would get a cup with my breakfast."

He felt her sapphire eyes fix on a spot between his shoulder blades, and he really wanted to twitch.

Finally she growled, "Drive the damn Coach."

He waited until he was sure she was occupied with fixing a plate of food before he allowed himself to grin.

And he did, eventually, get a cup of coffee with his breakfast.

Standing in the hallway beside Jaenelle, Daemon looked at the bedroom and the body—and swallowed hard.

It wasn't the blood. There had been times when he had drowned rooms in blood, so the sight of a sodden carpet and smears on the walls and furniture didn't bother him.

And it wasn't the body, which, from the shoulders down, looked relaxed, as if she'd fallen asleep on the floor.

It was the rage—the cold, dark, glittering rage—that

made him shiver. It filled the room and yet felt elusive, wispy. As if it could be brushed aside. And there was something more in that rage, some quality to it that he knew he should recognize.

"Mother Night," Jaenelle said softly.

"And may the Darkness be merciful," Daemon added.

"She came upstairs early, said she was tired," Lord Collyn, the aristo who owned the house, said. There was a bitterness in his voice, in his eyes. "She often got tired at house parties and went to bed earlier than the other guests."

"This wasn't her room?" Jaenelle asked.

"No," Collyn replied. "My wife and I were the last to retire, and when we were about to go upstairs, our butler mentioned that one of our guests left in a hurry and was very upset. Having heard about what had happened at Lady Rhea's country house"—he shot a nervous look at Daemon—"my wife went up to confirm that my 'friend' was in the guest room that had been assigned to her. She wasn't, of course, so my wife came to this room . . . and found her. I don't know what she could have been thinking. It was clear Vulchera was dead, but Rosalene touched the body. That's how she hurt her hands."

"What's wrong with her hands?" Daemon asked.

"The Healer isn't sure." Another nervous glance at Daemon. "Or doesn't want to say. But she's tried everything and hasn't been able to heal the wounds."

"I'll look at them in a few minutes," Jaenelle said. "Examining the body won't take long."

How do you know that? Daemon asked on a private psychic thread.

She didn't answer him. Instead, she removed her flowing, calf-length black jacket and vanished it. "You'll want to air walk when you're in this room."

"I've walked on blood-soaked ground before."

"That may be, Prince, but you don't want the scent of blood on you. Not this blood."

He watched her walk into the room, standing on air a finger's length above the floor. He made sure he was standing the same distance above the floor before he walked into the room.

Jaenelle circled the body slowly. Once. Twice. Thrice.

He circled the body too, and was almost certain they

weren't picking up the same information. At least, not all the same information.

If he'd come across a body like this when he'd lived in Terreille, he would have recognized there was nothing gentle about this death, despite there being no sense of violence in the room. That would have made him sufficiently wary to back away. Because it took more than control and power to do what had been done in this room.

Jaenelle crouched on one side of the body and stared at it. He crouched on the other side, trying to make sense of the pieces of information he could glean.

He put a Black shield around his hand, then reached for the shirt, intending to pull back the collar enough to see if there was a tailor's label.

Jaenelle grabbed his wrist. *Don't touch the shirt. I'm fairly certain the spell wasn't triggered until she put the shirt on, but now that the silk has been saturated with blood, I think it will hook into any flesh.*

My hand is shielded.

She looked at him, just looked at him. A chill went down his spine.

Releasing his wrist, she held one hand above the witch's chest. The Twilight's Dawn Jewel in her pendant changed to Red edged with Gray. The Jewel in her ring was the equivalent of Ebon-gray with veins of Black.

He couldn't tell what spell she used. The power that flowed out of her felt like nothing more than a puff of warm air.

But when that power flowed through the fabric, silvery strands shone in the blood-darkened silk. Silvery strands that had nothing to do with clothing and everything to do with a different kind of weaving.

Tangled web, Jaenelle said.

The silvery strands faded.

Can we remove it? Daemon asked.

No.

Can we destroy it?

She looked grim. *Yes. It . . . offers the answer to destroying it. But the Darkness only knows what that will unleash.*

*Jaenelle . . . *

*We need to talk about this. About all of this. But not

here. Not now. Right now, I want you to walk out of this room and close the door.*

Why?

Wood and stone remember.

He *couldn't* be understanding her. *You're going to use the Hourglass's Craft to recall what happened here and *watch* the execution?*

Yes.

Then I'll stay with you.

No. I want you out of this room, Daemon. Now.

And the Queen commands, he thought as he walked out of the room—and wondered if his heart could bruise his chest, the way it was pounding.

What was it she suspected that she didn't want him to see?

It felt like he'd been standing in that hallway for days, but when Jaenelle walked out of the room, he was fairly certain she'd been inside less time than it had taken for Vulchera to bleed out.

"You'll have to burn the body," Jaenelle told Lord Collyn. "If you don't, that shirt will continue to be a danger to your household."

"Can't we wait until the spell fades and then deal with the remains?" Collyn asked.

"The body will rot before those spells fade," she replied sharply. "Use Craft. Don't touch anything you don't have to. Build a bonfire, Warlord, because this has to *burn*. Use witchfire as well as natural fire. Both will be needed to break the spells. I'll leave a cleansing web Lady Yaslana and I developed to remove emotional residue from a room. That should make it possible for your people to be in the room long enough to take care of the physical cleaning."

Of course, it would be a long time—if ever—before any guest would willingly stay in that room, cleansed or not, Daemon thought.

"Now," Jaenelle said, "I'll see your wife."

Blood seeped from fine lines on Lady Rosalene's hands, as if she'd pressed down on wires that had cut deep into her skin. Except the skin wasn't cut. If you wiped away the blood, all that was visible were those silvery strands on the surface of her skin—until the blood welled up again from those strands.

Rosalene had pressed her hands on the shirt. She had walked into the bedroom, seen the body, seen the blood, and grabbed that bitch Vulchera's arm in some shocked effort to help before she saw the reason there was no possible way to help.

Silver strands. Like the tangled web that had been woven into that silk shirt.

Ignoring Collyn, who hovered in the doorway, not quite daring to come into the room, Daemon stood near Jaenelle and watched her clean the blood off Rosalene's hands again.

"I've tried everything I know." The Healer was a middle-aged woman who sounded both frustrated and anxious. "I've tried every healing spell I know, but there's nothing to actually *heal*."

Jaenelle called in a small, short-bladed Healer's knife and made a shallow cut in Rosalene's hand, following the path of one of those silvery strands. Setting that knife aside, she called in another and pricked her own finger.

Daemon snarled, a reflex to smelling his Queen's blood, to knowing her blood ran.

A phantom caress down his back—a caress that reassured enough for him to leash the instincts of a Warlord Prince.

As one drop of her blood fell on the shallow cut she had made in Rosalene's hand, Jaenelle said, "And the Blood shall sing to the Blood. And in the blood."

The Healer wet a small square of cloth with a healing lotion and handed it to Jaenelle, who murmured her thanks—and didn't grumble at him when he took the cloth and cleaned her pricked finger.

"Clean off her hands again," Jaenelle told the Healer.

The silvery strands showed once more, but this time when they faded, no blood seeped up through the skin.

"I didn't think to do that," the Healer said.

Jaenelle shook her head. "It wouldn't have made a difference if you had."

Because the spell was made to recognize your blood? Daemon asked.

And yours.

"I would recommend drinking a healing brew several times a day for the next couple of days," Jaenelle told Rosalene. "That will help your body regain its strength and replace the blood you've lost."

"I can take care of that," the Healer said.

"Then I think we're done here." Jaenelle looked at him, clearly letting him make the choice.

He was more than ready to get out of that house, but he had duties as the Warlord Prince of Dhemlan.

"Everyone needs some rest," he told Collyn, who was still hovering in the doorway. "I'll return this afternoon, and you and I can discuss what happened yesterday."

He escorted Jaenelle out of that room and down the stairs to the main floor . . . and escape.

Daemon, I know you have duties, but I don't want to stay in this house, Jaenelle said.

We're not going to, he said as they left the house and walked to the Coach. *Arrangements have already been made for us to stay at the estate house for as long as it takes to settle this.*

She stuttered a step. *Is that why Holt came with us? It seemed odd that Beale would assign a footman to look after us for a Coach ride, but I had other things on my mind.*

Holt went on to the house to let them know we're coming.

Ah.

She had seemed grimly calm while she'd looked at the body. She had taken care of Rosalene's hands with her usual skill as a Healer.

So he wasn't prepared when she flung herself in his arms and held on with shuddering distress the moment they were safely inside the Coach.

"Jaenelle . . ." He held her, not knowing what else to do—and more unnerved by this reaction than he'd been by anything else. "Jaenelle, what's wrong?"

"Not yet," she whispered. "Please. I don't want to talk about it yet, think about it yet. I don't want to be completely sober when we talk about this."

Mother Night. "Isn't there *anything* you can tell me?"

Her eyes were so haunted when she eased back enough to look at him. "Do you know the story of Zuulaman?"

*   *   *

They had a summer blanket tucked around them—more for the idea of comfort, since it couldn't relieve what chilled them—and they were both working on their third very large brandies before Jaenelle stopped shivering.

Daemon kept one arm wrapped around her. He would have preferred the privacy of the bedroom to a locked parlor, but he understood her choice. She wanted this conversation over with before they got into bed to offer each other some comfort and get some sleep.

"He's not sane, Daemon."

He wasn't sure he'd heard her correctly. "You think Saetan got so pissed off about this bitch that he decided to take a walk in the Twisted Kingdom in order to deal with her?"

"I don't think he decided anything," Jaenelle said. "I think something about this shoved him over the border. Free fall into madness—and the rage inside that madness is huge . . . and terrible."

He had walked in the Twisted Kingdom for eight years, lost in madness. He had lost none of his power during that time, but his madness had been self-destructive. If he'd understood Jaenelle's reference to Zuulaman, Saetan's madness tended to look outward. Toward an enemy.

"Why?" he asked. "What did you see in that room?"

She shook her head. "The spell in the shirt was an execution, a brutal kind of justice. He was in that room with her as the Executioner. But something changed toward the end."

Shivering, she tried to tuck herself closer to him. Since that wasn't possible, he put a warming spell on the blanket.

"It changed," Jaenelle said. "It became personal. For him. Personal enough to break something inside him."

She drained her glass, then used Craft to float the decanter of brandy from the table in front of the sofa. She filled her glass and topped off his before sending the decanter back to the table.

Daemon narrowed his eyes and considered the wobble as the decanter settled back on the wood. Then he considered his slightly glassy-eyed wife.

Yes, this *was* the first time she'd tossed back enough liquor to feel the effects since she'd healed and begun wearing Twilight's Dawn. She hadn't taken into account that since she no longer wore the Black, her body wouldn't burn up the liquor as fast.

So his darling was a lot less sober than she realized. Which meant he could ask the questions he didn't think she would have answered otherwise.

"He took Vulchera's head," he said, keeping his voice soothing. "Why did he take her head?"

"It was all he needed." Jaenelle sipped her brandy. "He didn't break her Jewels, didn't strip her power. She'll make the transition to demon-dead. He'll make sure of it."

"But . . . it's just her head."

"Which contains the brain, which contains the mind, which is the conduit to the Self. Or one of them, anyway. All he needs. He's going to finish the execution. She bled to death. Slowly. That was what the shirt was intended to do. Bleed her out. He would have sealed her into that room. She would have tried to get out, would have tried to get the shirt off. When she couldn't do either, when she knew she couldn't do either . . . There was so much fear in that room. Could you feel it?"

"Yes, I could."

"Bleeding out because she put on a shirt." Jaenelle laughed, but it was a hollow sound. "I imagine when they burn the body . . . Whatever spell that releases . . . I guess there will be a few men who will sleep better for whatever message rises from that fire."

There is nothing he has done that I couldn't have done, Daemon thought. *So why am I so uneasy?*

"That fear while she bled out, that was the first part of the execution," Jaenelle said. "After she makes the transition to demon-dead . . . That's when the pain truly begins."

"Why?"

She looked sleepy. Her body was relaxing against him.

"Because of you. This is about you, Daemon. About him . . . and you. That's why you need to be the one who helps him come back from the Twisted Kingdom. He'll answer you."

"I don't know how to do that," he protested. "I don't have any training to do that."

"You don't need training. This is about fathers and sons. Lucivar needs to go with you."

"Hell's fire, Jaenelle. Saetan is my father. Do you really think I'll need Lucivar there to watch my back?"

She smiled gently. "No, think of his being there as stacking the deck in your favor."

Suddenly exhausted, and scared sick of what he might be facing, he rested his cheek against her head. "When?"

"Tomorrow after sunset," Jaenelle replied. "He'll be done with the execution by then, and I think he'll go back to the Keep after that."

"All right." His breath came out in a shuddering sigh. "Come to bed with me. Just be with me."

They went to bed for rest, for comfort. And as he went through the motions of the rest of the day, talking to Lord Collyn and dealing with the aftermath of the kill, he tried not to think about what might be waiting for him at the Keep tomorrow.

TWENTY-SEVEN

"Psst. Gray."

Gray tensed. When he'd been in captivity, that sound usually preceded some boy's attempt to "befriend" him so that he could be blamed for whatever mischief the boy and his friends had done.

"Psst."

He turned toward the sound—and wondered why Ranon was hiding behind the stone shed.

He moved toward the other man slowly, reluctantly. Ranon seemed hesitant, uncertain. That in itself was a reason to be wary.

Then Ranon crouched and rested his hand above the ground. When he dropped the sight shield and revealed the wooden box, Gray rushed behind the shed to join him.

Plants. Lovely little plants ready for a garden.

"I talked to my people," Ranon said. "Some of the elders, along with the Queens, traveled to my home village to meet with me. To hear about the new Queen. I told them about Cassidy. I told them she knew about witchblood—a plant that is not unknown in the reserves even though we'd forgotten what it meant. I told them about the flower bed you wanted to plant for her. I mentioned that some of the flowers Cassidy's mother had sent looked similar to plants that grew in the southern part of Dena Nehele, so they sent these back with me. The Ladies sent notes with the plants." He called in several folded sheets of paper. "They said some are perennials, some are annuals. Some can winter over. They tried to give me more of a gardening lesson than I wanted, but I figured you'd know what they were talking about."

Each plant had a carefully written label attached to its pot. Gray touched each one gently, moved that strangers would be willing to help him make this special part of the garden.

He looked up, and was about to ask why Ranon was acting so uneasy about offering the plants. But when he looked into the other man's dark eyes, he understood the risk—and the hope—that had been carried with these plants.

Would someone from the house of Grayhaven accept plants that came from the Shalador reserves? Would the new Queen accept a gift from the Shalador people?

"Thank you," Gray said. "This will make the flower bed even more special."

Ranon's shoulders relaxed, and he smiled.

"I'll be ready to plant tomorrow," Gray said. "I just need to talk to Theran about keeping Cassie occupied for a few hours."

"Won't that be interesting?"

He wasn't sure what that meant, but judging by Ranon's amusement, he didn't think Theran would share the opinion that tomorrow would be "interesting."

Ebon Askavi

When Daemon arrived at the Keep at sunset, he didn't know what to expect.

What he found scared him to the bone.

A sparely furnished room that was heavily shielded, but he couldn't tell if the shields were Black or had been made by a power more ancient than the Blood—the power of the dragons, who had gifted the Blood with their magic long, long ago.

He also couldn't tell if the shields were meant to contain the man who waited for him in that room or contain the rage. The cold, dark, glittering rage.

He entered the room and walked toward the table that was set a few paces from the door. An awkward place for the thing, which made him think it had been placed there so that no one would have to cross the room under that feral gaze.

He moved toward the table and the man waiting beside it, and he swallowed hard. When he looked into Saetan's eyes, he saw the Warlord Prince who had destroyed an entire race so completely, there had been no trace of them left behind—including the islands they had called home.

And he saw a truth about himself.

"Prince," the High Lord said.

Oh, no. He had no chance of reaching the man if they kept to formal titles.

"Father," Daemon said—and saw a flicker of emotion in those glazed gold eyes. He stopped when he reached the edge of the table, still out of reach of lethally honed nails—and the venom in the snake tooth under Saetan's ring finger nail. "Father, talk to me. Please."

No response. Just a terrifying assessment being made by a powerful man who was walking who knew what roads in the Twisted Kingdom.

I can take him. If it comes to that, I'm strong enough to stop him.

Strong enough to win—maybe—but not strong enough to come out of that fight intact. Not when he'd be pitting a little extra raw power against thousands of years of experience.

Which made him glad Jaenelle had held Lucivar back instead of having both of them go to the Keep. One of them needed to survive to take care of the rest of the family.

If it came down to that.

Sweet Darkness, please don't let it come down to that.

"Father," Daemon said again.

Saetan looked at the table. Pressed the fingertips of his right hand on the polished wood. Two sheets of paper appeared beside his fingers.

Wary, Daemon took a step closer. "What are these?"

"Names," Saetan said, his voice a hoarse, singsong croon. "The names of men who didn't take the bait but were still caught by the trap."

Moving slowly, painfully alert in case a simple action gave offense, Daemon drew one of the sheets closer so he could read it.

Names and places.

He took her head, Daemon thought. *All he needed. What kind of pain did the High Lord extract along with these names in order to collect the full debt Vulchera owed the people she had harmed?*

"Words that were said cannot be unsaid," Saetan whispered. "But sometimes hearts can forgive when a lie is revealed, and maybe, for some, the truth will let them hold what is most dear."

Daemon frowned at the list as he sorted through the layers of messages in those words. Marriages had been broken by Vulchera's games. There weren't many women who would forgive a husband's betrayal of the marriage bed, especially when fidelity was one of the things a man offered as part of the marriage contract. But Jaenelle was sure Saetan's slide into the Twisted Kingdom was about him and was personal. So if it wasn't about the wives and broken marriages, it had to be about the children.

Daemon pushed aside the chill of fear. He couldn't afford to have Saetan pick up *that* particular psychic scent.

Children. Dangerous ground where the High Lord of Hell was concerned.

"You want me to contact the families of these men?" he asked.

Saetan's fingertips brushed the second sheet of paper. "Their lives were torn apart because of a lie. Because some bitch liked to play games."

The words started softly and ended in a savage snarl.

Who are we talking about? Daemon wondered—and felt something shiver through him.

The rage still filled the room, but something else was building under the rage. Something that could be the spark that would light the tinder and unleash the High Lord's temper.

"You don't know what it's like," Saetan whispered. "You don't know the agony a man can f-feel when he hears those three words: 'Paternity is denied.' "

The hoarseness in that deep voice. As if Saetan's throat had been strained by the effort of keeping the rage in—or by screaming to get some of the rage out.

Daemon had to choose. Had to commit to the fight. If Saetan lost control of that madness-driven rage, he had to strike without hesitation—because hesitating would, most likely, leave him open to an attack that would cripple him enough to take him out of the fight . . . and leave Lucivar standing alone on the killing field.

"Father. Talk to me."

The silence held for almost too long.

"When the burden of existing as demon-dead becomes too great, sometimes Hell's citizens will seek out the High Lord and ask him to finish what was begun," Saetan said. "So even though I wasn't informed by any of the Dhemlan Queens, as I should have been, I heard the story anyway."

"What happened?" Daemon asked, watching Saetan's eyes become lifeless and blank of everything but a memory.

"By his own admission, the Warlord had flirted a few times with the idea of becoming another woman's lover, but he hadn't done anything that would force his wife into making a choice about their marriage. They had a son who had gone through the Birthright Ceremony and was irrevocably his by law. But they also had a little girl who hadn't gone through the Ceremony yet.

"Whatever trouble he had with the woman, he adored the little girl, and it was for her sake that he trod so carefully when it came to his marriage vows.

"A few months before his daughter's Birthright Ceremony, he went to visit a close friend for a few days—an annual house party he and his wife had gone to for several years. But his wife didn't go with him that year because their boy was feeling poorly, so it was prudent to keep the children at home."

Daemon nodded, seeing where the next part of the story was going. "Vulchera was at the house party, playing her games. Did he take the bait?"

"No. He came close to it because he and his wife were growing more and more unhappy with each other, but he walked out of the bedroom and went to find his friend. By the time they got back to the room, the bitch was gone."

"She denied being in his bedroom?" Daemon said.

"Of course. But his friend's wife told her to pack her things and leave, and that didn't sit well with the *Lady.*"

"She sent a shirt to the Warlord's wife."

Saetan nodded. "With enough details about his body to make it clear she'd seen him undressed. The day before she'd set her trap, he'd gotten a soaking during some game the men were playing and had stripped off his wet shirt—which she had kindly offered to take into the laundry room, along with a few others.

"The marriage broke. He'd played too close to that line too many times, and his wife had not been as unaware as he'd believed. As sometimes happens, he began to regret the loss of what he'd had—including the woman, who hadn't seemed as exciting after she'd become familiar. And there was his daughter, his little girl, to consider.

"So they tried to rebuild what had been broken. He wasn't living with them, but he visited every evening, doing chores he'd previously resented, playing with his children. Talking to his wife and rediscovering the woman.

"A month before his daughter's Birthright Ceremony, he'd worked his way back to living at the family home half the time and had earned his way back into the marriage bed."

Daemon said nothing. Saetan's eyes still held that blankness, but Daemon felt a terrible *something* building under the words. Building and building.

"The Warlord going to his friend had caused problems for the *Lady*—the kind of problems that can be resolved only by relocating to another Province where her previous activities wouldn't be common knowledge. So she hired a young actress and purchased an illusion spell from a Black Widow to play a prank on a 'good friend.'

"The Warlord was going to move back to the family home after the Birthright Ceremony. His wife had already told him she would grant paternity, assuring his rights to his daughter, but his formal return as husband and father would come after the Ceremony. So he wasn't at the house when the package arrived with the second shirt and a note that was skillfully written and indicated that the Warlord had been leaving his wife's bed and going straight to his lover's for some real pleasure instead of duty sex.

"The words were meant to cripple a woman's pride and kill a piece of her heart. In that, they succeeded.

"That afternoon, the Warlord watched his little girl be gifted with her Birthright Jewel, and he waited for the last part of that ceremony that would give him back what he'd learned he held dear.

"Then his wife looked at him and said three words: 'Paternity is denied.' "

Saetan closed his eyes. "There are moments in a man's life when a decision is made, and once made, there is no going back, no changing it." When he opened his eyes, they were no longer blank. They were filled with a terrible, and growing, grief.

"The shock. The pain," Saetan said. "You don't know what it feels like to hear those words."

"It's a stupid law," Daemon said.

Saetan shook his head. "No, it's not. Considering the nature of Blood males, there are good reasons for that law. That was true when that irrevocable custom began, and it's still true. That law protects more than it harms. But it still . . . hurts."

"What happened to the Warlord?" Daemon asked.

"He backed away. He saw the shock on the faces of friends and family—people who had been aware of the reconciliation. He didn't know what happened, but he knew something had gone very wrong.

"So he backed away, but when he turned, *she* was standing there. And she laughed at him. That's all she needed to do. She laughed at him, laughed at his pain and his loss—and something inside him broke.

"He didn't remember what happened after that. She laughed, something inside him broke, and the next thing he remembered was standing in the middle of a slaughter. The witch, the young actress who had been hired to wear an enemy's face as a prank, was dead. So was the Warlord's closest friend, two of his cousins . . . and his daughter.

"When he saw his little girl . . . In that moment when he wondered, he dropped his shields, deliberately, and the blasts of power from other males fighting to defend friends and family ripped into his body and killed him."

"Mother Night," Daemon whispered. A terrible story, but he had the feeling that it was the crust holding back something even more terrible.

"Insane rage—and no memory of who had fallen by his hand," Saetan said. "And the feeling, the *fear*, that he had killed his little girl."

"Did he?"

Saetan finally looked up, finally looked him in the eyes.

"Yes." He smiled—and the insane rage within that gentle smile was a living thing. "She had been trying to reach him, had been trying to protect him with her newly acquired Jewel."

Daemon felt tears sting his eyes and blinked them away.

"His blast of power took half her face. Part of her shoulder," Saetan said too gently. "He made the transition to demon-dead, and when he reached the Dark Realm, he begged for an audience. Then he begged me to finish the kill."

"Did you give him mercy?"

"Yes, I finished the kill, and he became nothing more than a whisper in the Darkness."

Daemon's stomach rolled as another thought occurred to him. "The little girl became *cildru dyathe*, didn't she?"

"Yes, she did. But she didn't stay long. When I found her, I told her that her father loved her, and that he was very sorry she had gotten hurt, and if he could take that moment back and do it over, he would have walked away. For her sake. To keep her safe from what was inside him."

"Father . . ."

"It could have been you, Daemon. She could have been you."

He looked at those gold eyes glazed with madness and took a step back.

Pain. Shock. A moment to make a choice before insane rage eclipsed all ability to think.

Manny's words, when she finally told him about his father.

So he left. Went to that house you keep visiting, the house you and your mother lived in, and destroyed the study. Tore the books apart, shredded the curtains, broke every piece of furniture in the room. He couldn't get the rage out. When I finally dared open the door, he was kneeling in the middle of the room, his chest heaving, trying to get some air, a crazy look in his eyes.

When Dorothea betrayed Saetan at Daemon's Birthright Ceremony, the High Lord had walked away. Because he had known the depth of his rage. Because the boy, like the girl centuries later, would have tried to reach the father, would have gotten caught in the fight.

Would have died.

Saetan's eyes filled with tears. "It ... could have ... been you."

Here it is, Daemon thought. *Here is the cascade of memories that sent a strong man tumbling into the Twisted Kingdom—and almost ignited a cataclysmic rage.*

He didn't think. Didn't have to think. He threw his arms around his father and held on as Saetan broke down and wept.

"I'm here, Father. I'm here. I'm safe. I'm well. You protected me that day. You walked away and kept me safe." *And please, sweet Darkness, please don't let him think about what that boy's life had been like after that day. Not now.* "I'm here, Father. I've got you. I'm here."

Choices. And taking chances.

While Saetan wept, Daemon quietly descended until he stood in the abyss at the level of the Black.

I am my father's son. Not much to distinguish between their psychic scents or their power. He was counting on that as he carefully created a link between Saetan's Black power and his own—and began using his power to absorb Saetan's, draining them both in the process. Quietly. Carefully. It would leave them both vulnerable, but if he couldn't bring his father out of the Twisted Kingdom, Saetan wouldn't have a reserve of Black power, so he would end up tapping into his Birthright Red. Lucivar would be the dominant power coming into that fight—and Lucivar would do whatever needed to be done.

Thinking of his own Birthright Ceremony and the moment of that betrayal, Daemon wondered how much strength and courage a man needed to take that kind of emotional gutting and walk away in order to protect what was held dear.

"I'm here, Father. I'm safe. You kept me safe that day."

Running out of time. Draining the power faster and faster, hoping he could drain enough.

Another shock as a flick of temper sizzled along that link.

Saetan had been aware of being drained. Had been aware all along—and had *let* him drain the power instead of fighting.

Now the High Lord pushed back, shutting off his ability

to drain the Black without turning the effort into a fight. Saetan also pulled away from his embrace, turning toward the door.

He and Saetan were still linked, mind to mind, but it wasn't an intrusive connection, more an emotional awareness now. Enough to tell him that his father was still on the wrong side of the boundary between the Twisted Kingdom and sanity. Enough for Daemon to feel bristling temper being added to an already messy emotional stew.

As he wondered what had changed, Lucivar dropped the sight shield and spread his wings slowly, giving him an intimidating physical presence.

How long had Lucivar been standing there? He hadn't sensed his brother. He'd been too focused on his father. But Saetan had responded and had turned to face an adversary.

Red shield. Hell's fire, Lucivar needed more than that. *Knew* better than to come into a potential fight with less than his strongest shield.

Then Lucivar smiled the lazy, arrogant smile that always meant trouble, and Daemon realized the Red was simply hiding the Ebony shield in the Ring of Honor Jaenelle had given Lucivar years ago when she'd been cornered into accepting him into service.

"You've upset your daughter," Lucivar said in the conversational tone that he usually followed with a fist in someone's face. "You remember her? Well, you've upset her enough that she skipped over being pissed off about it and went straight to the scary kind of bitchy. You remember that mood? It's been a while since we've seen it."

There was still enough of a psychic link between them that Daemon felt Saetan's response to the emotional punch—the equivalent of a fist in the gut. And through that link came one flash of memory. One image of a large golden spider, an incredible tangled web—and one small strand of spider silk threaded with a chip of an Ebony Jewel.

Mother Night.

He tightened his own control, closed off more of his inner barriers. Now wasn't the time to share his own memories—especially since neither he nor Saetan had missed the threat under Lucivar's words.

Lucivar held up a stoppered bottle. "She sent me here

to give you this. It's a soothing brew. A few hours' sleep will help you regain your balance."

Saetan snarled.

Lucivar bared his teeth in a smile. "Now, we could tussle about this, which, personally, I think would be fun, but that would get Jaenelle mad at all of us. So I'll just give you a choice."

No, Lucivar, Daemon thought. *Not one of your choices.*

"You can drink this and get some rest—or I can let Daemonar loose in the library, unsupervised, and the only way you'll get your grandson away from all that old paper is by going through me."

Crackling tension—and something more.

Daemon felt Saetan recoil. Lucivar had drawn the line and would hold it with everything he had in him. And something about meeting Lucivar on a killing field was making the High Lord stumble away from that line.

Saetan sat on the table, called in a handkerchief, and blew his nose.

Cornered. Trapped. Nowhere for Saetan to turn that wouldn't bring him up against an adversary he didn't want to fight.

Grandson. Sons. Daughter.

Jaenelle had chosen her weapons well.

"You prick," Saetan finally snarled. "You'd really do it."

"Damn right I would," Lucivar said. "If you're going to scare the shit out of your sons, you deserve to be threatened."

Good. Fine. Wonderful. Let's just start a pissing contest and threaten the High Lord of Hell while he's in the Twisted Kingdom and might not remember who we are. Damn you, Lucivar.

Except it worked. The madness-driven rage faded, replaced by exasperation and annoyed amusement—maybe because no one but Lucivar would dare piss on the High Lord's foot.

Saetan took those last steps across the border and walked out of the Twisted Kingdom. His shoulders sagged. He looked exhausted, but he rallied enough to hold out a hand. "Give me the damn brew."

Lucivar pulled off the stopper and handed Saetan the bottle.

Saetan gulped down the brew and handed the bottle back. "Well," he said several moments later, "at least *this* brew of hers doesn't kick like a demented draft horse."

"Lucky for you." Lucivar vanished the bottle and hauled Saetan to his feet. "Come on, Papa. We'll all have a nice nap and then play round-robin snarling."

Daemon rolled his eyes and tucked a hand under Saetan's other elbow. Whatever was in that brew was hitting the High Lord hard and fast. They didn't bother trying to get him to his bedroom. The room they were in had a sofa long enough to accommodate a grown man, so they stripped off Saetan's tunic jacket and his shoes and settled him on the sofa, tucking blankets around him.

Barely awake, Saetan struggled to focus on them. "Lucivar . . ."

Lucivar grinned. "Nah. I won't let the little beast in the library until you're feeling frisky enough to chase him."

"You pri—"

They watched their father sleep for a couple of minutes to be sure he really was settled.

Lucivar shook his head. "She said he'd go down fast. I'm glad she was right."

Daemon tipped his head, an unspoken question.

Not here, Lucivar said on a psychic thread.

They found another sitting room nearby. One moment, they were staring at each other. The next moment, they were holding each other, shaking.

"You stupid prick," Daemon said. "What were you thinking of, drawing a line like that?"

"Me?" Lucivar squeezed hard enough to leave Daemon breathless. "You're the one who left yourself open to every kind of attack. Hell's fire, Bastard. You didn't even try to shield."

"Couldn't take the chance of igniting his rage."

"I know."

Daemon eased back enough to rest his forehead against his brother's. "Scared me, Lucivar. Seeing him like that. Watching you draw that line. All of it. Really scared me."

"Scared me too." Lucivar hesitated. "You would have killed him. If it came down to that, you would have killed him."

Daemon closed his eyes. "Yes. Would have tried to

anyway. Actually, I figured the best I could do was weaken him enough before he crippled me, so that you would be able to finish it."

"Well, that's good to know." Another hesitation, then Lucivar said, "We're not the only ones who have scars. He hides his better than most men, but he's got some."

"Yeah." He wasn't about to forget *this* particular scar anytime soon.

"Daemon . . ." Lucivar eased back a little more, but still kept his hands on Daemon's shoulders. "There's something I'd like to ask you. If you can't tell me, I'll understand."

"All right," Daemon replied, not liking the wariness now filling Lucivar's eyes.

"I meant what I said about Jaenelle's temper riding the scary kind of bitchy."

"Not the side of her temper a smart man would choose to tangle with."

"It was Witch's side of her temper. More than that. The look in her eyes . . ." Lucivar shook his head, frustrated. "For a moment, when I looked into her eyes, it felt like the abyss had opened up right under me and . . . I haven't felt that kind of power since . . ." He sighed. "Hell's fire. I don't even know what I'm asking."

Yes, you do, Daemon thought. Making a choice, he brushed lightly against Lucivar's inner barriers, asking to enter his brother's mind.

Lucivar hesitated a moment, then opened *all* his inner barriers, giving Daemon access to everything he was. Leaving himself completely vulnerable.

Daemon moved carefully and went deep because what he was about to give his brother was information that had to be kept secret.

When he reached the most protected part of Lucivar's mind, he offered two images: Saetan's memory of a tangled web that turned dreams into flesh, and his own memory of the Misty Place and a spiraling web of power—the power Witch had chosen to give up in order to have a more ordinary life.

"Mother Night," Lucivar whispered, his eyes widening. "Then the power is still there."

"It's still there."

"Could she claim it again?"

Didn't Lucivar understand?

"Could she survive if something pushed her into claiming it again?" Lucivar asked.

"I don't know if her body can still be a vessel for that much power. I think she could reclaim it . . . but I don't think she would survive very long." He swallowed hard. "That's why I'm going to make sure she never has to make that choice."

Lucivar gave his shoulders a friendly squeeze. "*We're* going to make sure she never has to make that choice."

Of course.

Daemon huffed out a laugh that also held a few tears. "I love you, Prick."

"I love you too, Bastard." Lucivar stepped back and rolled his shoulders. "We're going to camp here today and keep an eye on him? Make sure he really is stable when he wakes up?"

"Yes."

"So let's send a message to the scary little witch so she stops being scary, and then see what we can find to eat."

Neither of them would shake off the past hour quite that easily, but Daemon felt some of the weight slide off his shoulders. He smiled and slipped his hands in his trouser pockets. "Let's do that."

TWENTY-EIGHT

Terreille

With his ears still ringing from Gray's yappy list of instructions, Theran knocked on Cassidy's door. He hoped she'd still be taking a bath or otherwise occupied, so he'd have a little more time to figure out what to say, but she opened the door before he decided to knock a second time.

"Prince Theran."

Wary. Surprised to see him. And the look in her eyes told him plain enough that she remembered the other time he'd come knocking.

"May I come in?"

Hesitation. Then she stepped aside to let him enter her sitting room.

Who was with her? Not that it was any of his business. He was First Escort, not Consort, and the Queen could command the attention of any man in her court.

Except it would kill Gray if Cassidy had taken another lover.

"Am I intruding?" he asked when he heard some movement in her bedroom.

Her look said *Of course you are,* but she replied, "Not at all."

Which was when Vae nudged the bedroom door open and joined them.

"Just females here?"

"Gray isn't here, if that's what you're asking." Her voice had a snippy edge to it.

He knew that defensive tone. He'd used it enough times

in his youth when Talon had called him on something and he'd tried to slide around admitting he'd done something he wasn't supposed to do.

What did she think he was going to do if she *was* with Gray? Go running to the Keep to tell Yaslana so he could storm down here and pound on everyone?

Maybe that's exactly what she thought. They had to work to get along on their best days, and he had given her enough reasons to dislike him. But getting into an argument now would end with her stomping out to the garden, and that wouldn't make Gray happy.

Theran scratched his head and resisted the temptation to pull out some hair. "Look, it's like this. Gray is putting together a surprise for you, and my part of the task is to keep you occupied for a few hours."

Her face tightened, the pleasure of learning Gray was planning a surprise gone before it had been fully realized. She took a step back.

He almost asked why she was acting that way when he considered what he'd said and where they were.

"Not *that* way," he growled.

"That's good, because the sun will shine in Hell before *that* happens."

She didn't need to be so vehement about it. He gave a good accounting of himself in bed.

He bristled. Before he said something about the amount of work a man had to do in bed being in direct proportion to the attractiveness of his partner, he remembered why he'd come to Cassidy's suite to begin with.

"I thought we could go into town—not for an official visit or anything like that, but to . . . I don't know . . . shop . . . or whatever females do."

" 'Whatever females do'? Haven't you ever spent an afternoon with a girl when you didn't want sex?"

His temper slipped the leash, and he didn't try very hard to rein it in. "I grew up in the rogue camps in the Tamanara Mountains, not in some comfortable village where girls flirt with boys in order to have a packhorse for the afternoon's shopping."

"Girls don't need packhorses, you brainless ass," Cassidy snapped. "We're perfectly capable of carrying our own packages. You'd know that if you spent any time talking to women."

"There weren't many women in those camps, and there certainly weren't fancy shops. We were there to fight, to protect Dena Nehele, to escape being enslaved by a Ring of Obedience and made useless to our people. So I don't have town manners, *Lady*. I didn't need them in the mountains, and Talon didn't waste time teaching me anything I didn't need."

He saw her effort to pull back, to assess. And he saw something he hadn't expected—and didn't want: pity.

"My apologies, Prince Theran," Cassidy said quietly. "I didn't realize you had such a difficult life."

"I had a good life," Theran snapped. "I survived. A lot of men didn't."

He took a mental step back, regaining control of his temper with effort. They didn't like each other. So be it. He didn't care if she understood him. Gray was stupid in love with her, and there was nothing he could do about it. He had to tolerate her as best he could because Gray and that damn contract with Sadi chained him to her.

"Are we going to town or not?" he asked.

Cassidy looked away. "Yes. Give me a few minutes to change clothes."

"I'll get the pony cart and meet you at the front door." Because he needed air and open space.

Because standing here in her suite, he had the odd sense that something delicate was being weighed down by their words and feelings—and was about to break.

I survived. A lot of men didn't.

The words circled round and round in her mind.

Cassidy didn't want to get into a serious discussion, and Theran's stiff posture as he drove the pony cart into town didn't invite small talk. So she kept silent and absorbed the look and feel of the land during the short ride into town.

I survived. A lot of men didn't.

Those few words told her more about Theran Grayhaven than she'd learned in the past few weeks.

No, he didn't want pity. He wasn't the only boy who had been taken into the mountains to be trained to fight. He wasn't the only boy who had been hidden from the Queens who had been corrupted by Dorothea SaDiablo. And there had been other boys who had suffered far more than he had.

Gray, for instance.

But she saw his quest for a Queen differently because of those words. It hadn't been as simple as having a Queen who knew Protocol and the Old Ways of the Blood. It had been about having a Queen who could dazzle, who could restore the heart in men weary of fighting—men who might be asked to fight some more in order to restore Dena Nehele and then keep it safe from the Blood in the rest of Terreille.

The Queen was the heart of a land, its moral center.

Theran had needed a heart he could believe in without reservation. He hadn't found that. Not in her.

That was something she was going to have to think about. But not today. Today she would be a visitor from Kaeleer who was being given a tour of her host's home village. Today she would be Cassidy instead of a Queen.

Tomorrow was soon enough to think about who she would be in the days ahead.

As they entered the town of Grayhaven, she reviewed a mental list of what she could use against what she could shop for with a man trailing along. Yesterday she would have dragged Theran into shops that were bound to make most men uncomfortable. Now she considered which kinds of places her brother, Clayton, had gone into without balking; she figured those probably wouldn't discomfort Theran either.

"Any particular place you want to go?" Theran asked, sounding like he'd bitten into something sour.

"Like tends to gather with like, so every town has communities. I would like to ride through the town and see as much of it as possible, but, for now, I'd like to see the shops where the court usually makes purchases."

She'd made an effort to keep her tone "interested visitor" instead of Queen. He eyed her for a moment, as if he knew something had changed, but he wasn't sure what.

"All right," he finally said.

The shopping district had several carriage parks—plots of land where conveyances could be left while people were going about their business. Each park had a couple of youths who kept an eye on the horses and would even deliver a carriage if its owner didn't want to walk back and claim it.

Since that took care of the pony cart, Cassidy was quick to suggest walking and wondered why Theran hesitated.

She didn't wonder long. The men who recognized Theran nodded in greeting, then jolted when they saw her and realized who she must be.

"I gather the Blood here don't make a distinction between a formal and informal visit?" Cassidy asked, stopping in front of a shop window. She wasn't paying attention to the merchandise; she just wanted a moment to ask Theran about this behavior.

Which was when she focused on a movement close to the window and caught a glimpse of the proprietor's face before the man rabbited out of sight.

Theran placed a hand on her elbow and tugged her away from the window.

"What . . . ?"

"That particular shop caters to men."

"So?"

"Let's just say you were staring at things that most ladies pretend don't exist."

Which made her sorry she hadn't been paying attention, because she had no idea what he was talking about—and she was certain he wouldn't let her go back and look.

"What distinction?" Theran asked.

"What was in that window?"

He shook his head.

"If ladies aren't supposed to know about it, why were those things *in* the shop window?"

"Formal and informal," Theran said, getting that *Warlord Prince turning stubborn* tone in his voice.

Fine. She'd just make note of the shops nearby and she'd come back with Shira one day soon.

"When a Queen is going about her own business in her home village, she's treated like everyone else."

"I doubt that."

"All right, she might get a little extra attention from the shopkeepers, but the people we've passed . . . I don't know how to respond to them."

"They don't know how to respond to you either," Theran replied. "I don't think any of them has experienced an 'informal' visit from a Queen."

"The Queens declared Protocol to go *shopping*?"

He stopped walking. Since she didn't want to upset anyone else, she focused on his shoulder.

For the first time since she'd met him, she saw genuine amusement.

"We're standing in front of a bakery," he said. "You won't cause a scandal if you look in the window."

She knew her face was turning bright red, but she dutifully shifted positions so she could look in the window.

"I can't say for a fact," Theran said, "but I don't think any Queen has walked around this town informally in years. Might not be Protocol in the strictest sense, but the Queens didn't walk among the people casually."

"They've never done that here?"

"Not since Lia."

He frowned so fiercely after he said that, Cassidy ended up giving him a nudge with her elbow.

"If you keep glaring at those pastry things, you're going to turn the sweet cream sour," she said.

Oh, the expression on his face when he focused on what was in front of him!

His eyes slid sideways and looked at her. "Maybe we should buy a few, just to save other folk from that soured cream."

"Maybe we should," she agreed too politely.

Boy. Bakery. Memories of Clayton, the time he'd gone into a bakery with a fistful of coins and no parent to hold him back.

Ah, well. Theran wasn't eleven. Surely he had enough self-discipline to avoid eating himself sick.

When they entered the bakery, she wasn't sure if the baker was going to fawn or faint, but they walked out with a box of treats that Theran was more than happy to carry.

The morning was turning out better than he'd expected—although he probably shouldn't have eaten that last cream-filled pastry. But, Hell's fire, he'd always had a weakness for the damn things, and it had been a long time since he'd eaten one with any enjoyment.

Twelve years, as a matter of fact.

A boy who was hunted couldn't afford to have weaknesses—or habits that people noticed and would share for the right price.

There had been a handful of villages near the Tamanara Mountains that had been considered safe ground. Places where the rogues would get supplies, visit lovers or whores, collect news. Armed camps of a different kind, where people were trusted because they were loyal to Dena Nehele rather than the puppet Queens.

But everything has a price—including information about a boy with a weakness for cream-filled pastries.

Except, at fifteen, the lure of a woman proved stronger than the lure of a box of treats.

A young whore, not that much older than he was, who was willing to show one of the "brave fighters" some pleasure. He and Gray had slipped away from their escort—something that would have earned them a few licks of a strap if they'd both come back that day—so that he could romp with the girl. But he'd wanted that damn box of sweets too, so Gray went alone to the bakery they visited every time they came to that village, even though sweets of that kind didn't have much appeal for him.

That too was known. Which was why the Queen's guards who caught Gray coming out of the bakery were sure they'd captured Theran Grayhaven.

Gray still screamed when he saw one of those pastries, which was another reason it had been so long since Theran had tasted one.

None of which excused him from eating himself stupid this morning.

Still, Cassidy wasn't a torturous companion on a shopping trip. He'd caught a few wistful glances from her as they passed shops where, given a choice of going in or being whipped, he'd take the whipping, but she hadn't insisted on going inside.

Sadi would walk into a shop like that, Theran thought as he waited for Cassidy to finish purchasing a few books. *Hell's fire, Sadi wouldn't just walk into a shop like that; he'd dominate the place and have opinions about satin and lace and the advantages of each when worn against a woman's privates.*

Would Gray walk into a shop like that?

Cassidy turned away from the counter and studied him. "You look a little green."

Well, wasn't that just fine?

She shook her head. "I guess males don't outgrow it."

"Outgrow what?" Glad to be out of the stuffy shop, Theran took a deep breath. Didn't help. It was a fine summer morning, but it was starting to feel a bit too hot and sticky.

But that might have been him and not the weather.

"Put a man in a bakery and he turns into a boy."

"You're starting to sound like Vae." Who was home sulking because he wouldn't let her come with them. The townsfolk had enough to contend with, having a Queen trying to act like she was one of them, without a yappy dog around telling everyone what to do.

Cassidy bit her lip and shook her head.

Damn. And the morning had been going well. For the most part.

"It's almost time for the midday meal," Cassidy said.

"I don't think so."

"I want a steak, and you need one. Choose a dining house, Prince."

You turn Queen fast enough when you want something, Theran thought. But the idea of a steak—and just sitting still for a bit—had more appeal than he'd first thought, so he led them to a dining house that had an enclosed courtyard for private outdoor dining.

The courtyard needed to be cleansed by a Black Widow. Blood had dined there—and done other things there.

It was clear that the owners of the establishment had made an effort to scour away the past, so Cassidy said nothing to upset anyone. Such things were best done quietly anyway. And since they had been outlawed, finding a Black Widow might not be the easiest thing.

Maybe Shira would know how to get in touch with other Black Widows.

A task for another day, Cassidy thought. The food was excellent, and even though she was less comfortable than she might have been, she could see herself being a regular guest here.

As for Theran ... Well, the steak was waging war on the pastries, and judging by the color of his skin now, the steak was winning. So was the way a man who wore a Green Jewel burned food.

She waited until he'd eaten three-quarters of his steak. Then she reached over and snagged the rest with her fork.

"Hey," Theran protested. "I wasn't finished eating that."

"Yes, you were," Cassidy replied, setting that piece and the one she'd kept from her own meal on her bread plate.

"What ... ?" Theran stared at her as she put the bread plate on the ground beside her.

"There you go, Vae," Cassidy said.

Theran's eyes widened and his jaw dropped as the Sceltie dropped the sight shield and gave him a tail-tip wag. She sniffed the steak and wagged her tail with more enthusiasm.

"When did she get here?" Theran asked.

"She caught up to us when we left the carriage park," Cassidy said, giving him a wide smile.

"How'd she avoid being stepped on when no one could see her?"

"Grf."

Guess Vae is still sulking, Cassidy thought. *At least where Theran is concerned.*

"She can air walk," Cassidy said. "She was trotting above us." She fiddled with her spoon and wondered how to ask a question she knew wouldn't sit well with a warrior. Especially a Warlord Prince. "You weren't aware of her, were you?"

"No, I wasn't. Were you?"

"Yes. But kindred have a different feel from the human Blood, and it takes practice—and awareness—to detect their presence."

"If they're sight shielded and not yapping, they'd be hard to find," Theran said.

"Grf," Vae said, finishing the last bit of steak.

"They don't have to sight shield to go undetected," Cassidy said. "If there were twenty Scelties in a yard, could you pick out the one who was kindred? Especially if you weren't aware of the existence of kindred? Kindred Scelties and horses lived around humans for a lot of years with no one realizing they were Blood. They don't reveal their presence unless they choose to, Theran."

She watched him absorb her words. Someone who wore a darker Jewel could have gone undetected and followed him, but he should have sensed a Purple Dusk witch who had been trailing him for hours.

A witch is a witch, Theran. Don't dismiss one because she looks different from you.

A lesson the Blood in Kaeleer were still learning when it came to the kindred.

"Coffee?" he asked.

"Yes, please."

She wanted to linger a little longer, since it was a lovely summer day. And now that Vae's presence was acknowledged, she thought the two of them could persuade Theran to show her a particular part of town.

How did I get talked into this? Theran asked himself. He knew how. Sure he did. Two females yapping at him. One of them even growled at him when he'd refused to do this, and it wasn't Vae.

So here he was, driving the pony cart into the landen part of the town.

"Landens usually have their own villages," Cassidy said.

Theran nodded to the guards who patrolled this part of Grayhaven. Two nodded back and mounted their horses to provide an escort.

"Most still do," Theran replied, "but some landens were resettled as part of Blood villages after their own villages burned during the uprisings." *And making them live so close to the Blood kept them on a very short leash.*

That didn't mean the Blood liked having a landen slum attached to their town.

Bitterness laced his voice as he looked at the shops they passed and the people who watched them. "Damn landens are nothing but a boil on the town's backside."

"They're people," Cassidy said. "They belong to this land, same as you."

"They would have driven us out if they could. Took us two years to crush the uprisings."

"How many died in those two years?" Cassidy asked.

"More Blood than we could afford to lose."

"And how many landens?"

"Not enough."

She sighed. "All the more reason for me to see this part of the town."

Exactly the reason she *shouldn't* be there. But it was pointless to argue now that they'd crossed that boundary, and there were other Blood wandering these streets.

Market day, Theran realized. When power—and the unspoken threat of its being unleashed—was another marker on the table, a few coins could buy a Blood family provisions for a week at the landen markets.

"What's that?" Cassidy asked, sitting up straighter.

"A craftmen's courtyard," Theran replied, glancing in that direction. "Potters, weavers, and others of that sort put out their wares. Some even work on a piece to—"

"Stop," Cassidy said. "Theran, stop the cart, I want to—"

"No."

Theran? Theran!

Shit. The little bitch would yap at him for the rest of the day. And Cassidy wouldn't be much better.

He gave the guards a psychic tap to alert them as he reined in.

Cassidy and Vae were out of the cart and walking back the way they'd come before he could set the brake and tie off the reins.

One of the guards dismounted and came to stand at the horse's head. "I'll keep an eye on the cart, but you'd best shield those packages. Lots of quick fingers here could lift a package and be on the next street before you know you've been robbed."

"Thanks for the reminder." Theran put a Green shield around the back of the cart, then hurried to catch up to Cassidy. If the packages were stolen, it would give the Blood a reason to shake this part of town. If the Queen was injured ... Well, he wasn't sure who would be going to war with whom, especially once Sadi and Yaslana heard about it, but no matter who stepped onto the battleground, a lot of the town would burn before the fighting was done.

Cassidy had stopped before a weaver's table.

Family group, Theran decided. Man, woman, adolescent boy, and young girl. The man had a hard face and a look in his eyes Theran recognized.

Fighter.

"This is lovely work," Cassidy said, smiling at the girl. "And this is yours?"

"Y-yes, Lady."

Cassidy stepped closer to the loom and the unfinished piece—and the girl.

The man stiffened.

Theran descended to the depth of his Green Jewel and prepared to rise to the killing edge.

But Cassidy pointed at the loom, not touching child or work.

"What kind of pattern is this?"

"It's a traditional pattern, Lady," the woman said. "Dena Nehele has traditional patterns for each season. The girl is weaving a summer pattern."

"Lovely colors," Cassidy said, directing her remarks to the girl. "Did you choose them?"

The girl nodded.

"You have a good eye for color."

By now the other merchants and their customers had stopped their own bartering to watch this exchange. A few had even sidled closer.

But not too close. One slashing look from him was enough to have them reconsidering the wisdom of getting *too* close.

"Are you planning to sell this piece when it's done?" Cassidy asked.

Tension flashed through the landens, the emotion so strong it surprised a growl out of Vae in response.

"Why?" the man asked roughly.

"Because I'd like to buy it," Cassidy said, looking confused. "As I said, it's lovely work. The traditional design would appeal to my mother, so I'd like to buy it for her as a Winsol gift. If you think it would be completed by then," she added, once more addressing the girl.

The girl nodded.

"We would be pleased to make a gift of it," the man said.

If you were any more pleased, you'd choke on the words, Theran thought, hearing the man's anger and bitterness from being obliged over the years to provide a good number of "gifts" to keep his family safe.

Bristling, Cassidy straightened to her full height. "You'll do no such thing. If the piece is being made to sell, then you should make a reasonable profit on it. Besides, it's not for you to decide. This is between me and the young lady. When she delivers the piece to the Grayhaven estate, we'll sit down and discuss the price."

Landens in my home? Never!

But Theran saw the man's face turn white with fear, and he wondered what had happened to other landens who had gone up to the estate.

"Is it a bargain?" Cassidy asked, holding out a hand.

The girl glanced at her father, confused enough by the tension to hesitate.

★You are supposed to shake hands now,★ Vae said. ★That is what humans do for bargains.★

Stunned looks all around as the people stared at the Sceltie.

★I like this human puppy,★ Vae said, wagging her tail. ★She has good smells.★

The woman clapped a hand over her mouth. Her eyes were bright with laughter. The man looked like he'd been whacked in the head.

"I know the feeling," Theran muttered.

A flash of humor in the man's eyes.

Seeing the change in her father, and intrigued by a talking dog, the girl shook hands with Cassidy, sealing their bargain.

And that, thank the Darkness, would end this visit.

After bidding them all a good day, Cassidy headed back to the pony cart. She smiled at him as he fell into step beside her, as if nothing unusual had happened.

It hadn't, he realized. Not for her. This wasn't the first time she had purchased something from a landen.

What kind of place was Dharo that a Queen would shop in a landen village? Or was it that, wearing a Rose Jewel, Cassidy didn't feel as different from landens as the darker-Jeweled Blood?

He didn't have answers. Wasn't sure he wanted any. But he had to let the rest of the First Circle know about their Queen's potential for doing the unusual.

Vae growled. That was the only warning he had before he heard a child scream in pain and a man roar in outrage.

Theran spun around to meet the threat. When he saw the two adolescent Warlords standing a few paces away from the weaver's table, he hesitated.

Cassidy didn't. She ran back to the landen family.

He—and the guards—felt the punch of Rose power and saw one adolescent Warlord get knocked off his feet. The other young Warlord staggered under the punch, but he wore a Summer-sky Jewel and was able to absorb most of Cassidy's strike.

Rose shields went up in front of the landens. Rose shields went up around Cassidy as she called in a round-headed club and settled into a fighting stance.

"You bitch!" A man old enough to be the Warlords' father ran toward them. "I'll teach you a lesson, bitch."

Hell's fire.

Theran took a step toward Cassidy, intending to yank her out of a fight she shouldn't have gotten involved in, since it wasn't Blood against Blood.

Then Vae launched herself at the man, and Theran saw a small dog who knew her Craft yank a full-grown man off his feet.

And heard bone snap as jaws enhanced by Purple Dusk power closed on the man's forearm.

The Summer-sky Warlord launched himself at Cassidy. Theran received another shock when Cassidy bared her teeth and met the attack, using the club with enough savagery to break through shields stronger than her own and drive the Warlord back.

By then Vae was beside Cassidy, Purple Dusk shields around them both.

Theran? Theran!

Prince? one of the guards said. *What should we do?*

Damned if he knew. They shouldn't have been in this fight in the first place.

I smell blood, Vae said.

Of course you do, you little bitch, Theran thought. *You bit a man and tore up his arm.*

But Cassidy looked behind her, then screamed, "SHIRA!"

The Craft-enhanced sound probably wouldn't reach the estate, but it was going to shake up the Blood closest to this part of town.

"You hurt my boys!" the older Warlord shouted as he got to his feet, cradling the broken arm.

"They hurt the girl," Cassidy snarled.

"Landen slut," the Warlord snarled back.

"*Girl*. I am the Queen here, and that makes her one of mine. And *no one* lays a hand on one of mine."

"Queen, is it? Rose-Jeweled bitch, you don't have the power to be a Queen."

"Try me." Cassidy shifted her stance. "You want a fight? *Draw the line.*"

The Warlord hesitated. Theran felt the guards recoil in shock.

And he saw everything he'd hoped for going down in ruins because of Cassidy's foolish actions.

And he saw Gray breaking under the pain of losing her because she wouldn't survive this fight. Cassidy and Vae against those three Warlords? Even wounded, the males would rip the witches to pieces.

He hated her. In that moment, when he knew what he had to do and choked on the knowledge, he hated her.

But making a choice, he stepped across the boundary of that small battleground. "If you want to draw the line, you do that," he told the Warlord. "But you won't be meeting her. You'll be meeting me on the killing field."

"And me." Ranon dropped the sight shield as he moved to guard Cassidy's left side, his Shalador blade flashing in the sun.

"Us," Archerr said, flanking the three Warlords.

More sight shields were dropped. More blades flashed in the sun.

Except for Powell and Talon, the whole First Circle was there.

How . . . ? Theran asked Ranon.

Vae called us.

The bitter anger in Ranon's thoughts made it plain that he thought the First Escort should have been the one to call the court to the Queen's defense.

Which was true.

"I need Shira here," Cassidy said, glancing at Ranon.

"I'm here. Drop your shield, Cassidy, so I can get to the girl."

More shields. Layers of them going up in front of Cassidy

and curving around to close off the area where the landen family huddled.

Layers of shields formed by the Warlord Princes who served Cassidy.

But not the Green. His strength wasn't needed, and if he added it now, it would feel like a lie.

"You can drop your shield now, Lady," Ranon said.

The Rose shields behind Cassidy vanished. Shira rushed over to the girl, who was still wailing.

"Let me have a look." Shira pulled the girl's hands away from her face. "I'm a Healer. I'm going to help—"

"Shira?" Cassidy said.

"Hell's fire," Shira said. Then she looked at the girl's mother. "Give me a hand. Come on, darling. Come back here with us." She hustled the girl to the back of the family's space, where they had a canopy for shade and a small table and chairs.

"*Shira?*" Cassidy said.

"Let me work!"

It's bad, Theran thought, remembering other Healers who had that particular tone in their voices.

"That Healer should be looking after my arm, not some slut's face," the older Warlord said.

"If he's the one who threw the stone, I'll be happy to take care of his arm," Shira said. "And I promise there won't be much left of it when I get done."

All the men, even Ranon, looked startled by the words. Cassidy just nodded.

"Well," the older Warlord said, "I guess it's done. We'll be on our way."

"It isn't done," Cassidy said. "Everything has a price, and your little bit of sport is going to cost you."

"Now, look here . . . ," the Warlord began, taking a step toward Cassidy.

Blades were raised in warning. Cassidy and Vae bared their teeth and snarled.

"What is the Queen's will?" Theran asked.

Cassidy walked over to the loom and stared for too long before she turned back to the men.

"The weaving is ruined," she said. "From the smell of it, there's horse manure along with some other muck. Since the streets are dry, the only way to make this kind of shit soup is by making it somewhere else and bringing it here."

A quick glance at the youngsters' faces confirmed it.

"So that ruined piece of weaving will cost you one hundred gold marks," Cassidy said, her eyes filled with a wild fury as she stared at the older Warlord.

"What?" the Warlord yelled. "For that piece of—"

Vae snarled, and the sound rumbled through the whole street.

"One hundred gold marks as compensation for the lost work and as a penalty for not teaching your boys some manners. As for them ..." Cassidy's eyes focused on the two younger Warlords. "Ten days' labor, without using Craft, or ten lashes."

"I'll handle the whip if it comes to that," Ranon said. "And I'll strip flesh from bone."

"Shalador bastard," the Warlord growled.

"Since you understand the Shalador temper so well," Cassidy said, "*your* little bastards will work under Prince Ranon's supervision."

"Don't you insult my boys."

"Ten days or ten lashes," Cassidy snapped. "Choose."

"It's not right, making my boys work like landens," the Warlord protested.

"It will help them appreciate what someone without Craft has to do in order to accomplish a task. *Choose.*"

"You've got no right!" the Warlord shouted.

Something in the air. Something delicate being weighed down by words. Bending, bending. Almost breaking. If it broke ...

Theran stepped closer to Cassidy. "She is the Queen of Dena Nehele. Her will is the law. You've been given a choice, Warlords, and the Queen's First Circle stands witness." *And may the Darkness help me, I stand witness.*

The feeling in the air was gone, as if a question had been answered.

"Ten days' labor," the Warlord said. "And I'll bring the gold marks when—"

"No," Cassidy said. "The three of you are forbidden to set foot in the landen section of this town. You come here again, you'll be exiled from Dena Nehele."

The guards gasped. Even the Warlord Princes who supported her looked stunned.

"You will report to the Steward of the court and give the payment to him," Cassidy said.

"Can't come up with that much all at once," the Warlord said.

"Then you'll work out a payment arrangement with the Steward—and if you don't show up with the payment, the First Circle will be showing up on your doorstep to find out why. And they can take the payment however they see fit."

Mother Night, Cassidy, Theran said. *You've just told him the Warlord Princes can rip him apart without penalty.*

She looked at him with eyes still filled with fury.

He didn't know this woman. Didn't know this Queen.

But he knew with cold certainty that he was seeing the Old Ways of the Blood, and that under the same circumstances, the Warlord Princes in Kaeleer wouldn't hesitate to do the Queen's will.

And he wondered for the first time if bringing the Old Ways back to Dena Nehele had been a mistake.

"One other thing." Cassidy stared at the two younger Warlords, finally settling on the one who wore the Summersky Jewel. "If the girl loses her eye because of the stone you threw, you forfeit a hand. This is the Queen's Justice."

"Queen's Justice."

It was a shout, a battle cry. And Theran heard his own voice raised with the others.

No more fight in the Warlords. No more thinking they could somehow slide out from under what they had done. The predators had gathered and were held by the Queen's leash. And by nightfall, the whole town would know for certain that these Warlord Princes belonged to Cassidy.

"Prince?" asked one of the guards who had escorted the pony cart.

"Prince Ranon is the Master of the Guard's second-in-command," Theran said, nodding to Ranon, acknowledging another truth.

"Escort those three back to their home," Ranon told the guard. "Prince Archerr will assist you."

The guard glanced at Cassidy. "I'll inform the others of

the Queen's command. We'll make sure these Warlords don't come back to this part of town."

The Warlords were led away.

"Lady?"

At the sound of Shira's voice, they all turned.

Cassidy looked at Shira, then past her.

"The rock came damn close, but it didn't take the girl's eye," Shira said. "I can't say for sure yet that there isn't any damage. There was lots of muck and grit in the eye, plus the cut just beside it from the rock. But I've got the eye cleaned out and have the first stage of healing salves on the injury. I gave her a sedative. I'll give her mother another dose for the girl, since her face is going to hurt and sleep will help her heal. I'll come back tomorrow morning for the next stage of the healing."

The man stepped forward. "Lady, if we'd sold that piece in the market, we would have asked for fifty silver marks and been happy to have gotten thirty."

"Today it was worth one hundred gold marks," Cassidy said.

Theran felt her shudder. That was the only warning he had before her legs buckled.

He grabbed one arm. Ranon grabbed the other.

"Fetch a chair," the man told his son.

The youth darted under the canopy and came back with a chair. They dumped Cassidy in it and pushed her head down.

"Are you hurt?" Shira asked. "Is she hurt?"

"I feel wobbly," Cassidy said.

"Keep your head down," Theran said, tugging the club out of her hand.

"I've never attacked anyone before," Cassidy said. "Lucivar taught me how to use the club. He said I didn't have the right temper for a knife. I worked on the moves lots of times in practice—Lucivar has a lust for practice—and I kept practicing because it was good exercise and a kind of mental discipline. But I've never hit anyone before and meant it. Well, my brother, Clayton, but that's different."

"I'm not finding anything," Shira said. "What's wrong with her?"

"First-fight nerves," Ranon said. "She's just shaky."

"I've got a bit of something that might help that," the man said.

Theran exchanged a look with Ranon. They both knew about the "bit of something" that was brewed in stills and cost a lot less than the liquor that didn't require a man to bring his own container.

It will fuzz her nerves, Ranon said.

"Thanks," Theran said as he rose to follow the man.

The flask was tucked away with the water jugs and makings for tea. The man took a cup and saucer, then filled the cup halfway from the flask. He glanced at Theran, then poured a bit more.

Theran accepted the cup and took a sip. His eyeballs sang and his teeth danced.

"Mother Night," he wheezed.

"It's got some bite to it," the man agreed.

When he brought the cup over, Cassidy got a whiff of the stuff and refused to drink it until Shira snapped, "You can drink that tonic or I can make you one that tastes worse."

She gulped it down, draining the cup.

Her throat didn't catch on fire, and her lungs didn't explode.

Theran wasn't sure if he should admire her for that or be afraid of her.

"Give me a minute to check on the girl," Shira said. "Then I'll ride with you and help you get Lady Cassidy home."

"Um aright," Cassidy said.

"Uh-huh," Theran replied as he hauled her to her feet.

Vae was stretched out on the seat, looking quite pleased with herself. Theran dropped the Green shield around the packages and said, "In the back."

She grumbled a bit, but she stepped over the seat and walked on air while she nudged packages around until she'd made a Sceltie-sized spot. Then she lay down with a sigh.

Cassidy was more of a handful since the liquor and the fight were catching up to her and coordination became a vague concept. But he finally got her on the seat and wrapped a Green shield around her to keep her from falling out of the cart.

When he turned to find out what was keeping Shira, he

saw Ranon holding the Healer back—and the landen man standing within reach.

"I've got something to say to you," the man said.

Theran stiffened. "Then say it."

"What happened today ... What those boys did ... That's happened before. Not to me and mine, but to others."

He nodded.

"Been a long time since someone looked at us and saw people instead of *less*."

He nodded again, not knowing what to say or what this man wanted.

"I fought in the landen uprisings."

"So did I," Theran replied.

The man glanced at the cart. "If there had been someone like her around two years ago, maybe we wouldn't have felt the need to fight. I just wanted you to know that."

His throat closed. Something ached inside of him. He raised a hand in farewell, then climbed up to the seat. A moment later, Shira joined him, and they drove away with Ranon riding behind them as escort.

"Exciting day," Shira said.

"Yeah." Too many things had happened too fast. There were too many things to think about.

And he wasn't sure how he felt about any of them.

TWENTY-NINE

Kaeleer

Daemon shifted the wooden delivery box to one hand and knocked on the cottage door.

He understood Jaenelle's reason for waiting in solitude. Witch would not have been an easy companion last night, and Witch wouldn't have been soothed by the company of all the women who had rallied around Marian. Lucivar had placed the Eyrien warriors on alert, and that had been enough warning for the women. For the warriors, seeing Lucivar go to the Keep armed and shielded told them everything they needed to know. If a fight broke out at Ebon Askavi between the three strongest Warlord Princes in the Realm, it would shake the whole damn valley. Or worse.

So the Eyrien women had gathered to keep Marian company, to keep Daemonar distracted. To wait.

But the Queen would have waited in silence, in solitude. Because if she'd felt the need to reclaim what she had given up, she would have terrified all of them.

He wasn't sure who—or what—would open the door, and he began to worry when she didn't answer.

Then the door opened and Jaenelle stood there, studying him with those haunted sapphire eyes that always saw too much.

"Why were you knocking?" she asked, the tension visible in her stance—and audible in her voice.

"Because this is your private place."

Like his suite of rooms at the Hall.

Relaxing, she nodded, acknowledging his reason. "What did you bring?"

"A loving man—and breakfast."

Her lips twitched, fighting a smile. "In that case, Prince, come in."

He was so glad to see her, he didn't try to fight a smile. There were shadows under her eyes, testimony of a sleepless night, and her hair was sticking up every which way, making her look like a scruffy waif . . . who was wearing snug trousers and one of his silk shirts.

Screw breakfast, he thought as he set the box on the table. *I'll just nibble on her for an hour or two.*

Then Jaenelle peered into the box and her stomach growled so loudly, he figured it was prudent to change his priorities.

"Where did you get this?" Jaenelle asked.

"I stopped at The Tavern after seeing Lucivar home. There's a steak pie, a vegetable casserole, and some fruit."

"The Tavern isn't usually open this early."

Daemon hesitated, then wondered why he bothered. She would have been aware of the mood of the Blood in Riada. "They were just closing when I got there." Merry and Briggs had stayed open because so many had been sleepless and uneasy last night, and a gathering place offered comfort.

He reached into the box for the steak pie. "The food needs to be warmed a bit."

Her hands settled over his, stopping him.

"Daemon, why don't you say what you need to say? The food will settle better on an easy stomach—and an easy heart."

He removed his hands from the box and slipped them into his trouser pockets. He wanted to hold her, but he chose to keep the table between them.

"I am my father's son," he said.

She tipped her head. "That shouldn't come as a surprise to you, Prince. You're more than his son. You are your father's mirror."

"Yes, I am. But despite all the things I've done, that wasn't as clear to me before as it was last night."

He took a deep breath, then let it out slowly. He and Lucivar had taken shifts, one standing watch while the other rested, and during one of those vigils, as he replayed that dance with Saetan, he'd acknowledged a difficult truth.

"Last night I saw the man who had destroyed an entire race, and I understood something about myself. That kind of rage is in me, Jaenelle, in a way it's not in Lucivar. I am capable of doing what Saetan did to Zuulaman, and unlike my father, I wouldn't need to be drowning in grief or insane rage before I made that choice. Given the right provocation, I could do what he did."

"I know."

That stopped him, had him rocking back on his heels. When he'd first met her, those sapphire eyes had looked through him and she had made some decision about him, passed some judgment. Had she known then, at twelve, the depth of his temper, his potential for violence?

Probably.

"And yet you love me," he said, "despite what I am."

Jaenelle walked around the table and took his face in her hands. "No, Daemon. I love you because of what you are. Because of *all* that you are. Right now, you're feeling raw, which is understandable, and you're shining a light on one truth about a complex man and not seeing the rest. So I'll see the whole of who you are and not let you shine a light on one part for too long."

He wrapped his arms around her. "Do you know how much I love you? How much I need you?"

Her arms twined around his neck. "Why don't you show me—"

His stomach growled.

"—after breakfast?" she finished, laughing.

They ate, they slept, they made love. When they were heating up the remainder of the food for a midday meal, Daemon said, "Your strategy was quite brilliant. In case you were wondering."

"Strategy?" Jaenelle said, setting two plates on the counter in anticipation of simply dividing the food.

"Having Lucivar draw that particular line."

She gave him a puzzled look. "I told Lucivar to give Saetan a nudge that would remind him of his family as it is, here and now. You would be able to get him to the border, but that reminder is what Saetan would need to take those last steps out of the Twisted Kingdom."

Daemon laughed. "Well, it was a damn good bluff,

threatening to toss Daemonar into the library unsupervised and let him at the books."

Jaenelle dropped the silverware. "What? Lucivar said *what*?"

Daemon turned away from the stove and studied Jaenelle's pale face.

"That *was* your bluff, wasn't it?" Daemon asked, feeling the blood draining out of his head.

"I would *never* threaten Papa that way."

"Hell's fire."

"Daemon? *Daemon!*"

One moment he was standing by the stove. The next moment he was sitting on the floor with Jaenelle kneeling beside him.

"That wasn't your idea?" he asked weakly.

She shook her head.

"Lucivar is Eyrien."

"I know," she said.

"He wears Ebon-gray."

"I know."

"He doesn't bluff."

She plopped on the floor beside him. They sat there for several minutes before she said, "Did Saetan think it was a bluff?"

"I'm sure he did—at least after he woke up and thought, as I did, that you had told Lucivar to say that."

"Oh."

They pondered that for a few more minutes while their meal got cold.

"So," Jaenelle finally said, "how long do you want to wait before we explain this to Papa?"

No point having children who could match a man's temper if they weren't going to be a pain in the ass on occasion.

"Let's give him a couple of days," he said. "By then he won't be expecting anything."

"That's mean," Jaenelle said. "I like it."

Picturing the look on Saetan's face when he discovered the library threat *had* been Lucivar's idea, Daemon wrapped his arms around Jaenelle, lay back on the kitchen floor—and laughed.

THIRTY

Terreille

Shira walked into the Steward's office and shook her head in response to the men's unspoken question. "She wouldn't answer the door, and Vae says Cassidy still doesn't want to talk to anyone."

"Why not?" Gray said, hugging himself. "She didn't do anything wrong."

"She was in a fight, Gray," Theran said. "That's bound to unsettle anyone, and it would be more unsettling for a Queen."

A hard look from Ranon and an equally hard look from Talon, who had delayed going to his room when the sun rose in order to hear the morning report.

Since they'd come back from town three days ago, Cassidy hadn't left her suite, claiming to be unsettled by the fight—a fight Theran could have ended before it began.

Should have ended.

Talon had made that abundantly clear when he'd heard their account of what had happened.

And Gray . . . Since the two young Warlords were working on the estate to pay off their debt of ten days' labor, Gray had turned into a merciless taskmaster, and Ranon's job wasn't supervising the Warlords so much as holding Gray back and providing some balance.

Theran didn't know what to think, didn't know what to do. Cassidy hadn't been hurt, hadn't been harmed. Not really. Shaken up, sure, but not harmed.

Except she hadn't left her suite since it happened, hadn't talked to any of them.

Not even Gray.

What in the name of Hell was she thinking?

Cassidy brushed her fingers over the cover of each journal, as if touch could be a conduit, and wisdom would seep into her fingers from the leather.

She had been hiding in her room for the past three days. It was time to stop hiding. Time to do the right thing.

Lia had revealed her heart in the journals, but Cassidy had found no wisdom that would help a Queen who didn't belong. Could never belong. She'd shocked her court, shocked the Blood in the town. Hell's fire, she'd even shocked the landens by standing up for them. What had made her think she could rule these people when she saw and thought about things so differently from them? And what made her think any of them would accept the way she thought about things? She wasn't Lia. Could never be Lia.

"I wish I had found some of the journals from when you were my age," she said as she stacked the journals and set them on one side of the bed. "I wish . . ."

She opened the trinket box and took out each piece of jewelry. Memories. Family heirlooms. Talismans of a life filled with love. She would give the jewelry to Theran, along with the journals—and her resignation. This time, she wouldn't wait for the court to resign from her. She'd release these people from their unwilling loyalty, and she'd go home before the roots she'd begun putting down sank in too deep.

Before going would hurt as much as staying.

She put each piece of jewelry back in the box, one by one. Would Theran let her take one as a keepsake? Would she have the courage to ask him?

Her lower lip quivered and her vision blurred. She pressed her lips together hard enough to stop the quiver, then blinked back tears.

Just go. Just get it done.

She picked up the trinket box, intending to set it on the desk while she wrote the letter that would dissolve her court. She heard the *crack* as the bottom of the box broke and fell, spilling the jewelry over the bed.

"Hell's fire," Cassidy muttered, shaking her head. Something else she couldn't do right.

When she picked up the bottom of the box to see if it could be repaired, she discovered it was made of two thin layers of wood.

Then she discovered the paper that had been hidden between those layers.

And when she opened the paper, she found the map—and another key.

There are bad smells up here. Vae pressed against Cassidy's leg.

"I know." The psychic onslaught was bad enough for her. Who knew what else the dog might be sensing?

The attic was a graveyard of furniture. Nothing physically wrong with most of it from what she could see, but the psychic scents that had been absorbed by the wood—the pain and despair or the gleeful cruelty—had probably reached a saturation point where no one could stand being in the same room with the stuff.

Of course, piling it up here in the attic got the furniture out of sight but did nothing to cleanse the house. The weight of emotions pressed down on everyone living here, and most likely, none of them realized why.

Why would they? Cassidy thought. Theran and his family had returned to Grayhaven shortly before bringing her here, the rest of the court hadn't lived here before, and the servants were probably so used to these feelings, they had no reason to think things might be different.

They could be different. There were cleansing spells that could remove psychic residue from an object. Shira might know some, and if she didn't, Cassidy could ask Jaenelle and send the information back to Shira.

"And if that doesn't work, burn the damn stuff," Cassidy muttered.

Fire? The Sceltie sounded much too eager to use witchfire to take care of the bad smells.

"Not up here." Crouching, Cassidy held up the key. If Vae had been able to find the hiding place under the bed by smelling a key, maybe she could find what this key opened. "We're looking for the thing that fits this key, that has the same smell."

Vae sniffed the key. *Not much smell, even for kindred.*

Damn. Well, she hadn't expected this to be easy. "Come

on. Let's see if we can find the starting point that's shown on the map."

Grayhaven was a big mansion, so there were several ways up to the attic, and the map, by accident or deliberate omission, didn't indicate direction. So she was hot and dusty, and Vae's tail was veiled in cobwebs, by the time she found the attic entrance that looked like the starting point for this stage of the treasure hunt.

Of course, that assumed no one had removed or added windows in the past few centuries or made other structural changes to the house. And the map had been made long before generations of furniture had been disposed of by tossing it up here.

Cassidy tipped the paper toward the light to read the small print around the section of the attic that had been marked as the end of the search.

"We need to find a large wardrobe that has a mirror beside it and a clothes trunk in front of the mirror." She looked around at all the discarded furniture. "Hell's fire, Lia. Didn't you consider that someone else might toss a trunk or two up here?"

The attic had been divided into sections. The interior walls didn't go all the way up to the roof, but they did offer sufficient privacy. Would she find remnants of servants' quarters at the other end of the attic, or would she find more out-of-reach shelves?

"She tells me the number of paces from here to the treasure if I walk in a straight line," Cassidy muttered. "So were the walls here then, and she assumed whoever was searching would use Craft to pass through the wood, or were the walls added later?"

Cassie?

"Do we walk in a straight line as the map indicates, going through the walls and furniture?" Cassidy asked, more as a question to herself.

No. Vae shook herself. *Don't want to walk through the bad smells.*

The dog had a point. Cassidy was feeling mucky enough just being near this furniture. The thought of passing through it and having some of that psychic residue cling to her was nauseating.

"All right, then. I guess we do this the hard way."

* * *

"She's not in her room," Shira said when she returned to the Steward's office later that morning. Talon had gone to his room for some rest, which was a relief to her, but Powell, Ranon, Theran, and Gray were still waiting for her report.

Gray hugged himself. "Captured?"

The sharp look Ranon gave her said he was wondering the same thing. The fact that any of them would ask that question now . . .

She could almost feel Dena Nehele dying around her.

Shira shook her head. "No sign of struggle. No feel of anything wrong." She hesitated, then decided against mentioning the old, broken trinket box on Cassidy's bed. Might have been an heirloom Cassidy had brought with her, but Shira didn't think so. She'd been tempted to pick up one of the books that had been on the bed as well, but when she'd reached for one, she'd had the feeling that the moment she touched one, something important would go away, would be lost.

Because it wasn't time for her to touch one or read whatever was inside.

When a Black Widow sensed that kind of warning, she heeded it—especially when a friend was suddenly, and mysteriously, missing.

Which was why she had put locks and shields around Cassidy's rooms. Until they knew what had happened to the Queen, she wasn't taking a chance of anyone upsetting a delicate balance.

"Did you try contacting her on a psychic thread?" Theran asked.

Didn't you? Shira wondered as she nodded. "No answer."

"But she didn't"—Theran glanced at Gray—"pack up?"

She shook her head.

Poor Gray. Cassidy's retreat from all of them had been hard on him. Now Shira could see him breaking down, little by little, as the possibility of Cassidy disappearing for good began to take root.

"Well," she said, trying for a bracing tone and hoping no one—except Ranon—heard the worry, "at least we know Cassidy isn't alone."

"Why do you think that?" Ranon asked.

"Because I can't find Vae either."

*   *   *

"I guess when you get rid of a wardrobe, the mirror and trunk go with it," Cassidy said, rubbing her forehead with a grimy hand as she studied the latest combination of furniture. Why hadn't she thought to bring a jug of water? She was parched, and Vae was panting.

I'm certainly not going to tell anyone I didn't bring any water. Lucivar can't yell about what he doesn't know.

It was tempting to give up, since they had circled and wandered the damn attic long enough to have crossed their own footprints a few times, but the answer was up here. Somewhere.

Tired, Cassie, Vae said.

And there were times when sense should override a foolish need to do one thing right.

"Me too. Last one. If we don't find anything this time, we'll go downstairs and get some help looking." Maybe they could just pitch every mirror, trunk, and wardrobe onto the lawn until they found the right one. And Theran could damn well help with the pitching and searching. After all, this was his inheritance, not hers.

Taking a deep breath—and coughing from the dusty air—Cassidy crouched in front of the trunk and warily held out a hand. Some of the trunks . . . Whatever they contained was so vile, she couldn't get near them without feeling sick. This one . . .

Expectation. Anticipation. An odd feeling of hope.

She slipped the key into the trunk's lock . . .

. . . and the wardrobe door opened.

"Well, that's clever." She pulled the wardrobe door open a little more, then pushed the nearest box of whatevers against it to hold it open before she created a ball of witchlight.

"It's a room," Cassidy whispered. She stepped back and looked at the discarded furniture and boxes. Part real and part illusion? Had to be, but she wasn't sure her hands would be able to tell the difference, even now when so many centuries had passed since that spell had been cast.

"Vae, you stay out here."

Why?

"Because if that door closes and I get trapped in there, you'll need to find Theran and rescue me."

Vae sat down, wagged her tail in agreement—and sneezed.

"Let's see what Lia left for her heirs."

Trunks lined two of the walls. Sturdy shelves rose above them, filled with boxes and bags—and more journals. The third side, to her left, had racks for storing paintings.

She pulled out the first painting, easing away the protecting cloth—and wondered how a portrait of Theran had gotten up there. Then she uncovered the next painting and saw the same man, older. His arms were around a woman who wasn't pretty, but had her own kind of beauty.

Jared and Lia.

She wanted to uncover the rest of the paintings, wanted to spend hours studying these people who were still the heart of their land. But Theran and Gray should have the pleasure of that discovery, so she replaced the cloths over the paintings and began to check the shelves to get an idea of what was there before she went downstairs to tell the others what she'd found.

Bags of gold and silver coins. Even a few gold bars. Loose gemstones. Enough, she judged, to repair the estate and support a prudent Queen's court for several years so that the tithes could be put back into the Provinces and villages, helping Blood and landens alike to rebuild Dena Nehele.

And a few pieces of jewelry, carefully preserved in velvet-lined boxes and fit for a Queen.

Family heirlooms. Dishes and trinkets that were worth more for their history than for whatever price they might fetch.

Then there was the box with the sealed message resting on top.

For the Queen.

You have found what we left behind to help when it will be needed most.

Give this box to the Grayhaven heir. Once it is placed in the heir's hands, all the spells that have kept these items safe will end, and this room can be found by any eye.

May the Darkness embrace you, Sister. You have given Dena Nehele, and my family, more than you know.

Lia

*   *   *

"Where in the name of Hell have you been?" Theran said the moment Cassidy stepped out on the terrace, looking happy and incredibly dirty. "Gray's been frantic, worrying about you."

Hell's fire, was he relieved to see her! At that moment, he wanted to strangle her for scaring them all so much, but he was relieved to see her.

"Do you realize it's midafternoon now and there's been no sign of you—none!—since the maid found the breakfast tray outside your door?"

"So late?" She looked startled. "I didn't realize."

"Where have you been?" he shouted.

She shifted away from him. "I was up in the attic."

"What for? And why didn't you tell someone? We were ready to tear apart the town looking for you." Not to mention having to go to Sadi and tell him they had lost the Queen.

Vae joined them, so filthy he imagined the housekeeper was having a fit about the dog tramping through the house, and since he knew who would end up washing the little bitch, he wasn't quite as relieved to see her.

Especially when she growled at him.

"And you," he snapped, pointing at Vae. "You couldn't have told us where Cassidy had gone? You're always yapping about everything else."

I do not yap.

Theran snorted.

"Prince . . . ," Cassidy began.

"Cassie!"

He didn't need to watch Gray running for the house. He watched Cassidy . . . and the way her eyes lit up when she saw Gray.

At least that answered one question.

"Cassie!" Gray stopped at the edge of the terrace. "There's . . . there's something I want to show you."

She smiled. "I have some things to show you too."

"Mine first," Gray said.

Her smile widened. "All right." Then she looked at Theran and held out a rectangular wooden box, its top decorated with the Grayhaven seal. "This is for you."

As he took the box, his eyes asked the question.

"I found the treasure," Cassidy said, her face glowing with excitement under the grime. "It's up there, Theran, along with so much of your heritage." She took a step toward Gray, then turned back. "You look like him, you know. Jared. You look like him."

Stunned, he watched as Gray clasped her hand and tugged her to the surprise in the garden. Talon had told him that a few times, but how would Cassidy know?

"Gray, wait," Cassidy said. Too many emotions pouring off him. She couldn't tell if he was happy or upset, angry or excited.

Maybe all of them. Which meant her court would be equally upset by her unexpected absence.

Assuming any of them noticed or gave a damn.

You're tired, so you're bitchy, she scolded herself. "Gray, wait."

He stopped, but he looked like he was about to receive a crippling blow.

"I'm parched. Can I have some water before I see the surprise?"

"How did you know it was a surprise?"

Hell's fire. She wasn't supposed to know that. "Since I don't know what you want to show me, it must be a surprise."

As he rubbed a thumb over her cheek, he made one of those lightning shifts from boy to man.

"You're not hurt?" he asked.

"No, Gray, I'm not hurt. I was up in the attic and lost track of time. I didn't mean to worry you."

"Scared me, Cassie. That's a lot more than worry."

"Yes, it is, and I'm sorry."

He shook his head. "There were too many years when someone going missing meant they weren't coming back. Captured or killed. Sometimes Talon found what was left of them. Most times not."

"Oh, Gray."

He shook his head again. "Dena Nehele isn't a safe place yet. It will be, someday, but for now it's still not safe to go off on your own and not leave a direction for someone to follow."

"I'll remember that." *I'll miss you, Gray.*

"Let's get you some water."

She drank her fill. Then Gray worked the pump for her so she could wash some of the grime off her face and hands.

He called in a small towel and handed it to her, and there was a question in his eyes that she couldn't figure out.

"Close your eyes," he said.

When she obeyed, he put an arm around her shoulders and guided her around the garden.

"Open your eyes now."

She looked at the flower bed and thought, *Home.* Then she looked more closely.

"Common ground," Gray said quietly. "Not quite the same, but similar. Not quite home, but it could be home— if you wanted to put down roots. And if you don't, if you can't, maybe I could put down roots in Dharo."

It was her mother's garden, and yet it wasn't.

Then what he said sank in all the way.

"Dharo?" she asked, finally looking away from the flowers. "You want to live in Dharo?"

"I want to be with you." He drew her into his arms.

"Theran needs you," Cassidy said.

"And I need you. I know it's not easy for you because your ways are so different from what we've known here, but maybe we can find some common ground there too. Can't we try, Cassie? Can't we at least try?"

He kissed her slowly, deeply, as if she truly mattered.

As if she were the only thing that mattered.

"Cassie?"

She looked into his eyes. Not quite a man, but no longer a boy. She didn't know if they had a future together, but she did love him—and wasn't love the most fertile ground of all?

"I'd like to try, Gray," she said, her eyes filling with tears. "I really would like to try."

His alarmed expression changed to thoughtful. "Are those happy tears?"

She hugged him hard. "Yes, these are happy tears." Then she stepped back, rubbed her face, and smiled. "Show me the garden."

Theran watched Gray kiss Cassidy, but that quickly felt intrusive, so he turned away and opened the box.

"To the Heir of Grayhaven."

Under the wax-sealed paper was a Green Jewel that still held some of the psychic resonance of the woman who had worn it.

And some of the power, Theran realized as he felt that power fade, its last task completed.

The wax seal was so old, it crumbled when he tried to open it, but the words were clear enough.

> To the Heir of Grayhaven,
>
> If you are reading this, the treasure stands before you. Not the gold and jewels, although we hope those will help you rebuild what was destroyed, but the Queen who has the strength and heart to care for our land and our people. That is a treasure beyond price.
>
> But you already know that. Something has happened that tested her commitment and her courage—and you chose to stand with her. If you hadn't, the last key would have never been found, and Dena Nehele would fail within a decade, splintering until it was nothing more than a memory.
>
> Now you have a chance to remember who we were as a people. You have a chance to be a strong land again.
>
> The treasure stands before you. I hope you can cherish her as Jared cherished me.
>
> May the Darkness embrace you.
>
> Lia

"Theran?"

Talon stood inside the open terrace doors, out of the afternoon sunlight.

His throat was too tight for words, so Theran handed the letter to Talon and focused on Gray and Cassidy, who had their arms around each other's waists and were pointing at parts of the new flower bed Gray had planted for her.

"Mother Night," Talon said as he finished reading.

Theran opened the box.

"Lia's," Talon said, sounding hoarse. "I recognize it. It was her Birthright Jewel."

"I wish I could see her the way he does," Theran said as he turned, again, to watch Gray and Cassidy. "Not romantically. He loves her, and he deserves to be happy. But I wish

I could see the Queen he sees when he looks at her. The Queen you see when you look at her. I didn't stand with her for her sake, Talon. I did it for Gray. I did it because it would destroy him if something happened to her."

"You still made the choice to stand with her. First time in a long time the Grayhaven line has defended a Queen. I guess that was enough." Talon folded the letter and gave it back. "What are you going to do?"

Theran vanished the box and letter. "I'm going to learn how to be a good First Escort."

"For Gray's sake?"

"And for Dena Nehele. And for my own sake."

Ranon joined them, looked toward the garden, and grinned, his relief at seeing Cassidy evident on his face. "Looks like Gray found her. That's good." Then the grin faded, and he looked wary. "Remember the letter Cassidy wrote to the Shalador Queens?"

"I remember," Theran said.

"Well, they're here. And they would like to meet the Queen."

Theran probably looked as startled as Talon did. No one had expected the Shalador Queens to come out of hiding, much less leave the reserves.

He hesitated, automatically stalling for time until he could think of a reason why the other Queens couldn't meet with Cassidy.

As he looked at Talon and Ranon, he realized they expected him to make an excuse. Maybe it was time for him to stop feeling disappointed that he hadn't gotten what he'd wanted from this bargain, because Dena Nehele had gotten what it needed—a Queen who could help their land and all of its people.

It was time to be a First Escort.

"Wait here," he told Ranon.

Then he walked over to the new part of the garden, where Gray and Cassidy were still talking about the flowers they could see and the ones that were still just seeds in the dirt.

"My apologies for the interruption, Lady," Theran said.

Cassidy turned to look at him, her surprise at his formal address changing to wariness. "Is something wrong, Prince?"

He shook his head. "The Shalador Queens are here and have requested an audience."

"They came?"

Her joy changed her plain face. It wasn't pretty, would never be pretty, but for a moment, he almost understood what men like Ranon and Talon saw when they looked at her.

"Yes," he said, smiling. "They came." He held out his right hand, palm down.

She placed her left hand over his, an automatic response. Then she stopped, said, "Oh," and looked at Gray.

And Theran saw Gray take another step toward becoming the man he should have been.

"Go on," Gray said. "Right now, Dena Nehele needs the Queen. The garden and I will be here when you're done with the day's business."

They hadn't gone more than a couple of steps when Gray said, "Cassie? You might want to show them this flower bed. Some of the plants came from the reserves."

She flashed a smile at Gray over her shoulder, then lengthened her stride until she and Theran were almost running to the house. They bounded up the terrace steps.

"Mother Night!" Cassidy skidded to a stop, looked down at herself, and gave him, Talon, and Ranon a look of undiluted female panic. "I can't meet the Shalador Queens looking like this."

A week ago he would have thought her taking so long to remember her appearance was a sign that she didn't care how the people saw her. Now he understood it was a sign of how much the people mattered to her.

"Ranon and I can entertain the Ladies for a while and give you a chance to wash up," Theran said.

She flashed him a smile almost as brilliant as the one she'd given Gray, then dashed into the house.

"Well," Theran said, "we shouldn't keep the Ladies waiting."

But Ranon stepped outside, his expression a little dazed as he stared at the pots lining the terrace. "Look."

Theran looked. Then he smiled.

The honey pears were starting to grow.

Read on for an excerpt from Anne Bishop's
stunning *Black Jewels* novel

SHALADOR'S LADY

Available from Roc

Terreille

Cassidy closed her eyes and concentrated on breathing. Nerves and excitement. Her first official visit among the people she ruled. And the first time people outside the town of Grayhaven would see her First Circle working together as a First Circle.

She glanced at Theran. Ever since she had found the treasure hidden in the attic at Grayhaven, he had made an obvious effort to act like he wanted to serve in her court. But his forced courtesy was a daily reminder that he didn't belong to her the way the other men in her First Circle did.

In fact, his effort to serve felt too much like her previous court. They had lavished her with forced courtesy too— right before they broke her court and left her in order to serve another Queen.

This visit to Eyota, Ranon's home village, was harder for him to accept than it was for the rest of the First Circle. They had spent the days prior to this trip discussing the details of what was required to guard their Queen in an unfamiliar place. Theran had offered no comments, no suggestions, nothing. Had, in fact, voiced none of the concerns that a First Escort should have. Was he distancing himself because she had refused to cancel this visit—or because being on a Shalador reserve would make him look at the other side of his heritage? He was proud to be descended from Jared, but he seemed to resent having to acknowledge that Jared came from Shalador.

Then there was Gray, who was clinging to her hand despite the fact they were in a Coach that had a driver experienced with controlling a long enclosed furnished box designed to ride the Winds, those psychic webs through the Darkness. It wasn't being dependent on someone else's power and skill that made Gray cling to her. Captured at fifteen and given to Dena Nehele's Queen, he had survived two years of torture before being rescued. It had taken courage for him to go back to Grayhaven when Theran and Talon had announced they were going to be living there with the new Territory Queen. And she knew it had taken even more courage for him to leave Grayhaven and come with her to a place that was unfamiliar and spend time among strangers.

"The boardinghouse looks shabby, but it's solid, has running water and plumbing, a kitchen, and it's big enough to accommodate all of the First Circle," Ranon said.

Since this was the fourth time he'd told her that—and sounded both defensive and apologetic—Cassidy figured the Shalador Warlord Prince wasn't as calm or confident about this visit as he appeared to be. And Shira's composure had become more frayed as this day approached.

"It will be fine, Ranon," Cassidy said. "I'm sure everything will be fine." She hoped so, because the success of this visit would determine if she would be allowed to be a Queen to these people in the truest sense or only be a symbol the Warlord Princes would use to try to rebuild Dena Nehele. The witch storm unleashed by Jaenelle Angelline two years ago had swept away the Blood who had been tainted by Dorothea SaDiablo, and the landen uprisings that followed had killed so many more. The survivors not only had to worry about keeping peace within their own Territory—they had to remain strong enough to stop any Blood from other Territories who might try to encroach on Dena Nehele's land and take whatever resources could be won from a fight.

"It will be fine," Shira echoed.

Noticing the way Ranon stopped himself from looking at Shira, as if a look at that moment might betray some confidence, Cassidy wondered what the Black Widow knew that could make the two Shaladorans so doubtful that anything would be fine.

*   *   *

They were a proud, ragged people.

Since he wasn't an official member of Cassie's First Circle, Gray stood back and watched as Lady Nimarr, the eldest Shalador Queen, formally introduced Cassie to the other Queens who ruled in the Shalador reserves. Cassie had met several of the women a few days before when they came to Grayhaven and requested an audience, so Gray figured this introduction was for the benefit of the people who had gathered to get a look at the Queen of Dena Nehele.

Then some of the Tradition Keepers were introduced, including Ranon's grandfather Yairen, who was a Keeper of Music.

Gray looked at Theran, whose face seemed frozen in an expression between stubbornness and forced courtesy, then at Ranon, who stood tall and proud—but not confident, despite his effort to appear so. Too much depended on this meeting for Ranon to feel confident of the outcome.

Gray watched Cassie talking to the Tradition Keepers. Her eyes never left Lord Yairen's face, but he knew her well enough to appreciate how much effort it took for her not to look at the old man's crippled hands. And he was certain she understood that the crippling hadn't been caused by age or accident.

The Queens wore new dresses that were simple in design. Over those dresses were finely embroidered vests—old vests that were tended carefully and probably only worn for special occasions. The Tradition Keepers had worn their best clothes too, but even skilled seamstresses couldn't hide all the mending and patches in those clothes, and Gray admired the men and women for not using illusion spells to cover one truth about the reserves.

He had lived a rough life in the rogue camps hidden in the Tamanara Mountains. These people had lived a desperate life, had endured more—and worse—than anyone else in Dena Nehele because of Dorothea SaDiablo's hatred for Jared.

Was it any wonder that Ranon felt so bitter and angry about the way his people had been treated? Was it any wonder that he took every opportunity to call attention to the way the Shaladorans lived—and what they lived without?

But was Ranon hoping for more than Cassie could give?

*   *   *

Thank the Darkness, the ceremonies were over. At least until that evening when she would be the special guest at a feast held in her honor.

Honor, Cassidy thought as brushed her hair. The Shaladorans had held on to honor when they could hold on to nothing else. She saw that truth in their dark eyes, heard it in the quiet voices. Unlike Ranon, who was vocal on his people's behalf, the Queens and elders had said nothing. They didn't have to. Just looking at them, just hearing the dignity in their voices told her more than words.

The boardinghouse told her even more. Shabby? Yes. But there was a new mattress on the bed in her room, new linens. The room had been scrubbed free of every speck of dirt, although the wallpaper still showed signs of water stains. And *everything* was free of psychic scents. There was no psychic residue on the bed or linens or carpets to reveal the previous owners.

Who in the village had given up these new things in order to furnish this room for her visit?

She didn't know how much she could do for these people, but she knew where to begin—if the Shaladorans, and Theran, would let her do this much.

She looked at the door that opened into the adjoining bedroom. By rights it should have been her First Escort's room, but Ranon must have said something to the elders, and Gray had been assigned that room. His need to be close to her had been so obvious, Theran had said nothing about taking the room on the other side of hers—the room without an adjoining door. Ranon and Shira were across the hall from her, sharing a room. At some point she would ask Shira if the elders' eyes had widened because it was a Black Widow and a Warlord Prince sharing a room or just because it was unusual in the reserves for unmarried lovers to share a room so openly.

For now, she would go outside and take a look at the boardinghouse's gardens and see what she could do.

When she opened the bedroom door, there were no guards waiting for her in the hallway; there were no escorts. There were no males of any kind.

But there was a Sceltie, who took one look at her and said, *Hat, Cassie.*

"I'm just—"

Hat.

She fetched the brown open-weave hat she had bought for this visit. Gray insisted she wear a hat to protect her skin, and Shira had talked her into shopping for one and had gone so far as to buy a hat too, laughingly saying it would become a trademark of the court—any Lady serving in the First Circle would wear a hat as a symbol of her service to the Queen.

At the time, Cassidy had accepted the teasing and Shira's purchase of a hat without a second thought. Now she wondered how dear the cost of that hat had been for the Shalador witch. *Her* hat had been put on the court account, and its price would be deducted from the tithe the shopkeeper owed at the end of summer. But Shira had paid for her own hat.

Prince Sadi had offered to help pay some of her expenses while she was in Dena Nehele. Would he be willing to extend the Queen's gift to a small loan so she could pay her First Circle an advance against their quarterly wages? Would she have the courage to ask him?

Cassie?

She plunked the hat on her head and scowled at Vae. "See? I'm wearing the hat."

Yes. Vae gave Cassidy a tail-tip wag. *Now Gray will not worry about your face molting.*

The image of pieces of skin fluttering to the ground like discarded bird feathers made her queasy. Kindred tended to describe things in relation to an animal, but that wasn't always a comfortable picture for humans when they were the subject of the conversation.

Vae headed for the stairs, pausing long enough to make sure Cassidy was following her.

Gray is outside with Ranon and a young male who is a Warlord Prince, Vae said. *He is family to Ranon, and Ranon wants you to see him, but there are worry smells too.*

"Ranon has probably spent a lot of years keeping his relative hidden from the Queens," Cassidy replied. "It can't be easy for him to bring a young Warlord Prince into the open."

Why? You are Ranon's Queen. You are Dena Nehele's Queen. The pup belongs to you.

You can't claim what you can't find, Cassidy thought. *Hide some of the Queens so there will be someone left to rule. Hide the young Warlord Princes so that another generation can survive long enough to stand on a killing field and fight for their land.*

The world was simple for Vae. Not because she was a dog, but because she had grown up in the village the Queen of Scelt called home. Even if only a few actually served in a court, a Territory Queen held the life of every person in her hands, as well as the land itself. Lady Morghann was a strong Queen and a close friend of Jaenelle Angelline, and Morghann's husband, Lord Khardeen, ruled the village of Maghre on his Lady's behalf. So Vae had no reason to doubt that praise and punishment would be given fairly—and both would be given when deserved.

Vae wouldn't hesitate to bring someone who mattered to her to the attention of the Queen she served. For Ranon to bring the boy within sight of a Queen was a huge act of trust.

Cassidy stopped at the door leading outside as she thought about this young male Ranon had brought to the boardinghouse. Brother? Or son? Was that the reason he and Shira had been acting so uneasy? Was it *their* son or just *his* son?

Neither, Cassidy decided as she rounded the side of the house and saw the three men. The boy was in his late teens—too old to be anything but a brother or cousin to Ranon.

Gray's smile was warm and open when he saw her walking toward them. Ranon's expression was somewhere between determined and hopeful. And the youngster . . .

How many friends had he seen taken away only to be returned broken or crippled—or never to return at all? She had no sense that the Shalador Queens had mistreated their own people, but the Shalador Queens had had little power, controlled as they had been by the Province Queens.

She stopped when there was enough distance between her and the men that Ranon could dismiss the young Warlord Prince before approaching her, eliminating the requirement of an introduction.

She watched Ranon assess the distance, and knew the moment when he realized what it meant. A moment later, he signaled the youngster and approached her.

"Lady, may I introduce my younger brother?" Ranon asked.

"You may," Cassidy replied.

"Lady, this is Prince Janos. Our father was Lord Yairen's son. Janos, this is Lady Cassidy, the Queen of Dena Nehele."

"It is an honor to be introduced to so great a Queen," Janos replied, bowing too low for the act to be respectful since his Summer-sky Jewel outranked her Rose.

You bow too low, Vae said. *That is rude. Sniffing female parts is rude too. That is confusing because there are good smells there, but it is something you must learn or you will get smacked on the nose. Or nipped.*

Janos's face turned dusky red as he snapped upright, making it clear that the insult had been unintentional. Ranon's coloring wasn't much better.

And Gray looked a bit too curious about female smells.

Thank the Darkness, Cassidy thought when the back door opened and a young woman walked out. Sixteen years old. Maybe seventeen. And beautiful in a way that made the breath catch when she moved. Long dark hair and green eyes. And a Purple Dusk Jewel.

"What are you doing here, Reyhana?" Ranon growled.

Surprised by his animosity, Cassidy stared at him. Yes, he outranked the girl, but she was a Queen and should be shown some respect unless Reyhana had done something to earn his anger.

"I asked the elder Queens if I could work here as a service to the new Queen," Reyhana replied, her voice a shade too defiant.

"You're a Queen. You shouldn't be doing servants' work," Ranon snapped.

"Why not?" Cassidy asked.

The silence was more startling than a thunderclap would have been at that moment.

"Why not?" Ranon said. "She's a Queen!"

"A Queen who doesn't know how to work is of no use to her people," Reyhana said.

"Well put, Sister," Cassidy said. Ranon looked like he'd been clobbered with a fence post, and she was sorry for what she was about to do to him, but the girl was her priority now. "My family is not aristo, Prince Ranon. We never had servants. And even though by caste I am a Queen, I am also a daughter. So when my mother pulled out the rags and mops on cleaning day, I dusted and polished furniture, and mopped the floors right along with her. And when it was my turn to clean the bathroom, I had very bad thoughts about my brother." She looked Ranon right in the eyes. "Why is it that a man can hit the center of a bull's-eye at one hundred paces and can't manage to get all of his stream in the toilet bowl when he's standing right over it?"

Janos and Gray stood there with their mouths hanging open. Ranon, poor man, looked ready to slink away.

But it was the suppressed snort from the young Queen that told Cassidy she had achieved her goal. She'd talk to the girl later about the proper way to address a Warlord Prince when his Jewels were dominant.

She smiled at all of them. "Now, if you'll excuse me, I want to take a look at the vegetable garden." As she walked away, she added on a distaff thread, *Vae, keep an eye on the males. Make sure they're still breathing.*

One, two, three . . .

Ranon? Ranon! Are you breathing?

There, Cassidy thought. By the time Ranon, Gray, and Janos untangled themselves from Vae's attention, Reyhana would be safely among the older women—the ones Prince Ranon would not dare offend without good reason.

When she reached the vegetable garden, she stopped.

It should have been good soil, but it was parched, almost barren, and the plants struggling to grow wouldn't yield the bounty needed to feed these people. Not parched for water, the ground was still soft, a sure sign that there had been a long, soaking rain sometime in the past day or two. No, it was parched for the connection with a Queen, for that necessary give and take that kept the land healthy.

Why had the Shalador Queens neglected this? Cassidy wondered as she knelt at the edge of the bed. Surely they were aware of the need. Had they been so afraid to call attention to themselves that they hadn't done this one thing that would have helped so many? Or had they stopped because they realized that if they made this land richer than the rest of Dena Nehele by following traditions, it would have been taken away? Ranon had told them that the reserves were half the size they had been when Lady Grizelle and Lia had established those parts of Dena Nehele as a place that belonged to the Shalador people.

Well, it was time everyone stopped denying one of the duties of a Queen.

She didn't turn around. If she looked at him, Gray would join her—and raise too many objections. Ceremony could come later. First she would show them *why*; then she would show them *how*.

Cassidy called in a short-bladed knife and made a cut on each palm. As the blood flowed, she vanished the knife and pressed her hands into the soil—and sent her Rose-Jeweled power flowing through her blood and into the ground.

So parched. So needy. So empty for so long.

Power flowed, spreading through the vegetable garden like sweet rain.

The land was the true root and heart of the Blood's power. They were the caretakers of the Realms. That was more than society and cities. That was more than music and literature. That was more than ruling over the landens. A connection to the land was an important part of what made the Blood who and what they were, and the Queens were the bridge because their power supported the land.

So parched. So needy. Soaking up everything she was willing to give. She could feel the land responding under her hands, wanting more. Wanting everything.

"Cassie?"

A little more. She could give a little more. Saturation would come soon, and the land would stop draining her.

"Cassie."

So parched. So needy. To be wanted so much.

Then the power was draining too fast, too much. But she couldn't pull away, couldn't turn away when there was so much need.

Just a lit—

"CASSIE!"

The Black Jewels Series

by Anne Bishop

"Darkly mesmerizing...fascinatingly different."
—Locus

This is the story of the heir to a dark throne, a magic more powerful than that of the High Lord of Hell, and an ancient prophecy. These books tell of a ruthless game of politics and intrigue, magic and betrayal, love and sacrifice, destiny and fulfillment.

Daughter of the Blood

Heir to the Shadows

Queen of the Darkness

The Invisible Ring

Dreams Made Flesh

Tangled Webs

The Shadow Queen

Shalador's Lady

Available wherever books are sold or at
penguin.com

R420